Leutnant Gustl muß sich von einem Bäckermeister »dummer Bub« nennen lassen; dies scheint ihm mit seiner soldatischen Ehre nicht vereinbar; er glaubt, sich erschießen zu müssen, verlebt seine vermeintlich letzte Nacht im Prater, geht vor dem Selbstmord noch zum Frühstück ins Café, wo er erfährt, daß sein Beleidiger um Mitternacht vom Schlag tödlich getroffen wurde, so daß er nun weiter in den Tag leben kann wie bisher.

Fräulein Else, natur- und zeitgemäß einer gänzlich anderen Gesellschaft entstammend, aber nicht weniger intensiv in einen Konflikt gebracht zwischen der Scham und der Vorstellung, ihrer Familie verpflichtet zu sein, kommen keine für sie glücklichen Umstände zugute. Ihr Vater steht vor einem Skandal: Er hat Mündelgelder unterschlagen, die Tochter soll die Summe innerhalb von zwei Tagen von einem Geschäftsfreund zu leihen versuchen; dieser fordert als Gegenleistung, »eine Viertelstunde dastehen zu dürfen vor ihrer Schönheit« – sie soll nackt sein; sie stimmt in einem Brief zu, irrt dann aber in der Hotelhalle umher, bis sie umfällt, bis Traum und Realität sich mehr und mehr mischen und langsam ausklingen.

Gemeinsam ist diesen beiden Meistererzählungen aus den Jahren 1901 und 1924 das Formale, der innere Monolog, bei dem eine einzige Figur ihre eigenen Beobachtungen und Empfindungen von außen nach innen reflektiert, in die Innenwelt der Außenwelt. Sprunghaftigkeit der Assoziationen und Nervosität werden zum Stilmittel.

Arthur Schnitzler wurde am 15. Mai 1862 in Wien als Sohn eines Professors der Medizin geboren. Nach dem Studium der Medizin war er Assistenzarzt an der Poliklinik und dann praktischer Arzt in Wien, bis er sich mehr und mehr seinen literarischen Arbeiten widmete. Er starb am 21. Oktober 1931 als einer der bedeutendsten österreichischen Erzähler und Dramatiker der Gegenwart in Wien.

Arthur Schnitzler
Leutnant Gustl
Fräulein Else

Fischer
Taschenbuch
Verlag

Sonderausgabe
40 Jahre Fischer Taschenbücher
Veröffentlicht im Fischer Taschenbuch Verlag GmbH,
Frankfurt am Main, Januar 1992

Lizenzausgabe mit freundlicher Genehmigung des
S. Fischer Verlags GmbH, Frankfurt am Main
© 1961 S. Fischer Verlag GmbH, Frankfurt am Main
Umschlaggestaltung: Bartholl & Bartholl, Hamburg
Foto: Hänse Herrmann, ›Tilla Durieux‹, Berlin
Druck und Bindung: Clausen & Bosse, Leck
Printed in Germany
ISBN 3-596-11216-8

Inhalt

Leutnant Gustl

Leutnant Gustl

Wie lang' wird denn das noch dauern? Ich muß auf die Uhr
schauen... schickt sich wahrscheinlich nicht in einem so ernsten
Konzert. Aber wer sieht's denn? Wenn's einer sieht, so paßt er
gerade so wenig auf, wie ich, und vor dem brauch' ich mich
nicht zu genieren... Erst viertel auf zehn?... Mir kommt vor,
ich sitz' schon drei Stunden in dem Konzert. Ich bin's halt nicht
gewohnt... Was ist es denn eigentlich? Ich muß das Programm
anschauen.. Ja, richtig: Oratorium! Ich hab' gemeint: Messe.
Solche Sachen gehören doch nur in die Kirche! Die Kirche hat
auch das Gute, daß man jeden Augenblick fortgehen kann. –
Wenn ich wenigstens einen Ecksitz hätt'! – Also Geduld, Geduld! Auch Oratorien nehmen ein End'! Vielleicht ist es sehr
schön, und ich bin nur nicht in der Laune. Woher sollt' mir auch
die Laune kommen? Wenn ich denke, daß ich hergekommen
bin, um mich zu zerstreuen... Hätt' ich die Karte lieber dem
Benedek geschenkt, dem machen solche Sachen Spaß; er spielt ja
selber Violine. Aber da wär' der Kopetzky beleidigt gewesen. Es
war ja sehr lieb von ihm, wenigstens gut gemeint. Ein braver
Kerl, der Kopetzky! Der einzige, auf den man sich verlassen
kann... Seine Schwester singt ja mit unter denen da oben. Min-
destens hundert Jungfrauen, alle schwarz gekleidet; wie soll ich
sie da herausfinden? Weil sie mitsingt, hat er auch das Billett
gehabt, der Kopetzky... Warum ist er denn nicht selber gegangen? – Sie singen übrigens sehr schön. Es ist sehr erhebend –
sicher! Bravo! Bravo!... Ja, applaudieren wir mit. Der neben
mir klatscht wie verrückt. Ob's ihm wirklich so gut gefällt? –
Das Mädel drüben in der Loge ist sehr hübsch. Sieht sie mich an
oder den Herrn dort mit dem blonden Vollbart?... Ah, ein Solo!
Wer ist das? Alt: Fräulein Walker, Sopran: Fräulein Michalek...
das ist wahrscheinlich Sopran... Lang' war ich schon nicht in
der Oper. In der Oper unterhalt' ich mich immer, auch wenn's

langweilig ist. Übermorgen könnt' ich eigentlich wieder hineingeh'n, zur ›Traviata‹. Ja, übermorgen bin ich vielleicht schon eine tote Leiche! Ah, Unsinn, das glaub' ich selber nicht! Warten S' nur, Herr Doktor, Ihnen wird's vergeh'n, solche Bemerkungen zu machen! Das Nasenspitzel hau' ich Ihnen herunter...

Wenn ich die in der Loge nur genau sehen könnt'! Ich möcht' mir den Operngucker von dem Herrn neben mir ausleih'n, aber der frißt mich ja auf, wenn ich ihn in seiner Andacht stör'... In welcher Gegend die Schwester vom Kopetzky steht? Ob ich sie erkennen möcht'? Ich hab' sie ja nur zwei- oder dreimal gesehen, das letztemal im Offizierskasino... Ob das lauter anständige Mädeln sind, alle hundert? O jeh!... »Unter Mitwirkung des Singvereins«! – Singverein... komisch! Ich hab' mir darunter eigentlich immer so was Ähnliches vorgestellt, wie die Wiener Tanzsängerinnen, das heißt, ich hab' schon gewußt, daß es was anderes ist!.. Schöne Erinnerungen! Damals beim ›Grünen Tor‹... Wie hat sie nur geheißen? Und dann hat sie mir einmal eine Ansichtskarte aus Belgrad geschickt... Auch eine schöne Gegend! – Der Kopetzky hat's gut, der sitzt jetzt längst im Wirtshaus und raucht seine Virginia!...

Was guckt mich denn der Kerl dort immer an? Mir scheint, der merkt, daß ich mich langweil' und nicht herg'hör'... Ich möcht' Ihnen raten, ein etwas weniger freches Gesicht zu machen, sonst stell' ich Sie mir nachher im Foyer! – Schaut schon weg!... Daß sie alle vor meinem Blick so eine Angst hab'n... »Du hast die schönsten Augen, die mir je vorgekommen sind!« hat neulich die Steffi gesagt... O Steffi, Steffi, Steffi! – Die Steffi ist eigentlich schuld, daß ich dasitz' und mir stundenlang vorlamentieren lassen muß. – Ah, diese ewige Abschreiberei von der Steffi geht mir wirklich schon auf die Nerven! Wie schön hätt' der heutige Abend sein können. Ich hätt' große Lust, das Brieferl von der Steffi zu lesen. Da hab' ich's ja. Aber wenn ich die Brieftasche herausnehm', frißt mich der Kerl daneben auf! – Ich weiß ja, was drinsteht... sie kann nicht kommen, weil sie mit »ihm« nachtmahlen gehen muß... Ah, das war komisch vor acht Tagen, wie sie mit ihm in der Gartenbaugesellschaft gewesen ist, und ich vis-à-vis mit'm Kopetzky; und sie hat mir immer die Zeichen gemacht mit den Augerln, die verabredeten. Er hat nichts gemerkt – unglaublich! Muß übrigens ein Jud' sein! Freilich, in einer Bank ist er, und der schwarze Schnurrbart... Reserveleutnant soll er auch sein! Na, in mein Regiment sollt' er nicht zur Waffenübung kommen! Überhaupt, daß sie noch immer so viel Juden zu Offizieren machen – da pfeif' ich auf'n ganzen Antisemitismus! Neulich in der Gesellschaft, wo die G'schicht' mit dem Doktor passiert ist bei den Mannheimers... die Mannheimer selber sollen ja auch Juden sein, getauft natürlich... denen merkt man's aber gar nicht an – besonders die Frau... so blond, bildhübsch die Figur... War sehr amüsant im ganzen. Famoses Essen, großartige Zigarren... Na ja, wer hat's Geld?...

Bravo, bravo! Jetzt wird's doch bald aus sein? – Ja, jetzt steht die ganze G'sellschaft da droben auf... sieht sehr gut aus – imposant! – Orgel auch?... Orgel hab' ich sehr gern... So, das laß' ich mir g'fall'n – sehr schön! Es ist wirklich wahr, man sollt' öfter in Konzerte gehen... Wunderschön ist's g'wesen, werd' ich dem Kopetzky sagen... Werd' ich ihn heut' im Kaffeehaus treffen? – Ah, ich hab' gar keine Lust, ins Kaffeehaus zu geh'n; hab' mich gestern so gegiftet! Hundertsechzig Gulden auf einem Sitz verspielt – zu dumm! Und wer hat alles gewonnen? Der Ballert, grad' der, der's nicht notwendig hat... Der Ballert ist eigentlich schuld, daß ich in das blöde Konzert hab' geh'n müssen... Na ja, sonst hätt' ich heut' wieder spielen können, vielleicht doch was zurückgewonnen. Aber es ist ganz gut, daß ich mir selber das Ehrenwort gegeben hab', einen Monat lang keine Karte anzurühren... Die Mama wird wieder ein G'sicht machen, wenn sie meinen Brief bekommt! –

Ah, sie soll zum Onkel geh'n, der hat Geld wie Mist; auf die paar hundert Gulden kommt's ihm nicht an. Wenn ich's nur durchsetzen könnt', daß er mir eine regelmäßige Sustentation gibt... aber nein, um jeden Kreuzer muß man extra betteln. Dann heißt's wieder: Im vorigen Jahr war die Ernte schlecht!... Ob ich heuer im Sommer wieder zum Onkel fahren soll auf vier-

zehn Tag'? Eigentlich langweilt man sich dort zum Sterben...
Wenn ich die... wie hat sie nur geheißen?... Es ist merkwürdig,
ich kann mir keinen Namen merken!... Ah, ja: Etelka!... Kein
Wort deutsch hat sie verstanden, aber das war auch nicht notwendig... hab' gar nichts zu reden brauchen!... Ja, es wird ganz
gut sein, vierzehn Tage Landluft und vierzehn Nächt' Etelka
oder sonstwer... Aber acht Tag' sollt' ich doch auch wieder
beim Papa und bei der Mama sein... Schlecht hat sie ausg'seh'n
heuer zu Weihnachten... Na, jetzt wird die Kränkung schon
überwunden sein. Ich an ihrer Stelle wär' froh, daß der Papa in
Pension gegangen ist. – Und die Klara wird schon noch einen
Mann kriegen... Der Onkel kann schon was hergeben... Acht-
undzwanzig Jahr', das ist doch nicht so alt... Die Steffi ist sicher
nicht jünger... Aber es ist merkwürdig: die Frauenzimmer erhalten sich länger jung. Wenn man so bedenkt: die Maretti neulich in der ›Madame Sans-Gêne‹ – siebenunddreißig Jahr' ist sie
sicher, und sieht aus... Na, ich hätt' nicht Nein g'sagt! – Schad',
daß sie mich nicht g'fragt hat...

   Heiß wird's! Noch immer nicht aus? Ah, ich freu' mich so auf
die frische Luft! Werd' ein bißl spazieren geh'n, übern Ring...
Heut' heißt's: früh ins Bett, morgen nachmittag frisch sein! Komisch, wie wenig ich daran denk', so egal ist mir das! Das erstemal hat's mich doch ein bißl aufgeregt. Nicht, daß ich Angst
g'habt hätt'; aber nervos bin ich gewesen in der Nacht vorher...
Freilich, der Oberleutnant Bisanz war ein ernster Gegner. – Und
doch, nichts ist mir g'scheh'n!... Auch schon anderthalb Jahr'
her. Wie die Zeit vergeht! Und wenn mir der Bisanz nichts getan
hat, der Doktor wird mir schon gewiß nichts tun! Obzwar, gerade diese ungeschulten Fechter sind manchmal die gefährlich-
sten. Der Doschintzky hat mir erzählt, daß ihn ein Kerl, der das
erstemal einen Säbel in der Hand gehabt hat, auf ein Haar abge-
stochen hätt'; und der Doschintzky ist heut' Fechtlehrer bei der
Landwehr. Freilich – ob er damals schon so viel können hat...
Das Wichtigste ist: kaltes Blut. Nicht einmal einen rechten Zorn
hab' ich mehr in mir, und es war doch eine Frechheit – unglaublich! Sicher hätt' er sich's nicht getraut, wenn er nicht Champag-

ner getrunken hätt' vorher... So eine Frechheit! Gewiß ein Sozialist! Die Rechtsverdreher sind doch heutzutag' alle Sozialisten! Eine Bande... am liebsten möchten sie gleich 's ganze Militär abschaffen; aber wer ihnen dann helfen möcht', wenn die Chinesen über sie kommen, daran denken sie nicht. Blödisten! – Man muß gelegentlich ein Exempel statuieren. Ganz recht hab' ich g'habt. Ich bin froh, daß ich ihn nimmer auslassen hab' nach der Bemerkung. Wenn ich dran denk', werd' ich ganz wild! Aber ich hab' mich famos benommen; der Oberst sagt auch, es war absolut korrekt. Wird mir überhaupt nützen, die Sache. Ich kenn' manche, die den Burschen hätten durchschlüpfen lassen. Der Müller sicher, der wär' wieder objektiv gewesen oder so was. Mit dem Objektivsein hat sich noch jeder blamiert... »Herr Leutnant!«.. schon die Art, wie er »Herr Leutnant« gesagt hat, war unverschämt!... »Sie werden mir doch zugeben müssen«... – Wie sind wir denn nur d'rauf gekommen? Wieso hab' ich mich mit dem Sozialisten in ein Gespräch eingelassen? Wie hat's denn nur angefangen?... Mir scheint, die schwarze Frau, die ich zum Büfett geführt hab', ist auch dabei gewesen... und dann dieser junge Mensch, der die Jagdbilder malt – wie heißt er denn nur?... Meiner Seel', der ist an der ganzen Geschichte schuld gewesen! Der hat von den Manövern geredet; und dann erst ist dieser Doktor dazugekommen und hat irgendwas g'sagt, was mir nicht gepaßt hat, von Kriegsspielerei oder so was – aber wo ich noch nichts hab' reden können... Ja, und dann ist von den Kadettenschulen gesprochen worden... ja, so war's... und ich hab' von einem patriotischen Fest erzählt... und dann hat der Doktor gesagt – nicht gleich, aber aus dem Fest hat es sich entwickelt – »Herr Leutnant, Sie werden mir doch zugeben, daß nicht alle Ihre Kameraden zum Militär gegangen sind, ausschließlich um das Vaterland zu verteidigen!« So eine Frechheit! Das wagt so ein Mensch einem Offizier ins Gesicht zu sagen! Wenn ich mich nur erinnern könnt', was ich d'rauf geantwortet hab'?... Ah ja, etwas von Leuten, die sich in Dinge dreinmengen, von denen sie nichts versteh'n... Ja, richtig... und dann war einer da, der hat die Sache gütlich beilegen wollen, ein älterer Herr mit einem Stockschnupfen... Aber ich war zu wütend! Der Doktor hat das absolut in dem Ton gesagt, als wenn er direkt mich gemeint hätt'. Er hätt' nur noch sagen müssen, daß sie mich aus dem Gymnasium hinausg'schmissen haben und daß ich deswegen in die Kadettenschul' gesteckt worden bin... Die Leut' können eben unserein'n nicht versteh'n, sie sind zu dumm dazu... Wenn ich mich so erinner', wie ich das erstemal den Rock angehabt hab', so was erlebt eben nicht ein jeder... Im vorigen Jahr' bei den Manövern – ich hätt' was drum gegeben, wenn's plötzlich Ernst gewesen wär'... Und der Mirovic hat mir g'sagt, es ist ihm ebenso gegangen. Und dann, wie Seine Hoheit die Front abgeritten sind, und die Ansprache vom Obersten – da muß einer schon ein ordentlicher Lump sein, wenn ihm das Herz nicht höher schlägt... Und da kommt so ein Tintenfisch daher, der sein Lebtag nichts getan hat, als hinter den Büchern gesessen, und erlaubt sich eine freche Bemerkung!... Ah, wart' nur, mein Lieber – bis zur Kampfunfähigkeit... jawohl, du sollst so kampfunfähig werden...

Ja, was ist denn? Jetzt muß es doch bald aus sein?... »Ihr, seine Engel, lobet den Herrn«... – Freilich, das ist der Schlußchor... Wunderschön, da kann man gar nichts sagen. Wunderschön! Jetzt hab' ich ganz die aus der Loge vergessen, die früher zu kokettieren angefangen hat. Wo ist sie denn?... Schon fortgegangen... Die dort scheint auch sehr nett zu sein... Zu dumm, daß ich keinen Operngucker bei mir hab'! Der Brunnthaler ist ganz gescheit, der hat sein Glas immer im Kaffeehaus bei der Kassa liegen, da kann einem nichts g'scheh'n... Wenn sich die Kleine da vor mir nur einmal umdreh'n möcht'! So brav sitzt s' alleweil da. Das neben ihr ist sicher die Mama. – Ob ich nicht doch einmal ernstlich ans Heiraten denken soll? Der Willy war nicht älter als ich, wie er hineingesprungen ist. Hat schon was für sich, so immer gleich ein hübsches Weiberl zu Haus vorrätig zu haben... Zu dumm, daß die Steffi grad' heut' keine Zeit hat! Wenn ich wenigstens wüßte, wo sie ist, möcht' ich mich wieder vis-à-vis von ihr hinsetzen. Das wär' eine schöne G'schicht', wenn ihr der draufkommen möcht', da hätt' ich sie am Hals... Wenn ich so denk', was dem Fließ sein Verhältnis mit der Winterfeld kostet! Und dabei betrügt sie ihn hinten und vorn. Das nimmt noch einmal ein Ende mit Schrecken... Bravo, bravo! Ah, aus!... So, das tut wohl, aufsteh'n können, sich rühren... Na, vielleicht! Wie lang' wird der da noch brauchen, um sein Glas ins Futteral zu stecken?

»Pardon, pardon, wollen mich nicht hinauslassen?«...

Ist das ein Gedränge! Lassen wir die Leut' lieber vorbeipassieren... Elegante Person... ob das echte Brillanten sind?... Die da ist nett... Wie sie mich anschaut!... O ja, mein Fräulein, ich möcht' schon!... O, die Nase! – Jüdin... Noch eine... Es ist doch fabelhaft, da sind auch die Hälfte Juden... nicht einmal ein Oratorium kann man mehr in Ruhe genießen... So, jetzt schließen wir uns an... Warum drängt denn der Idiot hinter mir? Das werd' ich ihm abgewöhnen... Ah, ein älterer Herr!... Wer grüßt mich denn dort von drüben?... Habe die Ehre, habe die Ehre! Keine Ahnung hab' ich, wer das ist... Das Einfachste wär', ich ging gleich zum Leidinger hinüber nachtmahlen... oder soll ich in die Gartenbaugesellschaft? Am End' ist die Steffi auch dort? Warum hat sie mir eigentlich nicht geschrieben, wohin sie mit ihm geht? Sie wird's selber noch nicht gewußt haben. Eigentlich schrecklich, so eine abhängige Existenz... Armes Ding! – So, da ist der Ausgang... Ah, die ist aber bildschön! Ganz allein? Wie sie mich anlacht. Das wär' eine Idee, der geh' ich nach!... So, jetzt die Treppen hinunter: Oh, ein Major von Fünfundneunzig... Sehr liebenswürdig hat er gedankt... Bin doch nicht der einzige Offizier herin gewesen... Wo ist denn das hübsche Mädel? Ah, dort... am Geländer steht sie... So, jetzt heißt's noch zur Garderobe.. Daß mir die Kleine nicht auskommt... Hat ihm schon! So ein elender Fratz! Laßt sich da von einem Herrn abholen, und jetzt lacht sie noch auf mich herüber! – Es ist doch keine was wert... Herrgott, ist das ein Gedränge bei der Garderobe!... Warten wir lieber noch ein bisserl... So! Ob der Blödist meine Nummer nehmen möcht'?...

»Sie, zweihundertvierundzwanzig! Da hängt er! Na, hab'n Sie keine Augen? Da hängt er! Na, Gott sei Dank!... Also bitte!«..

Der Dicke da verstellt einem schier die ganze Garderobe..
»Bitte sehr!«...

»Geduld, Geduld!«

Was sagt der Kerl?

»Nur ein bisserl Geduld!«

Dem muß ich doch antworten... »Machen Sie doch Platz!«

»Na, Sie werden's auch nicht versäumen!«

Was sagt er da? Sagt er das zu mir? Das ist doch stark! Das kann ich mir nicht gefallen lassen! »Ruhig!«

»Was meinen Sie?«

Ah, so ein Ton! Da hört sich doch alles auf!

»Stoßen Sie nicht!«

»Sie, halten Sie das Maul!« Das hätt' ich nicht sagen sollen, ich war zu grob... Na, jetzt ist's schon g'scheh'n!

»Wie meinen?«

Jetzt dreht er sich um... Den kenn' ich ja! – Donnerwetter, das ist ja der Bäckermeister, der immer ins Kaffeehaus kommt... Was macht denn der da? Hat sicher auch eine Tochter oder so was bei der Singakademie... Ja, was ist denn das? Ja, was macht er denn? Mir scheint gar... ja, meiner Seel', er hat den Griff von meinem Säbel in der Hand... Ja, ist der Kerl verrückt?... »Sie, Herr...«

»Sie, Herr Leutnant, sein S' jetzt ganz stad.«

Was sagt er da? Um Gottes willen, es hat's doch keiner gehört? Nein, er red't ganz leise... Ja, warum laßt er denn meinen Säbel net aus?... Herrgott noch einmal... Ah, da heißt's rabiat sein... ich bring' seine Hand vom Griff nicht weg... nur keinen Skandal jetzt!... Ist nicht am End' der Major hinter mir?... Bemerkt's nur niemand, daß er den Griff von meinem Säbel hält? Er red't ja zu mir! Was red't er denn?

»Herr Leutnant, wenn Sie das geringste Aufsehen machen, so zieh' ich den Säbel aus der Scheide, zerbrech' ihn und schick' die Stück' an Ihr Regimentskommando. Versteh'n Sie mich, Sie dummer Bub?«

Was hat er g'sagt? Mir scheint, ich träum'! Red't er wirklich zu mir? Ich sollt' was antworten... Aber der Kerl macht ja Ernst –

der zieht wirklich den Säbel heraus. Herrgott – er tut's!... Ich spür's, er reißt schon d'ran! Was red't er denn?... Um Gottes willen, nur kein' Skandal – – Was red't er denn noch immer?

»Aber ich will Ihnen die Karriere nicht verderben... Also, schön brav sein!... So, hab'n S' keine Angst, 's hat niemand was gehört... es ist schon alles gut... so! Und damit keiner glaubt, daß wir uns gestritten haben, werd' ich jetzt sehr freundlich mit Ihnen sein! – Habe die Ehre, Herr Leutnant, hat mich sehr gefreut – habe die Ehre!«

Um Gottes willen, hab' ich geträumt?... Hat er das wirklich gesagt?... Wo ist er denn?... Da geht er... Ich müßt' ja den Säbel ziehen und ihn zusammenhauen – – Um Gottes willen, es hat's doch niemand gehört?... Nein, er hat ja nur ganz leise geredet, mir ins Ohr... Warum geh' ich denn nicht hin und hau' ihm den Schädel auseinander?... Nein, es geht ja nicht, es geht ja nicht... gleich hätt' ich's tun müssen... Warum hab' ich's denn nicht gleich getan?... Ich hab's ja nicht können... er hat ja den Griff nicht auslassen, und er ist zehnmal stärker als ich... Wenn ich noch ein Wort gesagt hätt', hätt' er mir wirklich den Säbel zerbrochen... Ich muß ja noch froh sein, daß er nicht laut geredet hat! Wenn's ein Mensch gehört hätt', so müßt' ich mich ja stante pede erschießen... Vielleicht ist es doch ein Traum gewesen... Warum schaut mich denn der Herr dort an der Säule so an? – Hat der am End' was gehört?... Ich werd' ihn fragen... Fragen? – Ich bin ja verrückt! – Wie schau' ich denn aus? – Merkt man mir was an? – Ich muß ganz blaß sein. – Wo ist der Hund?... Ich muß ihn umbringen!... Fort ist er... Überhaupt schon ganz leer... Wo ist denn mein Mantel?... Ich hab' ihn ja schon angezogen... Ich hab's gar nicht gemerkt... Wer hat mir denn geholfen?... Ah, der da... dem muß ich ein Sechserl geben... So!... Aber was ist denn das? Ist es denn wirklich gescheh'n? Hat wirklich einer so zu mir geredet? Hat mir wirklich einer »dummer Bub« gesagt? Und ich hab' ihn nicht auf der Stelle zusammengehauen?... Aber ich hab' ja nicht können... er hat ja eine Faust gehabt wie Eisen... ich bin ja dagestanden wie angenagelt... Nein, ich muß den Verstand verloren gehabt haben, sonst hätt' ich mit der anderen Hand ... Aber da hätt' er ja meinen Säbel herausgezogen und zerbrochen, und aus wär's gewesen – Alles wär' aus gewesen! Und nachher, wie er fortgegangen ist, war's zu spät ... ich hab' ihm doch nicht den Säbel von hinten in den Leib rennen können ...

Was, ich bin schon auf der Straße? Wie bin ich denn da herausgekommen? – So kühl ist es ... ah, der Wind, der ist gut ... Wer ist denn das da drüben? Warum schau'n denn die zu mir herüber? Am End' haben die was gehört ... Nein, es kann niemand was gehört haben ... ich weiß ja, ich hab' mich gleich nachher umgeschaut! Keiner hat sich um mich gekümmert, niemand hat was gehört ... Aber gesagt hat er's, wenn's auch niemand gehört hat; gesagt hat er's doch. Und ich bin dagestanden und hab' mir's gefallen lassen, wie wenn mich einer vor den Kopf geschlagen hätt'! ... Aber ich hab' ja nichts sagen können, nichts tun können; es war ja noch das einzige, was mir übrig geblieben ist: stad sein, stad sein! ... 's ist fürchterlich, es ist nicht zum Aushalten; ich muß ihn totschlagen, wo ich ihn treff'! ... Mir sagt das einer! Mir sagt das so ein Kerl, so ein Hund! Und er kennt mich ... Herrgott noch einmal, er kennt mich, er weiß, wer ich bin! ... Er kann jedem Menschen erzählen, daß er mir das g'sagt hat! ... Nein, nein, das wird er ja nicht tun, sonst hätt' er auch nicht so leise geredet ... er hat auch nur wollen, daß ich es allein hör'! ... Aber wer garantiert mir, daß er's nicht doch erzählt, heut' oder morgen, seiner Frau, seiner Tochter, seinen Bekannten im Kaffeehaus. – – Um Gottes willen, morgen seh' ich ihn ja wieder! Wenn ich morgen ins Kaffeehaus komm', sitzt er wieder dort wie alle Tag' und spielt seinen Tapper mit dem Herrn Schlesinger und mit dem Kunstblumenhändler ... Nein, nein, das geht ja nicht, das geht ja nicht ... Wenn ich ihn seh', so hau' ich ihn zusammen ... Nein, das darf ich ja nicht ... gleich hätt' ich's tun müssen, gleich! ... Wenn's nur gegangen wär'! ... Ich werd' zum Obersten geh'n und ihm die Sache melden ... ja, zum Obersten ... Der Oberst ist immer sehr freundlich – und ich werd' ihm sagen: Herr Oberst, ich melde gehorsamst, er hat den Griff gehalten, er hat ihn nicht aus'lassen; es war genau so, als wenn ich ohne Waffe gewesen wäre... – Was wird der Oberst sagen? – Was er sagen wird? – Aber da gibt's ja nur eins: quittieren mit Schimpf und Schand' – quittieren!... Sind das Freiwillige da drüben?... Ekelhaft, bei der Nacht schau'n sie aus, wie Offiziere... sie salutieren! – Wenn die wüßten – wenn die wüßten!... – Da ist das Café Hochleitner... Sind jetzt gewiß ein paar Kameraden drin... vielleicht auch einer oder der andere, den ich kenn'... Wenn ich's dem ersten Besten erzählen möcht', aber so, als wär's einem andern passiert?... – Ich bin ja schon ganz irrsinnig... Wo lauf' ich denn da herum? Was tu' ich denn auf der Straße? – Ja, aber wo soll ich denn hin? Hab' ich nicht zum Leidinger wollen? Haha, unter Menschen mich niedersetzen... ich glaub', ein jeder müßt' mir's anseh'n... Ja, aber irgendwas muß doch gescheh'n... Was soll denn gescheh'n?... Nichts, nichts – es hat ja niemand was gehört... es weiß ja niemand was... in dem Moment weiß niemand was... Wenn ich jetzt zu ihm in die Wohnung ginge und ihn beschwören möchte, daß er's niemandem erzählt?... – Ah, lieber gleich eine Kugel vor den Kopf, als so was!... Wär' so das Gescheiteste!... Das Gescheiteste? Das Gescheiteste? – Gibt ja überhaupt nichts anderes... gibt nichts anderes... Wenn ich den Oberst fragen möcht', oder den Kopetzky – oder den Blany – oder den Friedmaier: – jeder möcht' sagen: Es bleibt dir nichts anderes übrig!... Wie wär's, wenn ich mit dem Kopetzky spräch'?... Ja, es wär' doch das Vernünftigste... schon wegen morgen... Ja, natürlich – wegen morgen... um vier in der Reiterkasern'... ich soll mich ja morgen um vier Uhr schlagen... und ich darf's ja nimmer, ich bin satisfaktionsunfähig... Unsinn! Unsinn! Kein Mensch weiß was, kein Mensch weiß was! – Es laufen viele herum, denen ärgere Sachen passiert sind, als mir... Was hat man nicht alles von dem Deckener erzählt, wie er sich mit dem Rederow geschossen hat... und der Ehrenrat hat entschieden, das Duell darf stattfinden... Aber wie möcht' der Ehrenrat bei mir entscheiden? – Dummer Bub – dummer Bub... und ich bin dagestanden –! Heiliger Himmel, es ist doch ganz egal, ob ein anderer was weiß!... ich weiß es doch, und das ist die Hauptsache! Ich spür', daß ich jetzt wer

anderer bin, als vor einer Stunde – Ich weiß, daß ich satisfaktionsunfähig bin, und darum muß ich mich totschießen...
Keine ruhige Minute hätt' ich mehr im Leben... immer hätt' ich
die Angst, daß es doch einer erfahren könnt', so oder so... und
daß mir's einer einmal ins Gesicht sagt, was heut' abend gescheh'n ist! – Was für ein glücklicher Mensch bin ich vor einer
Stund' gewesen... Muß mir der Kopetzky die Karte schenken –
und die Steffi muß mir absagen, das Mensch! – Von so was hängt
man ab... Nachmittag war noch alles gut und schön, und jetzt
bin ich ein verlorener Mensch und muß mich totschießen...
Warum renn' ich denn so? Es lauft mir ja nichts davon... Wieviel schlagt's denn?... 1, 2, 3, 4, 5, 6, 7, 8, 9, 10, 11... elf, elf...
ich sollt' doch nachtmahlen geh'n! Irgendwo muß ich doch
schließlich hingeh'n... ich könnt' mich ja in irgendein Beisl setzen, wo mich kein Mensch kennt – schließlich, essen muß der
Mensch, auch wenn er sich nachher gleich totschießt... Haha,
der Tod ist ja kein Kinderspiel... wer hat das nur neulich gesagt?... Aber das ist ja ganz egal...

Ich möcht' wissen, wer sich am meisten kränken möcht'?...
Die Mama, oder die Steffi?... Die Steffi... Gott, die Steffi...
die dürft' sich ja nicht einmal was anmerken lassen, sonst gibt
»er« ihr den Abschied... Arme Person! – Beim Regiment – kein
Mensch hätt' eine Ahnung, warum ich's getan hab'... sie täten
sich alle den Kopf zerbrechen... warum hat sich denn der Gustl
umgebracht? – Darauf möcht' keiner kommen, daß ich mich
hab' totschießen müssen, weil ein elender Bäckermeister, so ein
niederträchtiger, der zufällig stärkere Fäust' hat... es ist ja zu
dumm, zu dumm! – Deswegen soll ein Kerl wie ich, so ein junger, fescher Mensch... Ja, nachher möchten's gewiß alle sagen:
das hätt' er doch nicht tun müssen, wegen so einer Dummheit;
ist doch schad'!... Aber wenn ich jetzt wen immer fragen tät',
jeder möcht' mir die gleiche Antwort geben... und ich selber,
wenn ich mich frag'... das ist doch zum Teufelholen... ganz
wehrlos sind wir gegen die Zivilisten... Da meinen die Leut',
wir sind besser dran, weil wir einen Säbel haben... und wenn
schon einmal einer von der Waffe Gebrauch macht, geht's über

uns her, als wenn wir alle die geborenen Mörder wären... In der Zeitung möcht's auch steh'n... »Selbstmord eines jungen Offiziers«... Wie schreiben sie nur immer?... »Die Motive sind in Dunkel gehüllt«... Haha!... »An seinem Sarge trauern...« – Aber es ist ja wahr... mir ist immer, als wenn ich mir eine Geschichte erzählen möcht'... aber es ist wahr... ich muß mich umbringen, es bleibt mir ja nichts anderes übrig – ich kann's ja nicht d'rauf ankommen lassen, daß morgen früh der Kopetzky und der Blany mir ihr Mandat zurückgeben und mir sagen: wir können dir nicht sekundieren!... Ich wär' ja ein Schuft, wenn ich's ihnen zumuten möcht'... So ein Kerl wie ich, der dasteht und sich einen dummen Buben heißen läßt... morgen wissen's ja alle Leut'... das ist zu dumm, daß ich mir einen Moment einbilde, so ein Mensch erzählt's nicht weiter... überall wird er's erzählen... seine Frau weiß's jetzt schon... morgen weiß es das ganze Kaffeehaus... die Kellner werd'n's wissen... der Herr Schlesinger – die Kassierin – – Und selbst, wenn er sich vorgenommen hat, er red't nicht davon, so sagt er's übermorgen... und wenn er's übermorgen nicht sagt, in einer Woche... Und wenn ihn heut' nacht der Schlag trifft, so weiß ich's... ich weiß es... und ich bin nicht der Mensch, der weiter den Rock trägt und den Säbel, wenn ein solcher Schimpf auf ihm sitzt!... So, ich muß es tun, und Schluß! – Was ist weiter dabei? – Morgen nachmittag könnt' mich der Doktor mit 'm Säbel erschlagen... so was ist schon einmal dagewesen... und der Bauer, der arme Kerl, der hat eine Gehirnentzündung 'kriegt und war in drei Tagen hin... und der Brenitsch ist vom Pferd gestürzt und hat sich 's Genick gebrochen... und schließlich und endlich: es gibt nichts anderes – für mich nicht, für mich nicht! – Es gibt ja Leut', die's leichter nähmen... Gott, was gibt's für Menschen!... Dem Ringeimer hat ein Fleischselcher, wie er ihn mit seiner Frau erwischt hat, eine Ohrfeige gegeben, und er hat quittiert und sitzt irgendwo auf'm Land und hat geheiratet... Daß es Weiber gibt, die so einen Menschen heiraten!... – Meiner Seel', ich gäb' ihm nicht die Hand, wenn er wieder nach Wien käm'... Also, hast's gehört, Gustl: – aus, aus, abgeschlossen mit dem

Leben! Punktum und Streusand d'rauf!... So, jetzt weiß ich's, die Geschichte ist ganz einfach... So! Ich bin eigentlich ganz ruhig... Das hab' ich übrigens immer gewußt: wenn's einmal dazu kommt, werd' ich ruhig sein, ganz ruhig... aber daß es so dazu kommt, das hab' ich doch nicht gedacht... daß ich mich umbringen muß, weil so ein... Vielleicht hab' ich ihn doch nicht recht verstanden... am End' hat er ganz was anderes gesagt... Ich war ja ganz blöd von der Singerei und der Hitz'... vielleicht bin ich verrückt gewesen, und es ist alles gar nicht wahr?... Nicht wahr, haha, nicht wahr! – Ich hör's ja noch... es klingt mir noch immer im Ohr... und ich spür's in den Fingern, wie ich seine Hand vom Säbelgriff hab' wegbringen wollen... Ein Kraftmensch ist er, ein Jagendorfer... Ich bin doch auch kein Schwächling... der Franziski ist der einzige im Regiment, der stärker ist als ich...

Die Aspernbrücke... Wie weit renn' ich denn noch? – Wenn ich so weiterrenn', bin ich um Mitternacht in Kagran... Haha! – Herrgott, froh sind wir gewesen, wie wir im vorigen September dort eingerückt sind. Noch zwei Stunden, und Wien... todmüd' war ich, wie wir angekommen sind... den ganzen Nachmittag hab' ich geschlafen wie ein Stock, und am Abend waren wir schon beim Ronacher... der Kopetzky, der Ladinser und... wer war denn nur noch mit uns? – Ja, richtig, der Freiwillige, der uns auf dem Marsch die jüdischen Anekdoten erzählt hat... Manchmal sind's ganz nette Burschen, die Einjährigen... aber sie sollten alle nur Stellvertreter werden – denn was hat das für einen Sinn? Wir müssen uns jahrelang plagen, und so ein Kerl dient ein Jahr und hat genau dieselbe Distinktion wie wir... es ist eine Ungerechtigkeit! – Aber was geht mich denn das alles an? – Was scher' ich mich denn um solche Sachen? – Ein Gemeiner von der Verpflegsbranche ist ja jetzt mehr als ich: ich bin ja überhaupt nicht mehr auf der Welt... es ist ja aus mit mir... Ehre verloren, alles verloren!... Ich hab' ja nichts anderes zu tun, als meinen Revolver zu laden und... Gustl, Gustl, mir scheint, du glaubst noch immer nicht recht d'ran? Komm' nur zur Besinnung... es gibt nichts anderes... wenn du auch dein Gehirn zermarterst, es gibt nichts anderes! – Jetzt heißt's nur mehr, im letzten Moment sich anständig benehmen, ein Mann sein, ein Offizier sein, so daß der Oberst sagt: Er ist ein braver Kerl gewesen, wir werden ihm ein treues Angedenken bewahren!... Wieviel Kompagnien rücken denn aus beim Leichenbegängnis von einem Leutnant?... Das müßt' ich eigentlich wissen... Haha! Wenn das ganze Bataillon ausrückt, oder die ganze Garnison, und sie feuern zwanzig Salven ab, davon wach' ich doch nimmer auf! – Vor dem Kaffeehaus, da bin ich im vorigen Sommer einmal mit dem Herrn von Engel gesessen, nach der Armee-Steeple-Chase... Komisch, den Menschen hab' ich seitdem nie wieder gesehn... Warum hat er denn das linke Aug' verbunden gehabt? Ich hab' ihn immer d'rum fragen wollen, aber es hätt' sich nicht gehört... Da geh'n zwei Artilleristen... die denken gewiß, ich steig' der Person nach... Muß sie mir übrigens anseh'n... O schrecklich! – Ich möcht' nur wissen, wie sich so eine ihr Brot verdient... da möcht' ich doch eher... Obzwar, in der Not frißt der Teufel Fliegen... in Przemysl – mir hat's nachher so gegraust, daß ich gemeint hab', nie wieder rühr' ich ein Frauenzimmer an... Das war eine gräßliche Zeit da oben in Galizien... eigentlich ein Mordsglück, daß wir nach Wien gekommen sind. Der Bokorny sitzt noch immer in Sambor und kann noch zehn Jahr' dort sitzen und alt und grau werden.. Aber wenn ich dort geblieben wär', wär' mir das nicht passiert, was mir heut' passiert ist... und ich möcht' lieber in Galizien alt und grau werden, als daß... als was? Als was? – Ja, was ist denn? Was ist denn? – Bin ich denn wahnsinnig, daß ich das immer vergeß'? – Ja, meiner Seel', vergessen tu' ich's jeden Moment... ist das schon je erhört worden, daß sich einer in ein paar Stunden eine Kugel durch'n Kopf jagen muß, und er denkt an alle möglichen Sachen, die ihn gar nichts mehr angeh'n? Meiner Seel', mir ist geradeso, als wenn ich einen Rausch hätt'! Haha! Ein schöner Rausch! Ein Mordsrausch! Ein Selbstmordsrausch! – Ha! Witze mach' ich, das ist sehr gut! – Ja, ganz gut aufgelegt bin ich – so was muß doch angeboren sein... Wahrhaftig, wenn ich's einem erzählen möcht', er würd' es nicht glauben. – Mir scheint, wenn ich das Ding bei mir hätt'... jetzt würd' ich abdrücken – in einer Sekunde ist alles vorbei... Nicht jeder hat's so gut – andere müssen sich monatelang plagen... meine arme Cousin', zwei Jahr' ist sie gelegen, hat sich nicht rühren können, hat die gräßlichsten Schmerzen g'habt – so ein Jammer!... Ist es nicht besser, wenn man das selber besorgt? Nur Obacht geben heißt's, gut zielen, daß einem nicht am End' das Malheur passiert, wie dem Kadett-Stellvertreter im vorigen Jahr... Der arme Teufel, gestorben ist er nicht, aber blind ist er geworden... Was mit dem nur geschehen ist? Wo er jetzt lebt? – Schrecklich, so herumlaufen, wie der – das heißt: herumlaufen kann er nicht, g'führt muß er werden – so ein junger Mensch, kann heut' noch keine Zwanzig sein.. seine Geliebte hat er besser getroffen... gleich war sie tot... Unglaublich, weswegen sich die Leut' totschießen! Wie kann man überhaupt nur eifersüchtig sein?... Mein Lebtag hab' ich so was nicht gekannt... Die Steffi ist jetzt gemütlich in der Gartenbaugesellschaft; dann geht sie mit »ihm« nach Haus... Nichts liegt mir d'ran, gar nichts! Hübsche Einrichtung hat sie – das kleine Badezimmer mit der roten Latern'. – Wie sie neulich in dem grünseidenen Schlafrock hereingekommen ist... den grünen Schlafrock werd' ich auch nimmer seh'n – und die ganze Steffi auch nicht... und die schöne, breite Treppe in der Gußhausstraße werd' ich auch nimmer hinaufgeh'n... Das Fräulein Steffi wird sich weiter amüsieren, als wenn gar nichts gescheh'n wär'... nicht einmal erzählen darf sie's wem, daß ihr lieber Gustl sich umgebracht hat... Aber weinen wirds' schon – ah ja, weinen wirds'... Überhaupt, weinen werden gar viele Leut'... Um Gottes willen, die Mama! – Nein, nein, daran darf ich nicht denken. – Ah, nein, daran darf absolut nicht gedacht werden... An Zuhaus wird nicht gedacht, Gustl, verstanden? – Nicht mit dem allerleisesten Gedanken...

Das ist nicht schlecht, jetzt bin ich gar im Prater... mitten in der Nacht... das hätt' ich mir auch nicht gedacht in der Früh', daß ich heut' nacht im Prater spazieren geh'n werd'... Was sich der Sicherheitswachmann dort denkt?... Na, geh'n wir nur weiter... es ist ganz schön... Mit'm Nachtmahlen ist's eh' nichts, mit dem Kaffeehaus auch nichts; die Luft ist angenehm, und ruhig ist es.. sehr.. Zwar, ruhig werd' ich's jetzt bald haben, so ruhig, als ich's mir nur wünschen kann. Haha! – Aber ich bin ja ganz außer Atem... ich bin ja gerannt wie nicht g'scheit... langsamer, langsamer, Gustl, versäumst nichts, hast gar nichts mehr zu tun – gar nichts, aber absolut nichts mehr! – Mir scheint gar, ich fröstel'? – Es wird halt doch die Aufregung sein... dann hab' ich ja nichts gegessen... Was riecht denn da so eigentümlich?... Es kann doch noch nichts blühen?... Was haben wir denn heut'? – Den vierten April... freilich, es hat viel geregnet in den letzten Tagen... aber die Bäume sind beinah' noch ganz kahl... und dunkel ist es, hu! Man könnt' schier Angst kriegen... Das ist eigentlich das einzigemal in meinem Leben, daß ich Furcht gehabt hab', als kleiner Bub, damals im Wald... aber ich war ja gar nicht so klein... vierzehn oder fünfzehn... Wie lang' ist das jetzt her? – Neun Jahr'... freilich – mit achtzehn war ich Stellvertreter, mit zwanzig Leutnant... und im nächsten Jahr werd' ich... Was werd' ich im nächsten Jahr? Was heißt das überhaupt: nächstes Jahr? Was heißt das: in der nächsten Woche? Was heißt das: übermorgen?... Wie? Zähneklappern? Oho! – Na, lassen wir's nur ein biss'l klappern... Herr Leutnant, Sie sind jetzt allein, brauchen niemandem einen Pflanz vorzumachen... es ist bitter, es ist bitter...

Ich will mich auf die Bank setzen... Ah! – Wie weit bin ich denn da? – So eine Dunkelheit! Das da hinter mir, das muß das zweite Kaffeehaus sein.. bin ich im vorigen Sommer auch einmal gewesen, wie unsere Kapelle konzertiert hat... mit'm Kopetzky und mit'm Rüttner – noch ein paar waren dabei.. – Ich bin aber müd'... nein, ich bin müd', als wenn ich einen Marsch von zehn Stunden gemacht hätt'... Ja, das wär' sowas, da einschlafen. – Ha! Ein obdachloser Leutnant.. Ja, ich sollt' doch eigentlich nach Haus... was tu' ich denn zu Haus? Aber was tu' ich denn im Prater? – Ah, mir wär' am liebsten, ich müßt' gar nicht aufsteh'n – da einschlafen und nimmer aufwachen... ja, das wär' halt bequem! – Nein, so bequem wird's Ihnen nicht gemacht, Herr Leutnant.. Aber wie und wann? – Jetzt könnt' ich mir doch endlich einmal die Geschichte ordentlich überlegen... überlegt muß ja alles werden... so ist es schon einmal im Leben... Also überlegen wir... Was denn?... – Nein, ist die Luft gut... man sollt' öfters bei der Nacht in' Prater geh'n... Ja, das hätt' mir eben früher einfallen müssen, jetzt ist's aus mit'm Prater, mit der Luft und mit'm Spazierengeh'n... Ja, also was ist denn? – Ah, fort mit dem Kappl; mir scheint, das drückt mir aufs Gehirn... ich kann ja gar nicht ordentlich denken... Ah... so!... Also jetzt Verstand zusammennehmen, Gustl... letzte Verfügungen treffen! Also morgen früh wird Schluß gemacht... morgen früh um sieben Uhr... sieben Uhr ist eine schöne Stund'. Haha! – Also um acht, wenn die Schul' anfangt, ist alles vorbei... der Kopetzky wird aber keine Schul' halten können, weil er zu sehr erschüttert sein wird.. Aber vielleicht weiß er's noch gar nicht... man braucht ja nichts zu hören... Den Max Lippay haben sie auch erst am Nachmittag gefunden, und in der Früh' hat er sich erschossen, und kein Mensch hat was davon gehört... Aber was geht mich das an, ob der Kopetzky Schul' halten wird oder nicht?... Ha! – Also um sieben Uhr! – Ja... na, was denn noch?... Weiter ist ja nichts zu überlegen. Im Zimmer schieß' ich mich tot, und dann is basta! Montag ist die Leich'... Einen kenn' ich, der wird eine Freud' haben: das ist der Doktor... Duell kann nicht stattfinden wegen Selbstmord des einen Kombattanten... Was sie bei Mannheimers sagen werden? – Na, er wird sich nicht viel d'raus machen... aber die Frau, die hübsche, blonde... mit der war was zu machen... O ja, mir scheint, bei der hätt' ich Chance gehabt, wenn ich mich nur ein bissl zusammengenommen hätt'... ja, das wär' doch was anders gewesen, als die Steffi, dieses Mensch... Aber faul darf man halt nicht sein... da heißt's: Cour machen, Blumen schicken, vernünftig reden... das geht nicht so, daß man sagt: Komm' morgen nachmittag zu mir in die Kasern'!... Ja, so eine anständige Frau, das wär' halt was g'wesen... Die Frau von meinem Hauptmann in Przemysl, das war ja doch keine anständige Frau... ich könnt' schwören: der Libitzky und der Wermutek und der schäbige Stellvertreter, der hat sie auch g'habt...

Aber die Frau Mannheimer ... ja, das wär' was anders, das wär' doch auch ein Umgang gewesen, das hätt' einen beinah' zu einem andern Menschen gemacht – da hätt' man doch noch einen andern Schliff gekriegt – da hätt' man einen Respekt vor sich selber haben dürfen. – – Aber ewig diese Menscher ... und so jung hab' ich ang'fangen – ein Bub war ich ja noch, wie ich damals den ersten Urlaub gehabt hab' und in Graz bei den Eltern zu Haus war ... der Riedl war auch dabei – eine Böhmin ist es gewesen ... die muß doppelt so alt gewesen sein wie ich – in der Früh bin ich erst nach Haus gekommen ... Wie mich der Vater ang'schaut hat ... und die Klara ... Vor der Klara hab' ich mich am meisten g'schämt ... Damals war sie verlobt ... warum ist denn nichts d'raus geworden? Ich hab' mich eigentlich nicht viel d'rum gekümmert ... Armes Hascherl, hat auch nie Glück gehabt – und jetzt verliert sie noch den einzigen Bruder ... Ja, wirst mich nimmer seh'n, Klara – aus! Was, das hast du dir nicht gedacht, Schwesterl, wie du mich am Neujahrstag zur Bahn begleitet hast, daß du mich nie wieder seh'n wirst? – Und die Mama ... Herrgott, die Mama ... nein, ich darf daran nicht denken ... wenn ich daran denk', bin ich imstand', eine Gemeinheit zu begehen ... Ah ... wenn ich zuerst noch nach Haus fahren möcht' ... sagen, es ist ein Urlaub auf einen Tag ... noch einmal den Papa, die Mama, die Klara seh'n, bevor ich einen Schluß mach' ... Ja, mit dem ersten Zug um sieben kann ich nach Graz fahren, um eins bin ich dort ... Grüß dich Gott, Mama ... Servus, Klara! Na, wie geht's euch denn? ... Nein, das ist eine Überraschung! ... Aber sie möchten was merken ... wenn niemand anders ... die Klara ... die Klara gewiß ... Die Klara ist ein so gescheites Mädel ... Wie lieb sie mir neulich geschrieben hat, und ich bin ihr noch immer die Antwort schuldig – und die guten Ratschläge, die sie mir immer gibt ... ein so seelengutes Geschöpf ... Ob nicht alles ganz anders geworden wär', wenn ich zu Haus geblieben wär'? Ich hätt' Ökonomie studiert, wär' zum Onkel gegangen ... sie haben's ja alle wollen, wie ich noch ein Bub war ... Jetzt wär' ich am End' schon verheiratet, ein liebes, gutes Mädel ... vielleicht die Anna, die hat mich so gern gehabt... auch jetzt hab' ich's noch gemerkt, wie ich das letztemal zu Haus war, obzwar sie schon einen Mann hat und zwei Kinder... ich hab's g'sehn', wie sie mich ang'schaut hat... Und noch immer sagt sie mir »Gustl« wie früher... Der wird's ordentlich in die Glieder fahren, wenn sie erfährt, was es mit mir für ein End' genommen hat – aber ihr Mann wird sagen: Das hab' ich vorausgesehen – so ein Lump! – Alle werden meinen, es ist, weil ich Schulden gehabt hab'... und es ist doch gar nicht wahr, es ist doch alles gezahlt... nur die letzten hundertsechzig Gulden – na, und die sind morgen da... Ja, dafür muß ich auch noch sorgen, daß der Ballert die hundertsechzig Gulden kriegt... das muß ich niederschreiben, bevor ich mich erschieß'... Es ist schrecklich, es ist schrecklich!... Wenn ich lieber auf und davon fahren möcht' – nach Amerika, wo mich niemand kennt... In Amerika weiß kein Mensch davon, was hier heut' abend gescheh'n ist... da kümmert sich kein Mensch d'rum... Neulich ist in der Zeitung gestanden von einem Grafen Runge, der hat fortmüssen wegen einer schmutzigen Geschichte, und jetzt hat er drüben ein Hotel und pfeift auf den ganzen Schwindel... Und in ein paar Jahren könnt' man ja wieder zurück... nicht nach Wien natürlich... auch nicht nach Graz... aber aufs Gut könnt' ich... und der Mama und dem Papa und der Klara möcht's doch tausendmal lieber sein, wenn ich nur lebendig blieb'... Und was geh'n mich denn die andern Leut' an? Wer meint's denn sonst gut mit mir? – Außer'm Kopetzky könnt' ich allen gestohlen werden... der Kopetzky ist doch der einzige... Und grad der hat mir heut' das Billett geben müssen... und das Billett ist an allem schuld... ohne das Billett wär' ich nicht ins Konzert gegangen, und alles das wär' nicht passiert... Was ist denn nur passiert?... Es ist grad, als wenn hundert Jahr' seitdem vergangen wären, und es kann noch keine zwei Stunden sein... Vor zwei Stunden hat mir einer »dummer Bub« gesagt und hat meinen Säbel zerbrechen wollen... Herrgott, ich fang' noch zu schreien an mitten in der Nacht! Warum ist denn das alles gescheh'n? Hätt' ich nicht länger warten können, bis's ganz leer wird in der Garderobe? Und warum hab' ich ihm denn nur gesagt: »Halten Sie's Maul!«? Wie ist mir denn das nur ausgerutscht? Ich bin doch sonst ein höflicher Mensch.. nicht einmal mit meinem Burschen bin ich sonst so grob... aber natürlich, nervos bin ich gewesen – alle die Sachen, die da zusammengekommen sind... das Pech im Spiel und die ewige Absagerei von der Steffi – und das Duell morgen nachmittag – und zu wenig schlafen tu' ich in der letzten Zeit – und die Rackerei in der Kasern' – das halt't man auf die Dauer nicht aus!... Ja, über kurz oder lang wär' ich krank geworden – hätt' um einen Urlaub einkommen müssen... Jetzt ist es nicht mehr notwendig – jetzt kommt ein langer Urlaub – mit Karenz der Gebühren – haha!...

Wie lang werd' ich denn da noch sitzen bleiben? Es muß Mitternacht vorbei sein... hab' ich's nicht früher schlagen hören? – Was ist denn das... ein Wagen fährt da? Um die Zeit? Gummiradler – kann mir schon denken... Die haben's besser wie ich – vielleicht ist es der Ballert mit der Bertha... Warum soll's grad der Ballert sein? – Fahr' nur zu! – Ein hübsches Zeug'l hat Seine Hoheit in Pzremysl gehabt... mit dem ist er immer in die Stadt hinunterg'fahren zu der Rosenberg... Sehr leutselig war Seine Hoheit – ein echter Kamerad, mit allen auf du und du.. War doch eine schöne Zeit.. obzwar.. die Gegend war trostlos und im Sommer zum Verschmachten... an einem Nachmittag sind einmal drei vom Sonnenstich getroffen worden... auch der Korporal von meinem Zug – ein so verwendbarer Mensch... Nachmittag haben wir uns nackt aufs Bett hingelegt. – Einmal ist plötzlich der Wiesner zu mir hereingekommen; ich muß grad geträumt haben und steh' auf und zieh' den Säbel, der neben mir liegt... muß gut ausg'schaut haben... der Wiesner hat sich halbtot gelacht – der ist jetzt schon Rittmeister... – Schad', daß ich nicht zur Kavallerie gegangen bin... aber das hat der Alte nicht wollen – wär' ein zu teurer Spaß gewesen – jetzt ist es ja doch alles eins... Warum denn? – Ja, ich ich weiß schon: sterben muß ich, darum ist es alles eins – sterben muß ich... Also wie? – Schau, Gustl, du bist doch extra da herunter in den Prater gegangen, mitten in der Nacht, wo dich keine Menschenseele stört –

jetzt kannst du dir alles ruhig überlegen... Das ist ja lauter Unsinn mit Amerika und quittieren, und du bist ja viel zu dumm, um was anderes anzufangen – und wenn du hundert Jahr' alt wirst, und du denkst d'ran, daß dir einer hat den Säbel zerbrechen wollen und dich einen dummen Buben g'heißen, und du bist dag'standen und hast nichts tun können – nein, zu überlegen ist da gar nichts – gescheh'n ist gescheh'n – auch das mit der Mama und mit der Klara ist ein Unsinn – die werden's schon verschmerzen – man verschmerzt alles... Wie hat die Mama gejammert, wie ihr Bruder gestorben ist – und nach vier Wochen hat sie kaum mehr d'ran gedacht... auf den Friedhof ist sie hinausgefahren... zuerst alle Wochen, dann alle Monat' – und jetzt nur mehr am Todestag. – – Morgen ist mein Todestag – fünfter April. – – Ob sie mich nach Graz überführen? Haha! Da werden die Würmer in Graz eine Freud' haben! – Aber das geht mich nichts an – darüber sollen sich die andern den Kopf zerbrechen... Also, was geht mich denn eigentlich an?... Ja, die hundertsechzig Gulden für den Ballert – das ist alles – weiter brauch' ich keine Verfügungen zu treffen. – Briefe schreiben? Wozu denn? An wen denn?... Abschied nehmen? – Ja, zum Teufel hinein, das ist doch deutlich genug, wenn man sich totschießt! – Dann merken's die andern schon, daß man Abschied genommen hat... Wenn die Leut' wüßten, wie egal mir die ganze Geschichte ist, möchten sie mich gar nicht bedauern – ist eh' nicht schad' um mich... Und was hab' ich denn vom ganzen Leben gehabt? – Etwas hätt' ich gern noch mitgemacht: einen Krieg – aber da hätt' ich lang' warten können... Und alles übrige kenn' ich... Ob so ein Mensch Steffi oder Kunigunde heißt, bleibt sich gleich. – – Und die schönsten Operetten kenn' ich auch – und im ›Lohengrin‹ bin ich zwölfmal d'rin gewesen – und heut' abend war ich sogar bei einem Oratorium – und ein Bäckermeister hat mich einen dummen Buben geheißen – meiner Seel', es ist grad' genug! – Und ich bin gar nimmer neugierig... – Also geh'n wir nach Haus, langsam, ganz langsam... Eile hab' ich ja wirklich keine. – Noch ein paar Minuten ausruhen da im Prater, auf einer Bank – obdachlos. – Ins Bett leg' ich mich ja doch nimmer – hab' ja genug Zeit zum Ausschlafen. – – Ah, die Luft! – Die wird mir abgeh'n...

Was ist denn? – He, Johann, bringen S' mir ein Glas frisches Wasser... Was ist?... Wo... Ja, träum' ich denn?... Mein Schädel... o, Donnerwetter... Fischamend... Ich bring' die Augen nicht auf! – Ich bin ja angezogen! – Wo sitz' ich denn? – Heiliger Himmel, eingeschlafen bin ich! Wie hab' ich denn nur schlafen können; es dämmert ja schon! – Wie lang' hab' ich denn geschlafen? – Muß auf die Uhr schau'n... Ich seh' nichts?... Wo sind denn meine Zündhölzeln?... Na, brennt eins an?... Drei... und ich soll mich um vier duellieren – nein, nicht duellieren – totschießen soll ich mich! – Es ist gar nichts mit dem Duell; ich muß mich totschießen, weil ein Bäckermeister mich einen dummen Buben genannt hat... Ja, ist es denn wirklich g'scheh'n? – Mir ist im Kopf so merkwürdig... wie in einem Schraubstock ist mein Hals – ich kann mich gar nicht rühren – das rechte Bein ist eingeschlafen. – Aufsteh'n! Aufsteh'n!... Ah, so ist es besser! – Es wird schon lichter... Und die Luft... ganz wie damals in der Früh', wie ich auf Vorposten war und im Wald kampiert hab'... Das war ein anderes Aufwachen – da war ein anderer Tag vor mir.. Mir scheint, ich glaub's noch nicht recht. – Da liegt die Straße, grau, leer – ich bin jetzt sicher der einzige Mensch im Prater. – Um vier Uhr früh war ich schon einmal herunten, mit'm Pausinger – geritten sind wir – ich auf dem Pferd vom Hauptmann Mirovic und der Pausinger auf seinem eigenen Krampen – das war im Mai, im vorigen Jahr – da hat schon alles geblüht – alles war grün. Jetzt ist's noch kahl – aber der Frühling kommt bald – in ein paar Tagen ist er schon da. – Maiglöckerln, Veigerln – schad', daß ich nichts mehr davon haben werd' – jeder Schubiak hat was davon, und ich muß sterben! Es ist ein Elend! Und die andern werden im Weingartl sitzen beim Nachtmahl, als wenn gar nichts g'wesen wär' – so wie wir alle im Weingartl g'sessen sind, noch am Abend nach dem Tag, wo sie den Lippay hinausgetragen haben... Und der Lippay war so beliebt... sie haben ihn lieber g'habt, als mich, beim Regiment – warum sollen sie denn nicht im Weingartl sitzen, wenn ich abkratz'? – Ganz warm ist es – viel wärmer als gestern – und so ein Duft – es muß doch schon blühen... Ob die Steffi mir Blumen bringen wird? – Aber fallt ihr ja gar nicht ein! Die wird grad hinausfahren... Ja, wenn's noch die Adel' wär'.. Nein, die Adel'! Mir scheint, seit zwei Jahren hab' ich an die nicht mehr gedacht... Was die für G'schichten gemacht hat, wie's aus war... mein Lebtag hab' ich kein Frauenzimmer so weinen geseh'n... Das war doch eigentlich das Hübscheste, was ich erlebt hab'... So bescheiden, so anspruchslos, wie die war – die hat mich gern gehabt, da könnt' ich d'rauf schwören. – War doch was ganz anderes, als die Steffi... Ich möcht' nur wissen, warum ich die aufgegeben hab'... so eine Eselei! Zu fad ist es mir geworden, ja, das war das Ganze... So jeden Abend mit ein und derselben ausgeh'n... Dann hab' ich eine Angst g'habt, daß ich überhaupt nimmer loskomm' – eine solche Raunzen – – Na, Gustl, hätt'st schon noch warten können – war doch die einzige, die dich gern gehabt hat... Was sie jetzt macht? Na, was wird's machen? – Jetzt wird's halt einen andern haben... Freilich, das mit der Steffi ist bequemer – wenn man nur gelegentlich engagiert ist und ein anderer hat die ganzen Unannehmlichkeiten, und ich hab' nur das Vergnügen... Ja, da kann man auch nicht verlangen, daß sie auf den Friedhof hinauskommt.. Wer ging' denn überhaupt mit, wenn er nicht müßt'! – Vielleicht der Kopetzky, und dann wär' Rest! – Ist doch traurig, so gar niemanden zu haben...

Aber so ein Unsinn! Der Papa und die Mama und die Klara... Ja, ich bin halt der Sohn, der Bruder... aber was ist denn weiter zwischen uns? Gern haben sie mich ja – aber was wissen sie denn von mir? – Daß ich meinen Dienst mach', daß ich Karten spiel' und daß ich mit Menschern herumlauf'... aber sonst? – Daß mich manchmal selber vor mir graust, das hab' ich ihnen ja doch nicht geschrieben – na, mir scheint, ich hab's auch selber gar nicht recht gewußt. – Ah was, kommst du jetzt mit solchen Sachen, Gustl? Fehlt nur noch, daß zu zum Weinen anfangst... pfui Teufel! – Ordentlich Schritt... so! Ob man zu einem

Rendezvous geht oder auf Posten oder in die Schlacht... wer hat
das nur gesagt?... Ah ja, der Major Lederer, in der Kantin', wie
man von dem Wingleder erzählt hat, der so blaß geworden ist
vor seinem ersten Duell – und gespieben hat... Ja: ob man zu
einem Rendezvous geht oder in den sicher'n Tod, am Gang und
am G'sicht läßt sich das der richtige Offizier nicht anerkennen! –
Also Gustl – der Major Lederer hat's g'sagt! Ha! –

Immer lichter... man könnt' schon lesen.... Was pfeift denn
da?.... Ah, drüben ist der Nordbahnhof.... Die Tegetthoff-
säule... so lang' hat sie noch nie ausg'schaut... Da drüben stehen Wagen... Aber nichts als Straßenkehrer auf der Straße...
meine letzten Straßenkehrer – ha! Ich muß immer lachen, wenn
ich d'ran denk'... das versteh' ich gar nicht... Ob das bei allen
Leuten so ist, wenn sie's einmal ganz sicher wissen? Halb vier auf
der Nordbahnuhr... jetzt ist nur die Frage, ob ich mich um sieben nach Bahnzeit oder nach Wiener Zeit erschieß?... Sieben...
ja, warum grad' sieben?... Als wenn's gar nicht anders sein
könnt'... Hunger hab' ich – meiner Seel', ich hab' Hunger –
kein Wunder... seit wann hab' ich denn nichts gegessen?... Seit
– seit gestern sechs Uhr abends im Kaffeehaus... ja! Wie mir der
Kopetzky das Billett gegeben hat – eine Melange und zwei Kip-
fel. – Was der Bäckermeister sagen wird, wenn er's erfahrt?...
Der verfluchte Hund! – Ah, der wird wissen, warum – dem wird
der Knopf aufgeh'n – der wird draufkommen, was es heißt: Offizier! – So ein Kerl kann sich auf offener Straße prügeln lassen,
und es hat keine Folgen, und unsereiner wird unter vier Augen
insultiert und ist ein toter Mann... Wenn sich so ein Fallot wenigstens schlagen möcht' – aber nein, da wär' er ja vorsichtiger,
da möcht' er sowas nicht riskieren... Und der Kerl lebt weiter,
ruhig weiter, während ich – krepieren muß! – Der hat mich doch
umgebracht... Ja, Gustl, merkst d' was? – Der ist es, der dich
umbringt! Aber so glatt soll's ihm doch nicht ausgeh'n! – Nein,
nein, nein! Ich werd' dem Kopetzky einen Brief schreiben, wo
alles drinsteht, die ganze G'schicht' schreib' ich auf... oder noch
besser: ich schreib's dem Obersten, ich mach' eine Meldung ans
Regimentskommando... ganz wie eine dienstliche Meldung...

Ja, wart', du glaubst, daß sowas geheim bleiben kann? – Du irrst dich – aufgeschrieben wird's zum ewigen Gedächtnis, und dann möcht' ich sehen, ob du dich noch ins Kaffeehaus traust! – Ha! – »Das möcht' ich sehen« ist gut!... Ich möcht' noch manches gern seh'n, wird nur leider nicht möglich sein – aus is! –

Jetzt kommt der Johann in mein Zimmer, jetzt merkt er, daß der Herr Leutnant nicht zu Haus geschlafen hat. – Na, alles mögliche wird er sich denken; aber daß der Herr Leutnant im Prater übernachtet hat, das, meiner Seel', das nicht... Ah, die Vierundvierziger! Zur Schießstätte marschieren s' – lassen wir sie vorübergeh'n... so stellen wir uns da her... – Da oben wird ein Fenster aufgemacht – hübsche Person – na, ich möcht' mir wenigstens ein Tüchel umnehmen, wenn ich zum Fenster geh'... Vorigen Sonntag war's zum letztenmal... Daß grad' die Steffi die letzte sein wird, hab' ich mir nicht träumen lassen. – Ach Gott, das ist doch das einzige reelle Vergnügen... Na ja, der Herr Oberst wird in zwei Stunden nobel nachreiten... die Herren haben's gut – ja, ja, rechts g'schaut! – Ist schon gut... Wenn ihr wüßtet, wie ich auf euch pfeif'! – Ah, das ist nicht schlecht: der Katzer... seit wann ist denn der zu den Vierundvierzigern übersetzt? – Servus, servus! – Was der für ein G'sicht macht?... Warum deut' er denn auf seinen Kopf? – Mein Lieber, dein Schädel interessiert mich sehr wenig... Ah, so! Nein, mein Lieber, du irrst dich: im Prater hab' ich übernachtet... wirst schon heut' im Abendblatt lesen. – »Nicht möglich!« wird er sagen; »heut' früh, wie wir zur Schießstätte ausgerückt sind, hab' ich ihn noch auf der Praterstraße getroffen!« – Wer wird denn meinen Zug kriegen? – Ob sie ihn dem Walterer geben werden? – Na, da wird was Schönes herauskommen – ein Kerl ohne Schneid – der hätt' auch lieber Schuster werden sollen... Was, geht schon die Sonne auf? – Das wird heut' ein schöner Tag – so ein rechter Frühlingstag... Ist doch eigentlich zum Teufelholen! – Der Komfortabelkutscher wird noch um achte in der Früh' auf der Welt sein, und ich... na, was ist denn das? He, das wär' sowas – noch im letzten Moment die Contenance verlieren wegen einem Komfortabelkutscher... Was ist denn das, daß ich auf einmal so ein blödes Herzklopfen krieg'? – Das wird doch nicht deswegen sein.. Nein, o nein... es ist, weil ich so lang' nichts gegessen hab'. – – Aber Gustl, sei doch aufrichtig mit dir selber: – Angst hast du – Angst, weil du's noch nie probiert hast... Aber das hilft dir ja nichts, die Angst hat noch keinem was geholfen, jeder muß es einmal durchmachen, der eine früher, der andere später, und du kommst halt früher d'ran... Viel wert bist du ja nie gewesen, so benimm dich wenigstens anständig zu guter Letzt, das verlang' ich von dir! – So, jetzt heißt's nur überlegen – aber was denn?... Immer will ich mir was überlegen... ist doch ganz einfach: – im Nachtkastelladel liegt er, geladen ist er auch, heißt's nur: losdrucken – das wird doch keine Kunst sein! – –

Die geht schon ins G'schäft... die armen Mädeln! Die Adel' war auch in einem G'schäft – ein paarmal hab' ich sie am Abend abg'holt... Wenn sie in einem G'schäft sind, werd'n sie doch keine solchen Menscher... Wenn die Steffi mir allein g'hören möcht', ich ließ sie Modistin werden oder sowas... Wie wird sie's denn erfahren? – Aus der Zeitung!... Sie wird sich ärgern, daß ich ihr's nicht geschrieben hab'... Mir scheint, ich schnapp' doch noch über... Was geht denn das mich an, ob sie sich ärgert... Wie lang' hat denn die ganze G'schicht gedauert?... Seit'm Jänner?... Ah nein, es muß doch schon vor Weihnachten gewesen sein... ich hab' ihr ja aus Graz Zuckerln mitgebracht, und zu Neujahr hat sie mir ein Brieferl g'schickt... Richtig, die Briefe, die ich zu Haus hab', – sind keine da, die ich verbrennen sollt'?... Hm, der vom Fallsteiner – wenn man den Brief findet... der Bursch könnt' Unannehmlichkeiten haben... Was mir das schon aufliegt! – Na, es ist ja keine große Anstrengung... aber hervorsuchen kann ich den Wisch nicht... Das beste ist, ich verbrenn' alles zusammen... wer braucht's denn? Ist lauter Makulatur. – – Und meine paar Bücher könnt' ich dem Blany vermachen. – ›Durch Nacht und Eis‹... schad', daß ich's nimmer auslesen kann... bin wenig zum Lesen gekommen in der letzten Zeit... Orgel – ah, aus der Kirche... Frühmesse – bin schon lang' bei keiner gewesen... das letztemal im Feber, wie mein Zug dazu kommandiert war... Aber das galt nichts –

ich hab' auf meine Leut' aufgepaßt, ob sie andächtig sind und sich ordentlich benehmen... – Möcht' in die Kirche hineingeh'n... am End' ist doch was d'ran... – Na, heut' nach Tisch werd' ich's schon genau wissen... Ah, »nach Tisch« ist sehr gut!... Also, was ist, soll ich hineingeh'n? – Ich glaub', der Mama wär's ein Trost, wenn sie das wüßt'!... Die Klara gibt weniger d'rauf... Na, geh'n wir hinein – schaden kann's ja nicht!

Orgel – Gesang – hm! – Was ist denn das? – Mir ist ganz schwindlig... O Gott, o Gott, o Gott! Ich möcht' einen Menschen haben, mit dem ich ein Wort reden könnt' vorher! – Das wär' so was – zur Beicht' geh'n! Der möcht' Augen machen, der Pfaff', wenn ich zum Schluß sagen möcht': Habe die Ehre, Hochwürden; jetzt geh' ich mich umbringen!... – Am liebsten läg' ich da auf dem Steinboden und tät' heulen... Ah nein, das darf man nicht tun! Aber weinen tut manchmal so gut... Setzen wir uns einen Moment – aber nicht wieder einschlafen wie im Prater!... – Die Leut', die eine Religion haben, sind doch besser d'ran... Na, jetzt fangen mir gar die Händ' zu zittern an!... Wenn's so weitergeht, werd' ich mir selber auf die Letzt' so ekelhaft, daß ich mich vor lauter Schand' umbring'! – Das alte Weib da – um was betet denn die noch?... Wär' eine Idee, wenn ich ihr sagen möcht': Sie, schließen Sie mich auch ein... ich hab' das nicht ordentlich gelernt, wie man das macht... Ha! Mir scheint, das Sterben macht blöd'! – Aufsteh'n! – Woran erinnert mich denn nur die Melodie? – Heiliger Himmel! Gestern abend! – Fort, fort! Das halt' ich gar nicht aus!... Pst! Keinen solchen Lärm, nicht mit dem Säbel scheppern – die Leut' nicht in der Andacht stören – so! – doch besser im Freien... Licht... Ah, es kommt immer näher – wenn es lieber schon vorbei wär'! – Ich hätt's gleich tun sollen – im Prater... man sollt' nie ohne Revolver ausgeh'n... Hätt' ich gestern abend einen gehabt... Herrgott noch einmal! – In das Kaffeehaus könnt' ich geh'n frühstükken... Hunger hab' ich... Früher ist's mir immer sonderbar vorgekommen, daß die Leut', die verurteilt sind, in der Früh' noch ihren Kaffee trinken und ihr Zigarrl rauchen... Donnerwetter, geraucht hab' ich gar nicht! Gar keine Lust zum Rauchen! – Es ist komisch: ich hätt' Lust, in mein Kaffeehaus zu geh'n... Ja, aufgesperrt ist schon, und von uns ist jetzt doch keiner dort – und wenn schon... ist höchstens ein Zeichen von Kaltblütigkeit. »Um sechs hat er noch im Kaffeehaus gefrühstückt, und um sieben hat er sich erschossen«... – Ganz ruhig bin ich wieder... das Gehen ist so angenehm – und das Schönste ist, daß mich keiner zwingt. – Wenn ich wollt' könnt' ich noch immer den ganzen Krempel hinschmeißen... Amerika... Was ist das: »Krempel«? Was ist ein »Krempel«? Mir scheint, ich hab' den Sonnenstich!... Oho, bin ich vielleicht deshalb so ruhig, weil ich mir noch immer einbild', ich muß nicht?... Ich muß! Ich muß! Nein, ich will! – Kannst du dir denn überhaupt vorstellen, Gustl, daß du dir die Uniform ausziehst und durchgehst? Und der verfluchte Hund lacht sich den Buckel voll – und der Kopetzky selbst möcht' dir nicht mehr die Hand geben... Mir kommt vor, ich bin jetzt ganz rot geworden. – – Der Wachmann salutiert mir... ich muß danken... »Servus!« – Jetzt hab' ich gar »Servus« gesagt!... Das freut so einen armen Teufel immer... Na, über mich hat sich keiner zu beklagen gehabt – außer Dienst war ich immer gemütlich. – Wie wir auf Manöver waren, hab' ich den Chargen von der Kompagnie Britannikas geschenkt; – einmal hab' ich gehört, wie ein Mann hinter mir bei den Gewehrgriffen was von »verfluchter Rackerei« g'sagt hat, und ich hab' ihn nicht zum Rapport geschickt – ich hab' ihm nur gesagt: »Sie, passen S' auf, das könnt' einmal wer anderer hören – da ging's Ihnen schlecht!«... Der Burghof... Wer ist denn heut' auf Wach'? – Die Bosniaken – schau'n gut aus – der Oberstleutnant hat neulich g'sagt: Wie wir im 78er Jahr unten waren, hätt' keiner geglaubt, daß uns die einmal so parieren werden!... Herrgott, bei so was hätt' ich dabei sein mögen! – Da steh'n sie alle auf von der Bank. – Servus, servus! – Das ist halt zuwider, daß unsereiner nicht dazu kommt. – Wär' doch schöner gewesen, auf dem Feld der Ehre, fürs Vaterland, als so... Ja, Herr Doktor, Sie kommen eigentlich gut weg!... Ob das nicht einer für mich übernehmen könnt'? – Meiner Seel', das sollt' ich hinterlassen, daß sich der Kopetzky oder der Wymetal an meiner Statt mit dem Kerl schlagen... Ah, so leicht sollt' der doch nicht davonkommen! – Ah, was! Ist das nicht egal, was nachher geschieht? Ich erfahr's ja doch nimmer! – Da schlagen die Bäume aus... Im Volksgarten hab' ich einmal eine angesprochen – ein rotes Kleid hat sie angehabt – in der Strozzigasse hat sie gewohnt – nachher hat sie der Rochlitz übernommen... Mir scheint, er hat sie noch immer, aber er red't nichts mehr davon – er schämt sich vielleicht... Jetzt schlaft die Steffi noch... so lieb sieht sie aus, wenn sie schlaft... als wenn sie nicht bis fünf zählen könnt'! – Na, wenn sie schlafen, schau'n sie alle so aus! – Ich sollt' ihr doch noch ein Wort schreiben... warum denn nicht? Es tut's ja doch ein jeder, daß er vorher noch Briefe schreibt. – Auch der Klara sollt' ich schreiben, daß sie den Papa und die Mama tröstet – und was man halt so schreibt! – und dem Kopetzky doch auch... Meiner Seel', mir kommt vor, es wär' viel leichter, wenn man ein paar Leuten Adieu gesagt hätt'... Und die Anzeige an das Regimentskommando – und die hundertsechzig Gulden für den Ballert... eigentlich noch viel zu tun... Na, es hat's mir ja keiner g'schafft, daß ich's um sieben tu'... von acht an ist noch immer Zeit genug zum Totsein!... Totsein, ja – so heißt's – da kann man nichts machen...

Ringstraße – jetzt bin ich ja bald in meinem Kaffeehaus... Mir scheint gar, ich freu' mich aufs Frühstück... es ist nicht zum glauben. – – Ja, nach dem Frühstück zünd' ich mir eine Zigarr' an, und dann geh' ich nach Haus und schreib'... Ja, vor allem mach' ich die Anzeige ans Kommando; dann kommt der Brief an die Klara – dann an den Kopetzky – dann an die Steffi... Was soll ich denn dem Luder schreiben... »Mein liebes Kind, Du hast wohl nicht gedacht«... Ah, was, Unsinn! – »Mein liebes Kind, ich danke Dir sehr«... – »Mein liebes Kind, bevor ich von hinnen gehe, will ich es nicht verabsäumen«... – Na, Briefschreiben war auch nie meine starke Seite... »Mein liebes Kind, ein letztes Lebewohl von Deinem Gustl«... – Die Augen, die sie machen wird! Ist doch ein Glück, daß ich nicht in sie verliebt war... das muß traurig sein, wenn man eine gern hat und so...

Na, Gustl, sei gut: so ist es auch traurig genug... Nach der Steffi wär' ja noch manche andere gekommen, und am End' auch eine, die was wert ist – junges Mädel aus guter Familie mit Kaution – es wär' ganz schön gewesen... – Der Klara muß ich ausführlich schreiben, daß ich nicht hab' anders können... »Du mußt mir verzeihen, liebe Schwester, und bitte, tröste auch die lieben Eltern. Ich weiß, daß ich Euch allen manche Sorge gemacht habe und manchen Schmerz bereitet; aber glaube mir, ich habe Euch alle immer sehr lieb gehabt, und ich hoffe, Du wirst noch einmal glücklich werden, meine liebe Klara, und Deinen unglücklichen Bruder nicht ganz vergessen«... Ah, ich schreib' ihr lieber gar nicht!... Nein, da wird mir zum Weinen... es beißt mich ja schon in den Augen, wenn ich d'ran denk'... Höchstens dem Kopetzky schreib' ich – ein kameradschaftliches Lebewohl, und er soll's den andern ausrichten... – Ist's schon sechs? – Ah, nein: halb – dreiviertel. – Ist das ein liebes G'sichtel!... Der kleine Fratz mit den schwarzen Augen, den ich so oft in der Florianigasse treff'! – Was die sagen wird? – Aber die weiß ja gar nicht, wer ich bin – die wird sich nur wundern, daß sie mich nimmer sieht... Vorgestern hab' ich mir vorgenommen, das nächstemal sprech' ich sie an. – Kokettiert hat sie genug... so jung war die – am End' war die gar noch eine Unschuld!... Ja, Gustl! Was du heute kannst besorgen, das verschiebe nicht auf morgen!... Der da hat sicher auch die ganze Nacht nicht geschlafen. – Na, jetzt wird er schön nach Haus geh'n und sich niederlegen – ich auch! – Haha! Jetzt wird's ernst, Gustl, ja!... Na, wenn nicht einmal das biss'l Grausen wär', so wär' ja schon gar nichts d'ran – und im ganzen, ich muß's schon selber sagen, halt' ich mich brav... Ah, wohin denn noch? Da ist ja schon mein Kaffeehaus... auskehren tun sie noch... Na, geh'n wir hinein...

Da hinten ist der Tisch, wo die immer Tarock spielen... Merkwürdig, ich kann mir's gar nicht vorstellen, daß der Kerl, der immer da hinten sitzt an der Wand, derselbe sein soll, der mich... – Kein Mensch ist noch da... Wo ist denn der Kellner?... He! Da kommt er aus der Küche... er schlieft schnell in den Frack hinein... Ist wirklich nimmer notwendig!... Ah, für ihn schon... er muß heut' noch andere Leut' bedienen! –

»Habe die Ehre, Herr Leutnant!«

»Guten Morgen.«

»So früh heute, Herr Leutnant?«

»Ah, lassen S' nur – ich hab' nicht viel Zeit, ich kann mit'm Mantel dasitzen.«

»Was befehlen Herr Leutnant?«

»Eine Melange mit Haut.«

»Bitte gleich, Herr Leutnant!«

Ah, da liegen ja Zeitungen... schon heutige Zeitungen?... Ob schon was drinsteht?... Was denn? – Mir scheint, ich will nachseh'n, ob drinsteht, daß ich mich umgebracht hab'! Haha! – Warum steh' ich denn noch immer?... Setzen wir uns da zum Fenster... Er hat mir ja schon die Melange hingestellt... So, den Vorhang zieh' ich zu; es ist mir zuwider, wenn die Leut' hereingucken.. Es geht zwar noch keiner vorüber.. Ah, gut schmeckt der Kaffee – doch kein leerer Wahn, das Frühstükken!... Ah, ein ganz anderer Mensch wird man – der ganze Blödsinn ist, daß ich nicht genachtmahlt hab'... Was steht denn der Kerl schon wieder da? – Ah, die Semmeln hat er mir gebracht...

»Haben Herr Leutnant schon gehört?«...

»Was denn?« Ja, um Gotteswillen, weiß der schon was?... Aber, Unsinn, es ist ja nicht möglich!

»Den Herrn Habetswallner...«

Was? So heißt ja der Bäckermeister... was wird der jetzt sagen?... Ist der am End' schon dagewesen? Ist er am End' gestern schon dagewesen und hat's erzählt?... Warum red't er denn nicht weiter?... Aber er red't ja...

»... hat heut' nacht um zwölf der Schlag getroffen.«

»Was?«... Ich darf nicht so schreien... nein, ich darf mir nichts anmerken lassen... aber vielleicht träum' ich... ich muß ihn noch einmal fragen... »Wen hat der Schlag getroffen?« – Famos, famos! – Ganz harmlos hab' ich das gesagt! –

»Den Bäckermeister, Herr Leutnant!.. Herr Leutnant werd'n

ihn ja kennen... na, den Dicken, der jeden Nachmittag neben die Herren Offiziere seine Tarockpartie hat... mit'n Herrn Schlesinger und'n Herrn Wasner von der Kunstblumenhandlung vis-à-vis!«

Ich bin ganz wach – stimmt alles – und doch kann ich's noch nicht recht glauben – ich muß ihn noch einmal fragen... aber ganz harmlos...

»Der Schlag hat ihn getroffen?... Ja, wieso denn? Woher wissen S' denn das?«

»Aber Herr Leutnant, wer soll's denn früher wissen, als unsereiner – die Semmel, die der Herr Leutnant da essen, ist ja auch vom Herrn Habetswallner. Der Bub, der uns das Gebäck um halber fünfe in der Früh bringt, hat's uns erzählt.«

Um Himmelswillen, ich darf mich nicht verraten... ich möcht' ja schreien... ich möcht' ja lachen... ich möcht' ja dem Rudolf ein Bussel geben... Aber ich muß ihn noch was fragen!... Vom Schlag getroffen werden, heißt noch nicht: tot sein... ich muß fragen, ob er tot ist... aber ganz ruhig, denn was geht mich der Bäckermeister an – ich muß in die Zeitung schau'n, während ich den Kellner frag'..

»Ist er tot?«

»Na, freilich, Herr Leutnant; auf'm Fleck ist er tot geblieben.«

O, herrlich, herrlich! – Am End' ist das alles, weil ich in der Kirchen g'wesen bin...

»Er ist am Abend im Theater g'wesen; auf der Stiegen ist er umg'fallen – der Hausmeister hat den Krach gehört... na, und dann haben s' ihn in die Wohnung getragen, und wie der Doktor gekommen ist, war's schon lang' aus.«

»Ist aber traurig. Er war doch noch in den besten Jahren.« – Das hab' ich jetzt famos gesagt – kein Mensch könnt' mir was anmerken... und ich muß mich wirklich zurückhalten, daß ich nicht schrei' oder aufs Billard spring'...

»Ja, Herr Leutnant, sehr traurig; war ein so lieber Herr, und zwanzig Jahr' ist er schon zu uns kommen – war ein guter Freund von unserm Herrn. Und die arme Frau...«

Ich glaub', so froh bin ich in meinem ganzen Leben nicht gewesen... Tot ist er – tot ist er! Keiner weiß was, und nichts ist g'scheh'n! – Und das Mordsglück, daß ich in das Kaffeehaus gegangen bin... sonst hätt' ich mich ja ganz umsonst erschossen – es ist doch wie eine Fügung des Schicksals... Wo ist denn der Rudolf? – Ah, mit dem Feuerburschen red't er... – Also, tot ist er – tot ist er – ich kann's noch gar nicht glauben! Am liebsten möcht' ich hingeh'n, um's zu seh'n. – – Am End' hat ihn der Schlag getroffen aus Wut, aus verhaltenem Zorn... Ah, warum, ist mir ganz egal! Die Hauptsach' ist: er ist tot, und ich darf leben, und alles g'hört wieder mein!... Komisch, wie ich mir da immerfort die Semmel einbrock', die mir der Herr Habetswallner gebacken hat! Schmeckt mir ganz gut, Herr von Habetswallner! Famos! – So, jetzt möcht' ich noch ein Zigarrl rauchen...

»Rudolf! Sie, Rudolf! Sie, lassen S' mir den Feuerburschen dort in Ruh'!«

»Bitte, Herr Leutnant!«

»Trabucco«... – Ich bin so froh, so froh!... Was mach' ich denn nur?... Was mach ich denn nur?... Es muß ja was gescheh'n, sonst trifft mich auch noch der Schlag vor lauter Freud'!... In einer Viertelstund' geh' ich hinüber in die Kasern' und laß mich vom Johann kalt abreiben... um halb acht sind die Gewehrgriff', und um halb zehn ist Exerzieren. – Und der Steffi schreib' ich, sie muß sich für heut' abend frei machen, und wenn's Graz gilt! Und nachmittag um vier... na wart', mein Lieber, wart', mein Lieber! Ich bin grad gut aufgelegt... Dich hau' ich zu Krenfleisch!

Reichenau, 13.–17. Juli 1900.

Fräulein Else

Fräulein Else

»Du willst wirklich nicht mehr weiterspielen, Else?« – »Nein, Paul, ich kann nicht mehr. Adieu. – Auf Wiedersehen, gnädige Frau.« – *»Aber Else, sagen Sie mir doch: Frau Cissy. – Oder lieber noch: Cissy, ganz einfach.«* – »Auf Wiedersehen, Frau Cissy.« – *»Aber warum gehen Sie denn schon, Else? Es sind noch volle zwei Stunden bis zum Dinner.«* – »Spielen Sie nur Ihr Single mit Paul, Frau Cissy, mit mir ist's doch heut' wahrhaftig kein Vergnügen.« – *»Lassen Sie sie, gnädige Frau, sie hat heut' ihren ungnädigen Tag. – Steht dir übrigens ausgezeichnet zu Gesicht, das Ungnädigsein, Else. – Und der rote Sweater noch besser.«* – »Bei Blau wirst du hoffentlich mehr Gnade finden, Paul. Adieu.«

Das war ein ganz guter Abgang. Hoffentlich glauben die Zwei nicht, daß ich eifersüchtig bin. – Daß sie was miteinander haben, Cousin Paul und Cissy Mohr, darauf schwör' ich. Nichts auf der Welt ist mir gleichgültiger. – Nun wende ich mich noch einmal um und winke ihnen zu. Winke und lächle. Sehe ich nun gnädig aus? – Ach Gott, sie spielen schon wieder. Eigentlich spiele ich besser als Cissy Mohr; und Paul ist auch nicht gerade ein Matador. Aber gut sieht er aus – mit dem offenen Kragen und dem Bösen-Jungen-Gesicht. Wenn er nur weniger affektiert wäre. Brauchst keine Angst zu haben, Tante Emma...

Was für ein wundervoller Abend! Heut' wär' das richtige Wetter gewesen für die Tour auf die Rosetta-Hütte. Wie herrlich der Cimone in den Himmel ragt! – Um fünf Uhr früh wär' man aufgebrochen. Anfangs wär' mir natürlich übel gewesen, wie gewöhnlich. Aber das verliert sich. – Nichts köstlicher als das Wandern im Morgengrauen. – Der einäugige Amerikaner auf der Rosetta hat ausgesehen wie ein Boxkämpfer. Vielleicht hat ihm beim Boxen wer das Aug' ausgeschlagen. Nach Amerika würd' ich ganz gern heiraten, aber keinen Amerikaner. Oder ich heirat' einen Amerikaner und wir leben in Europa. Villa an der

Riviera. Marmorstufen ins Meer. Ich liege nackt auf dem Marmor. – Wie lang ist's her, daß wir in Mentone waren? Sieben oder acht Jahre. Ich war dreizehn oder vierzehn. Ach ja, damals waren wir noch in besseren Verhältnissen. – Es war eigentlich ein Unsinn, die Partie aufzuschieben. Jetzt wären wir jedenfalls schon zurück. – Um vier, wie ich zum Tennis gegangen bin, war der telegraphisch angekündigte Expreßbrief von Mama noch nicht da. Wer weiß, ob jetzt. Ich hätt' noch ganz gut ein Set spielen können. – Warum grüßen mich diese zwei jungen Leute? Ich kenn' sie gar nicht. Seit gestern wohnen sie im Hotel, sitzen beim Essen links am Fenster, wo früher die Holländer gesessen sind. Hab' ich ungnädig gedankt? Oder gar hochmütig? Ich bin's ja gar nicht. Wie sagte Fred auf dem Weg vom ›Coriolan‹ nach Hause? Frohgemut. Nein, hochgemut. Hochgemut sind Sie, nicht hochmütig, Else. – Ein schönes Wort. Er findet immer schöne Worte. – Warum geh' ich so langsam? Fürcht' ich mich am Ende vor Mamas Brief? Nun, Angenehmes wird er wohl nicht enthalten. Expreß! Vielleicht muß ich wieder zurückfahren. O weh. Was für ein Leben – trotz rotem Seidensweater und Seidenstrümpfen. Drei Paar! Die arme Verwandte, von der reichen Tante eingeladen. Sicher bereut sie's schon. Soll ich's dir schriftlich geben, teure Tante, daß ich an Paul nicht im Traum denke? Ach, an niemanden denke ich. Ich bin nicht verliebt. In niemanden. Und war noch nie verliebt. Auch in Albert bin ich's nicht gewesen, obwohl ich es mir acht Tage lang eingebildet habe. Ich glaube, ich kann mich nicht verlieben. Eigentlich merkwürdig. Denn sinnlich bin ich gewiß. Aber auch hochgemut und ungnädig Gott sei Dank. Mit dreizehn war ich vielleicht das einzige Mal wirklich verliebt. In den Van Dyck – oder vielmehr in den Abbé Des Grieux, und in die Renard auch. Und wie ich sechzehn war, am Wörthersee. – Ach nein, das war nichts. Wozu nachdenken, ich schreibe ja keine Memoiren. Nicht einmal ein Tagebuch wie die Bertha. Fred ist mir sympathisch, nicht mehr. Vielleicht, wenn er eleganter wäre. Ich bin ja doch ein Snob. Der Papa findet's auch und lacht mich aus. Ach, lieber Papa, du machst mir viel Sorgen. Ob er die Mama einmal betrogen hat? Sicher. Öfters. Mama ist ziemlich dumm. Von mir hat sie keine Ahnung. Andere Menschen auch nicht. Fred? – Aber eben nur eine Ahnung. – Himmlischer Abend. Wie festlich das Hotel aussieht. Man spürt: Lauter Leute, denen es gutgeht und die keine Sorgen haben. Ich zum Beispiel. Haha! Schad'. Ich wär' zu einem sorgenlosen Leben geboren. Es könnt' so schön sein. Schad'. – Auf dem Cimone liegt ein roter Glanz. Paul würde sagen: Alpenglühen. Das ist noch lang' kein Alpenglühen. Es ist zum Weinen schön. Ach, warum muß man wieder zurück in die Stadt!

»*Guten Abend, Fräulein Else.*« – »Küss' die Hand, gnädige Frau.« – »*Vom Tennis?*« – Sie sieht's doch, warum fragt sie? »Ja, gnädige Frau. Beinah drei Stunden lang haben wir gespielt. – Und gnädige Frau machen noch einen Spaziergang?« – »*Ja, meinen gewohnten Abendspaziergang. Den Rolleweg. Der geht so schön zwischen den Wiesen, bei Tag ist er beinahe zu sonnig.*« – »Ja, die Wiesen hier sind herrlich. Besonders im Mondenschein von meinem Fenster aus.*« –

»*Guten Abend, Fräulein Else. – Küss' die Hand, gnädige Frau.*« – »Guten Abend, Herr von Dorsday.« – »*Vom Tennis, Fräulein Else?*« – »Was für ein Scharfblick, Herr von Dorsday.« – »*Spotten Sie nicht, Else.*« – Warum sagt er nicht ›Fräulein Else?‹ – »*Wenn man mit dem Rakett so gut ausschaut, darf man es gewissermaßen auch als Schmuck tragen.*« – Esel, darauf antworte ich gar nicht. »Den ganzen Nachmittag haben wir gespielt. Wir waren leider nur Drei. Paul, Frau Mohr und ich.« – »*Ich war früher ein engagierter Tennisspieler.*« – »Und jetzt nicht mehr?« – »*Jetzt bin ich zu alt dazu.*« – »Ach, alt, in Marienlust, da war ein fünfundsechzigjähriger Schwede, der spielte jeden Abend von sechs bis acht Uhr. Und im Jahr vorher hat er sogar noch bei einem Turnier mitgespielt.« – »*Nun, fünfundsechzig bin ich Gott sei Dank noch nicht, aber leider auch kein Schwede.*« – Warum leider? Das hält er wohl für einen Witz. Das Beste, ich lächle höflich und gehe. »Küss' die Hand, gnädige Frau. Adieu, Herr von Dorsday.« Wie tief er sich verbeugt und was für Augen er macht. Kalbsaugen. Hab' ich ihn am Ende verletzt mit dem fünfundsechzigjährigen Schweden?

Schad't auch nichts. Frau Winawer muß eine unglückliche Frau sein. Gewiß schon nah an Fünfzig. Diese Tränensäcke, – als wenn sie viel geweint hätte. Ach wie furchtbar, so alt zu sein. Herr von Dorsday nimmt sich ihrer an. Da geht er an ihrer Seite. Er sieht noch immer ganz gut aus mit dem graumelierten Spitzbart. Aber sympathisch ist er nicht. Schraubt sich künstlich hinauf. Was hilft Ihnen Ihr erster Schneider, Herr von Dorsday? Dorsday! Sie haben sicher einmal anders geheißen. – Da kommt das süße kleine Mädel von Cissy mit ihrem Fräulein. – »Grüß dich Gott, Fritzi. Bon soir, Mademoiselle. Vous allez bien?« – »*Merci, Mademoiselle. Et vous?* « – »Was seh' ich, Fritzi, du hast ja einen Bergstock. Willst du am End' den Cimone besteigen?« – »*Aber nein, so hoch hinauf darf ich noch nicht.* « – »Im nächsten Jahr wirst du es schon dürfen. Pah, Fritzi. A bientôt, Mademoiselle.« – »*Bon soir, Mademoiselle.* «

Eine hübsche Person. Warum ist sie eigentlich Bonne? Noch dazu bei Cissy. Ein bitteres Los. Ach Gott, kann mir auch noch blühen. Nein, ich wüßte mir jedesfalls was Besseres. Besseres? – Köstlicher Abend. ›Die Luft ist wie Champagner‹, sagte gestern Doktor Waldberg. Vorgestern hat es auch einer gesagt. – Warum die Leute bei dem wundervollen Wetter in der Halle sitzen? Unbegreiflich. Oder wartet jeder auf einen Expreßbrief? Der Portier hat mich schon gesehen; – wenn ein Expreßbrief für mich da wäre, hätte er mir ihn sofort hergebracht. Also keiner da. Gott sei Dank. Ich werde mich noch ein bißl hinlegen vor dem Diner. Warum sagt Cissy ›Dinner‹? Dumme Affektation. Passen zusammen, Cissy und Paul. – Ach, wär der Brief lieber schon da. Am Ende kommt er während des ›Dinner‹. Und wenn er nicht kommt, hab' ich eine unruhige Nacht. Auch die vorige Nacht hab' ich so miserabel geschlafen. Freilich, es sind gerade diese Tage. Drum hab' ich auch das Ziehen in den Beinen. Dritter September ist heute. Also wahrscheinlich am sechsten. Ich werde heute Veronal nehmen. O, ich werde mich nicht daran gewöhnen. Nein, lieber Fred, du mußt nicht besorgt sein. In Gedanken bin ich immer per Du mit ihm. – Versuchen sollte man alles, – auch Haschisch. Der Marinefähnrich Brandel hat

sich aus China, glaub' ich, Haschisch mitgebracht. Trinkt man oder raucht man Haschisch? Man soll prachtvolle Visionen haben. Brandel hat mich eingeladen mit ihm Haschisch zu trinken oder – zu rauchen – Frecher Kerl. Aber hübsch. –
»*Bitte sehr, Fräulein, ein Brief.*« – Der Portier! Also doch! – Ich wende mich ganz unbefangen um. Es könnte auch ein Brief von der Karoline sein oder von der Bertha oder von Fred oder Miß Jackson? »Danke schön.« Doch von Mama. Expreß. Warum sagt er nicht gleich: ein Expreßbrief? »O, ein Expreß!« Ich mach' ihn erst auf dem Zimmer auf und les' ihn in aller Ruhe. – Die Marchesa. Wie jung sie im Halbdunkel aussieht. Sicher fünfundvierzig. Wo werd' ich mit fünfundvierzig sein? Vielleicht schon tot. Hoffentlich. Sie lächelt mich so nett an, wie immer. Ich lasse sie vorbei, nicke ein wenig, – nicht als wenn ich mir eine besondere Ehre daraus machte, daß mich eine Marchesa anlächelt. – »*Buona sera.*« – Sie sagt mir buona sera. Jetzt muß ich mich doch wenigstens verneigen. War das zu tief? Sie ist ja um so viel älter. Was für einen herrlichen Gang sie hat. Ist sie geschieden? Mein Gang ist auch schön. Aber – ich weiß es. Ja, das ist der Unterschied. – Ein Italiener könnte mir gefährlich werden. Schade, daß der schöne Schwarze mit dem Römerkopf schon wieder fort ist. ›Er sieht aus wie ein Filou‹, sagte Paul. Ach Gott, ich hab' nichts gegen Filous, im Gegenteil. – So, da wär' ich. Nummer siebenundsiebzig. Eigentlich eine Glücksnummer. Hübsches Zimmer. Zirbelholz. Dort steht mein jungfräuliches Bett. – Nun ist es richtig ein Alpenglühen geworden. Aber Paul gegenüber werde ich es abstreiten. Eigentlich ist Paul schüchtern. Ein Arzt, ein Frauenarzt! Vielleicht gerade deshalb. Vorgestern im Wald, wie wir so weit voraus waren, hätt' er schon etwas unternehmender sein dürfen. Aber dann wäre es ihm übel ergangen. Wirklich unternehmend war eigentlich mir gegenüber noch niemand. Höchstens am Wörthersee vor drei Jahren im Bad. Unternehmend? Nein, unanständig war er ganz einfach. Aber schön. Apoll vom Belvedere. Ich hab' es ja eigentlich nicht ganz verstanden damals. Nun ja mit – sechzehn Jahren. Meine himmlische Wiese! Meine –! Wenn man sich die nach

Wien mitnehmen könnte. Zarte Nebel. Herbst? Nun ja, dritter September, Hochgebirge.

Nun, Fräulein Else, möchten Sie sich nicht doch entschließen, den Brief zu lesen? Er muß sich ja gar nicht auf den Papa beziehen. Könnte es nicht auch etwas mit meinem Bruder sein? Vielleicht hat er sich verlobt mit einer seiner Flammen? Mit einer Choristin oder einem Handschuhmädel. Ach nein, dazu ist er wohl doch zu gescheit. Eigentlich weiß ich ja nicht viel von ihm. Wie ich sechzehn war und er einundzwanzig, da waren wir eine Zeitlang geradezu befreundet. Von einer gewissen Lotte hat er mir viel erzählt. Dann hat er plötzlich aufgehört. Diese Lotte muß ihm irgend etwas angetan haben. Und seitdem erzählt er mir nichts mehr. – Nun ist er offen, der Brief, und ich hab' gar nicht bemerkt, daß ich ihn aufgemacht habe. Ich setze mich aufs Fensterbrett und lese ihn. Achtgeben, daß ich nicht hinunterstürze. Wie uns aus San Martino gemeldet wird, hat sich dort im Hotel Fratazza ein beklagenswerter Unfall ereignet. Fräulein Else T., ein neunzehnjähriges bildschönes Mädchen, Tochter des bekannten Advokaten... Natürlich würde es heißen, ich hätte mich umgebracht aus unglücklicher Liebe oder weil ich in der Hoffnung war. Unglückliche Liebe, ah nein.

›Mein liebes Kind‹ – Ich will mir vor allem den Schluß anschaun. – ›Also nochmals, sei uns nicht böse, mein liebes gutes Kind und sei tausendmal‹ – Um Gottes willen, sie werden sich doch nicht umgebracht haben! Nein, – in dem Fall wär' ein Telegramm von Rudi da. – ›Mein liebes Kind, du kannst mir glauben, wie leid es mir tut, daß ich dir in deine schönen Ferialwochen‹ – Als wenn ich nicht immer Ferien hätt', leider – ›mit einer so unangenehmen Nachricht hineinplatze.‹ – Einen furchtbaren Stil schreibt Mama – ›Aber nach reiflicher Überlegung bleibt mir wirklich nichts anderes übrig. Also, kurz und gut, die Sache mit Papa ist akut geworden. Ich weiß mir nicht zu raten, noch zu helfen.‹ – Wozu die vielen Worte? – ›Es handelt sich um eine verhältnismäßig lächerliche Summe – dreißigtausend Gulden‹, lächerlich? – ›die in drei Tagen herbeigeschafft sein müssen, sonst ist alles verloren.‹ – Um Gottes willen, was heißt das? –

›Denk dir, mein geliebtes Kind, daß der Baron Höning‹, – wie, der Staatsanwalt? – ›sich heut' früh den Papa hat kommen lassen. Du weißt ja, wie der Baron den Papa hochschätzt, ja geradezu liebt. Vor anderthalb Jahren, damals, wie es auch an einem Haar gehangen hat, hat er persönlich mit den Hauptgläubigern gesprochen und die Sache noch im letzten Moment in Ordnung gebracht. Aber diesmal ist absolut nichts zu machen, wenn das Geld nicht beschafft wird. Und abgesehen davon, daß wir alle ruiniert sind, wird es ein Skandal, wie er noch nicht da war. Denk' dir, ein Advokat, ein berühmter Advokat, – der, – nein, ich kann es gar nicht niederschreiben. Ich kämpfe immer mit den Tränen. Du weißt ja, Kind, du bist ja klug, wir waren ja, Gott sei's geklagt, schon ein paar Mal in einer ähnlichen Situation und die Familie hat immer herausgeholfen. Zuletzt hat es sich gar um hundertzwanzigtausend gehandelt. Aber damals hat der Papa einen Revers unterschreiben müssen, daß er niemals wieder an die Verwandten, speziell an den Onkel Bernhard, herantreten wird.‹ – Na weiter, weiter, wo will denn das hin? Was kann denn ich dabei tun? – ›Der Einzige, an den man eventuell noch denken könnte, wäre der Onkel Viktor, der befindet sich aber unglücklicherweise auf einer Reise zum Nordkap oder nach Schottland‹ – Ja, der hat's gut, der ekelhafte Kerl – ›und ist absolut unerreichbar, wenigstens für den Moment. An die Kollegen, speziell Dr. Sch., der Papa schon öfter ausgeholfen hat‹ – Herrgott, wie stehn wir da – ›ist nicht mehr zu denken, seit er sich wieder verheiratet hat‹ – also was denn, was denn, was wollt ihr denn von mir? – ›Und da ist nun dein Brief gekommen, mein liebes Kind, wo du unter andern Dorsday erwähnst, der sich auch im Fratazza aufhält, und das ist uns wie ein Schicksalswink erschienen. Du weißt ja, wie oft Dorsday in früheren Jahren zu uns gekommen ist‹ – na, gar so oft – ›es ist der reine Zufall, daß er sich seit zwei, drei Jahren seltener blicken läßt; er soll in ziemlich festen Banden sein – unter uns, nichts sehr Feines‹ – warum ›unter uns?‹ – ›Im Residenzklub hat Papa jeden Donnerstag noch immer seine Whistpartie mit ihm, und im verflossenen Winter hat er ihm im Prozeß gegen einen andern Kunsthändler ein hübsches

Stück Geld gerettet. Im übrigen, warum sollst du es nicht wissen, er ist schon früher einmal dem Papa beigesprungen.‹ – Hab’ ich mir gedacht – ›Es hat sich damals um eine Bagatelle gehandelt, achttausend Gulden, – aber schließlich – dreißig bedeuten für Dorsday auch keinen Betrag. Darum hab’ ich mir gedacht, ob du uns nicht die Liebe erweisen und mit Dorsday reden könntest‹ – Was? – ›Dich hat er ja immer besonders gern gehabt‹ – Hab’ nichts davon gemerkt. Die Wange hat er mir gestreichelt, wie ich zwölf oder dreizehn Jahre alt war. ›Schon ein ganzes Fräulein.‹ – ›Und da Papa seit den achttausend glücklicherweise nicht mehr an ihn herangetreten ist, so wird er ihm diesen Liebesdienst nicht verweigern. Neulich soll er an einem Rubens, den er nach Amerika verkauft hat, allein achtzigtausend verdient haben. Das darfst du selbstverständlich nicht erwähnen.‹ – Hältst du mich für eine Gans, Mama? – ›Aber im übrigen kannst du ganz aufrichtig zu ihm reden. Auch, daß der Baron Höning sich den Papa hat kommen lassen, kannst du erwähnen, wenn es sich so ergeben sollte. Und daß mit den dreißigtausend tatsächlich das Schlimmste abgewendet ist, nicht nur für den Moment, sondern, so Gott will, für immer.‹ – Glaubst du wirklich, Mama? – ›Denn der Prozeß Erbesheimer, der glänzend steht, trägt dem Papa sicher hunderttausend, aber selbstverständlich kann er gerade in diesem Stadium von den Erbesheimers nichts verlangen. Also, ich bitte dich, Kind, sprich mit Dorsday. Ich versichere dich, es ist nichts dabei. Papa hätte ihm ja einfach telegraphieren können, wir haben es ernstlich überlegt, aber es ist doch etwas ganz anderes, Kind, wenn man mit einem Menschen persönlich spricht. Am sechsten um zwölf muß das Geld da sein, Doktor F.‹ – Wer ist Doktor F.? Ach ja, Fiala – ›ist unerbittlich. Natürlich ist da auch persönliche Rancune dabei. Aber da es sich unglücklicherweise um Mündelgelder handelt‹ – Um Gottes willen! Papa, was hast du getan? – ›kann man nichts machen. Und wenn das Geld am fünften um zwölf Uhr mittags nicht in Fialas Händen ist, wird der Haftbefehl erlassen, vielmehr so lange hält der Baron Höning ihn noch zurück. Also Dorsday müßte die Summe telegraphisch durch seine Bank an Doktor F. überweisen lassen. Dann sind wir gerettet. Im andern Fall weiß Gott was geschieht. Glaub' mir, du vergibst dir nicht das Geringste, mein geliebtes Kind. Papa hatte ja anfangs Bedenken gehabt. Er hat sogar noch Versuche gemacht auf zwei verschiedenen Seiten. Aber er ist ganz verzweifelt nach Hause gekommen.‹ – Kann Papa überhaupt verzweifelt sein? – ›Vielleicht nicht einmal so sehr wegen des Geldes, als darum, weil die Leute sich so schändlich gegen ihn benehmen. Der eine von ihnen war einmal Papas bester Freund. Du kannst dir denken, wen ich meine.‹ – Ich kann mir gar nichts denken. Papa hat so viel beste Freunde gehabt und in Wirklichkeit keinen. Warnsdorf vielleicht? – ›Um ein Uhr ist Papa nach Hause gekommen, und jetzt ist es vier Uhr früh. Jetzt schläft er endlich, Gott sei Dank.‹ – Wenn er lieber nicht aufwachte, das wär' das beste für ihn. – ›Ich gebe den Brief in aller früh selbst auf die Post, expreß, da mußt du ihn vormittag am dritten haben.‹ – Wie hat sich Mama das vorgestellt? Sie kennt sich doch in diesen Dingen nie aus. – ›Also sprich sofort mit Dorsday, ich beschwöre dich und telegraphiere sofort, wie es ausgefallen ist. Vor Tante Emma laß dir um Gottes willen nichts merken, es ist ja traurig genug, daß man sich in einem solchen Fall an die eigene Schwester nicht wenden kann, aber da könnte man ja ebensogut zu einem Stein reden. Mein liebes, liebes Kind, mir tut es ja so leid, daß du in deinen jungen Jahren solche Dinge mitmachen mußt, aber glaub' mir, der Papa ist zum geringsten Teil selber daran schuld.‹ – Wer denn, Mama? – ›Nun, hoffen wir zu Gott, daß der Prozeß Erbesheimer in jeder Hinsicht einen Abschnitt in unserer Existenz bedeutet. Nur über diese paar Wochen müssen wir hinaus sein. Es wäre doch ein wahrer Hohn, wenn wegen der dreißigtausend Gulden ein Unglück geschähe?‹ – Sie meint doch nicht im Ernst, daß Papa sich selber... Aber wäre – das andere nicht noch schlimmer? – ›Nun schließe ich, mein Kind, ich hoffe, du wirst unter allen Umständen‹ – Unter allen Umständen? – ›noch über die Feiertage, wenigstens bis neunten oder zehnten in San Martino bleiben können. Unseretwegen mußt du keineswegs zurück. Grüße die Tante, sei nur weiter nett mit ihr. Also nochmals, sei uns nicht böse, mein liebes gutes Kind, und sei tausendmal‹ – ja, das weiß ich schon.

Also, ich soll Herrn Dorsday anpumpen... Irrsinnig. Wie stellt sich Mama das vor? Warum hat sich Papa nicht einfach auf die Bahn gesetzt und ist hergefahren? – Wär' grad' so geschwind gegangen wie der Expreßbrief. Aber vielleicht hätten sie ihn auf dem Bahnhof wegen Fluchtverdacht – – Furchtbar, furchtbar! Auch mit den dreißigtausend wird uns ja nicht geholfen sein. Immer diese Geschichten! Seit sieben Jahren! Nein – länger. Wer möcht' mir das ansehen? Niemand sieht mir was an, auch dem Papa nicht. Und doch wissen es alle Leute. Rätselhaft, daß wir uns immer noch halten. Wie man alles gewöhnt! Dabei leben wir eigentlich ganz gut. Mama ist wirklich eine Künstlerin. Das Souper am letzten Neujahrstag für vierzehn Personen – unbegreiflich. Aber dafür meine zwei Paar Ballhandschuhe, die waren eine Affäre. Und wie der Rudi neulich dreihundert Gulden gebraucht hat, da hat die Mama beinah' geweint. Und der Papa ist dabei immer gut aufgelegt. Immer? Nein. O nein. In der Oper neulich bei Figaro sein Blick, – plötzlich ganz leer – ich bin erschrocken. Da war er wie ein ganz anderer Mensch. Aber dann haben wir im Grand Hotel soupiert und er war so glänzend aufgelegt wie nur je.

Und da halte ich den Brief in der Hand. Der Brief ist ja irrsinnig. Ich soll mit Dorsday sprechen? Zu Tod' würde ich mich schämen. – – Schämen, ich mich? Warum? Ich bin ja nicht schuld. – Wenn ich doch mit Tante Emma spräche? Unsinn. Sie hat wahrscheinlich gar nicht so viel Geld zur Verfügung. Der Onkel ist ja ein Geizkragen. Ach Gott, warum habe ich kein Geld? Warum hab' ich mir noch nichts verdient? Warum habe ich nichts gelernt? O, ich habe was gelernt! Wer darf sagen, daß ich nichts gelernt habe? Ich spiele Klavier, ich kann Französisch, Englisch, auch ein bißl Italienisch, habe kunstgeschichtliche Vorlesungen besucht – Haha! Und wenn ich schon was Gescheiteres gelernt hätte, was hülfe es mir? Dreißigtausend Gulden hätte ich mir keineswegs erspart. – –

Aus ist es mit dem Alpenglühen. Der Abend ist nicht mehr

wunderbar. Traurig ist die Gegend. Nein, nicht die Gegend, aber das Leben ist traurig. Und ich sitz' da ruhig auf dem Fensterbrett. Und der Papa soll eingesperrt werden. Nein. Nie und nimmer. Es darf nicht sein. Ich werde ihn retten. Ja, Papa, ich werde dich retten. Es ist ja ganz einfach. Ein paar Worte ganz nonchalant, das ist ja mein Fall, ›hochgemut‹, – haha, ich werde Herrn Dorsday behandeln, als wenn es eine Ehre für ihn wäre, uns Geld zu leihen. Es ist ja auch eine. – Herr von Dorsday, haben Sie vielleicht einen Moment Zeit für mich? Ich bekomme da eben einen Brief von Mama, sie ist in augenblicklicher Verlegenheit, – vielmehr der Papa – – ›Aber selbstverständlich, mein Fräulein, mit dem größten Vergnügen. Um wieviel handelt es sich denn?‹ – Wenn er mir nur nicht so unsympathisch wäre. Auch die Art, wie er mich ansieht. Nein, Herr Dorsday, ich glaube Ihnen Ihre Eleganz nicht und nicht Ihr Monokel und nicht Ihre Noblesse. Sie könnten ebensogut mit alten Kleidern handeln wie mit alten Bildern. – Aber Else! Else, was fällt dir denn ein. – O, ich kann mir das erlauben. Mir sieht's niemand an. Ich bin sogar blond, rötlichblond, und Rudi sieht absolut aus wie ein Aristokrat. Bei der Mama merkt man es freilich gleich, wenigstens im Reden. Beim Papa wieder gar nicht. Übrigens sollen sie es merken. Ich verleugne es durchaus nicht und Rudi erst recht nicht. Im Gegenteil. Was täte der Rudi, wenn der Papa eingesperrt würde? Würde er sich erschießen? Aber Unsinn! Erschießen und Kriminal, all die Sachen gibt's ja gar nicht, die stehn nur in der Zeitung.

Die Luft ist wie Champagner. In einer Stunde ist das Diner, das ›Dinner‹. Ich kann die Cissy nicht leiden. Um ihr Mäderl kümmert sie sich überhaupt nicht. Was zieh' ich an? Das Blaue oder das Schwarze? Heut' wär vielleicht das Schwarze richtiger. Zu dekolletiert? Toilette de circonstance heißt es in den französischen Romanen. Jedenfalls muß ich berückend aussehen, wenn ich mit Dorsday rede. Nach dem Dinner, nonchalant. Seine Augen werden sich in meinen Ausschnitt bohren. Widerlicher Kerl. Ich hasse ihn. Alle Menschen hasse ich. Muß es gerade Dorsday sein? Gibt es denn wirklich nur diesen Dorsday auf der

Welt, der dreißigtausend Gulden hat? Wenn ich mit Paul spräche? Wenn er der Tante sagte, er hat Spielschulden, – da würde
sie sich das Geld sicher verschaffen können. –

Beinah schon dunkel. Nacht, Grabesnacht. Am liebsten
möcht' ich tot sein. – Es ist ja gar nicht wahr. Wenn ich jetzt
gleich hinunterginge, Dorsday noch vor dem Diner spräche?
Ah, wie entsetzlich! – Paul, wenn du mir die dreißigtausend ver-
schaffst, kannst du von mir haben, was du willst. Das ist ja schon
wieder aus einem Roman. Die edle Tochter verkauft sich für den
geliebten Vater, und hat am End' noch ein Vergnügen davon.
Pfui Teufel! Nein, Paul, auch für dreißigtausend kannst du von
mir nichts haben. Niemand. Aber für eine Million? – Für ein
Palais? Für eine Perlenschnur? Wenn ich einmal heirate, werde
ich es wahrscheinlich billiger tun. Ist es denn gar so schlimm?
Die Fanny hat sich am Ende auch verkauft. Sie hat mir selber
gesagt, daß sie sich vor ihrem Manne graust. Nun, wie wär's,
Papa, wenn ich mich heute Abend versteigerte? Um dich vor
dem Zuchthaus zu retten. Sensation –! Ich habe Fieber, ganz gewiß. Oder bin ich schon unwohl? Nein, Fieber habe ich. Vielleicht von der Luft. Wie Champagner. – Wenn Fred hier wäre,
könnte er mir raten? Ich brauche keinen Rat. Es gibt ja auch
nichts zu raten. Ich werde mit Herrn Dorsday aus Eperies sprechen, werde ihn anpumpen, ich die Hochgemute, die Aristokra-
tin, die Marchesa, die Bettlerin, die Tochter des Defraudanten.
Wie komm' ich dazu? Wie komm' ich dazu? Keine klettert so gut
wie ich, keine hat so viel Schneid, – sporting girl, in England
hätte ich auf die Welt kommen sollen, oder als Gräfin.

Da hängen die Kleider im Kasten! Ist das grüne Loden überhaupt schon bezahlt, Mama? Ich glaube nur eine Anzahlung.
Das Schwarze zieh' ich an. Sie haben mich gestern alle angestarrt. Auch der blasse kleine Herr mit dem goldenen Zwicker.
Schön bin ich eigentlich nicht, aber interessant. Zur Bühne hätte
ich gehen sollen. Bertha hat schon drei Liebhaber, keiner nimmt
es ihr übel... In Düsseldorf war es der Direktor. Mit einem verheirateten Manne war sie in Hamburg und hat im Atlantic gewohnt, Appartement mit Badezimmer. Ich glaub' gar, sie ist

stolz darauf. Dumm sind sie alle. Ich werde hundert Geliebte haben, tausend, warum nicht? Der Ausschnitt ist nicht tief genug; wenn ich verheiratet wäre, dürfte er tiefer sein. – Gut, daß ich Sie treffe, Herr von Dorsday, ich bekomme da eben einen Brief aus Wien... Den Brief stecke ich für alle Fälle zu mir. Soll ich dem Stubenmädchen läuten? Nein, ich mache mich allein fertig. Zu dem schwarzen Kleid brauche ich niemanden. Wäre ich reich, würde ich nie ohne Kammerjungfer reisen.

Ich muß Licht machen. Kühl wird es. Fenster zu. Vorhang herunter? – Überflüssig. Steht keiner auf dem Berg drüben mit einem Fernrohr. Schade. – Ich bekomme da eben einen Brief, Herr von Dorsday. – Nach dem Dinner wäre es doch vielleicht besser. Man ist in leichterer Stimmung. Auch Dorsday – ich könnt' ja ein Glas Wein vorher trinken. Aber wenn die Sache vor dem Dinner abgetan wäre, würde mir das Essen besser schmekken. Pudding à la merveille, fromage et fruits divers. Und wenn Herr von Dorsday Nein sagt? – Oder wenn er gar frech wird? Ah nein, mit mir ist noch keiner frech gewesen. Das heißt, der Marineleutnant Brandl, aber es war nicht bös gemeint. – Ich bin wieder etwas schlanker geworden. Das steht mir gut. – Die Dämmerung starrt herein. Wie ein Gespenst starrt sie herein. Wie hundert Gespenster. Aus meiner Wiese herauf steigen die Gespenster. Wie weit ist Wien? Wie lange bin ich schon fort? Wie allein bin ich da! Ich habe keine Freundin, ich habe auch keinen Freund. Wo sind sie alle? Wen werd' ich heiraten? Wer heiratet die Tochter eines Defraudanten? – Eben erhalte ich einen Brief, Herr von Dorsday. – ›Aber es ist doch gar nicht der Rede wert, Fräulein Else, gestern erst habe ich einen Rembrandt verkauft, Sie beschämen mich, Fräulein Else.‹ Und jetzt reißt er ein Blatt aus seinem Scheckbuch und unterschreibt mit seiner goldenen Füllfeder; und morgen früh fahr' ich mit dem Scheck nach Wien. Jedesfalls; auch ohne Scheck. Ich bleibe nicht mehr hier. Ich könnte ja gar nicht, ich dürfte ja gar nicht. Ich lebe hier als elegante junge Dame und Papa steht mit einem Fuß im Grab – nein im Kriminal. Das vorletzte Paar Seidenstrümpfe. Den kleinen Riß grad unterm Knie merkt niemand. Niemand? Wer weiß.

Nicht frivol sein, Else. – Bertha ist einfach ein Luder. Aber ist die Christine um ein Haar besser? Ihr künftiger Mann kann sich freuen. Mama war gewiß immer eine treue Gattin. Ich werde nicht treu sein. Ich bin hochgemut, aber ich werde nicht treu sein. Die Filous sind mir gefährlich. Die Marchesa hat gewiß einen Filou zum Liebhaber. Wenn Fred mich wirklich kennte, dann wäre es aus mit seiner Verehrung. – ›Aus Ihnen hätte alles Mögliche werden können, Fräulein, eine Pianistin, eine Buchhalterin, eine Schauspielerin, es stecken so viele Möglichkeiten in Ihnen. Aber es ist Ihnen immer zu gut gegangen.‹ Zu gut gegangen. Haha. Fred überschätzt mich. Ich hab' ja eigentlich zu nichts Talent. – Wer weiß? So weit wie Bertha hätte ich es auch noch gebracht. Aber mir fehlt es an Energie. Junge Dame aus guter Familie. Ha, gute Familie. Der Vater veruntreut Mündelgelder. Warum tust du mir das an, Papa? Wenn du noch etwas davon hättest! Aber an der Börse verspielt! Ist das der Mühe wert? Und die dreißigtausend werden dir auch nichts helfen. Für ein Vierteljahr vielleicht. Endlich wird er doch durchgehen müssen. Vor anderthalb Jahren war es ja fast schon soweit. Da kam noch Hilfe. Aber einmal wird sie nicht kommen – und was geschieht dann mit uns? Rudi wird nach Rotterdam gehen zu Vanderhulst in die Bank. Aber ich? Reiche Partie. O, wenn ich es darauf anlegte! Ich bin heute wirklich schön. Das macht wahrscheinlich die Aufregung. Für wen bin ich schön? Wäre ich froher, wenn Fred hier wäre? Ach Fred ist im Grunde nichts für mich. Kein Filou! Aber ich nähme ihn, wenn er Geld hätte. Und dann käme ein Filou – und das Malheur wäre fertig. – Sie möchten wohl gern ein Filou sein, Herr von Dorsday? – Von weitem sehen Sie manchmal auch so aus. Wie ein verlebter Vicomte, wie ein Don Juan – mit Ihrem blöden Monocle und Ihrem weißen Flanellanzug. Aber ein Filou sind Sie noch lange nicht. – Habe ich alles? Fertig zum ›Dinner‹? – Was tue ich aber eine Stunde lang, wenn ich Dorsday nicht treffe? Wenn er mit der unglücklichen Frau Winawer spazieren geht? Ach, sie ist gar nicht unglücklich, sie braucht keine dreißigtausend Gulden. Also ich werde mich in die Halle setzen, großartig in einen Fauteuil, schau mir die ›Illustrated News‹ an und die ›Vie parisienne‹, schlage die Beine übereinander, – den Riß unter dem Knie wird man nicht sehen. Vielleicht ist gerade ein Milliardär angekommen. – Sie oder keine. – Ich nehme den weißen Schal, der steht mir gut. Ganz ungezwungen lege ich ihn um meine herrlichen Schultern. Für wen habe ich sie denn, die herrlichen Schultern? Ich könnte einen Mann sehr glücklich machen. Wäre nur der rechte Mann da. Aber Kind will ich keines haben. Ich bin nicht mütterlich. Marie Weil ist mütterlich. Mama ist mütterlich, Tante Irene ist mütterlich. Ich habe eine edle Stirn und eine schöne Figur. – ›Wenn ich Sie malen dürfte, wie ich wollte, Fräulein Else.‹ – Ja, das möchte Ihnen passen. Ich weiß nicht einmal seinen Namen mehr. Tizian hat er keineswegs geheißen, also war es eine Frechheit. – Eben erhalte ich einen Brief, Herr von Dorsday. – Noch etwas Puder auf den Nacken und Hals, einen Tropfen Verveine ins Taschentuch, Kasten zusperren, Fenster wieder auf, ah, wie wunderbar! Zum Weinen. Ich bin nervös. Ach, soll man nicht unter solchen Umständen nervös sein. Die Schachtel mit dem Veronal hab' ich bei den Hemden. Auch neue Hemden brauchte ich. Das wird wieder eine Affäre sein. Ach Gott.

Unheimlich, riesig der Cimone, als wenn er auf mich herunterfallen wollte! Noch kein Stern am Himmel. Die Luft ist wie Champagner. Und der Duft von den Wiesen! Ich werde auf dem Land leben. Einen Gutsbesitzer werde ich heiraten und Kinder werde ich haben. Doktor Froriep war vielleicht der Einzige, mit dem ich glücklich geworden wäre. Wie schön waren die beiden Abende hintereinander, der erste bei Kniep, und dann der auf dem Künstlerball. Warum ist er plötzlich verschwunden – wenigstens für mich? Wegen Papa vielleicht? Wahrscheinlich. Ich möchte einen Gruß in die Luft hinausrufen, ehe ich wieder hinuntersteige unter das Gesindel. Aber zu wem soll der Gruß gehen? Ich bin ja ganz allein. Ich bin ja so furchtbar allein, wie es sich niemand vorstellen kann. Sei gegrüßt, mein Geliebter. Wer? Sei gegrüßt, mein Bräutigam! Wer? Sei gegrüßt, mein Freund! Wer? – Fred? – Aber keine Spur. So, das Fenster bleibt offen.

Wenn's auch kühl wird. Licht abdrehen. So. – Ja richtig, den Brief. Ich muß ihn zu mir nehmen für alle Fälle. Das Buch aufs Nachtkastel, ich lese heut' nacht noch weiter in ›Notre Coeur‹, unbedingt, was immer geschieht. Guten Abend, schönstes Fräulein im Spiegel, behalten Sie mich in gutem Angedenken, auf Wiedersehen…

Warum sperre ich die Tür zu? Hier wird nichts gestohlen. Ob Cissy in der Nacht ihre Türe offen läßt? Oder sperrt sie ihm erst auf, wenn er klopft? Ist es denn ganz sicher? Aber natürlich. Dann liegen sie zusammen im Bett. Unappetitlich. Ich werde kein gemeinsames Schlafzimmer haben mit meinem Mann und mit meinen tausend Geliebten. – Leer ist das ganze Stiegenhaus! Immer um diese Zeit. Meine Schritte hallen. Drei Wochen bin ich jetzt da. Am zwölften August bin ich von Gmunden abgereist. Gmunden war langweilig. Woher hat der Papa das Geld gehabt, Mama und mich aufs Land zu schicken? Und Rudi war sogar vier Wochen auf Reisen. Weiß Gott wo. Nicht zweimal hat er geschrieben in der Zeit. Nie werde ich unsere Existenz verstehen. Schmuck hat die Mama freilich keinen mehr. – Warum war Fred nur zwei Tage in Gmunden? Hat sicher auch eine Geliebte! Vorstellen kann ich es mir zwar nicht. Ich kann mir überhaupt gar nichts vorstellen. Acht Tage sind es, daß er mir nicht geschrieben hat. Er schreibt schöne Briefe. – Wer sitzt denn dort an dem kleinen Tisch? Nein, Dorsday ist es nicht. Gott sei Dank. Jetzt vor dem Diner wäre es doch unmöglich, ihm etwas zu sagen. – Warum schaut mich der Portier so merkwürdig an? Hat er am Ende den Expreßbrief von der Mama gelesen? Mir scheint, ich bin verrückt. Ich muß ihm nächstens wieder ein Trinkgeld geben. – Die Blonde da ist auch schon zum Diner angezogen. Wie kann man so dick sein! – Ich werde noch vors Hotel hinaus und ein bißchen auf und abgehen. Oder ins Musikzimmer? Spielt da nicht wer? Eine Beethovensonate! Wie kann man hier eine Beethovensonate spielen! Ich vernachlässige mein Klavierspiel. In Wien werde ich wieder regelmäßig üben. Überhaupt ein anderes Leben anfangen. Das müssen wir alle. So darf es nicht weitergehen. Ich werde einmal ernsthaft mit Papa sprechen – wenn noch Zeit dazu sein sollte. Es wird, es wird. Warum habe ich es noch nie getan? Alles in unserem Haus wird mit Scherzen erledigt, und keinem ist scherzhaft zumut. Jeder hat eigentlich Angst vor dem andern, jeder ist allein. Die Mama ist allein, weil sie nicht gescheit genug ist und von niemandem was weiß, nicht von mir, nicht von Rudi und nicht vom Papa. Aber sie spürt es nicht und Rudi spürt es auch nicht. Er ist ja ein netter eleganter Kerl, aber mit einundzwanzig hat er mehr versprochen. Es wird gut für ihn sein, wenn er nach Holland geht. Aber wo werde ich hingehen? Ich möchte fortreisen und tun können was ich will. Wenn Papa nach Amerika durchgeht, begleite ich ihn. Ich bin schon ganz konfus... Der Portier wird mich für wahnsinnig halten, wie ich da auf der Lehne sitze und in die Luft starre. Ich werde mir eine Zigarette anzünden. Wo ist meine Zigarettendose? Oben. Wo nur? Das Veronal habe ich bei der Wäsche. Aber wo habe ich die Dose? Da kommen Cissy und Paul. Ja, sie muß sich endlich umkleiden zum ›Dinner‹, sonst hätten sie noch im Dunkeln weitergespielt. – Sie sehen mich nicht. Was sagt er ihr denn? Warum lacht sie so blitzdumm? Wär' lustig, ihrem Gatten einen anonymen Brief nach Wien zu schreiben. Wäre ich so was imstande? Nie. Wer weiß? Jetzt haben sie mich gesehen. Ich nicke ihnen zu. Sie ärgert sich, daß ich so hübsch aussehe. Wie verlegen sie ist.

»Wie, Else, Sie sind schon fertig zum Diner?« – Warum sagt sie jetzt Diner und nicht Dinner. Nicht einmal konsequent ist sie. – »Wie Sie sehen, Frau Cissy.« – *»Du siehst wirklich entzückend aus, Else, ich hätte große Lust, dir den Hof zu machen.«* – »Erspar' dir die Mühe, Paul, gib mir lieber eine Zigarette.« – *»Aber mit Wonne.«* – »Dank' schön. Wie ist das Single ausgefallen?« – *»Frau Cissy hat mich dreimal hintereinander geschlagen.«* – *»Er war nämlich zerstreut. Wissen Sie übrigens, Else, daß morgen der Kronprinz von Griechenland hier ankommt?«* – Was kümmert mich der Kronprinz von Griechenland? »So wirklich?« O Gott, – Dorsday mit Frau Winawer! Sie grüßen. Sie gehen weiter. Ich habe zu höflich zurückgegrüßt. Ja, ganz anders als sonst. O, was bin ich für eine Person. – *»Deine Zigarette brennt ja nicht, Else?«* – »Also, gib mir

noch einmal Feuer. Danke. « – »*Ihr Schal ist sehr hübsch, Else, zu dem schwarzen Kleid steht er Ihnen fabelhaft. Übrigens muß ich mich jetzt auch umziehen.*« – Sie soll lieber nicht weggehen, ich habe Angst vor Dorsday. – »*Und für sieben habe ich mir die Friseurin bestellt, sie ist famos. Im Winter ist sie in Mailand. Also adieu, Else, adieu, Paul.*« – »*Küss' die Hand, gnädige Frau.*« – »Adieu, Frau Cissy.« – Fort ist sie. Gut, daß Paul wenigstens da bleibt. »*Darf ich mich einen Moment zu dir setzen, Else, oder stör' ich dich in deinen Träumen?*« – »Warum in meinen Träumen? Vielleicht in meinen Wirklichkeiten.« Das heißt eigentlich gar nichts. Er soll lieber fortgehen. Ich muß ja doch mit Dorsday sprechen. Dort steht er noch immer mit der unglücklichen Frau Winawer, er langweilt sich, ich seh' es ihm an, er möchte zu mir herüberkommen. – »*Gibt es denn solche Wirklichkeiten, in denen du nicht gestört sein willst?*« – Was sagt er da? Er soll zum Teufel gehen. Warum lächle ich ihn so kokett an? Ich mein' ihn ja gar nicht. Dorsday schielt herüber. Wo bin ich? Wo bin ich? »*Was hast du denn heute, Else?*« – »Was soll ich denn haben?« – »*Du bist geheimnisvoll, dämonisch, verführerisch.*« – »Red' keinen Unsinn, Paul.« – »*Man könnte geradezu toll werden, wenn man dich ansieht.*« – Was fällt ihm denn ein? Wie redet er denn zu mir? Hübsch ist er. Der Rauch meiner Zigarette verfängt sich in seinen Haaren. Aber ich kann ihn jetzt nicht brauchen. – »*Du siehst so über mich hinweg. Warum denn, Else?*« – Ich antworte gar nichts. Ich kann ihn jetzt nicht brauchen. Ich mache mein unausstehliches Gesicht. Nur keine Konversation jetzt. – »*Du bist mit deinen Gedanken ganz woanders.*« – »Das dürfte stimmen.« Er ist Luft für mich. Merkt Dorsday, daß ich ihn erwarte? Ich sehe nicht hin, aber ich weiß, daß er hersieht. – »*Also, leb' wohl, Else.*« – Gott sei Dank. Er küßt mir die Hand. Das tut er sonst nie. »Adieu, Paul.« Wo hab' ich die schmelzende Stimme her? Er geht, der Schwindler. Wahrscheinlich muß er noch etwas abmachen mit Cissy wegen heute nacht. Wünsche viel Vergnügen. Ich ziehe den Schal um meine Schulter und stehe auf und geh' vors Hotel hinaus. Wird freilich schon etwas kühl sein. Schad', daß ich meinen Mantel – Ah, ich habe ihn ja heute früh in die Portierloge hineingehängt. Ich fühle den Blick von Dorsday auf meinem Nacken, durch den Schal. Frau Winawer geht jetzt hinauf in ihr Zimmer. Wieso weiß ich denn das? Telepathie. »Ich bitte Sie, Herr Portier –« – »*Fräulein wünschen den Mantel?*« – »Ja, bitte.« – »*Schon etwas kühl die Abende, Fräulein. Das kommt bei uns so plötzlich.*« – »Danke.« Soll ich wirklich vors Hotel? Gewiß, was denn? Jedesfalls zur Türe hin. Jetzt kommt einer nach dem andern. Der Herr mit dem goldenen Zwicker. Der lange Blonde mit der grünen Weste. Alle sehen sie mich an. Hübsch ist diese kleine Genferin. Nein, aus Lausanne ist sie. Es ist eigentlich gar nicht so kühl.

»*Guten Abend, Fräulein Else.*« – Um Gottes willen, er ist es. Ich sage nichts von Papa. Kein Wort. Erst nach dem Essen. Oder ich reise morgen nach Wien. Ich gehe persönlich zu Doktor Fiala. Warum ist mir das nicht gleich eingefallen? Ich wende mich um mit einem Gesicht, als wüßte ich nicht, wer hinter mir steht. »Ah, Herr von Dorsday.« – »*Sie wollen noch einen Spaziergang machen, Fräulein Else?*« – »Ach, nicht gerade einen Spaziergang, ein bißchen auf und abgehen vor dem Diner.« – »*Es ist fast noch eine Stunde bis dahin.*« – »Wirklich?« Es ist gar nicht so kühl. Blau sind die Berge. Lustig wär's, wenn er plötzlich um meine Hand anhielte. – »*Es gibt doch auf der Welt keinen schöneren Fleck als diesen hier.*« – »Finden Sie, Herr von Dorsday? Aber bitte, sagen Sie nicht, daß die Luft hier wie Champagner ist.« – »*Nein, Fräulein Else, das sage ich erst von zweitausend Metern an. Und hier stehen wir kaum sechzehnhundertfünfzig über dem Meeresspiegel.*« – »Macht das einen solchen Unterschied?« – »*Aber selbstverständlich. Waren Sie schon einmal im Engadin?*« – »Nein, noch nie. Also dort ist die Luft wirklich wie Champagner?« – »*Man könnte es beinah' sagen. Aber Champagner ist nicht mein Lieblingsgetränk. Ich ziehe diese Gegend vor. Schon wegen der wundervollen Wälder.*« – Wie langweilig er ist. Merkt er das nicht? Er weiß offenbar nicht recht, was er mit mir reden soll. Mit einer verheirateten Frau wäre es einfacher. Man sagt eine kleine Unanständigkeit und die Konversation geht weiter. – »*Bleiben Sie noch längere Zeit hier in San Martino, Fräulein Else?*« – Idiotisch. Warum schau' ich ihn so kokett an? Und schon lächelt er in der gewissen Weise. Nein, wie

dumm die Männer sind. »Das hängt zum Teil von den Disposi-
tionen meiner Tante ab.« Ist ja gar nicht wahr. Ich kann ja allein
nach Wien fahren. »Wahrscheinlich bis zum zehnten.« – »*Die
Mama ist wohl noch in Gmunden?*« – »Nein, Herr von Dorsday.
Sie ist schon in Wien. Schon seit drei Wochen. Papa ist auch in
Wien. Er hat sich heuer kaum acht Tage Urlaub genommen. Ich
glaube, der Prozeß Erbesheimer macht ihm sehr viel Arbeit.« –
»*Das kann ich mir denken. Aber Ihr Papa ist wohl der Einzige, der
Erbesheimer herausreißen kann ... Es bedeutet ja schon einen Erfolg,
daß es überhaupt eine Zivilsache geworden ist.*« – Das ist gut, das ist
gut. »Es ist mir angenehm zu hören, daß auch Sie ein so günsti-
ges Vorgefühl haben.« – »*Vorgefühl? Inwiefern?*« – »Ja, daß der
Papa den Prozeß für Erbesheimer gewinnen wird.« – »*Das will
ich nicht einmal mit Bestimmtheit behauptet haben.*« – Wie, weicht er
schon zurück? Das soll ihm nicht gelingen. »O, ich halte etwas
von Vorgefühlen und von Ahnungen. Denken Sie, Herr von
Dorsday, gerade heute habe ich einen Brief von zu Hause bekommen.« Das war nicht sehr geschickt. Er macht ein etwas
verblüfftes Gesicht. Nur weiter, nicht schlucken. Er ist ein guter
alter Freund von Papa. Vorwärts. Vorwärts. Jetzt oder nie.
»Herr von Dorsday, Sie haben eben so lieb von Papa gesprochen, es wäre geradezu häßlich von mir, wenn ich nicht ganz
aufrichtig zu Ihnen wäre.« Was macht er denn für Kalbsaugen?
O weh, er merkt was. Weiter, weiter. »Nämlich in dem Brief ist
auch von Ihnen die Rede, Herr von Dorsday. Es ist nämlich ein
Brief von Mama.« – »*So.*« – »Eigentlich ein sehr trauriger Brief.
Sie kennen ja die Verhältnisse in unserem Haus, Herr von Dorsday.« – Um Himmels willen, ich habe ja Tränen in der Stimme.
Vorwärts, vorwärts, jetzt gibt es kein Zurück mehr. Gott sei
Dank. »Kurz und gut, Herr von Dorsday, wir wären wieder
einmal soweit.« – Jetzt möchte er am liebsten verschwinden.
»Es handelt sich – um eine Bagatelle. Wirklich nur um eine Bagatelle, Herr von Dorsday. Und doch, wie Mama schreibt, steht
alles auf dem Spiel.« Ich rede so blöd' daher wie eine Kuh. –
»*Aber beruhigen Sie sich doch, Fräulein Else.*« – Das hat er nett
gesagt. Aber meinen Arm brauchte er darum nicht zu berühren.

– »*Also, was gibt's denn eigentlich, Fräulein Else? Was steht denn in dem traurigen Brief von Mama?*« – »Herr von Dorsday, der Papa« – Mir zittern die Knie. »Die Mama schreibt mir, daß der Papa« – »*Aber um Gottes willen, Else, was ist Ihnen denn? Wollen Sie nicht lieber – hier ist eine Bank. Darf ich Ihnen den Mantel umgeben? Es ist etwas kühl.*« – »Danke, Herr von Dorsday, o, es ist nichts, gar nichts besonderes.« So, da sitze ich nun plötzlich auf der Bank. Wer ist die Dame, die da vorüberkommt? Kenn' ich gar nicht. Wenn ich nur nicht weiterreden müßte. Wie er mich ansieht! Wie konntest du das von mir verlangen, Papa? Das war nicht recht von dir, Papa. Nun ist es einmal geschehen. Ich hätte bis nach dem Diner warten sollen. – »*Nun, Fräulein Else?*« – Sein Monokel baumelt. Dumm sieht das aus. Soll ich ihm antworten? Ich muß ja. Also geschwind, damit ich es hinter mir habe. Was kann mir denn passieren? Er ist ein Freund von Papa. »Ach Gott, Herr von Dorsday, Sie sind ja ein alter Freund unseres Hauses.« Das habe ich sehr gut gesagt. »Und es wird Sie wahrscheinlich nicht wundern, wenn ich Ihnen erzähle, daß Papa sich wieder einmal in einer recht fatalen Situation befindet.« Wie merkwürdig meine Stimme klingt. Bin das ich, die da redet? Träume ich vielleicht? Ich habe gewiß jetzt auch ein ganz anderes Gesicht als sonst. – »*Es wundert mich allerdings nicht übermäßig. Da haben Sie schon recht, liebes Fräulein Else, – wenn ich es auch lebhaft bedauere.*« – Warum sehe ich denn so flehend zu ihm auf? Lächeln, lächeln. Geht schon. – »*Ich empfinde für Ihren Papa eine so aufrichtige Freundschaft, für Sie alle.*« – Er soll mich nicht so ansehen, es ist unanständig. Ich will anders zu ihm reden und nicht lächeln. Ich muß mich würdiger benehmen. »Nun, Herr von Dorsday, jetzt hätten Sie Gelegenheit, Ihre Freundschaft für meinen Vater zu beweisen.« Gott sei Dank, ich habe meine alte Stimme wieder. »Es scheint nämlich, Herr von Dorsday, daß alle unsere Verwandten und Bekannten – die Mehrzahl ist noch nicht in Wien – sonst wäre Mama wohl nicht auf die Idee gekommen. – Neulich habe ich nämlich zufällig in einem Brief an Mama Ihrer Anwesenheit hier in Martino Erwähnung getan – unter anderm natürlich.« – »*Ich vermutete gleich, Fräulein Else, daß ich nicht das einzige Thema Ihrer Korrespondenz mit Mama vorstelle.«* – Warum drückt er seine Knie an meine, während er da vor mir steht. Ach, ich lasse es mir gefallen. Was tut's! Wenn man einmal so tief gesunken ist. – »Die Sache verhält sich nämlich so, Doktor Fiala ist es, der diesmal dem Papa besondere Schwierigkeiten zu bereiten scheint.« – »*Ach Doktor Fiala.«* – Er weiß offenbar auch, was er von diesem Fiala zu halten hat. »Ja, Doktor Fiala. Und die Summe, um die es sich handelt, soll am fünften, das ist übermorgen um zwölf Uhr Mittag, – vielmehr, sie muß in seinen Händen sein, wenn nicht der Baron Höning – ja, denken Sie, der Baron hat Papa zu sich bitten lassen, privat, er liebt ihn nämlich sehr.« Warum red' ich denn von Höning, das wär' ja gar nicht notwendig gewesen. – »*Sie wollen sagen, Else, daß andernfalls eine Verhaftung unausbleiblich wäre?«* – Warum sagt er das so hart? Ich antworte nicht, ich nicke nur. »Ja.« Nun habe ich doch ja gesagt. – »*Hm, das ist ja – schlimm, das ist ja wirklich sehr – dieser hochbegabte geniale Mensch. – Und um welchen Betrag handelt es sich denn eigentlich, Fräulein Else?«* – Warum lächelt er denn? Er findet es schlimm und er lächelt. Was meint er mit seinem Lächeln? Daß es gleichgültig ist wieviel? Und wenn er Nein sagt! Ich bring' mich um, wenn er Nein sagt. Also, ich soll die Summe nennen. »Wie, Herr von Dorsday, ich habe noch nicht gesagt, wieviel? Eine Million.« Warum sag' ich das? Es ist doch jetzt nicht der Moment zum Spaßen? Aber wenn ich ihm dann sage, um wieviel weniger es in Wirklichkeit ist, wird er sich freuen. Wie er die Augen aufreißt? Hält er es am Ende wirklich für möglich, daß ihn der Papa um eine Million – »Entschuldigen Sie, Herr von Dorsday, daß ich in diesem Augenblick scherze. Es ist mir wahrhaftig nicht scherzhaft zumute.« – Ja, ja, drück' die Knie nur an, du darfst es dir ja erlauben. »Es handelt sich natürlich nicht um eine Million, es handelt sich im ganzen um dreißigtausend Gulden, Herr von Dorsday, die bis übermorgen mittag um zwölf Uhr in den Händen des Herrn Doktor Fiala sein müssen. Ja. Mama schreibt mir, daß Papa alle möglichen Versuche gemacht hat, aber wie gesagt, die Verwandten, die in Betracht kämen, befinden sich nicht in Wien.« – O, Gott, wie ich mich erniedrige. – »Sonst wäre es dem Papa natürlich nicht eingefallen, sich an Sie zu wenden, Herr von Dorsday, respektive mich zu bitten –« – Warum schweigt er? Warum bewegt er keine Miene? Warum sagt er nicht Ja? Wo ist das Scheckbuch und die Füllfeder? Er wird doch um Himmels willen nicht Nein sagen? Soll ich mich auf die Knie vor ihm werfen? O Gott! O Gott –

»*Am fünften sagten Sie, Fräulein Else?*« – Gott sei Dank, er spricht. »Jawohl übermorgen, Herr von Dorsday, um zwölf Uhr mittags. Es wäre also nötig – ich glaube, brieflich ließe sich das kaum mehr erledigen.« – »*Natürlich nicht, Fräulein Else, das müßten wir wohl auf telegraphischem Wege*« – ›Wir‹, das ist gut, das ist sehr gut. – »*Nun, das wäre das wenigste. Wieviel sagten Sie, Else?*« – Aber er hat es ja gehört, warum quält er mich denn? »Dreißigtausend, Herr von Dorsday. Eigentlich eine lächerliche Summe.« Warum habe ich das gesagt? Wie dumm. Aber er lächelt. Dummes Mädel, denkt er. Er lächelt ganz liebenswürdig. Papa ist gerettet. Er hätte ihm auch fünfzigtausend geliehen, und wir hätten uns allerlei anschaffen können. Ich hätte mir neue Hemden gekauft. Wie gemein ich bin. So wird man. – »*Nicht ganz so lächerlich, liebes Kind*« – Warum sagt er ›liebes Kind‹? Ist das gut oder schlecht? – »*wie Sie sich das vorstellen. Auch dreißigtausend Gulden wollen verdient sein.*« – »Entschuldigen Sie, Herr von Dorsday, nicht so habe ich es gemeint. Ich dachte nur, wie traurig es ist, daß Papa wegen einer solchen Summe, wegen einer solchen Bagatelle« – Ach Gott, ich verhasple mich ja schon wieder. »Sie können sich gar nicht denken, Herr von Dorsday, – wenn Sie auch einen gewissen Einblick in unsere Verhältnisse haben, wie furchtbar es für mich und besonders für Mama ist.« – Er stellt den einen Fuß auf die Bank. Soll das elegant sein – oder was? – »*O, ich kann mir schon denken, liebe Else.*« – Wie seine Stimme klingt, ganz anders, merkwürdig. – »*Und ich habe mir selbst schon manchesmal gedacht: schade, schade um diesen genialen Menschen.*« – Warum sagt er ›schade‹? Will er das Geld nicht hergeben? Nein, er meint es nur im allgemeinen. Warum sagt er nicht endlich Ja? Oder nimmt er das als selbstverständlich an?

Wie er mich ansieht! Warum spricht er nicht weiter? Ah, weil die zwei Ungarinnen vorbeigehen. Nun steht er wenigstens wieder anständig da, nicht mehr mit dem Fuß auf der Bank. Die Krawatte ist zu grell für einen älteren Herrn. Sucht ihm die seine Geliebte aus? Nichts besonders Feines ›unter uns‹, schreibt Mama. Dreißigtausend Gulden! Aber ich lächle ihn ja an. Warum lächle ich denn? O, ich bin feig. – »*Und wenn man wenigstens annehmen dürfte, mein liebes Fräulein Else, daß mit dieser Summe wirklich etwas getan wäre? Aber – Sie sind doch ein so kluges Geschöpf, Else, was wären diese dreißigtausend Gulden? Ein Tropfen auf einen heißen Stein.*« – Um Gottes willen, er will das Geld nicht hergeben? Ich darf kein so erschrockenes Gesicht machen. Alles steht auf dem Spiel. Jetzt muß ich etwas Vernünftiges sagen und energisch. »O nein, Herr von Dorsday, diesmal wäre es kein Tropfen auf einen heißen Stein. Der Prozeß Erbesheimer steht bevor, vergessen Sie das nicht, Herr von Dorsday, und der ist schon heute so gut wie gewonnen. Sie hatten ja selbst diese Empfindung, Herr von Dorsday. Und Papa hat auch noch andere Prozesse. Und außerdem habe ich die Absicht, Sie dürfen nicht lachen, Herr von Dorsday, mit Papa zu sprechen, sehr ernsthaft. Er hält etwas auf mich. Ich darf sagen, wenn jemand einen gewissen Einfluß auf ihn zu nehmen imstande ist, so bin es noch am ehesten ich.« – »*Sie sind ja ein rührendes, ein entzückendes Geschöpf, Fräulein Else.*« – Seine Stimme klingt schon wieder. Wie zuwider ist mir das, wenn es so zu klingen anfängt bei den Männern. Auch bei Fred mag ich es nicht. – »*Ein entzückendes Geschöpf in der Tat.*« – Warum sagt er ›in der Tat‹? Das ist abgeschmackt. Das sagt man doch nur im Burgtheater. »*Aber so gern ich Ihren Optimismus teilen möchte – wenn der Karren einmal so verfahren ist.*« – »Das ist er nicht, Herr von Dorsday. Wenn ich an Papa nicht glauben würde, wenn ich nicht ganz überzeugt wäre, daß diese dreißigtausend Gulden« – Ich weiß nicht, was ich weiter sagen soll. Ich kann ihn doch nicht geradezu anbetteln. Er überlegt. Offenbar. Vielleicht weiß er die Adresse von Fiala nicht? Unsinn. Die Situation ist unmöglich. Ich sitze da wie eine arme Sünderin. Er steht vor mir und bohrt mir das Monokel in die Stirn und schweigt. Ich werde jetzt aufstehen, das ist das beste. Ich lasse mich nicht so behandeln. Papa soll sich umbringen. Ich werde mich auch umbringen. Eine Schande dieses Leben. Am besten wär's, sich dort von dem Felsen hinunterzustürzen und aus wär's. Geschähe euch recht, allen. Ich stehe auf. – »Fräulein Else.« – »Entschuldigen Sie, Herr von Dorsday, daß ich Sie unter diesen Umständen überhaupt bemüht habe. Ich kann Ihr ablehnendes Verhalten natürlich vollkommen verstehen.« – So, aus, ich gehe. – »Bleiben Sie, Fräulein Else.« – Bleiben Sie, sagt er? Warum soll ich bleiben? Er gibt das Geld her. Ja. Ganz bestimmt. Er muß ja. Aber ich setze mich nicht noch einmal nieder. Ich bleibe stehen, als wär' es nur für eine halbe Sekunde. Ich bin ein bißchen größer als er. – »Sie haben meine Antwort noch nicht abgewartet, Else. Ich war ja schon einmal, verzeihen Sie, Else, daß ich das in diesem Zusammenhang erwähne« – Er müßte nicht so oft Else sagen – »in der Lage, dem Papa aus einer Verlegenheit zu helfen. Allerdings mit einer – noch lächerlicheren Summe als diesmal, und schmeichelte mir keineswegs mit der Hoffnung, diesen Betrag jemals wiedersehen zu dürfen, – und so wäre eigentlich kein Grund vorhanden, meine Hilfe diesmal zu verweigern. Und gar wenn ein junges Mädchen wie Sie, Else, wenn Sie selbst als Fürbitterin vor mich hintreten –« – Worauf will er hinaus? Seine Stimme ›klingt‹ nicht mehr. Oder anders! Wie sieht er mich denn an? Er soll achtgeben!! – »Also, Else, ich bin bereit – Doktor Fiala soll übermorgen um zwölf Uhr mittags die dreißigtausend Gulden haben – unter einer Bedingung« – Er soll nicht weiterreden, er soll nicht. »Herr von Dorsday, ich, ich persönlich übernehme die Garantie, daß mein Vater diese Summe zurückerstatten wird, sobald er das Honorar von Erbesheimer erhalten hat. Erbesheimers haben bisher überhaupt noch nichts gezahlt. Noch nicht einmal einen Vorschuß – Mama selbst schreibt mir« – »Lassen Sie doch, Else, man soll niemals eine Garantie für einen anderen Menschen übernehmen, – nicht einmal für sich selbst.« – Was will er? Seine Stimme klingt schon wieder. Nie hat mich ein Mensch so angeschaut. Ich ahne, wo er hinauswill. Wehe ihm! – »Hätte ich es vor einer Stunde für möglich gehalten, daß ich in einem solchen Falle überhaupt mir jemals einfallen

lassen würde, eine Bedingung zu stellen? Und nun tue ich es doch. Ja,
Else, man ist eben nur ein Mann, und es ist nicht meine Schuld, daß Sie
so schön sind, Else.« – Was will er? Was will er –? – *»Vielleicht hätte*
ich heute oder morgen das Gleiche von Ihnen erbeten, was ich jetzt
erbitten will, auch wenn Sie nicht eine Million, pardon – dreißigtau-
send Gulden von mir gewünscht hätten. Aber freilich, unter anderen
Umständen hätten Sie mir wohl kaum Gelegenheit vergönnt, so lange
Zeit unter vier Augen mit Ihnen zu reden.« – »O, ich habe Sie wirklich allzu lange in Anspruch genommen, Herr von Dorsday.«
Das habe ich gut gesagt. Fred wäre zufrieden. Was ist das? Er
faßt nach meiner Hand? Was fällt ihm denn ein? – *»Wissen Sie es*
denn nicht schon lange, Else?« – Er soll meine Hand loslassen!
Nun, Gott sei Dank, er läßt sie los. Nicht so nah, nicht so nah. –
»Sie müßten keine Frau sein, Else, wenn Sie es nicht gemerkt hätten. Je
vous désire.« – Er hätte es auch deutsch sagen können, der Herr
Vicomte. – *»Muß ich noch mehr sagen?«* – »Sie haben schon zuviel
gesagt, Herr Dorsday.« Und ich stehe noch da. Warum denn?
Ich gehe, ich gehe ohne Gruß. – *»Else! Else!«* – Nun ist er wieder
neben mir. – *»Verzeihen Sie mir, Else. Auch ich habe nur einen*
Scherz gemacht, geradeso wie Sie vorher mit der Million. Auch meine
Forderung stelle ich nicht so hoch – als Sie gefürchtet haben, wie ich
leider sagen muß, – so daß die geringere Sie vielleicht angenehm überra-
schen wird. Bitte, bleiben Sie doch stehen, Else.« – Ich bleibe wirklich stehen. Warum denn? Da stehen wir uns gegenüber. Hätte
ich ihm nicht einfach ins Gesicht schlagen sollen? Wäre nicht
noch jetzt Zeit dazu? Die zwei Engländer kommen vorbei. Jetzt
wäre der Moment. Gerade darum. Warum tu' ich es denn nicht?
Ich bin feig, ich bin zerbrochen, ich bin erniedrigt. Was wird er
nun wollen statt der Million? Einen Kuß vielleicht? Darüber
ließe sich reden. Eine Million zu dreißigtausend verhält sich wie
– – Komische Gleichungen gibt es. – *»Wenn Sie wirklich einmal*
eine Million brauchen sollten, Else, – ich bin zwar kein reicher Mann,
dann wollen wir sehen. Aber für diesmal will ich genügsam sein, wie
Sie. Und für diesmal will ich nichts anderes, Else als – Sie sehen.« – Ist
er verrückt? Er sieht mich doch. – Ah, so meint er das, so!
Warum schlage ich ihm nicht ins Gesicht, dem Schuften! Bin ich

rot geworden oder blaß? Nackt willst du mich sehen? Das möchte mancher. Ich bin schön, wenn ich nackt bin. Warum schlage ich ihm nicht ins Gesicht? – Riesengroß ist sein Gesicht. Warum so nah, du Schuft? Ich will deinen Atem nicht auf meinen Wangen. Warum lasse ich ihn nicht einfach stehen? Bannt mich sein Blick? Wir schauen uns ins Auge wie Todfeinde. Ich möchte ihm Schuft sagen, aber ich kann nicht. Oder will ich nicht? – »Sie sehen mich an, Else, als wenn ich verrückt wäre. Ich bin es vielleicht ein wenig, denn es geht ein Zauber von Ihnen aus, Else, den Sie selbst wohl nicht ahnen. Sie müssen fühlen, Else, daß meine Bitte keine Beleidigung bedeutet. Ja, ›Bitte‹ sage ich, wenn sie auch einer Erpressung zum Verzweifeln ähnlich sieht. Aber ich bin kein Erpresser, ich bin nur ein Mensch, der mancherlei Erfahrungen gemacht hat, – unter andern die, daß alles auf der Welt seinen Preis hat und daß einer, der sein Geld verschenkt, wenn er in der Lage ist, einen Gegenwert dafür zu bekommen, ein ausgemachter Narr ist. Und – was ich mir diesmal kaufen will, Else, so viel es auch ist, Sie werden nicht ärmer dadurch, daß Sie es verkaufen. Und daß es ein Geheimnis bleiben würde zwischen Ihnen und mir, das schwöre ich Ihnen, Else, bei – bei all den Reizen, durch deren Enthüllung Sie mich beglücken würden.« – Wo hat er so reden gelernt? Es klingt wie aus einem Buch. – »Und ich schwöre Ihnen auch, daß ich – von der Situation keinen Gebrauch machen werde, der in unserem Vertrag nicht vorgesehen war. Nichts anderes verlange ich von Ihnen, als eine Viertelstunde dastehen dürfen in Andacht vor Ihrer Schönheit. Mein Zimmer liegt im gleichen Stockwerk wie das Ihre, Else, Nummer fünfundsechzig, leicht zu merken. Der schwedische Tennisspieler, von dem Sie heut' sprachen, war doch gerade fünfundsechzig Jahre alt?« – Er ist verrückt! Warum lasse ich ihn weiterreden? Ich bin gelähmt. – »Aber wenn es Ihnen aus irgendeinem Grunde nicht paßt, mich auf Zimmer Nummer fünfundsechzig zu besuchen, Else, so schlage ich Ihnen einen kleinen Spaziergang nach dem Diner vor. Es gibt eine Lichtung im Walde, ich habe sie neulich ganz zufällig entdeckt, kaum fünf Minuten weit von unserem Hotel. – Es wird eine wundervolle Sommernacht heute, beinahe warm, und das Sternenlicht wird Sie herrlich kleiden.« – Wie zu einer Sklavin spricht er. Ich spucke ihm ins Gesicht. – »Sie sollen mir *nicht gleich antworten, Else. Überlegen Sie. Nach dem Diner werden Sir mir gütigst Ihre Entscheidung kundtun.«* – Warum sagt er denn ›kundtun‹? Was für ein blödes Wort: kundtun. – *»Überlegen Sie in aller Ruhe. Sie werden vielleicht spüren, daß es nicht einfach ein Handel ist, den ich Ihnen vorschlage.«* – Was denn, du klingender Schuft! – *»Sie werden möglicherweise ahnen, daß ein Mann zu Ihnen spricht, der ziemlich einsam und nicht besonders glücklich ist und der vielleicht einige Nachsicht verdient.«* – Affektierter Schuft. Spricht wie ein schlechter Schauspieler. Seine gepflegten Finger sehen aus wie Krallen. Nein, nein, ich will nicht. Warum sag' ich es denn nicht? Bring' dich um, Papa! Was will er denn mit meiner Hand? Ganz schlaff ist mein Arm. Er führt meine Hand an seine Lippen. Heiße Lippen. Pfui! Meine Hand ist kalt. Ich hätte Lust, ihm den Hut herunterzublasen. Ha, wie komisch wär' das. Bald ausgeküßt, du Schuft? – Die Bogenlampen vor dem Hotel brennen schon. Zwei Fenster stehen offen im dritten Stock. Das, wo sich der Vorhang bewegt, ist meines. Oben auf dem Schrank glänzt etwas. Nichts liegt oben, es ist nur der Messingbeschlag. – *»Also auf Wiedersehen, Else.«* – Ich antworte nichts. Regungslos stehe ich da. Er sieht mir ins Auge. Mein Gesicht ist undurchdringlich. Er weiß gar nichts. Er weiß nicht, ob ich kommen werde oder nicht. Ich weiß es auch nicht. Ich weiß nur, daß alles aus ist. Ich bin halbtot. Da geht er. Ein wenig gebückt. Schuft! Er fühlt meinen Blick auf seinem Nacken. Wen grüßt er denn? Zwei Damen. Als wäre er ein Graf, so grüßt er. Paul soll ihn fordern und ihn totschießen. Oder Rudi. Was glaubt er denn eigentlich? Unverschämter Kerl! Nie und nimmer. Es wird dir nichts anderes übrigbleiben, Papa, du mußt dich umbringen. – Die Zwei kommen offenbar von einer Tour. Beide hübsch, er und sie. Haben sie noch Zeit, sich vor dem Diner umzukleiden? Sind gewiß auf der Hochzeitsreise oder vielleicht gar nicht verheiratet. Ich werde nie auf einer Hochzeitsreise sein. Dreißigtausend Gulden. Nein, nein, nein! Gibt es keine dreißigtausend Gulden auf der Welt? Ich fahre zu Fiala. Ich komme noch zurecht. Gnade, Gnade, Herr Doktor Fiala. Mit Vergnügen, mein Fräulein. Bemühen Sie sich in mein Schlafzimmer. – Tu mir doch den Gefallen, Paul, verlange dreißigtausend Gulden von deinem Vater. Sage, du hast Spielschulden, du mußt dich sonst erschießen. Gern, liebe Kusine. Ich habe Zimmer Nummer soundsoviel, um Mitternacht erwarte ich dich. O, Herr von Dorsday, wie bescheiden sind Sie. Vorläufig. Jetzt kleidet er sich um. Smoking. Also entscheiden wir uns. Wiese im Mondenschein oder Zimmer Nummer fünfundsechzig? Wird er mich im Smoking in den Wald begleiten?

Es ist noch Zeit bis zum Diner. Ein bißchen spazierengehen und die Sache in Ruhe überlegen. Ich bin ein einsamer alter Mann, haha. Himmlische Luft, wie Champagner. Gar nicht mehr kühl – dreißigtausend... dreißigtausend... Ich muß mich jetzt sehr hübsch ausnehmen in der weiten Landschaft. Schade, daß keine Leute mehr im Freien sind. Dem Herrn dort am Waldesrand gefalle ich offenbar sehr gut. O, mein Herr, nackt bin ich noch viel schöner, und es kostet einen Spottpreis, dreißigtausend Gulden. Vielleicht bringen Sie Ihre Freunde mit, dann kommt es billiger. Hoffentlich haben Sie lauter hübsche Freunde, hübschere und jüngere als Herr von Dorsday? Kennen Sie Herrn von Dorsday? Ein Schuft ist er – ein klingender Schuft...

Also überlegen, überlegen... Ein Menschenleben steht auf dem Spiel. Das Leben von Papa. Aber nein, er bringt sich nicht um, er wird sich lieber einsperren lassen. Drei Jahre schwerer Kerker oder fünf. In dieser ewigen Angst lebt er schon fünf oder zehn Jahre... Mündelgelder... Und Mama geradeso. Und ich doch auch. – Vor wem werde ich mich das nächste Mal nackt ausziehen müssen? Oder bleiben wir der Einfachheit wegen bei Herrn Dorsday? Seine jetzige Geliebte ist ja nichts Feines ›unter uns gesagt‹. Ich wäre ihm gewiß lieber. Es ist gar nicht so ausgemacht, ob ich viel feiner bin. Tun Sie nicht vornehm, Fräulein Else, ich könnte Geschichten von Ihnen erzählen... einen gewissen Traum zum Beispiel, den Sie schon dreimal gehabt haben – von dem haben Sie nicht einmal Ihrer Freundin Bertha erzählt. Und die verträgt doch was. Und wie war denn das heuer in Gmunden in der Früh um sechs auf dem Balkon, mein vornehmes Fräulein Else? Haben Sie die zwei jungen Leute im Kahn vielleicht gar nicht bemerkt, die Sie angestarrt haben? Mein Gesicht haben sie vom See aus freilich nicht genau ausnehmen können, aber daß ich im Hemd war, das haben sie schon bemerkt. Und ich hab' mich gefreut. Ah, mehr als gefreut. Ich war wie berauscht. Mit beiden Händen hab' ich mich über die Hüften gestrichen und vor mir selber hab' ich getan, als wüßte ich nicht, daß man mich sieht. Und der Kahn hat sich nicht vom Fleck bewegt. Ja, so bin ich, so bin ich. Ein Luder, ja. Sie spüren es ja alle. Auch Paul spürt es. Natürlich, er ist ja Frauenarzt. Und der Marineleutnant hat es ja auch gespürt und der Maler auch. Nur Fred, der dumme Kerl spürt es nicht. Darum liebt er mich ja. Aber gerade vor ihm möchte ich nicht nackt sein, nie und nimmer. Ich hätte gar keine Freude davon. Ich möchte mich schämen. Aber vor dem Filou mit dem Römerkopf – wie gern. Am allerliebsten vor dem. Und wenn ich gleich nachher sterben müßte. Aber es ist ja nicht notwendig gleich nachher zu sterben. Man überlebt es. Die Bertha hat mehr überlebt. Cissy liegt sicher auch nackt da, wenn Paul zu ihr schleicht durch die Hotelgänge, wie ich heute Nacht zu Herrn von Dorsday schleichen werde.

Nein, nein. Ich will nicht. Zu jedem andern – aber nicht zu ihm. Zu Paul meinetwegen. Oder ich such' mir einen aus heute abend beim Diner. Es ist ja alles egal. Aber ich kann doch nicht jedem sagen, daß ich dreißigtausend Gulden dafür haben will! Da wäre ich ja wie ein Frauenzimmer von der Kärntnerstraße. Nein, ich verkaufe mich nicht. Niemals. Nie werde ich mich verkaufen. Ich schenke mich her. Ja, wenn ich einmal den Rechten finde, schenke ich mich her. Aber ich verkaufe mich nicht. Ein Luder will ich sein, aber nicht eine Dirne. Sie haben sich verrechnet, Herr von Dorsday. Und der Papa auch. Ja, verrechnet hat er sich. Er muß es ja vorher gesehen haben. Er kennt ja die Menschen. Er kennt doch den Herrn von Dorsday. Er hat sich doch denken können, daß der Herr Dorsday nicht für nichts und wieder nichts. – Sonst hätte er doch telegraphieren oder selber herreisen können. Aber so war es bequemer und sicherer, nicht wahr, Papa? Wenn man eine so hübsche Tochter hat, wozu braucht man ins Zuchthaus zu spazieren? Und die Mama, dumm wie sie ist, setzt sich hin und schreibt den Brief. Der Papa hat sich nicht getraut. Da hätte ich es ja gleich merken müssen. Aber es soll euch nicht glücken. Nein, du hast zu sicher auf meine kindliche Zärtlichkeit spekuliert, Papa, zu sicher darauf gerechnet, daß ich lieber jede Gemeinheit erdulden würde als dich die Folgen deines verbrecherischen Leichtsinns tragen zu lassen. Ein Genie bist du ja. Herr von Dorsday sagt es, alle Leute sagen es. Aber was hilft mir das. Fiala ist eine Null, aber er unterschlägt keine Mündelgelder, sogar Waldheim ist nicht in einem Atem mit dir zu nennen... Wer hat das nur gesagt? Der Doktor Froriep. Ein Genie ist Ihr Papa. – Und ich hab' ihn erst einmal reden gehört! – Im vorigen Jahr im Schwurgerichtssaal – – zum ersten- und letztenmal! Herrlich! Die Tränen sind mir über die Wangen gelaufen. Und der elende Kerl, den er verteidigt hat, ist freigesprochen worden. Er war vielleicht gar kein so elender Kerl. Er hat jedenfalls nur gestohlen, keine Mündelgelder veruntreut, um Bakkarat zu spielen und auf der Börse zu spekulieren. Und jetzt wird der Papa selber vor den Geschworenen stehen. In allen Zeitungen wird man es lesen. Zweiter Verhandlungstag, dritter Verhandlungstag; der Verteidiger erhob sich zu einer Replik. Wer wird denn sein Verteidiger sein? Kein Genie. Nichts wird ihm helfen. Einstimmig schuldig. Verurteilt auf fünf Jahre. Stein, Sträflingskleid, geschorene Haare. Einmal im Monat darf man ihn besuchen. Ich fahre mit Mama hinaus, dritter Klasse. Wir haben ja kein Geld. Keiner leiht uns was. Kleine Wohnung in der Lerchenfelderstraße, so wie die, wo ich die Näherin besucht habe vor zehn Jahren. Wir bringen ihm etwas zu essen mit. Woher denn? Wir haben ja selber nichts. Onkel Viktor wird uns eine Rente aussetzen. Dreihundert Gulden monatlich. Rudi wird in Holland sein bei Vanderhulst – wenn man noch auf ihn reflektiert. Die Kinder des Sträflings! Roman von Temme in drei Bänden. Der Papa empfängt uns im gestreiften Sträflingsanzug. Er schaut nicht bös drein, nur traurig. Er kann ja gar nicht bös dreinschauen. – Else, wenn du mir damals das

Geld verschafft hättest, das wird er sich denken, aber er wird nichts sagen. Er wird nicht das Herz haben, mir Vorwürfe zu machen. Er ist ja seelengut, nur leichtsinnig ist er. Sein Verhängnis ist die Spielleidenschaft. Er kann ja nichts dafür, es ist eine Art von Wahnsinn. Vielleicht spricht man ihn frei, weil er wahnsinnig ist. Auch den Brief hat er vorher nicht überlegt. Es ist ihm vielleicht gar nicht eingefallen, daß Dorsday die Gelegenheit benützen könnte und so eine Gemeinheit von mir verlangen wird. Er ist ein guter Freund unseres Hauses, er hat dem Papa schon einmal achttausend Gulden geliehen. Wie soll man so was von einem Menschen denken. Zuerst hat der Papa sicher alles andere versucht. Was muß er durchgemacht haben, ehe er die Mama veranlaßt hat, diesen Brief zu schreiben? Von einem zum andern ist er gelaufen, von Warsdorf zu Burin, von Burin zu Wertheimstein und weiß Gott noch zu wem. Bei Onkel Karl war er gewiß auch. Und alle haben sie ihn im Stich gelassen. Alle die sogenannten Freunde. Und nun ist Dorsday seine Hoffnung, seine letzte Hoffnung. Und wenn das Geld nicht kommt, so bringt er sich um. Natürlich bringt er sich um. Er wird sich doch nicht einsperren lassen. Untersuchungshaft, Verhandlung, Schwurgericht, Kerker, Sträflingsgewand. Nein, nein! Wenn der Haftbefehl kommt, erschießt er sich oder hängt sich auf. Am Fensterkreuz wird er hängen. Man wird herüberschicken vom Haus vis-à-vis, der Schlosser wird aufsperren müssen und ich bin schuld gewesen. Und jetzt sitzt er zusammen mit Mama im selben Zimmer, wo er übermorgen hängen wird, und raucht eine Havannazigarre. Woher hat er immer noch Havannazigarren? Ich höre ihn sprechen, wie er die Mama beruhigt. Verlaß dich drauf, Dorsday weist das Geld an. Bedenke doch, ich habe ihm heuer im Winter eine große Summe durch meine Intervention gerettet. Und dann kommt der Prozeß Erbesheimer... – Wahrhaftig. – Ich höre ihn sprechen. Telepathie! Merkwürdig. Auch Fred seh ich in diesem Moment. Er geht mit einem Mädel im Stadtpark am Kursalon vorbei. Sie hat eine hellblaue Bluse und lichte Schuhe und ein bißl heiser ist sie. Das weiß ich alles ganz bestimmt. Wenn ich nach Wien komme, werde ich Fred fragen, ob er am dritten September zwischen halb acht und acht Uhr abends mit seiner Geliebten im Stadtpark war.

Wohin denn noch? Was ist denn mit mir? Beinahe ganz dunkel. Wie schön und ruhig. Weit und breit kein Mensch. Nun sitzen sie alle schon beim Diner. Telepathie? Nein, das ist noch keine Telepathie. Ich habe ja früher das Tamtam gehört. Wo ist die Else? wird sich Paul denken. Es wird allen auffallen, wenn ich zur Vorspeise noch nicht da bin. Sie werden zu mir heraufschicken. Was ist das mit Else? Sie ist doch sonst so pünktlich? Auch die zwei Herren am Fenster werden denken: Wo ist denn heute das schöne junge Mädel mit dem rötlichblonden Haar? Und Herr von Dorsday wird Angst bekommen. Er ist sicher feig. Beruhigen Sie sich, Herr von Dorsday, es wird Ihnen nichts geschehen. Ich verachte Sie ja so sehr. Wenn ich wollte, morgen abend wären Sie ein toter Mann. – Ich bin überzeugt, Paul würde ihn fordern, wenn ich ihm die Sache erzählte. Ich schenke Ihnen das Leben, Herr von Dorsday.

Wie ungeheur weit die Wiesen und wie riesig schwarz die Berge. Keine Sterne beinahe. Ja doch, drei, vier, – es werden schon mehr. Und so still der Wald hinter mir. Schön, hier auf der Bank am Waldesrand zu sitzen. So fern, so fern das Hotel und so märchenhaft leuchtet es her. Und was für Schufte sitzen drin. Ach nein, Menschen, arme Menschen, sie tun mir alle so leid. Auch die Marchesa tut mir leid, ich weiß nicht warum, und die Frau Winawer und die Bonne von Cissys kleinem Mädel. Sie sitzt nicht an der Table d'hôte, sie hat schon früher mit Fritzi gesessen. Was ist das nur mit Else? fragt Cissy. Wie, auf ihrem Zimmer ist sie auch nicht? Alle haben sie Angst um mich, ganz gewiß. Nur ich habe keine Angst. Ja, da bin ich in Martino di Castrozza, sitze auf einer Bank am Waldesrand und die Luft ist wie Champagner und mir scheint gar, ich weine. Ja, warum weine ich denn? Es ist doch kein Grund zu weinen. Das sind die Nerven. Ich muß mich beherrschen. Ich darf mich nicht so gehenlassen. Aber das Weinen ist gar nicht unangenehm. Das Weinen tut mir immer wohl. Wie ich unsere alte Französin besucht habe im Krankenhaus, die dann gestorben ist, habe ich auch geweint. Und beim Begräbnis von der Großmama, und wie die Bertha nach Nürnberg gereist ist, und wie das Kleine von der Agathe gestorben ist, und im Theater bei der Kameliendame hab' ich auch geweint. Wer wird weinen, wenn ich tot bin? O, wie schön wäre das tot zu sein. Aufgebahrt liege ich im Salon, die Kerzen brennen. Lange Kerzen. Zwölf lange Kerzen. Unten steht schon der Leichenwagen. Vor dem Haustor stehen Leute. Wie alt war sie denn? Erst neunzehn. Wirklich erst neunzehn? – Denken Sie sich, ihr Papa ist im Zuchthaus. Warum hat sie sich denn umgebracht? Aus unglücklicher Liebe zu einem Filou. Aber was fällt Ihnen denn ein? Sie hätte ein Kind kriegen sollen. Nein, sie ist vom Cimone heruntergestürzt. Es ist ein Unglücksfall. Guten Tag, Herr Dorsday, Sie erweisen der kleinen Else auch die letzte Ehre? Kleine Else, sagt das alte Weib. – Warum denn? Natürlich, ich muß ihr die letzte Ehre erweisen. Ich habe ihr ja auch die erste Schande erwiesen. O, es war der Mühe wert, Frau Winawer, ich habe noch nie einen so schönen Körper gesehen. Es hat mich nur dreißig Millionen gekostet. Ein Rubens kostet dreimal soviel. Mit Haschisch hat sie sich vergiftet. Sie wollte nur schöne Visionen haben, aber sie hat zuviel genommen und ist nicht mehr aufgewacht. Warum hat er denn ein rotes Monokel der Herr Dorsday? Wem winkt er denn mit dem Taschentuch? Die Mama kommt die Treppe herunter und küßt ihm die Hand. Pfui, pfui. Jetzt flüstern sie miteinander. Ich kann nichts verstehen, weil ich aufgebahrt bin. Der Veilchenkranz um meine Stirn ist von Paul. Die Schleifen fallen bis auf den Boden. Kein Mensch traut sich ins Zimmer. Ich stehe lieber auf und schaue zum Fenster hinaus. Was für ein großer blauer See! Hundert Schiffe mit gelben Segeln –. Die Wellen glitzern. So viel Sonne. Regatta. Die Herren haben alle Ruderleibchen. Die Damen sind im Schwimmkostüm. Das ist unanständig. Sie bilden sich ein, ich bin nackt. Wie dumm sie sind. Ich habe ja schwarze Trauerkleider an, weil ich tot bin. Ich werde es euch beweisen. Ich lege mich gleich wieder auf die Bahre hin. Wo ist sie denn? Fort ist sie. Man hat sie davongetragen. Man hat sie unterschlagen. Darum ist der Papa im Zuchthaus. Und sie haben ihn doch freigesprochen auf drei Jahre. Die Geschworenen sind alle bestochen von Fiala. Ich werde jetzt zu Fuß auf den Friedhof gehen, da erspart die Mama das Begräbnis. Wir müssen uns einschränken. Ich gehe so schnell, daß mir keiner nachkommt. Ah, wie schnell ich gehen kann. Da bleiben sie alle auf den Straßen stehen und wundern sich. Wie darf man jemanden so anschaun, der tot ist! Das ist zudringlich. Ich gehe lieber übers Feld, das ist ganz blau von Vergißmeinnicht und Veilchen. Die Marineoffiziere stehen Spalier. Guten Morgen, meine Herren. Öffnen Sie das Tor, Herr Matador. Erkennen Sie mich nicht? Ich bin ja die Tote... Sie müssen mir darum nicht die Hand küssen... Wo ist denn meine Gruft? Hat man die auch unterschlagen? Gott sei Dank, es ist gar nicht der Friedhof. Das ist ja der Park in Mentone. Der Papa wird sich freuen, daß ich nicht begraben bin. Vor den Schlangen habe ich keine Angst. Wenn mich nur keine in den Fuß beißt. O weh.

Was ist denn? Wo bin ich denn? Habe ich geschlafen? Ja. Geschlafen habe ich. Ich muß sogar geträumt haben. Mir ist so kalt in den Füßen. Im rechten Fuß ist mir kalt. Wieso denn? Da ist am Knöchel ein kleiner Riß im Strumpf. Warum sitze ich denn noch im Wald? Es muß ja längst geläutet haben zum Dinner. Dinner.

O Gott, wo war ich denn? So weit war ich fort. Was hab' ich denn geträumt? Ich glaube ich war schon tot. Und keine Sorgen habe ich gehabt und mir nicht den Kopf zerbrechen müssen. Dreißigtausend, dreißigtausend... ich habe sie noch nicht. Ich muß sie mir erst verdienen. Und da sitz' ich allein am Waldesrand. Das Hotel leuchtet bis her. Ich muß zurück. Es ist schrecklich, daß ich zurück muß. Aber es ist keine Zeit mehr zu verlieren. Herr von Dorsday erwartet meine Entscheidung. Entscheidung. Entscheidung! Nein. Nein, Herr von Dorsday, kurz und gut, nein. Sie haben gescherzt, Herr von Dorsday, selbstverständlich. Ja, das werde ich ihm sagen. O, das ist ausgezeichnet. Ihr Scherz war nicht sehr vornehm, Herr von Dorsday, aber ich will Ihnen verzeihen. Ich telegraphiere morgen früh an Papa, Herr von Dorsday, daß das Geld pünktlich in Doktor Fialas Händen sein wird. Wunderbar. Das sage ich ihm. Da bleibt ihm nichts übrig, er muß das Geld abschicken. Muß? Muß er? Warum muß er denn? Und wenn er's täte, so würde er sich dann rächen irgendwie. Er würde es so einrichten, daß das Geld zu spät kommt. Oder er würde das Geld schicken und dann überall erzählen, daß er mich gehabt hat. Aber er schickt ja das Geld gar nicht ab. Nein, Fräulein Else, so haben wir nicht gewettet. Telegraphieren Sie dem Papa, was Ihnen beliebt, ich schicke das Geld nicht ab. Sie sollen nicht glauben, Fräulein Else, daß ich mich von so einem kleinen Mädel übertölpeln lasse, ich, der Vicomte von Eperies.

Ich muß vorsichtig gehen. Der Weg ist ganz dunkel. Sonderbar, es ist mir wohler als vorher. Es hat sich doch gar nichts geändert und mir ist wohler. Was habe ich denn nur geträumt? Von einem Matador? Was war denn das für ein Matador? Es ist doch weiter zum Hotel, als ich gedacht habe. Sie sitzen gewiß noch alle beim Diner. Ich werde mich ruhig an den Tisch setzen und sagen, daß ich Migräne gehabt habe und lasse mir nachservieren. Herr von Dorsday wird am Ende selbst zu mir kommen und mir sagen, daß das Ganze nur ein Scherz war. Entschuldigen Sie, Fräulein Else, entschuldigen Sie den schlechten Spaß, ich habe schon an meine Bank telegraphiert. Aber er wird es nicht sagen. Er hat nicht telegraphiert. Es ist alles noch genauso wie früher. Er wartet. Herr von Dorsday wartet. Nein, ich will ihn nicht sehen. Ich kann ihn nicht mehr sehen. Ich will niemanden mehr sehen. Ich will nicht mehr ins Hotel, ich will nicht mehr nach Hause, ich will nicht nach Wien, zu niemandem will ich, zu keinem Menschen, nicht zu Papa und nicht zu Mama, nicht zu Rudi und nicht zu Fred, nicht zu Bertha und nicht zu Tante Irene. Die ist noch die Beste, die würde alles verstehen. Aber ich habe nichts mehr mit ihr zu tun und mit niemandem mehr. Wenn ich zaubern könnte, wäre ich ganz woanders in der Welt. Auf irgendeinem herrlichen Schiff im Mittelländischen Meer, aber nicht allein. Mit Paul zum Beispiel. Ja, das könnte ich mir ganz gut vorstellen. Oder ich wohnte in einer Villa am Meer, und wir lägen auf den Marmorstufen, die ins Wasser führen, und er hielte mich fest in seinen Armen und bisse mich in die Lippen, wie es Albert vor zwei Jahren getan hat beim Klavier, der unverschämte Kerl. Nein. Allein möchte ich am Meer liegen auf den Marmorstufen und warten. Und endlich käme einer oder mehrere, und ich hätte die Wahl und die andern, die ich verschmähe, die stürzen sich aus Verzweiflung alle ins Meer. Oder sie müßten Geduld haben bis zum nächsten Tag. Ach, was wäre das für ein köstliches Leben. Wozu habe ich denn meine herrlichen Schultern und meine schönen schlanken Beine? Und wozu bin ich denn überhaupt auf der Welt? Und es geschähe ihnen ganz recht, ihnen allen, sie haben mich ja doch nur daraufhin erzogen, daß ich mich verkaufe, so oder so. Vom Theaterspielen haben sie nichts wissen wollen. Da haben sie mich ausgelacht. Und es wäre ihnen ganz recht gewesen im vorigen Jahr, wenn ich den Doktor Wilomitzer geheiratet hätte, der bald fünfzig ist. Nur daß sie mir nicht zugeredet haben. Da hat sich der Papa doch geniert. Aber die Mama hat ganz deutliche Anspielungen gemacht.

Wie riesig es dasteht das Hotel, wie eine ungeheuere beleuchtete Zauberburg. Alles ist so riesig. Die Berge auch. Man könnte sich fürchten. Noch nie waren sie so schwarz. Der Mond ist noch nicht da. Der geht erst zur Vorstellung auf, zur großen Vorstellung auf der Wiese, wenn der Herr von Dorsday seine Sklavin nackt tanzen läßt. Was geht mich denn der Herr Dorsday an? Nun, Mademoiselle Else, was machen Sie denn für Geschichten? Sie waren doch schon bereit auf und davon zu gehen, die Geliebte von fremden Männern zu werden, von einem nach dem andern. Und auf die Kleinigkeit, die Herr von Dorsday von Ihnen verlangt, kommt es Ihnen an? Für einen Perlenschmuck, für schöne Kleider, für eine Villa am Meer sind Sie bereit sich zu verkaufen? Und das Leben Ihres Vaters ist Ihnen nicht soviel wert? Es wäre gerade der richtige Anfang. Es wäre dann gleich die Rechtfertigung für alles andere. Ihr wart es, könnt ich sagen, Ihr habt mich dazu gemacht, Ihr alle seid schuld, daß ich so geworden bin, nicht nur Papa und Mama. Auch der Rudi ist schuld und der Fred und alle, alle, weil sich ja niemand um einen kümmert. Ein bißchen Zärtlichkeit, wenn man hübsch aussieht, und ein bißl Besorgtheit, wenn man Fieber hat, und in die Schule schicken sie einen, und zu Hause lernt man Klavier und Französisch, und im Sommer geht man aufs Land und zum Geburtstag kriegt man Geschenke und bei Tisch reden sie über allerlei. Aber was in mir vorgeht und was in mir wühlt und Angst hat, habt ihr euch darum je gekümmert? Manchmal im Blick von Papa war eine Ahnung davon, aber ganz flüchtig. Und dann war gleich wieder der Beruf da, und die Sorgen und das Börsenspiel – und wahrscheinlich irgendein Frauenzimmer ganz im geheimen, ›nichts sehr Feines unter uns‹, – und ich war wieder allein. Nun, was tätst du Papa, was tätst du heute, wenn ich nicht da wäre?

Da stehe ich, ja da stehe ich vor dem Hotel. – Furchtbar, da hineingehen zu müssen, alle die Leute sehen, den Herrn von Dorsday, die Tante, Cissy. Wie schön war das früher auf der Bank am Waldesrand, wie ich schon tot war. Matador – wenn ich nur drauf käm', was – eine Regatta war es, richtig und ich habe vom Fenster aus zugesehen. Aber wer war der Matador? – Wenn ich nur nicht so müd wäre, so furchtbar müde. Und da soll ich bis Mitternacht aufbleiben und mich dann ins Zimmer von Herrn von Dorsday schleichen? Vielleicht begegne ich der Cissy auf dem Gang. Hat sie was an unter dem Schlafrock, wenn sie zu ihm kommt? Es ist schwer, wenn man in solchen Dingen nicht geübt ist. Soll ich sie nicht um Rat fragen, die Cissy? Natürlich würde ich nicht sagen, daß es sich um Dorsday handelt, sondern sie müßte sich denken, ich habe ein nächtliches Rendezvous mit einem von den hübschen jungen Leuten hier im Hotel. Zum Beispiel mit dem langen blonden Menschen, der die leuchtenden Augen hat. Aber der ist ja nicht mehr da. Plötzlich war er verschwunden. Ich habe doch gar nicht an ihn gedacht bis zu diesem Augenblick. Aber es ist leider nicht der lange blonde Mensch mit den leuchtenden Augen, auch der Paul ist es nicht, es ist der Herr von Dorsday. Also wie mach' ich es denn? Was sage ich ihm? Einfach Ja? Ich kann doch nicht zu Herrn Dorsday ins Zimmer kommen. Er hat sicher lauter elegante Flakons auf dem Waschtisch, und das Zimmer riecht nach französischem Parfüm. Nein, nicht um die Welt zu ihm. Lieber im Freien. Da

geht er mich nichts an. Der Himmel ist so hoch und die Wiese ist
so groß. Ich muß gar nicht an den Herrn Dorsday denken. Ich
muß ihn nicht einmal anschauen. Und wenn er es wagen würde,
mich anzurühren, einen Tritt bekäme er mit meinen nackten Füßen. Ach, wenn es doch ein anderer wäre, irgendein anderer.
Alles, alles könnte er von mir haben heute nacht, jeder andere,
nur Dorsday nicht. Und gerade der! Gerade der! Wie seine
Augen stechen und bohren werden. Mit dem Monokel wird er
dastehen und grinsen. Aber nein, er wird nicht grinsen. Er wird
ein vornehmes Gesicht schneiden. Elegant. Er ist ja solche Dinge
gewohnt. Wie viele hat er schon so gesehen? Hundert oder tausend? Aber war schon eine darunter wie ich? Nein, gewiß nicht.
Ich werde ihm sagen, daß er nicht der Erste ist, der mich so sieht.
Ich werde ihm sagen, daß ich einen Geliebten habe. Aber erst,
wenn die dreißigtausend Gulden an Fiala abgesandt sind. Dann
werde ich ihm sagen, daß er ein Narr war, daß er mich auch hätte
haben können um dasselbe Geld. – Daß ich schon zehn Liebhaber gehabt habe, zwanzig, hundert. – Aber das wird er mir ja
alles nicht glauben. – Und wenn er es mir glaubt, was hilft es
mir? – Wenn ich ihm nur irgendwie die Freude verderben
könnte. Wenn noch einer dabei wäre? Warum nicht? Er hat ja
nicht gesagt, daß er mit mir allein sein muß. Ach, Herr von
Dorsday, ich habe solche Angst vor Ihnen. Wollen Sie mir nicht
freundlichst gestatten, einen guten Bekannten mitzubringen?
O, das ist keineswegs gegen die Abrede, Herr von Dorsday.
Wenn es mir beliebte, dürfte ich das ganze Hotel dazu einladen,
und Sie wären trotzdem verpflichtet, die dreißigtausend Gulden
abzuschicken. Aber ich begnüge mich damit, meinen Vetter
Paul mitzubringen. Oder ziehen Sie etwa einen andern vor? Der
lange blonde Mensch ist leider nicht mehr da und der Filou mit
dem Römerkopf leider auch nicht. Aber ich find' schon noch
wen andern. Sie fürchten Indiskretion? Darauf kommt es ja
nicht an. Ich lege keinen Wert auf Diskretion. Wenn man einmal
so weit ist wie ich, dann ist alles ganz egal. Das ist heute ja nur
der Anfang. Oder denken Sie, aus diesem Abenteuer fahre ich
wieder nach Hause als anständiges Mädchen aus guter Familie?

Nein, weder gute Familie noch anständiges junges Mädchen. Das wäre erledigt. Ich stelle mich jetzt auf meine eigenen Beine. Ich habe schöne Beine, Herr von Dorsday, wie Sie und die übrigen Teilnehmer des Festes bald zu bemerken Gelegenheit haben werden. Also die Sache ist in Ordnung, Herr von Dorsday. Um zehn Uhr, während alles noch in der Halle sitzt, wandern wir im Mondenschein über die Wiese, durch den Wald nach Ihrer berühmten selbstentdeckten Lichtung. Das Telegramm an die Bank bringen Sie für alle Fälle gleich mit. Denn eine Sicherheit darf ich doch wohl verlangen von einem solchen Spitzbuben wie Sie. Und um Mitternacht können Sie wieder nach Hause gehen, und ich bleibe mit meinem Vetter oder sonstwem auf der Wiese im Mondenschein. Sie haben doch nichts dagegen, Herr von Dorsday? Das dürfen Sie gar nicht. Und wenn ich morgen früh zufällig tot sein sollte, so wundern Sie sich weiter nicht. Dann wird eben Paul das Telegramm aufgeben. Dafür wird schon gesorgt sein. Aber bilden Sie sich dann um Gottes willen nicht ein, daß Sie, elender Kerl, mich in den Tod getrieben haben. Ich weiß ja schon lange, daß es so mit mir enden wird. Fragen Sie doch nur meinen Freund Fred, ob ich es ihm nicht schon öfters gesagt habe. Fred, das ist nämlich Herr Friedrich Wenkheim, nebstbei der einzige anständige Mensch, den ich in meinem Leben kennengelernt habe. Der einzige, den ich geliebt hätte, wenn er nicht ein gar so anständiger Mensch wäre. Ja, ein so verworfenes Geschöpf bin ich. Bin nicht geschaffen für eine bürgerliche Existenz, und Talent habe ich auch keines. Für unsere Familie wäre es sowieso das Beste, sie stürbe aus. Mit dem Rudi wird auch schon irgendein Malheur geschehen. Der wird sich in Schulden stürzen für eine holländische Chansonette und bei Vanderhulst defraudieren. Das ist schon so in unserer Familie. Und der jüngste Bruder von meinem Vater, der hat sich erschossen, wie er fünfzehn Jahre alt war. Kein Mensch weiß warum. Ich habe ihn nicht gekannt. Lassen Sie sich die Photographie zeigen, Herr von Dorsday. Wir haben sie in einem Album... Ich soll ihm ähnlich sehen. Kein Mensch weiß, warum er sich umgebracht hat. Und von mir wird es auch keiner wissen. Ihretwegen keinesfalls, Herr von Dorsday. Die Ehre tue ich Ihnen nicht an. Ob mit neunzehn oder einundzwanzig, das ist doch egal. Oder soll ich Bonne werden oder Telephonistin oder einen Herrn Wilomitzer heiraten oder mich von Ihnen aushalten lassen? Es ist alles gleich ekelhaft, und ich komme überhaupt gar nicht mit Ihnen auf die Wiese. Nein, das ist alles viel zu anstrengend und zu dumm und zu widerwärtig. Wenn ich tot bin, werden Sie schon die Güte haben und die paar tausend Gulden für den Papa absenden, denn es wäre doch zu traurig, wenn er gerade an dem Tage verhaftet würde, an dem man meine Leiche nach Wien bringt. Aber ich werde einen Brief hinterlassen mit testamentarischer Verfügung: Herr von Dorsday hat das Recht, meinen Leichnam zu sehen. Meinen schönen nackten Mädchenleichnam. So können Sie sich nicht beklagen, Herr von Dorsday, daß ich Sie übers Ohr gehaut habe. Sie haben doch was für Ihr Geld. Daß ich noch lebendig sein muß, das steht nicht in unserem Kontrakt. O nein. Das steht nirgends geschrieben. Also den Anblick meines Leichnams vermache ich dem Kunsthändler Dorsday, und Herrn Fred Wenkheim vermache ich mein Tagebuch aus meinem siebzehnten Lebensjahr – weiter habe ich nichts geschrieben – und dem Fräulein bei Cissy vermache ich die fünf Zwanzigfranks-Stücke, die ich vor Jahren aus der Schweiz mitgebracht habe. Sie liegen im Schreibtisch neben den Briefen. Und Bertha vermache ich das schwarze Abendkleid. Und Agathe meine Bücher. Und meinem Vetter Paul, dem vermache ich einen Kuß auf meine blassen Lippen. Und der Cissy vermache ich mein Rakett, weil ich edel bin. Und man soll mich gleich hier begraben in San Martino di Castrozza auf dem schönen kleinen Friedhof. Ich will nicht mehr zurück nach Hause. Auch als Tote will ich nicht mehr zurück. Und Papa und Mama sollen sich nicht kränken, mir geht es besser als ihnen. Und ich verzeihe ihnen. Es ist nicht schade um mich. – Haha, was für ein komisches Testament. Ich bin wirklich gerührt. Wenn ich denke, daß ich morgen um die Zeit, während die andern beim Diner sitzen, schon tot bin? – Die Tante Emma wird natürlich nicht zum Diner herunterkommen und Paul auch nicht. Sie werden sich auf dem Zimmer servieren lassen. Neugierig bin ich, wie sich Cissy benehmen wird. Nur werde ich es leider nicht erfahren. Gar nichts mehr werde ich erfahren. Oder vielleicht weiß man noch alles, solange man nicht begraben ist? Und am Ende bin ich nur scheintot. Und wenn der Herr von Dorsday an meinen Leichnam tritt, so erwache ich und schlage die Augen auf, da läßt er vor Schreck das Monokel fallen.

Aber es ist ja leider alles nicht wahr. Ich werde nicht scheintot sein und tot auch nicht. Ich werde mich überhaupt gar nicht umbringen, ich bin ja viel zu feig. Wenn ich auch eine couragierte Kletterin bin, feig bin ich doch. Und vielleicht habe ich nicht einmal genug Veronal. Wieviel Pulver braucht man denn? Sechs glaube ich. Aber zehn ist sicherer. Ich glaube, es sind noch zehn. Ja, das werden genug sein.

Zum wievielten Mal lauf' ich jetzt eigentlich um das Hotel herum? Also was jetzt? Da steh' ich vor dem Tor. In der Halle ist noch niemand. Natürlich – sie sitzen ja noch alle beim Diner. Seltsam sieht die Halle aus so ganz ohne Menschen. Auf dem Sessel dort liegt ein Hut, ein Touristenhut, ganz fesch. Hübscher Gemsbart. Dort im Fauteuil sitzt ein alter Herr. Hat wahrscheinlich keinen Appetit mehr. Liest Zeitung. Dem geht's gut. Er hat keine Sorgen. Er liest ruhig Zeitung, und ich muß mir den Kopf zerbrechen, wie ich dem Papa dreißigtausend Gulden verschaffen soll. Aber nein. Ich weiß ja wie. Es ist ja so furchtbar einfach. Was will ich denn? Was will ich denn? Was tu' ich denn da in der Halle? Gleich werden sie alle kommen vom Diner. Was soll ich denn tun? Herr von Dorsday sitzt gewiß auf Nadeln. Wo bleibt sie, denkt er sich. Hat sie sich am Ende umgebracht? Oder engagiert sie jemanden, daß er mich umbringt? Oder hetzt sie ihren Vetter Paul auf mich? Haben Sie keine Angst, Herr von Dorsday, ich bin keine so gefährliche Person. Ein kleines Luder bin ich, weiter nichts. Für die Angst, die Sie ausgestanden haben, sollen Sie auch Ihren Lohn haben. Zwölf Uhr, Zimmer Nummer fünfundsechzig. Im Freien wäre es mir doch zu kühl. Und von Ihnen aus, Herr von Dorsday, begebe ich mich direkt zu meinem Vetter Paul. Sie haben doch nichts dagegen, Herr von Dorsday?

»Else! Else!«

Wie? Was? Das ist ja Pauls Stimme. Das Diner schon aus? – *»Else!«* – »Ach, Paul, was gibt's denn, Paul?« – Ich stell' mich ganz unschuldig. – *»Ja, wo steckst du denn, Else?«* – »Wo soll ich denn stecken? Ich bin spazierengegangen.« – *»Jetzt, während des Diners?«* – »Na, wann denn? Es ist doch die schönste Zeit dazu.« Ich red' Blödsinn. – *»Die Mama hat sich schon alles Mögliche eingeredet. Ich war an deiner Zimmertür, hab' geklopft.«* – »Hab' nichts gehört.« – *»Aber im Ernst, Else, wie kannst du uns in eine solche Unruhe versetzen! Du hättest Mama doch wenigstens verständigen können, daß du nicht zum Diner kommst.«* – »Du hast ja recht, Paul, aber wenn du eine Ahnung hättest, was ich für Kopfschmerzen gehabt habe.« Ganz schmelzend red' ich. O, ich Luder. – *»Ist dir jetzt wenigstens besser?«* – »Könnt' ich eigentlich nicht sagen.« – *»Ich will vor allem der Mama«* – »Halt Paul, noch nicht. Entschuldige mich bei der Tante, ich will nur für ein paar Minuten auf mein Zimmer, mich ein bißl herrichten. Dann komme ich gleich herunter und werde mir eine Kleinigkeit nachservieren lassen.« – *»Du bist so blaß, Else? – Soll ich dir die Mama hinaufschicken?«* – »Aber mach' doch keine solchen Geschichten mit mir, Paul, und schau' mich nicht so an. Hast du noch nie ein weibliches Wesen mit Kopfschmerzen gesehen? Ich komme bestimmt noch herunter. In zehn Minuten spätestens. Grüß dich Gott, Paul.« – *»Also auf Wiedersehen Else.«* – Gott sei Dank, daß er geht. Dummer Bub', aber lieb. Was will denn der Portier von mir? Wie, ein Telegramm? »Danke. Wann ist denn die Depesche gekommen, Herr Portier?« – *»Vor einer Viertelstunde, Fräulein.«* – Warum schaut er mich denn so an, so – bedauernd. Um Himmels willen, was wird denn da drin stehn? Ich mach' sie erst oben auf, sonst fall' ich vielleicht in Ohnmacht. Am Ende hat sich der Papa – Wenn der Papa tot ist, dann ist ja alles in Ordnung, dann muß ich nicht mehr mit Herrn von Dorsday auf die Wiese gehn... O, ich elende Person. Lieber Gott, mach', daß in der Depesche nichts Böses steht. Lieber Gott, mach', daß der Papa lebt. Verhaftet meinetwegen, nur nicht tot. Wenn nichts Böses drin steht, dann will ich ein Opfer bringen. Ich werde Bonne, ich nehme eine

Stellung in einem Bureau an. Sei nicht tot, Papa. Ich bin ja bereit. Ich tue ja alles, was du willst...

Gott sei Dank, daß ich oben bin. Licht gemacht, Licht gemacht. Kühl ist es geworden. Das Fenster war zu lange offen. Courage, Courage. Ha, vielleicht steht drin, daß die Sache geordnet ist. Vielleicht hat der Onkel Bernhard das Geld hergegeben und sie telegraphieren mir: Nicht mit Dorsday reden. Ich werde es ja gleich sehen. Aber wenn ich auf den Plafond schaue, kann ich natürlich nicht lesen, was in der Depesche steht. Trala, trala, Courage. Es muß ja sein. ›Wiederhole flehentlich Bitte mit Dorsday reden. Summe nicht dreißig, sondern fünfzig. Sonst alles vergeblich. Adresse bleibt Fiala.‹ – Sondern fünfzig. Sonst alles vergeblich. Trala, trala. Fünfzig. Adresse bleibt Fiala. Aber gewiß, ob fünfzig oder dreißig, darauf kommt es ja nicht an. Auch dem Herrn von Dorsday nicht. Das Veronal liegt unter der Wäsche, für alle Fälle. Warum habe ich nicht gleich gesagt: fünfzig. Ich habe doch daran gedacht! Sonst alles vergeblich. Also hinunter, geschwind, nicht da auf dem Bett sitzen bleiben. Ein kleiner Irrtum, Herr von Dorsday, verzeihen Sie. Nicht dreißig, sondern fünfzig, sonst alles vergeblich. Adresse bleibt Fiala. ›Sie halten mich wohl für einen Narren, Fräulein Else?‹ Keineswegs, Herr Vicomte, wie sollte ich. Für fünfzig müßte ich jedenfalls entsprechend mehr fordern, Fräulein. Sonst alles vergeblich, Adresse bleibt Fiala. Wie Sie wünschen, Herr von Dorsday. Bitte, befehlen Sie nur. Vor allem aber, schreiben Sie die Depesche an Ihr Bankhaus, natürlich, sonst habe ich ja keine Sicherheit. –

Ja, so mach' ich es. Ich komme zu ihm ins Zimmer und erst, wenn er vor meinen Augen die Depesche geschrieben – ziehe ich mich aus. Und die Depesche behalte ich in der Hand. Ha, wie unappetitlich. Und wo soll ich denn meine Kleider hinlegen? Nein, nein, ich ziehe mich schon hier aus und nehme den großen schwarzen Mantel um, der mich ganz einhüllt. So ist es am bequemsten. Für beide Teile. Adresse bleibt Fiala. Mir klappern die Zähne. Das Fenster ist noch offen. Zugemacht. Im Freien? Den Tod hätte ich davon haben können. Schuft! Fünfzigtausend. Er kann nicht Nein sagen. Zimmer fünfundsechzig. Aber vorher sag' ich Paul, er soll in seinem Zimmer auf mich warten. Von Dorsday geh' ich direkt zu Paul und erzähle ihm alles. Und dann soll Paul ihn ohrfeigen. Ja, noch heute nacht. Ein reichhaltiges Programm. Und dann kommt das Veronal. Nein, wozu denn? Warum denn sterben? Keine Spur. Lustig, lustig, jetzt fängt ja das Leben erst an. Ihr sollt euere Freude haben. Ihr sollt stolz werden auf euer Töchterlein. Ein Luder will ich werden, wie es die Welt noch nicht gesehen hat. Adresse bleibt Fiala. Du sollst deine fünfzigtausend Gulden haben, Papa. Aber die nächsten, die ich mir verdiene, um die kaufe ich mir neue Nachthemden mit Spitzen besetzt, ganz durchsichtig und köstliche Seidenstrümpfe. Man lebt nur einmal. Wozu schaut man denn so aus wie ich. Licht gemacht, – die Lampe über dem Spiegel schalt' ich ein. Wie schön meine blondroten Haare sind, und meine Schultern; meine Augen sind auch nicht übel. Hu, wie groß sie sind. Es wär' schad' um mich. Zum Veronal ist immer noch Zeit. – Aber ich muß ja hinunter. Tief hinunter. Herr Dorsday wartet, und er weiß noch nicht einmal, daß es indes fünfzigtausend geworden sind. Ja, ich bin im Preis gestiegen, Herr von Dorsday. Ich muß ihm das Telegramm zeigen, sonst glaubt er mir am Ende nicht und denkt, ich will ein Geschäft bei der Sache machen. Ich werde die Depesche auf sein Zimmer schicken und etwas dazu schreiben. Zu meinem lebhaften Bedauern sind es nun fünfzigtausend geworden, Herr von Dorsday, das kann Ihnen ja ganz egal sein. Und ich bin überzeugt, Ihre Gegenforderung war gar nicht ernstgemeint. Denn Sie sind ein Vicomte und ein Gentleman. Morgen früh werden Sie die fünfzigtausend, an denen das Leben meines Vaters hängt, ohne weiters an Fiala senden. Ich rechne darauf. – ›Selbstverständlich, mein Fräulein, ich sende für alle Fälle gleich hunderttausend, ohne jede Gegenleistung und verpflichte mich überdies, von heute an für den Lebensunterhalt Ihrer ganzen Familie zu sorgen, die Börsenschulden Ihres Herr Papas zu zahlen und sämtliche veruntreute Mündelgelder zu ersetzen.‹ Adresse bleibt Fiala. Hahaha! Ja, genauso ist der Vicomte von Eperies. Das ist ja alles

Unsinn. Was bleibt mir denn übrig? Es muß ja sein, ich muß es ja tun, alles muß ich tun, was Herr von Dorsday verlangt, damit der Papa morgen das Geld hat, – damit er nicht eingesperrt wird, damit er sich nicht umbringt. Und ich werde es auch tun. Ja, ich werde es tun, obzwar doch alles für die Katz' ist. In einem halben Jahr sind wir wieder gerade soweit wie heute! In vier Wochen! – Aber dann geht es mich nichts mehr an. Das eine Opfer bringe ich – und dann keines mehr. Nie, nie, niemals wieder. Ja, das sage ich dem Papa, sobald ich nach Wien komme. Und dann fort aus dem Haus, wo immer hin. Ich werde mich mit Fred beraten. Er ist der einzige, der mich wirklich gern hat. Aber soweit bin ich ja noch nicht. Ich bin nicht in Wien, ich bin noch in Martino di Castrozza. Noch nichts ist geschehen. Also wie, wie, was? Da ist das Telegramm. Was tue ich denn mit dem Telegramm? Ich habe es ja schon gewußt. Ich muß es ihm auf sein Zimmer schikken. Aber was sonst? Ich muß ihm etwas dazu schreiben. Nun ja, was soll ich ihm schreiben? Erwarten Sie mich um zwölf. Nein, nein, nein! Den Triumph soll er nicht haben. Ich will nicht, will nicht, will nicht. Gott sei Dank, daß ich die Pulver da habe. Das ist die einzige Rettung. Wo sind sie denn? Um Gottes willen, man wird sie mir doch nicht gestohlen haben. Aber nein, da sind sie ja. Da in der Schachtel. Sind sie noch alle da? Ja, da sind sie. Eins, zwei, drei, vier, fünf, sechs. Ich will sie ja nur ansehen, die lieben Pulver. Es verpflichtet ja zu nichts. Auch daß ich sie ins Glas schütte, verpflichtet ja zu nichts. Eins, zwei, – aber ich bringe mich ja sicher nicht um. Fällt mir gar nicht ein. Drei, vier, fünf – davon stirbt man auch noch lange nicht. Es wäre schrecklich, wenn ich das Veronal nicht mithätte. Da müßte ich mich zum Fenster hinunterstürzen und dazu hätt' ich doch nicht den Mut. Aber das Veronal, – man schläft langsam ein, wacht nicht mehr auf, keine Qual, keinen Schmerz. Man legt sich ins Bett; in einem Zuge trinkt man es aus, träumt, und alles ist vorbei. Vorgestern habe ich auch ein Pulver genommen und neulich sogar zwei. Pst, niemandem sagen. Heut' werden es halt ein bißl mehr sein. Es ist ja nur für alle Fälle. Wenn es mich gar gar zu sehr grausen sollte. Aber warum soll es mich denn

grausen? Wenn er mich anrührt, so spucke ich ihm ins Gesicht.
Ganz einfach.

Aber wie soll ich ihm denn den Brief zukommen lassen? Ich kann
doch nicht dem Herrn von Dorsday durch das Stubenmädchen
einen Brief schicken. Das beste, ich gehe hinunter und rede mit ihm
und zeige ihm das Telegramm. Hinunter muß ich ja jedenfalls. Ich
kann doch nicht da heroben im Zimmer bleiben. Ich hielte es ja
gar nicht aus, drei Stunden lang – bis der Moment kommt. Auch
wegen der Tante muß ich hinunter. Ha, was geht mich denn die
Tante an. Was gehen mich die Leute an? Sehen Sie, meine Herrschaften, da steht das Glas mit dem Veronal. So, jetzt nehme ich es
in die Hand. So, jetzt führe ich es an die Lippen. Ja, jeden Moment
kann ich drüben sein, wo es keine Tanten gibt und keinen Dorsday und keinen Vater, der Mündelgelder defraudiert...

Aber ich werde mich nicht umbringen. Das habe ich nicht
notwendig. Ich werde auch nicht zu Herrn von Dorsday ins Zimmer gehen. Fällt mir gar nicht ein. Ich werde mich doch nicht um
fünfzigtausend Gulden nackt hinstellen vor einen alten Lebe-
mann, um einen Lumpen vor dem Kriminal zu retten. Nein, nein,
entweder oder. Wie kommt denn der Herr von Dorsday dazu?
Gerade der? Wenn einer mich sieht, dann sollen mich auch andere
sehen. Ja! – Herrlicher Gedanke!– Alle sollen sie mich sehen. Die
ganze Welt soll mich sehen. Und dann kommt das Veronal. Nein,
nicht das Veronal, – wozu denn?! dann kommt die Villa mit den
Marmorstufen und die schönen Jünglinge und die Freiheit und die
weite Welt! Guten Abend, Fräulein Else, so gefallen Sie mir.
Haha. Da unten werden sie meinen, ich bin verrückt geworden.
Aber ich war noch nie so vernünftig. Zum erstenmal in meinem
Leben bin ich wirklich vernünftig. Alle, alle sollen sie mich sehen!
– Dann gibt es kein Zurück, kein nach Hause zu Papa und Mama,
zu den Onkeln und Tanten. Dann bin ich nicht mehr das Fräulein
Else, das man an irgendeinen Direktor Wilomitzer verkuppeln
möchte; alle hab' ich sie so zum Narren; – den Schuften Dorsday
vor allem – und komme zum zweitenmal auf die Welt... sonst
alles vergeblich – Adresse bleibt Fiala. Haha!

Keine Zeit mehr verlieren, nicht wieder feig werden. Herunter das Kleid. Wer wird der erste sein? Wirst du es sein, Vetter Paul? Dein Glück, daß der Römerkopf nicht mehr da ist. Wirst du diese schönen Brüste küssen heute nacht? Ah, wie bin ich schön. Bertha hat ein schwarzes Seidenhemd. Raffiniert. Ich werde noch viel raffinierter sein. Herrliches Leben. Fort mit den Strümpfen, das wäre unanständig. Nackt, ganz nackt. Wie wird mich Cissy beneiden! Und andere auch. Aber sie trauen sich nicht. Sie möchten ja alle so gern. Nehmt euch ein Beispiel. Ich, die Jungfrau, ich traue mich. Ich werde mich ja zu Tod lachen über Dorsday. Da bin ich, Herr von Dorsday. Rasch auf die Post. Fünfzigtausend. Soviel ist es doch wert?

Schön, schön bin ich! Schau' mich an, Nacht! Berge schaut mich an! Himmel schau' mich an, wie schön ich bin. Aber ihr seid ja blind. Was habe ich von euch. Die da unten haben Augen. Soll ich mir die Haare lösen? Nein. Da säh' ich aus wie eine Verrückte. Aber ihr sollt mich nicht für verrückt halten. Nur für schamlos sollt ihr mich halten. Für eine Kanaille. Wo ist das Telegramm? Um Gottes willen, wo habe ich denn das Telegramm? Da liegt es, friedlich neben dem Veronal. ›Wiederhole flehentlich – fünfzigtausend – sonst alles vergeblich. Adresse bleibt Fiala.‹ Ja, das ist das Telegramm. Das ist ein Stück Papier und da stehen Worte darauf. Aufgegeben in Wien vier Uhr dreißig. Nein, ich träume nicht, es ist alles wahr. Und zu Hause warten sie auf die fünfzigtausend Gulden. Und Herr von Dorsday wartet auch. Er soll nur warten. Wir haben ja Zeit. Ah, wie hübsch ist es, so nackt im Zimmer auf- und abzuspazieren. Bin ich wirklich so schön wie im Spiegel? Ach, kommen Sie doch näher, schönes Fräulein. Ich will Ihre blutroten Lippen küssen. Ich will Ihre Brüste an meine Brüste pressen. Wie schade, daß das Glas zwischen uns ist, das kalte Glas. Wie gut würden wir uns miteinander vertragen. Nicht wahr? Wir brauchten gar niemanden andern. Es gibt vielleicht gar keine andern Menschen. Es gibt Telegramme und Hotels und Berge und Bahnhöfe und Wälder, aber Menschen gibt es nicht. Die träumen wir nur. Nur der Doktor Fiala existiert mit der Adresse. Es bleibt immer dieselbe. O, ich bin keineswegs verrückt. Ich bin nur ein wenig erregt. Das ist doch ganz selbstverständlich, bevor man zum zweitenmal auf die Welt kommt. Denn die frühere Else ist schon gestorben. Ja, ganz bestimmt bin ich tot. Da braucht man kein Veronal dazu. Soll ich es nicht weggießen? Das Stubenmädel könnte es aus Versehen trinken. Ich werde einen Zettel hinlegen und darauf schreiben: Gift; nein, lieber: Medizin, – damit dem Stubenmädel nichts geschieht. So edel bin ich. So. Medizin, zweimal unterstrichen und drei Ausrufungszeichen. Jetzt kann nichts passieren. Und wenn ich dann heraufkomme und keine Lust habe mich umzubringen und nur schlafen will, dann trinke ich eben nicht das ganze Glas aus, sondern nur ein Viertel davon oder noch weniger. Ganz einfach. Alles habe ich in meiner Hand. Am einfachsten wäre, ich liefe hinunter – so wie ich bin über Gang und Stiegen. Aber nein, da könnte ich aufgehalten werden, ehe ich unten bin – und ich muß doch die Sicherheit haben, daß der Herr von Dorsday dabei ist! Sonst schickt er natürlich das Geld nicht ab, der Schmutzian. – Aber ich muß ihm ja noch schreiben. Das ist doch das Wichtigste. O, kalt ist die Sessellehne, aber angenehm. Wenn ich meine Villa am italienischen See haben werde, dann werde ich in meinem Park immer nackt herumspazieren... Die Füllfeder vermache ich Fred, wenn ich einmal sterbe. Aber vorläufig habe ich etwas Gescheiteres zu tun als zu sterben. ›Hochverehrter Herr Vicomte‹ – also vernünftig Else, keine Aufschrift, weder hochverehrt, noch hochverachtet. ›Ihre Bedingung, Herr von Dorsday, ist erfüllt‹ – – – ›In dem Augenblick, da Sie diese Zeilen lesen, Herr von Dorsday, ist Ihre Bedingung erfüllt, wenn auch nicht ganz in der von Ihnen vorgesehenen Weise.‹ – ›Nein, wie gut das Mädel schreibt‹, möcht' der Papa sagen. – ›Und so rechne ich darauf, daß Sie Ihrerseits Ihr Wort halten und die fünfzigtausend Gulden telegraphisch an die bekannte Adresse unverzüglich anweisen lassen werden. Else.‹ Nein, nicht Else. Gar keine Unterschrift. So. Mein schönes gelbes Briefpapier! Hab' ich zu Weihnachten bekommen. Schad' drum. So – und jetzt Telegramm und Brief ins Kuvert. – ›Herrn von Dorsday‹, Zimmer Nummer fünfundsechzig. Wozu die Nummer? Ich lege ihm den Brief einfach vor die Tür im Vorbeigehen. Aber ich muß nicht. Ich muß überhaupt gar nichts. Wenn es mir beliebt, kann ich mich jetzt auch ins Bett legen und schlafen und mich um nichts mehr kümmern. Nicht um den Herrn von Dorsday und nicht um den Papa. Ein gestreifter Sträflingsanzug ist auch ganz elegant. Und erschossen haben sich schon viele. Und sterben müssen wir alle.

Aber du hast ja das alles vorläufig nicht nötig, Papa. Du hast ja deine herrlich gewachsene Tochter, und Adresse bleibt Fiala. Ich werde eine Sammlung einleiten. Mit dem Teller werde ich herumgehen. Warum sollte nur Herr von Dorsday zahlen? Das wäre ein Unrecht. Jeder nach seinen Verhältnissen. Wieviel wird Paul auf den Teller legen? Und wieviel der Herr mit dem goldenen Zwicker? Aber bildet euch nur ja nicht ein, daß das Vergnügen lange dauern wird. Gleich hülle ich mich wieder ein, laufe die Treppen hinauf in mein Zimmer, sperre mich ein und, wenn es mir beliebt, trinke ich das ganze Glas auf einen Zug. Aber es wird mir nicht belieben. Es wäre nur eine Feigheit. Sie verdienen gar nicht soviel Respekt, die Schufte. Schämen vor euch? Ich mich schämen vor irgendwem? Das habe ich wirklich nicht nötig. Laß dir noch einmal in die Augen sehen, schöne Else. Was du für Riesenaugen hast, wenn man näher kommt. Ich wollte, es küßte mich einer auf meine Augen, auf meinen blutroten Mund. Kaum über die Knöchel reicht mein Mantel. Man wird sehen, daß meine Füße nackt sind. Was tut's, man wird noch mehr sehen! Aber ich bin nicht verpflichtet. Ich kann gleich wieder umkehren, noch bevor ich unten bin. Im ersten Stock kann ich umkehren. Ich muß überhaupt nicht hinuntergehen. Aber ich will ja. Ich freue mich drauf. Hab' ich mir nicht mein ganzes Leben lang so was gewüscht?

Worauf warte ich denn noch? Ich bin ja bereit. Die Vorstellung kann beginnen. Den Brief nicht vergessen. Eine aristokratische Schrift, behauptet Fred. Auf Wiedersehen, Else. Du bist schön mit dem Mantel. Florentinerinnen haben sich so malen lassen. In den Galerien hängen ihre Bilder und es ist eine Ehre für sie. – Man muß gar nichts bemerken, wenn ich den Mantel umhabe. Nur die Füße, nur die Füße. Ich nehme die schwarzen Lack-

schuhe, dann denkt man, es sind fleischfarbene Strümpfe. So
werde ich durch die Halle gehen, und kein Mensch wird ahnen,
daß unter dem Mantel nichts ist, als ich, ich selber. Und dann
kann ich immer noch herauf... – Wer spielt denn da unten so
schön Klavier? Chopin? – Herr von Dorsday wird etwas nervös
sein. Vielleicht hat er Angst vor Paul. Nur Geduld, Geduld,
wird sich alles finden. Ich weiß noch gar nichts, Herr von Dorsday, ich bin selber schrecklich gespannt. Licht ausschalten! Ist
alles in Ordnung in meinem Zimmer? Leb' wohl, Veronal, auf
Wiedersehen. Leb' wohl, mein heißgeliebtes Spiegelbild. Wie
du im Dunkel leuchtest. Ich bin schon ganz gewohnt, unter dem
Mantel nackt zu sein. Ganz angenehm. Wer weiß, ob nicht manche so in der Halle sitzen und keiner weiß es? Ob nicht manche
Dame so ins Theater geht und so in ihrer Loge sitzt – zum Spaß
oder aus anderen Gründen.

   Soll ich zusperren? Wozu? Hier wird ja nichts gestohlen. Und
wenn auch – ich brauche ja nichts mehr. Schluß... Wo ist denn
Nummer fünfundsechzig? Niemand ist auf dem Gang. Alles
noch unten beim Diner. Einundsechzig... zweiundsechzig...
das sind ja riesige Bergschuhe, die da vor der Türe stehen. Da
hängt eine Hose am Haken. Wie unanständig. Vierundsechzig,
fünfundsechzig. So. Da wohnt er, der Vicomte... Da unten
lehn' ich den Brief hin, an die Tür. Da muß er ihn gleich sehen.
Es wird ihn doch keiner stehlen? So, da liegt er... Macht
nichts... Ich kann noch immer tun, was ich will. Hab' ich ihn
halt zum Narren gehalten... Wenn ich ihm nur jetzt nicht auf
der Treppe begegne. Da kommt ja... nein, das ist er nicht!
... Der ist viel hübscher als der Herr von Dorsday, sehr elegant,
mit dem kleinen schwarzen Schnurrbart. Wann ist denn der angekommen? Ich könnte eine kleine Probe veranstalten – ein ganz
klein wenig den Mantel lüften. Ich habe große Lust dazu.
Schauen Sie mich nur an, mein Herr. Sie ahnen nicht, an wem
Sie da vorübergehen. Schade, daß Sie gerade jetzt sich heraufbe-
mühen. Warum bleiben Sie nicht in der Halle? Sie versäumen
etwas. Große Vorstellung. Warum halten Sie mich nicht auf?
Mein Schicksal liegt in Ihrer Hand. Wenn Sie mich grüßen, so

kehre ich wieder um. So grüßen Sie mich doch. Ích sehe Sie doch so liebenswürdig an... Er grüßt nicht. Vorbei ist er. Er wendet sich um, ich spüre es. Rufen Sie, grüßen Sie! Retten Sie mich! Vielleicht sind Sie an meinem Tode schuld, mein Herr! Aber Sie werden es nie erfahren. Adresse bleibt Fiala...

Wo bin ich? Schon in der Halle? Wie bin ich dahergekommen? So wenig Leute und so viele Unbekannte. Oder sehe ich so schlecht? Wo ist Dorsday? Er ist nicht da. Ist es ein Wink des Schicksals? Ich will zurück. Ich will einen andern Brief an Dorsday schreiben. Ich erwarte Sie in meinem Zimmer um Mitternacht. Bringen Sie die Depesche an Ihre Bank mit. Nein. Er könnte es für eine Falle halten. Könnte auch eine sein. Ich könnte Paul bei mir versteckt haben, und er könnte ihn mit dem Revolver zwingen, uns die Depesche auszuliefern. Erpressung. Ein Verbrecherpaar. Wo ist Dorsday? Dorsday, wo bist du? Hat er sich vielleicht umgebracht aus Reue über meinen Tod? Im Spielzimmer wird er sein. Gewiß. An einem Kartentisch wird er sitzen. Dann will ich ihm von der Tür aus mit den Augen ein Zeichen geben. Er wird sofort aufstehen. ›Hier bin ich, mein Fräulein.‹ Seine Stimme wird klingen. ›Wollen wir ein wenig promenieren, Herr Dorsday?‹ ›Wie es beliebt, Fräulein Else.‹ Wir gehen über den Marienweg zum Walde hin. Wir sind allein. Ich schlage den Mantel auseinander. Die fünfzigtausend sind fällig. Die Luft ist kalt, ich bekomme eine Lungenentzündung und sterbe... Warum sehen mich die zwei Damen an? Merken sie was? Warum bin ich denn da? Bin ich verrückt? Ich werde zurückgehen in mein Zimmer, mich geschwind ankleiden, das blaue, drüber den Mantel wie jetzt, aber offen, da kann niemand glauben, daß ich vorher nichts angehabt habe... Ich kann nicht zurück. Ich will auch nicht zurück. Wo ist Paul? Wo ist Tante Emma? Wo ist Cissy? Wo sind sie denn alle? Keiner wird es merken... Man kann es ja gar nicht merken. Wer spielt so schön? Chopin? Nein, Schumann.

Ich irre in der Halle umher wie eine Fledermaus. Fünfzigtausend! Die Zeit vergeht. Ich muß diesen verfluchten Herrn von Dorsday finden. Nein, ich muß in mein Zimmer zurück... Ich werde Veronal trinken. Nur einen kleinen Schluck, dann werde ich gut schlafen... Nach getaner Arbeit ist gut ruhen... Aber die Arbeit ist noch nicht getan... Wenn der Kellner den schwarzen Kaffee dem alten Herrn dort serviert, so geht alles gut aus. Und wenn er ihn dem jungen Ehepaar in der Ecke bringt, so ist alles verloren. Wieso? Was heißt das? Zu dem alten Herrn bringt er den Kaffee. Triumph! Alles geht gut aus. Ha, Cissy und Paul! Da draußen vor dem Hotel gehen sie auf und ab. Sie reden ganz vergnügt miteinander. Er regt sich nicht sonderlich auf wegen meiner Kopfschmerzen. Schwindler! ... Cissy hat keine so schöne Brüste wie ich. Freilich, sie hat ja ein Kind... Was reden die Zwei? Wenn man es hören könnte! Was geht es mich an, was sie reden? Aber ich könnte auch vors Hotel gehen, ihnen guten Abend wünschen und dann weiter, weiterflattern über die Wiese, in den Wald, hinaufsteigen, klettern, immer höher, bis auf den Cimone hinauf, mich hinlegen, einschlafen, erfrieren. Geheimnisvoller Selbstmord einer jungen Dame der Wiener Gesellschaft. Nur mit einem schwarzen Abendmantel bekleidet, wurde das schöne Mädchen an einer unzugänglichen Stelle des Cimone della Pala tot aufgefunden... Aber vielleicht findet man mich nicht... Oder erst im nächsten Jahr. Oder noch später. Verwest. Als Skelett. Doch besser, hier in der geheizten Halle sein und nicht erfrieren. Nun, Herr von Dorsday, wo stecken Sie denn eigentlich? Bin ich verpflichtet zu warten? Sie haben mich zu suchen, nicht ich Sie. Ich will noch im Spielsaal nachschauen. Wenn er dort nicht ist, hat er sein Recht verwirkt. Und ich schreibe ihm: Sie waren nicht zu finden, Herr von Dorsday, Sie haben freiwillig verzichtet; das entbindet Sie nicht von der Verpflichtung, das Geld sofort abzuschicken. Das Geld. Was für ein Geld denn? Was kümmert mich das? Es ist mir doch ganz gleichgültig, ob er das Geld abschickt oder nicht. Ich habe nicht das geringste Mitleid mehr mit Papa. Mit keinem Menschen habe ich Mitleid. Auch mit mir selber nicht. Mein Herz ist tot. Ich glaube, es schlägt gar nicht mehr. Vielleicht habe ich das Veronal schon getrunken... Warum schaut mich die holländische Familie so an? Man kann doch unmöglich was merken. Der

Portier sieht mich auch so verdächtig an. Ist vielleicht noch eine Depesche angekommen? Achtzigtausend? Hunderttausend? Adresse bleibt Fiala. Wenn eine Depesche da wäre, würde er es mir sagen. Er sieht mich hochachtungsvoll an. Er weiß nicht, daß ich unter dem Mantel nichts an habe. Niemand weiß es. Ich gehe zurück in mein Zimmer. Zurück, zurück, zurück! Wenn ich über die Stufen stolperte, das wäre eine nette Geschichte. Vor drei Jahren auf dem Wörthersee ist eine Dame ganz nackt hinausgeschwommen. Aber noch am selben Nachmittag ist sie abgereist. Die Mama hat gesagt, es ist eine Operettensängerin aus Berlin. Schumann? Ja, Karneval. Die oder der spielt ganz schön. Das Kartenzimmer ist aber rechts. Letzte Möglichkeit, Herr von Dorsday. Wenn er dort ist, winke ich ihn mit den Augen zu mir her und sage ihm, um Mitternacht werde ich bei Ihnen sein, Sie Schuft. – Nein, Schuft sage ich ihm nicht. Aber nachher sage ich es ihm... Irgendwer geht mir nach. Ich wende mich nicht um. Nein, nein. –

»Else!« – Um Gottes willen die Tante. Weiter, weiter! »Else!« – Ich muß mich umdrehen, es hilft mir nichts. »O, guten Abend, Tante.« – »Ja, Else, was ist denn mit dir? Grad wollte ich zu dir hinaufschauen. Paul hat mir gesagt – – Ja, wie schaust du denn aus?« – »Wie schau ich denn aus, Tante? Es geht mir schon ganz gut. Ich habe auch eine Kleinigkeit gegessen.« Sie merkt was, sie merkt was. – »Else – du hast ja – keine Strümpfe an!« – »Was sagst du da, Tante? Meiner Seel, ich habe keine Strümpfe an. Nein –!« – »Ist dir nicht wohl, Else? Deine Augen – du hast Fieber.« – »Fieber? Ich glaub' nicht. Ich hab' nur so furchtbare Kopfschmerzen gehabt, wie nie in meinem Leben noch.« – »Du mußt sofort zu Bett, Kind, du bist totenblaß.« – »Das kommt von der Beleuchtung, Tante. Alle Leute sehen hier blaß aus in der Halle.« Sie schaut so sonderbar an mir herab. Sie kann doch nichts merken? Jetzt nur die Fassung bewahren. Papa ist verloren, wenn ich nicht die Fassung bewahre. Ich muß etwas reden. »Weißt du, Tante, was mir heuer in Wien passiert ist? Da bin ich einmal mit einem gelben und einem schwarzen Schuh auf die Straße gegangen.« Kein Wort ist wahr. Ich muß weiterreden. Was sag' ich nur?

»Weißt du, Tante, nach Migräneanfällen habe ich manchmal solche Anfälle von Zerstreutheit. Die Mama hat das auch früher gehabt.« Nicht ein Wort ist wahr. – »*Ich werde jedesfalls um den Doktor schicken.*« – »Aber ich bitte dich, Tante, es ist ja gar keiner im Hotel. Man müßt' einen aus einer anderen Ortschaft holen. Der würde schön lachen, daß man ihn holen läßt, weil ich keine Strümpfe anhabe. Haha.« Ich sollte nicht so laut lachen. Das Gesicht von der Tante ist angstverzerrt. Die Sache ist ihr unheimlich. Die Augen fallen ihr heraus. – »*Sag', Else, hast du nicht zufällig Paul gesehen?*« – Ah, sie will sich Sukkurs verschaffen. Fassung, alles steht auf dem Spiel. »Ich glaube, er geht auf und ab vor dem Hotel mit Cissy Mohr, wenn ich nicht irre.« – »*Vor dem Hotel? Ich werde sie beide hereinholen. Wir wollen noch alle einen Tee trinken, nicht wahr?*« – »Gern.« Was für ein dummes Gesicht sie macht. Ich nicke ihr ganz freundlich und harmlos zu. Fort ist sie. Ich werde jetzt in mein Zimmer gehen. Nein, was soll ich denn in meinem Zimmer tun? Es ist höchste Zeit, höchste Zeit. Fünfzigtausend, fünfzigtausend. Warum laufe ich denn so? Nur langsam, langsam... Was will ich denn? Wie heißt der Mann? Herr von Dorsday. Komischer Name... Da ist ja das Spielzimmer. Grüner Vorhang vor der Tür. Man sieht nichts. Ich stelle mich auf die Zehenspitzen. Die Whistpartie. Die spielen jeden Abend. Dort spielen zwei Herren Schach. Herr von Dorsday ist nicht da. Viktoria. Gerettet! Wieso denn? Ich muß weitersuchen. Ich bin verdammt, Herrn von Dorsday zu suchen bis an mein Lebensende. Er sucht mich gewiß auch. Wir verfehlen uns immerfort. Vielleicht sucht er mich oben. Wir werden uns auf der Stiege treffen. Die Holländer sehen mich wieder an. Ganz hübsch die Tochter. Der alte Herr hat eine Brille, eine Brille, eine Brille... Fünfzigtausend. Es ist ja nicht soviel. Fünfzigtausend, Herr von Dorsday. Schumann? Ja, Karneval... Hab' ich auch einmal studiert. Schön spielt sie. Warum denn sie? Vielleicht ist es ein Er? Vielleicht ist es eine Virtuosin? Ich will einen Blick in den Musiksalon tun.

Da ist ja die Tür. – – Dorsday! Ich falle um. Dorsday! Dort

steht er am Fenster und hört zu. Wie ist das möglich? Ich ver-
zehre mich – ich werde verrückt – ich bin tot – und er hört einer
fremden Dame Klavierspielen zu. Dort auf dem Diwan sitzen
zwei Herren. Der Blonde ist erst heute angekommen. Ich hab'
ihn aus dem Wagen steigen sehen. Die Dame ist gar nicht mehr
jung. Sie ist schon ein paar Tage lang hier. Ich habe nicht gewußt, daß sie so schön Klavier spielt. Sie hat es gut. Alle Menschen haben es gut... nur ich bin verdammt... Dorsday! Dorsday! Ist er das wirklich? Er sieht mich nicht. Jetzt schaut er aus,
wie ein anständiger Mensch. Er hört zu. Fünfzigtausend! Jetzt

oder nie. Leise die Tür aufgemacht. Da bin ich, Herr von Dorsday! Er sieht mich nicht. Ich will ihm nur ein Zeichen mit den
Augen geben, dann werde ich den Mantel ein wenig lüften, das
ist genug. Ich bin ja ein junges Mädchen. Bin ein anständiges
junges Mädchen aus guter Familie. Bin ja keine Dirne... Ich will
fort. Ich will Veronal nehmen und schlafen. Sie haben sich ge-
irrt, Herr von Dorsday, ich bin keine Dirne. Adieu, adieu!
...Ha, er schaut auf. Da bin ich, Herr von Dorsday. Was für

Augen er macht. Seine Lippen zittern. Er bohrt seine Augen in meine Stirn. Er ahnt nicht, daß ich nackt bin unter dem Mantel. Lassen Sie mich fort, lassen Sie mich fort! Seine Augen glühen. Seine Augen drohen. Was wollen Sie von mir? Sie sind ein Schuft. Keiner sieht mich als er. Sie hören zu. So kommen Sie doch, Herr von Dorsday! Merken Sie nichts? Dort im Fauteuil – Herrgott, im Fauteuil – das ist ja der Filou! Himmel, ich danke dir. Er ist wieder da, er ist wieder da! Er war nur auf einer Tour! Jetzt ist er wieder da. Der Römerkopf ist wieder da. Mein Bräutigam, mein Geliebter. Aber er sieht mich nicht. Er soll mich auch nicht sehen. Was wollen Sie, Herr von Dorsday? Sie schauen mich an, als wenn ich Ihre Sklavin wäre. Ich bin nicht Ihre Sklavin. Fünfzigtausend! Bleibt es bei unserer Abmachung, Herr von Dorsday? Ich bin bereit. Da bin ich. Ich bin ganz ruhig. Ich lächle. Verstehen Sie meinen Blick? Sein Auge spricht zu mir: komm! Sein Auge spricht: ich will dich nackt sehen. Nun, du Schuft, ich bin ja nackt. Was willst du denn noch? Schick die Depesche ab... Sofort... Es rieselt durch meine Haut. Die Dame spielt weiter. Köstlich rieselt es durch meine Haut. Wie wundervoll ist es nackt zu sein. Die Dame spielt weiter, sie weiß nicht, was hier geschieht. Niemand weiß es. Keiner noch sieht mich. Filou, Filou! Nackt stehe ich da. Dorsday reißt die Augen auf. Jetzt endlich glaubt er es. Der Filou steht auf. Seine Augen leuchten. Du verstehst mich, schöner Jüngling. »Haha!« Die Dame spielt nicht mehr. Der Papa ist gerettet. Fünfzigtausend! Adresse bleibt Fiala! »Ha, ha, ha!« Wer lacht denn da? Ich selber? »Ha, ha, ha!« Was sind denn das für Gesichter um mich? »Ha, ha, ha!« Zu dumm, daß ich lache. Ich will nicht lachen, ich will nicht. »Haha!« *»Else!«* – Wer ruft Else? Das ist Paul. Er muß hinter mir sein. Ich spüre einen Luftzug über meinen nackten Rücken. Es saust in meinen Ohren. Vielleicht bin ich schon tot? Was wollen Sie, Herr von Dorsday? Warum sind Sie so groß und stürzen über mich her? »Ha, ha, ha!«

Was habe ich denn getan? Was habe ich getan? Was habe ich getan? Ich falle um. Alles ist vorbei. Warum ist denn keine Mu-

sik mehr? Ein Arm schlingt sich um meinen Nacken. Das ist
Paul. Wo ist denn der Filou? Da lieg ich. »Ha, ha, ha!« Der Mantel fliegt auf mich herab. Und ich liege da. Die Leute halten mich
für ohnmächtig. Nein, ich bin nicht ohnmächtig. Ich bin bei
vollem Bewußtsein. Ich bin hundertmal wach, ich bin tausendmal wach. Ich will nur immer lachen. »Ha, ha, ha!« Jetzt haben
Sie Ihren Willen, Herr von Dorsday, Sie müssen Geld für Papa
schicken. Sofort. »Haaaah!« Ich will nicht schreien, und ich muß
immer schreien. Warum muß ich denn schreien? – Meine Augen
sind zu. Niemand kann mich sehen. Papa ist gerettet. – »*Else!*« –
Das ist die Tante. – »*Else! Else!*« – »*Ein Arzt, ein Arzt!*« – »*Geschwind zum Portier!*« – »*Was ist denn passiert?*« – »*Das ist ja nicht
möglich.*« – »*Das arme Kind.*« – Was reden sie denn da? Was mur-
meln sie denn da? Ich bin kein armes Kind. Ich bin glücklich.
Der Filou hat mich nackt gesehen. O, ich schäme mich so. Was
habe ich getan? Nie wieder werde ich die Augen öffnen. – »*Bitte,
die Türe schließen.*«. – Warum soll man die Türe schließen? Was
für Gemurmel. Tausend Leute sind um mich. Sie halten mich

alle für ohnmächtig. Ich bin nicht ohnmächtig. Ich träume nur. – »Beruhigen Sie sich doch, gnädige Frau.« – »Ist schon um den Arzt geschickt?« – »Es ist ein Ohnmachtsanfall.« – Wie weit sie alle weg sind. Sie sprechen alle vom Cimone herunter. – »Man kann sie doch nicht auf dem Boden liegen lassen.« – »Hier ist ein Plaid.« – »Eine Decke.« – »Decke oder Plaid, das ist ja gleichgültig.« – »Bitte doch um Ruhe.« – »Auf den Diwan.« – »Bitte doch endlich die Türe zu schließen.« – »Nicht so nervös sein, sie ist ja geschlossen.« – »Else! Else!« – Wenn die Tante nur endlich still wär! – »Hörst du mich Else?« – »Du siehst doch, Mama, daß sie ohnmächtig ist.« – Ja, Gott sei Dank, für euch bin ich ohnmächtig. Und ich bleibe auch ohnmächtig. – »Wir müssen sie auf ihr Zimmer bringen.« – »Was ist denn da geschehen? Um Gottes willen!« – Cissy. Wie kommt denn Cissy auf die Wiese. Ach, es ist ja nicht die Wiese. – »Else!« – »Bitte um Ruhe.« – »Bitte ein wenig zurückzutreten.« – Hände, Hände unter mir. Was wollen sie denn? Wie schwer ich bin. Pauls Hände. Fort, fort. Der Filou ist in meiner Nähe, ich spüre es. Und Dorsday ist fort. Man muß ihn suchen. Er darf sich nicht umbringen, ehe er die fünfzigtausend abgeschickt hat. Meine Herrschaften, er ist mir Geld schuldig. Verhaften sie ihn. »Hast du eine Ahnung, von wem die Depesche war, Paul?« – »Guten Abend, meine Herrschaften.« – »Else, hörst du mich?« – »Lassen Sie sie doch, Frau Cissy.« – »Ach Paul.« – »Der Direktor sagt, es kann vier Stunden dauern, bis der Doktor da ist.« – »Sie sieht aus, als wenn sie schliefe.« – Ich liege auf dem Diwan. Paul hält meine Hand, er fühlt mir den Puls. Richtig, er ist ja Arzt. – »Von Gefahr ist keine Rede, Mama. Ein – Anfall.« »Keinen Tag länger bleibe ich im Hotel.« – »Bitte dich, Mama.« – »Morgen früh reisen wir ab.« – »Aber einfach über die Dienerschaftsstiege. Die Tragbare wird sofort hier sein.« – Bahre? Bin ich nicht heute schon auf einer Bahre gelegen? War ich nicht schon tot? Muß ich denn noch einmal sterben? – »Wollen Sie nicht dafür sorgen, Herr Direktor, daß die Leute sich endlich von der Türe entfernen.« – »Rege dich doch nicht auf, Mama.« – »Es ist eine Rücksichtslosigkeit von den Leuten.« – Warum flüstern sie denn alle? Wie in einem Sterbezimmer. Gleich wird die Bahre da sein. Mach' auf das Tor, Herr Matador! – »Der Gang ist frei.« – »Die

*Leute könnten doch wenigstens so viel Rücksicht haben.« – »Ich bitte
dich, Mama, beruhige dich doch.« – »Bitte, gnädige Frau.« – »Wollen
Sie sich nicht ein wenig meiner Mutter annehmen, Frau Cissy?«* – Sie
ist seine Geliebte, aber sie ist nicht so schön wie ich. Was ist denn
schon wieder? Was geschieht denn da? Sie bringen die Bahre. Ich
sehe es mit geschlossenen Augen. Das ist die Bahre, auf der sie
die Verunglückten tragen. Auf der ist auch der Doktor Zig-
mondi gelegen, der vom Cimone abgestürzt ist. Und jetzt
werde ich auf der Bahre liegen. Ich bin auch abgestürzt. »Ha!«
Nein, ich will nicht noch einmal schreien. Sie flüstern. Wer
beugt sich über meinen Kopf? Es riecht gut nach Zigaretten.
Seine Hand ist unter meinem Kopf. Hände unter meinem Rük-
ken, Hände unter meinen Beinen. Fort, fort, rührt mich nicht
an. Ich bin ja nackt. Pfui, pfui. Was wollt Ihr denn? Laßt mich in
Ruhe. Es war nur für Papa. – *»Bitte vorsichtig, so, langsam.«* –
»Der Plaid?« – *»Ja, danke, Frau Cissy.«* – Warum dankt er ihr?
Was hat sie denn getan? Was geschieht mit mir? Ah, wie gut, wie
gut. Ich schwebe. Ich schwebe. Ich schwebe hinüber. Man trägt
mich, man trägt mich, man trägt mich zu Grabe. – *»Aber mir sein
das g'wohnt, Herr Doktor. Da sind schon Schwerere darauf gelegen.
Im vorigen Herbst einmal zwei zugleich.«* – *»Pst, pst.«* – *»Vielleicht
sind Sie so gut, vorauszugehen, Frau Cissy, und sehen, ob in Elses
Zimmer alles in Ordnung ist.«* – Was hat Cissy in meinem Zimmer
zu tun? Das Veronal, das Veronal! Wenn sie es nur nicht weggießen. Dann müßte ich mich doch zum Fenster hinunterstürzen. –
»Danke sehr, Herr Direktor, bemühen Sie sich nicht weiter.« – *»Ich
werde mir erlauben, später wieder nachzufragen.«* – Die Treppe
knarrt, die Träger haben schwere Bergstiefel. Wo sind meine
Lackschuhe? Im Musikzimmer geblieben. Man wird sie stehlen.
Ich habe sie der Agathe vermachen wollen. Fred kriegt meine
Füllfeder. Sie tragen mich, sie tragen mich. Trauerzug. Wo ist
Dorsday, der Mörder? Fort ist er. Auch der Filou ist fort. Er ist
gleich wieder auf die Wanderschaft gegangen. Er ist nur zurück-
gekommen, um einmal meine weißen Brüste zu sehen. Und
jetzt ist er wieder fort. Er geht einen schwindligen Weg zwischen Felsen und Abgrund; – leb' wohl, leb' wohl. – Ich

schwebe, ich schwebe. Sie sollen mich nur hinauftragen, immer weiter, bis zum Dache, bis zum Himmel. Das wäre so bequem. – »*Ich habe es ja kommen gesehen, Paul.*« – Was hat die Tante kommen gesehen? – »*Schon die ganzen letzten Tage habe ich so etwas kommen gesehen. Sie ist überhaupt nicht normal. Sie muß natürlich in eine Anstalt.*« – »*Aber Mama, jetzt ist doch nicht der Moment davon zu reden.*« – Anstalt –? Anstalt –?! – »*Du denkst doch nicht, Paul, daß ich in ein und demselben Coupé mit dieser Person nach Wien fahren werde. Da könnte man schöne Sachen erleben.*« – »*Es wird nicht das Geringste passieren, Mama. Ich garantiere dir, daß du keinerlei Ungelegenheiten haben wirst.*« – »*Wie kannst du das garantieren?*« – Nein, Tante, du sollst keine Ungelegenheiten haben. Niemand wird Ungelegenheiten haben. Nicht einmal Herr von Dorsday. Wo sind wir denn? Wir bleiben stehen. Wir sind im zweiten Stock. Ich werde blinzeln. Cissy steht in der Tür und spricht mit Paul. – »*Hieher bitte. So. So. Hier. Danke. Rücken Sie die Bahre ganz nah ans Bett heran.*« – Sie heben die Bahre. Sie tragen mich. Wie gut. Nun bin ich wieder zu Hause. Ah! – »*Danke. So, es ist schon recht. Bitte die Türe zu schließen. – Wenn Sie so gut sein wollten mir zu helfen, Cissy.*« – »*O, mit Vergnügen, Herr Doktor.*« – »*Langsam, bitte. Hier, bitte, Cissy, fassen Sie sie an. Hier an den Beinen. Vorsichtig. Und dann – – Else – –? Hörst du mich, Else?*« – Aber natürlich höre ich dich, Paul. Ich höre alles. Aber was geht euch das an. Es ist ja so schön, ohnmächtig zu sein. Ach, macht, was ihr wollt. – »*Paul!*« – »*Gnädige Frau?*« – »*Glaubst du wirklich, daß sie bewußtlos ist, Paul?*« – Du? Sie sagt ihm du. Hab' ich euch erwischt! Du sagt sie ihm! – »*Ja, sie ist vollkommen bewußtlos. Das kommt nach solchen Anfällen gewöhnlich vor.*« – »*Nein, Paul, du bist zum Kranklachen, wenn du dich so erwachsen als Doktor benimmst.*« – Hab' ich euch, Schwindelbande! Hab' ich euch? – »*Still, Cissy.*« – »*Warum denn, wenn sie nichts hört?!*« – Was ist denn geschehen? Nackt liege ich im Bett unter der Decke. Wie haben sie das gemacht? – »*Nun, wie geht's? Besser?*« – Das ist ja die Tante. Was will sie denn da? – »*Noch immer ohnmächtig?*« – Auf den Zehenspitzen schleicht sie heran. Sie soll zum Teufel gehen. Ich laß mich in keine Anstalt bringen. Ich bin nicht irrsinnig. – »*Kann man sie nicht zum Be-*

wußtsein erwecken?« – »Sie wird bald wieder zu sich kommen, Mama. Jetzt braucht sie nichts als Ruhe. Übrigens du auch, Mama. Möchtest du nicht schlafen gehen? Es besteht absolut keine Gefahr. Ich werde zusammen mit Frau Cissy bei Else Nachtwache halten.« – »Jawohl, gnädige Frau, ich bin die Gardedame. Oder Else, wie man's nimmt.« – Elendes Frauenzimmer. Ich liege hier ohnmächtig und sie macht Späße *»Und ich kann mich darauf verlassen, Paul, daß du mich wecken läßt, sobald der Arzt kommt?« – »Aber Mama, der kommt nicht vor morgen früh.« – »Sie sieht aus, als wenn sie schliefe. Ihr Atem geht ganz ruhig.« – »Es ist ja auch eine Art von Schlaf, Mama.« – »Ich kann mich noch immer nicht fassen, Paul, ein solcher Skandal! – Du wirst sehen, es kommt in die Zeitung!« – »Mama!« – »Aber sie kann doch nichts hören, wenn sie ohnmächtig ist. Wir reden doch ganz leise.«* – *»In diesem Zustand sind die Sinne manchmal unheimlich geschärft.«* – *»Sie haben einen so gelehrten Sohn, gnädige Frau.« – »Bitte dich, Mama, geh' zu Bette.« – »Morgen reisen wir ab unter jeder Bedingung. Und in Bozen nehmen wir eine Wärterin für Else.« –* Was? Eine Wärterin? Da werdet ihr euch aber täuschen. – *»Über all' das reden wir morgen, Mama. Gute Nacht, Mama.« – »Ich will mir einen Tee aufs Zimmer bringen lassen und in einer Viertelstunde schau ich noch einmal her.« – »Das ist doch absolut nicht notwendig, Mama.«* – Nein, notwendig ist es nicht. Du sollst überhaupt zum Teufel gehen. Wo ist das Veronal? Ich muß noch warten. Sie begleiten die Tante zur Türe. Jetzt sieht mich niemand. Auf dem Nachttisch muß es ja stehen, das Glas mit dem Veronal. Wenn ich es austrinke, ist alles vorbei. Gleich werde ich es trinken. Die Tante ist fort. Paul und Cissy stehen noch an der Tür. Ha. Sie küßt ihn. Sie küßt ihn. Und ich liege nackt unter der Decke. Schämt ihr euch denn gar nicht? Sie küßt ihn wieder. Schämt ihr euch nicht? – *»Siehst du, Paul, jetzt weiß ich, daß sie ohnmächtig ist. Sonst wäre sie mir unbedingt an die Kehle gesprungen.« »Möchtest du mir nicht den Gefallen tun und schweigen, Cissy?« – »Aber was willst du denn, Paul? Entweder ist sie wirklich bewußtlos. Dann hört und sieht sie nichts. Oder sie hält uns zum Narren. Dann geschieht ihr ganz recht.« – »Es hat geklopft, Cissy.« – »Mir kam es auch so vor.« – »Ich will leise aufmachen und sehen wer es ist. – Guten Abend Herr* *von Dorsday.«* – *»Verzeihen Sie, ich wollte nur fragen, wie sich die Kranke«* – Dorsday! Dorsday! Wagt er es wirklich? Alle Bestien sind losgelassen. Wo ist er denn? Ich höre sie flüstern vor der Tür. Paul und Dorsday. Cissy stellt sich vor den Spiegel hin. Was machen Sie vor dem Spiegel dort? Mein Spiegel ist es. Ist nicht mein Bild noch drin? Was reden sie draußen vor der Tür, Paul und Dorsday? Ich fühle Cissys Blick. Vom Spiegel aus sieht sie zu mir her. Was will sie denn? Warum kommt sie denn näher? Hilfe! Hilfe! Ich schreie doch, und keiner hört mich. Was wollen Sie an meinem Bett, Cissy?! Warum beugen Sie sich herab? Wollen Sie mich erwürgen? Ich kann mich nicht rühren. – *»Else!«* – Was will sie denn? – *»Else! Hören Sie mich, Else?«* – Ich höre, aber ich schweige. Ich bin ohnmächtig, ich muß schweigen. – *»Else, Sie haben uns in einen schönen Schreck versetzt.«* – Sie spricht zu mir. Sie spricht zu mir, als wenn ich wach wäre. Was will sie denn? – *»Wissen Sie, was Sie getan haben, Else? Denken Sie, nur mit dem Mantel bekleidet sind Sie ins Musikzimmer getreten, sind plötzlich nackt dagestanden vor allen Leuten und dann sind Sie ohnmächtig hingefallen. Ein hysterischer Anfall wird behauptet. Ich glaube kein Wort davon. Ich glaube auch nicht, daß Sie bewußtlos sind. Ich wette, Sie hören jedes Wort, das ich rede.«* – Ja, ich höre, ja, ja, ja. Aber sie hört mein Ja nicht. Warum denn nicht? Ich kann meine Lippen nicht bewegen. Darum hört sie mich nicht. Ich kann mich nicht rühren. Was ist denn mit mir? Bin ich tot? Bin ich scheintot? Träume ich? Wo ist das Veronal? Ich möchte mein Veronal trinken. Aber ich kann den Arm nicht ausstrecken. Gehen Sie fort, Cissy. Warum sind Sie über mich gebeugt? Fort, fort! Nie wird sie wissen, daß ich sie gehört habe. Niemand wird es je wissen. Nie wieder werde ich zu einem Menschen sprechen. Nie wache ich wieder auf. Sie geht zur Türe. Sie wendet sich noch einmal nach mir um. Sie öffnet die Türe. Dorsday! Dort steht er. Ich habe ihn gesehen mit geschlossenen Augen. Nein, ich sehe ihn wirklich. Ich habe ja die Augen offen. Die Türe ist angelehnt. Cissy ist auch draußen. Nun flüstern sie alle. Ich bin allein. Wenn ich mich jetzt rühren könnte.

Ha, ich kann ja, kann ja. Ich bewege die Hand, ich rege die Finger, ich strecke den Arm, ich sperre die Augen weit auf. Ich sehe, ich sehe. Da steht mein Glas. Geschwind, ehe sie wieder ins Zimmer kommen. Sind es nur Pulver genug?! Nie wieder darf ich erwachen. Was ich zu tun hatte auf der Welt, habe ich getan. Der Papa ist gerettet. Niemals könnte ich wieder unter Menschen gehen. Paul guckt durch die Türspalte herein. Er denkt, ich bin noch ohnmächtig. Er sieht nicht, daß ich den Arm beinahe schon ausgestreckt habe. Nun stehen sie wieder alle drei draußen vor der Tür, die Mörder! – Alle sind sie Mörder. Dorsday und Cissy und Paul, auch Fred ist ein Mörder und die Mama ist eine Mörderin. Alle haben sie mich gemordet und machen sich nichts wissen. Sie hat sich selber umgebracht, werden sie sagen. Ihr habt mich umgebracht, ihr alle, ihr alle! Hab' ich es endlich? Geschwind, geschwind! Ich muß. Keinen Tropfen verschütten. So. Geschwind. Es schmeckt gut. Weiter, weiter. Es ist gar kein Gift. Nie hat mir was so gut geschmeckt. Wenn ihr wüßtet, wie gut der Tod schmeckt! Gute Nacht, mein Glas. Klirr, klirr! Was ist denn das? Auf dem Boden liegt das Glas. Unten liegt es. Gute Nacht. – *»Else, Else!«* – Was wollt ihr denn? – *»Else!«* – Seid ihr wieder da? Guten Morgen. Da lieg' ich bewußtlos mit geschlossenen Augen. Nie wieder sollt ihr meine Augen sehen. – *»Sie muß sich bewegt haben, Paul, wie hätte es sonst herunterfallen können?«* – *»Eine unwillkürliche Bewegung, das wäre schon möglich.«* – *»Wenn sie nicht wach ist.«* – *»Was fällt dir ein, Cissy. Sieh sie doch nur an.«* – Ich habe Veronal getrunken. Ich werde sterben. Aber es ist geradeso wie vorher. Vielleicht war es nicht genug... Paul faßt meine Hand. – *»Der Puls geht ruhig. Lach' doch nicht, Cissy. Das arme Kind.«* – *»Ob du mich auch ein armes Kind nennen würdest, wenn ich mich im Musikzimmer nackt hingestellt hätte?«* – *»Schweig' doch, Cissy.«* – *»Ganz nach Belieben, mein Herr. Vielleicht soll ich mich entfernen, dich mit dem nackten Fräulein allein lassen. Aber bitte, geniere dich nicht. Tu' als ob ich nicht da wäre.«* – Ich habe Veronal getrunken. Es ist gut. Ich werde sterben. Gott sei Dank. – *»Übrigens weißt du, was mir vorkommt. Daß dieser Herr von Dorsday in das nackte Fräulein verliebt ist. Er war* *so erregt, als ginge ihn die Sache persönlich an.«* – Dorsday, Dorsday! Das ist ja der – Fünfzigtausend! Wird er sie abschicken? Um Gottes willen, wenn er sie nicht abschickt? Ich muß es ihnen sagen. Sie müssen ihn zwingen. Um Gottes willen, wenn alles umsonst gewesen ist? Aber jetzt kann man mich noch retten. Paul! Cissy! Warum hört ihr mich denn nicht? Wißt ihr denn nicht, daß ich sterbe? Aber ich spüre nichts. Nur müde bin ich, Paul! Ich bin müde. Hörst du mich denn nicht? Ich bin müde, Paul. Ich kann die Lippen nicht öffnen. Ich kann die Zunge nicht bewegen, aber ich bin noch nicht tot. Das ist das Veronal. Wo seid ihr denn? Gleich schlafe ich ein. Dann wird es zu spät sein! Ich höre sie gar nicht reden. Sie reden und ich weiß nicht was. Ihre Stimmen brausen so. So hilf mir doch, Paul! Die Zunge ist mir so schwer. – *»Ich glaube, Cissy, daß sie bald erwachen wird. Es ist, als wenn sie sich schon mühte, die Augen zu öffnen. Aber Cissy, was tust du denn?«* – *»Nun, ich umarme dich. Warum denn nicht? Sie hat sich auch nicht geniert.«* – Nein, ich habe mich nicht geniert. Nackt bin ich dagestanden vor allen Leuten. Wenn ich nur reden könnte, so würdet ihr verstehen warum. Paul! Paul! Ich will, daß ihr mich hört. Ich habe Veronal getrunken, Paul, zehn Pulver, hundert. Ich hab' es nicht tun wollen. Ich war verrückt. Ich will nicht sterben. Du sollst mich retten, Paul. Du bist ja Doktor. Rette mich! – *»Jetzt scheint sie wieder ganz ruhig geworden. Der Puls – der Puls ist ziemlich regelmäßig.«* – Rette mich, Paul. Ich beschwöre dich. Laß mich doch nicht sterben. Jetzt ist's noch Zeit. Aber dann werde ich einschlafen und ihr werdet es nicht wissen. Ich will nicht sterben. So rette mich doch. Es war nur wegen Papa. Dorsday hat es verlangt. Paul! Paul! – *»Schau mal her, Cissy, scheint dir nicht, daß sie lächelt?«* – *»Wie sollte sie nicht lächeln, Paul, wenn du immerfort zärtlich ihre Hand hältst.«* – Cissy, Cissy, was habe ich dir denn getan, daß du so böse zu mir bist. Behalte deinen Paul – aber laßt mich nicht sterben. Ich bin noch so jung. Die Mama wird sich kränken. Ich will noch auf viele Berge klettern. Ich will noch tanzen. Ich will auch einmal heiraten. Ich will noch reisen. Morgen machen wir die Partie auf den Cimone. Morgen wird ein wunderschöner Tag sein. Der Filou soll mitkommen. Ich lade ihn ergebenst ein. Lauf' ihm doch nach, Paul, er geht einen so schwindligen Weg. Er wird dem Papa begegnen. Adresse bleibt Fiala, vergiß nicht. Es sind nur fünfzigtausend, und dann ist alles in Ordnung. Da marschieren sie alle im Sträflingsgewand und singen. Mach' auf das Tor, Herr Matador! Das ist ja alles nur ein Traum. Da geht auch Fred mit dem heiseren Fräulein und unter dem freien Himmel steht das Klavier. Der Klavierstimmer wohnt in der Bartensteinstraße, Mama! Warum hast du ihm denn nicht geschrieben, Kind? Du vergißt aber alles. Sie sollten mehr Skalen üben, Else. Ein Mädel mit dreizehn Jahren sollte fleißiger sein. – Rudi war auf dem Maskenball und ist erst um acht Uhr früh nach Hause gekommen. Was hast du mir mitgebracht, Papa? Dreißigtausend Puppen. Da brauch ich ein eigenes Haus dazu. Aber sie können auch im Garten spazierengehen. Oder auf den Maskenball mit Rudi. Grüß dich Gott, Else. Ach Bertha, bist du wieder aus Neapel zurück? Ja, aus Sizilien. Erlaube, daß ich dir meinen Mann vorstelle, Else. Enchanté, Monsieur. – *»Else, hörst du mich, Else? Ich bin es, Paul.«* – Haha, Paul. Warum sitzest du denn auf der Giraffe im Ringelspiel? – *»Else, Else!«* – So reit' mir doch nicht davon. Du kannst mich doch nicht hören, wenn du so schnell durch die Hauptallee reitest. Du sollst mich ja retten. Ich habe Veronalica genommen. Das läuft mir über die Beine, rechts und links, wie Ameisen. Ja, fang' ihn nur, den Herrn von Dorsday. Dort läuft er. Siehst du ihn denn nicht? Da springt er über den Teich. Er hat ja den Papa umgebracht. So lauf' ihm doch nach. Ich laufe mit. Sie haben mir die Bahre auf den Rücken geschnallt, aber ich laufe mit. Meine Brüste zittern so. Aber ich laufe mit. Wo bist du denn, Paul? Fred, wo bist du? Mama, wo bist du? Cissy? Warum laßt ihr mich denn allein durch die Wüste laufen? Ich habe ja Angst so allein. Ich werde lieber fliegen. Ich habe ja gewußt, daß ich fliegen kann.

»Else!« . . .

»Else!« . . .

Wo seid ihr denn? Ich höre euch, aber ich sehe euch nicht.

»Else!» . . .

»Else!« . . .

»Else! . . .«

Was ist denn das? Ein ganzer Chor? Und Orgel auch? Ich singe mit. Was ist es denn für ein Lied? Alle singen mit. Die Wälder auch und die Berge und die Sterne. Nie habe ich etwas so Schönes gehört. Noch nie habe ich eine so helle Nacht gesehen. Gib mir die Hand, Papa. Wir fliegen zusammen. So schön ist die Welt, wenn man fliegen kann. Küss' mir doch nicht die Hand. Ich bin ja dein Kind, Papa.

»Else! Else!«

Sie rufen von so weit! Was wollt ihr denn? Nicht wecken. Ich schlafe ja so gut. Morgen früh. Ich träume und fliege. Ich fliege . . . fliege . . . fliege . . . schlafe und träume . . . und fliege . . . nicht wecken . . . morgen früh . . .

»El . . .«

Ich fliege . . . ich träume . . . ich schlafe . . . ich träu . . . träu – ich flie . . . . . .

SPECIAL MESSAGE TO READERS

THE ULVERSCROFT FOUNDATION
(registered UK charity number 264873)

was established in 1972 to provide funds for
research, diagnosis and treatment of eye diseases.
Examples of major projects funded by
the Ulverscroft Foundation are:-

- The Children's Eye Unit at Moorfields Eye Hospital, London
- The Ulverscroft Children's Eye Unit at Great Ormond Street Hospital for Sick Children
- Funding research into eye diseases and treatment at the Department of Ophthalmology, University of Leicester
- The Ulverscroft Vision Research Group, Institute of Child Health
- Twin operating theatres at the Western Ophthalmic Hospital, London
- The Chair of Ophthalmology at the Royal Australian College of Ophthalmologists

You can help further the work of the Foundation
by making a donation or leaving a legacy.
Every contribution is gratefully received. If you
would like to help support the Foundation or
require further information, please contact:

THE ULVERSCROFT FOUNDATION
The Green, Bradgate Road, Anstey
Leicester LE7 7FU, England
Tel: (0116) 236 4325

website: www.foundation.ulverscroft.com

NO WAY BACK

Cole Rickard returns to the Arizona town of Maverick, hoping to make amends for an ignominious departure five years previously. His status as the Reno Kid, a ruthless bounty hunter and fast gun, has made him the target of young hotheads eager to snatch away what he now considers to be a crown of thorns. Cole wants nothing more than to settle down. But shucking such a dubious reputation is tough: there will always be somebody waiting to call him out . . .

Books by Ethan Flagg
in the Linford Western Library:

TWO FOR TEXAS
DIVIDED LOYALTIES
DYNAMITE DAZE
APACHE RIFLES
DUEL AT DEL NORTE
OUTLAW QUEEN
WHEN LIGHTNING STRIKES
PRAISE BE TO SILVER
A NECKTIE FOR GIFFORD
NAVAJO SUNRISE
SHOTGUN CHARADE
BLACKJACKS OF NEVADA
DERBY JOHN'S ALIBI
LONG RIDE TO PURGATORY

ETHAN FLAGG

NO WAY BACK

Complete and Unabridged

LINFORD
Leicester

First published in Great Britain in 2015 by
Robert Hale Limited
London

First Linford Edition
published 2017
by arrangement with
Robert Hale
an imprint of The Crowood Press
Wiltshire

A catalogue record for this book is available
from the British Library.

ISBN 978–1–4448–3235–8

Published by
F. A. Thorpe (Publishing)
Anstey, Leicestershire

Set by Words & Graphics Ltd.
Anstey, Leicestershire
Printed and bound in Great Britain by
T. J. International Ltd., Padstow, Cornwall

This book is printed on acid-free paper

1

Dark in the Afternoon

The hot sun shone down from a cloudless sky of deepest blue. Sitting astride a sorrel mare, the rider removed his black Stetson and wiped a sleeve across a sweat-beaded brow. His hand strayed to the water bottle hanging from the saddle horn. A tongue like tough cinch leather filled his mouth making it difficult to swallow. It reminded him too late that more than one water bottle was essential in this bleak country. He shook it.

The turgid slosh indicated there was insufficient to slake his raging thirst. But just enough to revive his flagging mount. In this harsh and arid land, the last thing a man needed was to be cast afoot. His horse had to come first.

Dismounting, he emptied the tepid contents onto his bandanna and rubbed the sorrel's muzzle, squeezing the remains into the open mouth. The animal snickered in appreciation. Its noble head quivered as the life-giving elixir was gratefully imbibed.

'Not much further, old gal,' he murmured into the twitching nostrils. A note of concern crept into the optimistic assessment of his grim situation. 'At least I hope not.' Eyes squinted in the bright sunlight as he peered across at the bleak expanse of endless sand and rock.

He leaned down and picked up a pebble, popping it into his mouth. This would have to do until he could find water. A poor substitute but enough to stimulate a few drops of saliva to keep him going.

That was the claim from an old prospector he had encountered up in the Mogollon country two days before. The sourdough miner had been working a creek with his rocker box. He had shared his meagre rations with the traveller, airing some much appreciated snippets of advice for survival in this harsh terrain.

The pebble trick was one such. Only time would tell if it worked.

Stretching the stiffness from tired muscles, the rangy guy ran a hand through his thick black hair, scraping it back off his forehead.

Age was fast coming up on the outside to overtake him. Clear evidence was the streaks of grey that had become far too well established. Lines akin to a ploughed field creased his tanned features making him look a decade older than his thirty-six years.

He pushed back his hat and fingered the livid scar on the side of his head, remembering how it had been acquired. Someday he would find the conniving rat who had caused it.

The trail-weary appearance was not just the result of Arizona's unforgiving climate. Cole Rickard was a bounty hunter. A profession, if such it could be termed, that took its toll on the men who chose this precarious way of life. Shunned by both sides of the law, these men had to be constantly on their guard.

3

But the rewards could be high. It was the lucrative payouts that kept most manhunters in the game. That and the excitement of the chase were addictive, not to mention the kudos of acquiring the reputation of a fast gun.

Very few of these knights of the frontier survived to reach old age. There was always going to be somebody just that little bit faster on the draw. Young pretenders, always eager to snatch the crown from the current King Colt. Yet still they clung to the illusory belief of being invincible. A fatal blend of arrogance and mule-headedness that invariably cost them dear.

Cole Rickard was the best, and the most feared of the bounty men. But that did not stop reckless hot-heads from calling him out. Boot Hill cemeteries across the West were filled with those who had tried and failed. He had once attempted to figure out how many, but had given up when the tally reached double figures.

Now he was heading back to the town of Maverick in Arizona's San Carlos

Valley. He had been away for five long years. Another four days should see him there. Home at long last. He could hardly wait. At least, he hoped it would still be his home. There were no guarantees that he would be made welcome.

A fervent anticipation that he could make a fresh start had persuaded him to take this little-used but direct trail across the Natanes Plateau. He was beginning to think it would have been a sight easier and quicker to have taken the longer route by way of Tucson. Too late for regrets now. He was committed.

Known as the Reno Kid, he wanted out of the gun-fighting caper. Just plain Cole Rickard would suit him fine. If only he could finally bury that reputation. Once regarded as an exciting adventure, it was now like an albatross hanging round his neck. All he craved was to make amends for past indiscretions and to settle down once again with his wife and son.

And this time it would be for good. His mind was made up.

At one time such a life would have

seemed dull and mundane. Domestic drudgery fit only for poor suckers who had no ambition. Yet now it was all he yearned for. The regular pattern of familial routine beckoned invitingly. No more constantly looking over your shoulder waiting for the next challenge. But it all depended on whether Marcia would have him back.

Young Joey would be eight years old now. How had he faired during the time his wayward pa had been absent? Was he doing his school work and helping his ma with the household chores? Had Marcia managed to keep him on the straight and narrow without the guiding hand of a father? All these questions and more were what Cole yearned to have answered.

He shook his head at the idiotic notions that had led him into the foolhardy lifestyle where a six-shooter was his tool of trade. Sure, it had brought him plenty of dough, most of which had been frittered away, and a reputation that saw men step aside when he walked down the street.

Excitement in abundance with the thrill of danger that the next pursuit would bring.

But had it all been worth it? That was the question now dogging his troubled mind. At the age of thirty-six, he had grown up. Taking on young gunslingers who sought to wrest a hard-won status no longer seemed important. Indeed, it was becoming increasingly irksome. The Reno Kid was still well capable of holding his own in any gunfight, yet he knew that sooner or later some dude would best him. It was inevitable. No reputation could last for ever.

Reno sensed his comeuppance was fast approaching. A leery smirk creased his gaunt features. The Reno Kid! And they still called him that, even though he was well past any association with his youth.

It had been acquired from a town marshal in the Nevada town of that name after bringing in the second owlhooter that month. Sarcasm loosely disguised as envy had prompted the old lawman to

7

announce, 'The Reno Kid strikes again. Don't spend all that dough in the same candy store.'

The marshal's attempt to unsettle the newly commissioned young manhunter failed. Cole Rickard liked the sound of it. And so the Reno Kid was born.

But a lot of water had flowed down the creek since those thrilling early days when the world was his oyster. He dismounted and sat down on a rock beside an old juniper tree. The gnarled roots, twisted and warped like a tangled ball of string, reminded the ruminating traveller of his own churned up innards.

A smoke would help ease the tightness in his guts. Cole hooked out the makings and rolled himself a quirly. Drawing the smoke deep into his lungs helped to focus his thoughts as he cast back to how it had come to this depressing state of affairs.

The Reno Kid's encounter with the lovely Marcia Kemp had been at the monthly hoedown in Maverick back in '73.

He had recently delivered an outlaw

to the sheriff's office. Wanted in three states for murder and robbery, Kansas Bob Jacket was worth a cool thousand dollars. Reno had been trailing him for two months, finally catching up with the critter in the Arizona badlands north of Safford.

The hunter had caught Jacket, literally, with his pants down. Reno couldn't contain his delight at catching the notorious bandit thus encumbered. Even though considerably disadvantaged in his moment of personal relief, Jacket had refused to come quietly. A hangman's rope was awaiting him following the inevitable guilty verdict from the twelve good men and true. Knowing Reno's reputation did not deter him from making his play.

'Sooner go down in a blaze of glory than choking at the end of a rope,' was his final response to the bounty hunter's chuckling encouragement to surrender.

The result was as expected. Dead or Alive, as it said on the poster, made no difference to the Reno Kid. Bob Jacket had opted for the former and paid the ultimate price. In fact it was far easier if these brigands did balk at getting arrested. A dead outlaw was much easier to handle than one always searching for a way out on the long ride to incarceration.

That was not the choice of receiving lawmen who lost the opportunity of an extra fee earned from a trial.

'I been hearing about how you bring all your marks in over a saddle, Kid,' the sardonic lawman jeered. If truth be told, Sheriff Chalk Fenton held a sneaking admiration for these guys. It irked that he himself did not have the bottle demanded of such a lifestyle. 'News like that spreads quickly.'

The bounty hunter fixed a jaundiced eye on the speaker. He had heard this quibble numerous times before.

'This *hombre* was given the chance to quit, Sheriff.' He gave the comment a nonchalant shrug. 'Ain't my fault he made the wrong choice.' He held out his hand. 'Now if'n you don't mind, it's been a thirsty ride. Which is the best drinking parlour in town?'

Fenton huffed some but had no option but to pay up. 'Hell's Acre is the right joint for jaspers of your calling.' With a sneering reluctance born of jealousy, Fenton paid the bounty hunter off. This was more dough than a humble lawdog could earn in a month of Sundays.

Reno casually flicked through the wad of greenbacks. A half-smile creased his handsome features. 'Looks like it's all there. Much obliged, Sheriff. I'll make sure not to spend it all at once.' A patronizing smirk left the tinstar fuming helplessly as Reno exited the office.

The bounty hunter fully intended to avoid the recommended drinking den known as Hell's Acre. Ambling down the main street, it was the Buckeye that caught his attention due to its well-maintained exterior. A fresh paint job and clean windows beckoned invitingly. He was not disappointed.

Cole had hung around Maverick for a few more days. Sheriff Fenton would have much preferred the bounty hunter to move on, but unless he broke the law, the starpacker was powerless to act. Cole took a room at the National Hotel. He liked the town. And the people seemed friendly enough. Within a week he reverted to his God-given name of Cole Rickard to help allay any suspicions as to his intentions.

Marcia Kemp came into his life at the next Saturday dance. She was a breath of fresh air in an otherwise sordid existence. Cole began to realize that there was more to life than strutting his stuff about town gaining attention through the creation of fear and awe.

The handsome school ma'am was flattered by the attentions of the good-looking stranger in their midst. Soon they were walking out. After three months of courtship, they were married. A child inevitably followed.

By seeking out this remote backwater, Cole was confident of having covered his steps. Only by a freakish accident could anybody find him here. And as time passed, so his notoriety would likewise fade into oblivion. His dubious earnings from the Jacket bounty enabled him to buy a half share in the Buckeye saloon.

Flush Harry Donovan was well aware of Reno's reputation but respected his desire to forge a new life far removed from his gunslinging days. Although it was never mentioned, other issues played their part in his enthusiastic welcome of the ex-manhunter into the business. Reno's past reputation would act as a tempering influence on those who might have otherwise caused trouble.

As his nickname suggested, Donovan ran the gambling side of the business. His penchant was for poker, always seeming to favour a Royal Flush hand.

Had Cole known about his partner's surreptitious motive, he might well have sought an investment elsewhere. It was Donovan's clandestine use of his partner's professional infamy that was to have devastating consequences.

2

Blast from the Past

For three years everything ran smoothly.

The saloon prospered, young Joey was growing up into a fine boy and most of all, his love for Marcia strengthened with each passing day. Yes indeed, life could not have been better for Cole Rickard. The Reno Kid had finally been laid to rest. A bright future looked assured.

Many of the current residents of Maverick knew nothing of his violent past. Even Sheriff Chalk Fenton had softened his attitude to the notorious gunslinger now living in his town.

Cole felt safe and secure. But it was all an illusion, a tantalizing chimera. And just as night follows day, the bubble was sure to burst. He ought to have realized that a hard-bitten reputation such as that attained by the Reno Kid would never truly be expunged. And so it came to pass one fine July afternoon in 1876.

Cole was discussing with his partner the idea of expanding the business to include a theatre and dance hall. The premises adjacent to the Buckeye had recently become vacant and would make the perfect venue for attracting top entertainers from around the country. It would also provide an ideal venue for the monthly hoedowns, at present held in barns dispersed throughout the valley.

They were about to work out some figures in the office when a cutting retort sliced through the general conversation of men drinking and playing cards. This was no ordinary hollering, but aimed specifically at Cole Rickard. A hoarse growl, jarring on the nerves, it instantly silenced the inane jabbering. All eyes turned towards the sudden interjection.

A large bear of a man stood framed in the doorway, his profile a dark silhouette.

'It's taken me a long while to catch up with you, Reno,' the man snarled. 'Now fill your hand and let's get to shooting.'

Doyle, the burly tough, hunkered down into the gunman's stance, his hands hovering above the twin Smith & Wesson .44s.

The name Reno didn't immediately strike a chord with the saloon's patrons. Furrowed brows displayed mystification. What was this guy claiming? Puzzled eyes swung between the two participants.

One man whispered what all the others were now thinking. 'Is Cole Rickard really none other than the Reno Kid?' Gasps circulated as the import of what had been suggested took hold like a wild bush fire.

'But I thought he only operated up north,' mouthed another drinker.

Nods of agreement responded to this poignant comment. But it was Doyle who confirmed what was merely a piece of idle speculation.

'That's right, boys,' he rasped out in answer to their baffled expressions. 'You've been living with that lowlife skunk in your midst all this time. This turkey is none other than the Reno Kid.

But not for much longer. You ready for this, Reno?'

A brief moment of silence hung heavy in the long narrow room as the implications of the assertion struck home. Then, as one, chairs scraped and tumbled over as the patrons sought to remove themselves from the field of conflict. Tables were upended as men took cover on the floor. Within seconds, only Cole Rickard and his partner were left standing as the challenger moved inside the saloon.

Flush Harry swallowed. He had lived in dread of this happening.

Using the Kid's name to scare off trouble was something he now bitterly regretted. The incident in question had occurred one Saturday night. Some drunken cowhands were passing through on their way back from a trail drive. They had been threatening trouble when some of the girls had denigrated their lecherous suggestions. Donovan had mentioned the name of the Reno Kid being in town and that he was a good friend. That piece of news soon curbed their unwelcome passion.

The man himself, however, had been in Globe at the time on business.

The cowboys must have spoken of the incident to others. Such talk gets around. Passed on from mouth to mouth by saddletramps and drifters. Donovan rightly assumed that talk of the incident had come to the ears of Wesco Doyle. This was not the first time that Cole's partner had played the Reno card. But it was the first time it had brought more trouble than he could ever have imagined.

The gambler quickly shrugged off his shocked reaction. 'You know this guy, Cole?' he asked in a voice crackly and shaking due to the tension of the moment.

'Never met him before,' came the terse reply. So intent was he on watching the movements of this man mountain that his partner's jumpiness washed over him.

The newcomer moved across to the bar. Eyes glued to his quarry, the big man snatched up a bottle standing on the counter and tipped a hefty slug down his throat.

18

A sarcastic chortle greeted the denial. 'The name's Wesco Doyle. You know my brother, Leroy. Or should I say you did until you shot him down.' Doyle's voice was growing louder in conjunction with his rising anger. 'I've been tracking you for over three years. Figured the scent had gone cold. Then I heard your name mentioned up north in Snowflake.'

Doyle took another long slug of hooch then nonchalantly tossed the bottle across the room. Gasps of fear and alarm issued from numerous throats as the bottle smashed against an iron post. The gunman never batted an eyelid.

'Well I'm here to see that justice is finally done. A varmint that shoots a guy in the back ain't no better than a snake in the grass. But I ain't like you, Reno. So I'm giving you an even break. Now are you gonna take me on, or is that a yellow streak I see painted across your miserable brow?'

A muttering could be heard from the cowering patrons of the saloon. If one thing was likely to incense frontiersmen it was backshooting. And the accusation was aimed squarely at the man they had all come to admire and respect.

Cole immediately sensed that he had to act quickly. His hard-won reputation as an upright citizen was in jeopardy of being wiped out. And it was due to a mistake he had hoped was long since buried.

How could he ever forget the shooting of Leroy Doyle?

That was the only time the Reno Kid had ever shot an adversary in the back. And it had haunted him ever since. Leroy was just another young hothead who had tried to gain the reputation as the man who shot the Reno Kid. The unforgettable incident had occurred six months before Cole had arrived in Maverick. The mining camp of Telluride up north in Colorado was the fateful setting.

But it was Doyle who had tried to shoot *him* in the back.

A warning from the barman had averted certain death by the merest whisker as the bullet had scraped Reno's ribcage.

Attuned to instant reactions, the bounty hunter had swung on his boot heels, drawing his own revolver and snapped off two shots at the bush-whacker. Doyle had been turning to flee the scene of his contemptible skulduggery when he was drilled squarely in the back.

Nobody blamed Reno. His reactions had been instinctive. Everybody in Telluride agreed that Doyle had deserved his plot on Boot Hill. Clearly, though, there was one person who held a grudge. And he was now standing here in Maverick.

Wesco Doyle was urgently seeking to even the score. And it was obvious that no amount of excuses would satisfy him. The guy wanted blood. Not the life-giving force running through Cole Rickard's veins, but the blood of the Reno Kid. And now that the sorry episode had been resurrected, the clientele of the Buckeye would also expect a spirited response from such a notable gunfighter.

Backing down would turn him into a pariah within the community. His name would be reviled and trailed through the mud. The Reno Kid had to stand firm and meet the challenge head on to enable Cole Rickard to maintain his standing in the Maverick community. It was Flush Harry who butted in on his thoughts.

'There's no need for any shooting, mister,' Donovan appealed, hoping to calm the irate bruiser down. 'Let's sit down over a drink and talk this through.'

'I ain't come all this way to jaw,' rapped Doyle. 'Now move out the way if'n you don't want some of the same.'

'Best do as he says, Harry,' Cole advised pushing his friend back. 'This turkey is in no mood for listening to reason.'

Donovan was relieved to get out of the firing line. But he tried one more tack to prevent certain bloodshed. 'The sheriff won't take kindly to gunplay in this town. You'll be arrested.'

Again Doyle laughed. It had a hollow ring. 'No lawdog is gonna interfere with a hogleg contest. That's the unwritten law of the West. There ain't a judge in the territory who would convict the winner of a one-on-one challenge where both

parties are in agreement.' He sneered at
the man he knew only as the Reno Kid.
'There is another way out, of course. The
sneaking rat could always walk away with
his tail between his legs. Is that how it's
gonna be, backshooter?'

Cole was sweating. His hackles were
rising. Being labelled a backshooter and
a coward were insults that could have
only one outcome. The problem was
that he had not fired a gun in anger for
three years. Could he handle a practised
gunman like Wesco Doyle and come out
on top? The guy was obviously adept.
Nobody wore a twin rig like that unless
he could use it.

His hands flexed. They felt stiff. Or was
that just nervous tension?

With slow deliberation he raised his
arms. 'I ain't carrying, Doyle.'

It was a futile attempt to gain some
much needed time to gather his wits
together for the inevitable showdown.

In slow motion, the gunman purposefully lifted one of the pistols from its
holster and slid it along the bar. The shiny

revolver settled ominously, six inches from Cole's resting hand.

'You have now,' leered Doyle squaring his broad shoulders. 'We've wasted enough time already. Now get to shooting, or crawl away on your ass.'

At that moment the saloon door burst open. Emitting a cry of alarm, a woman rushed into the room. It was Marcia Rickard. She dashed over to where her husband was standing.

'Aveline Beddows was passing the saloon when she saw what was happening. It's lucky I was close by. You have to stop this now,' Marcia pleaded grabbing her husband's arm. 'What happened before you came to Maverick is all in the past. It's the future that matters now. Our future. Joey's future.'

The words tumbled out as the comely woman tried desperately to avert a catastrophe. 'You are a husband and a father now, Cole. I don't want my son growing up knowing his father is a killer. Or worse still, that he has no father at all. Is that what you want?' She hurried on, not giving him chance to speak. 'Stop this now and come away before it's too late.'

She clawed at her husband's sleeve, the earnest appeal willing him to see reason.

But it was to no avail and fell on deaf ears. Cole's frosty regard was glued firmly to the challenging hulk of Wesco Doyle. Without shifting his look, he gently prised his wife's hand off.

'Too late for that, Marcia. The cards have been dealt and I have to play this hand to a conclusion. Winner takes all. There's no other choice.'

'This isn't a game, Cole,' snapped the petrified female. 'There's always a choice. You can walk away right now and nobody will think any the worse of you.'

'You gonna hide behind a woman's skirts, Reno?' Doyle goaded his adversary. 'That would sure be the action of a backshooter.'

Cole bristled angrily. His normally placid temper was rapidly shredding at the edges. A look chock full of venom speared the hovering gunman. Then, with slow deliberation and breathing deeply, his gaze shifted to his beautiful wife's gravely beseeching countenance. 'You know that ain't true, Marcia. A man has to be able to hold his head up. Life wouldn't be worth a dime in Maverick if'n I were to walk away from this now.'

The whole saloon was hanging on his every word. He could see nods and grunts of accord. He would be labelled a coward, no better than a rabid cur.

No man could live with that hanging over him. At best he and his family would have to up sticks and leave Maverick. But things like that were apt to follow a man round. Wherever he went, whispered voices and pointing fingers would mark him out as the cocky gunslinger with the yellow streak.

Marcia tried one last tack to persuade her beloved husband that his paternal responsibilities overshadowed all else. Her declaration was pitched low and even, but fizzled with suppressed emotion. 'Go through with this, Cole, and you could end up dead. But whatever happens, I could not live with a man who put

26

stubborn arrogant pride above duty to his family. Joey is staying with Aveline at the moment. If you insist on continuing on this road to destruction, you will never see him again.'

She gave him one last look, an imploring petition that tugged at the ex-manhunter's heartstrings. Sure it did. Who but a stone-hearted moron could not be so moved? And he dearly wanted to turn his back on Wesco Doyle and join his wife.

And he almost did just that. Marcia's threat was no idle throwaway. She meant every word.

On the other hand, Cole Rickard was a man of gentle and insistent persuasion. He had done it before. Why not again? Surely she would not reject all they had built up in Maverick. Yet in his heart, he knew that she was serious. Continue with this life or death struggle, and he could say goodbye to all he held dear.

But once again, the shame of backing down and being branded a craven milksop raised its ugly head. His mind was made up. There was no other way. The straight back stiffened, shoulders squared as a hard glint showed in the staring eyes.

He signalled to Harry Donovan to remove his wife from the field of battle. His partner quickly hustled the crying woman away. Her sobs had fallen on deaf ears.

'Now make your play, Doyle. I'm ready anytime you are.'

The gunman dug into his pocket and extracted a silver dollar. He placed it on the thumb of his left hand intending to flick it into the air. 'When this coin hits the floor, go for your piece. Agreed?'

Reno nodded. His hand rested on the bar top, the fingers twitching one final time seeking to retrieve that masterly touch.

The clock on the wall ticked away the seconds. An ominous reminder of man's mortality. The unassailable fact that time on this earth is limited and can easily be cut short. Everybody was holding their breath, waiting on the gunman's call.

Wesco was enjoying the notoriety he had created. He was confident that the

Reno Kid's three years of sedentary habits would have noticeably slowed his reactions. With due purpose, he delayed the moment of truth. The ugly smirk urged his opponent to lose his nerve. But Reno held firm. The delaying tactics had actually strengthened his resolve. Old habits had flooded back through his veins. His mindset had reverted to that of the ruthless bounty hunter of old.

'When you're ready, Doyle.' The terse retort was hissed out, removing the gunman's smug conceit. 'We don't want to keep these good folks waiting, do we?'

Somewhat deflated that his strategy had failed to pay dividends, Wesco Doyle's blotched visage twisted into an ugly grimace.

The coin rose into the thick air. Sunlight beaming in through the front window caught the spinning facets. Reaching its zenith, the twisting harbinger of doom began a flight towards destiny. Fate now hung in the balance. As if in slow motion the coin moved inexorably towards the point of no return.

Chhiiinnngg!

The sharp rattle as the coin touched ground echoed around the room. Both protagonists grabbed for their weapons. Each fired at almost the same moment. Two shots blending into one. A scream could be heard from behind the closed door of the back office. But nobody paid it any heed. Smoke belched from the two revolvers. An oil lamp behind Reno's head shattered into a myriad fragments.

But it was Doyle who clutched at his chest. A look of surprise, total and absolute, was etched across the startled visage. Too late the fact registered in his rapidly failing brain that he had sadly underestimated his opponent.

Then he slid to the floor. The Kid walked across and stood over the dying gunman, his own weapon trained on the guy's chest, just in case there was still any fight left in the shattered frame. But the oozing spread of scarlet across his shirt said otherwise.

'I judged you wrong, Reno ...' Doyle gasped out. 'Guess a man ... never does lose … that ability…' His head dropped onto his chest; a harsh rasping in his throat told of only seconds remaining.

'I never meant to shoot your brother in the back, Wesco,' Reno assured his dying adversary, bending down. 'It was a mistake. He turned away.'

'Gee … I know that…But a man has to try and … salvage some family pride … And maybe I was secretly hoping to take over … where Leroy failed …' A gurgle meant to be a guffaw rumbled inside the heaving torso. More urgent gasps. One final lifting of the large head followed as Doyle's watery gaze settled on the Reno Kid. 'More fool me … eh? Maybe next time…'

But there would be no second chance for Wesco Doyle.

The gunman slid over on to his face. One more death chalked up to the infamous bounty hunter known as the Reno Kid. The killer felt no sense of euphoria, no satisfaction. Indeed, he felt deflated by the whole sorry incident. Placing the revolver on the bar top he hurried to the back office.

Marcia had already left. Cole headed for the back door intending to follow and plead his case, but Flush Harry barred his way.

'Leave her be, Cole,' he cautioned although his voice held a note of warning as well. 'You've sunk your boats where Marcia is concerned. She don't want any more to do with you. And she meant it.'

'But you know that I wasn't given any choice, Harry. I had to face him down.' There were tears in his eyes knowing that the new life he had established in Maverick was falling apart.

The gambler led him back to a chair. He poured out a liberal shot of whiskey and handed it to his partner and best friend. 'Sure I do. And so does every man in this town. They'll all back your play.' He paused, not quite knowing how to voice his next announcement. 'But Marcia don't see it that way. She reckons you never really abandoned your old ways.'

'That ain't true!' Cole blurted out.

Donovan ignored the interruption. 'She figures that killing Doyle is only the start. And she has a point, Cole. It's only a matter of time before the news gets out and other scum of his ilk drift down here to try their luck.' He was now thinking of his own standing in the community and what the arrival of numerous young guns eager for a shoot-out would mean for the town.

Cole stood up. 'I have to see her. To explain.'

'Too late for that,' Donovan insisted. 'She's taking Joey to stay with her mother over in Dragoon Wells. She gave me strict instructions to prevent any contact between the three of you.'

'So what are you saying, Harry?' It was now Cole Rickard's voice that had hardened as the grim reality of what he had set in motion struck home like a gun barrel over the head.

'I'm sorry, Cole. Looks like it's the end.' Donovan hurried on. 'You'll have to leave town, old buddy. That's another choice you have forfeited. Of course, I'll buy out your share of the business. But you can't stay here now.'

Cole Rickard gritted his teeth. He was now more angry than upset. 'A leopard never changes its spots. Is that it? My past reputation will never be forgotten until some young tearaway ends it permanently.'

The gambler shrugged. 'You said it, not me. I suggest you head home and pack your gear. I'll have the dough ready when you return.'

What Flush Harry had failed to divulge was that the arrival of Wesco Doyle had been his doing. Now that Doyle was dead, there was nobody left to divulge his fatal indiscretion. He was hugely thankful that the dead man had not revealed the source of his knowledge. And if the Reno Kid also left town, there was no reason for trouble to raise its ugly head in Maverick.

Nevertheless, the unpleasant occurrence had left him shaken and ashen-faced.

Luckily for Donovan, Cole was not thinking of how Doyle had discovered his whereabouts. He was too wrapped up in his own sorry predicament. After gathering up his meagre belongings, he returned to the Buckeye for the final farewell.

'Good luck to you, Cole,' the gambler said as they shook hands. 'Take care out there. And watch how you go.' The beads of sweat bubbling on his rotund face passed unnoticed by the woebegone bounty hunter.

So after three good years, it was *término*! There was no more to be said. Cole Rickard, now once again having to don the despised persona of the Reno Kid, pushed his ex-partner aside and left the saloon by the back door.

3

Happy Jack

The recollection of that fateful day in Maverick had left Cole morose and dejected.

Was he heading down a box canyon where the only way out was back the way he had come? Surely, after all this time, Marcia would have mellowed and would be prepared to at least talk it through. Try to see their schism from his point of view. Or was he only fooling himself? Would he never be able to shrug off the past except by booking that plot in the graveyard?

He had come this far. There was only one way to discover what destiny had in store for the Reno Kid. With a heavy heart he mounted up and nudged the sorrel back into motion. He could only hope and pray that his exhortations would pay dividends.

The narrow trail pursued a meandering course between clusters of orange sandstone. Wind-scoured buttes rose up on either side with clumps of juniper and greasewood scrabbling for life amidst the arid wilderness. After pushing over the rimrock, the trail began a lazy descent towards the sprawling plateau land below.

If his figuring was right, the town of Happy Jack ought to be just over that next range of foothills.

It was the following afternoon when the narrow deer track he had been following crested a low rise. Below, on the level plain, sat a tiny cluster of buildings. Reno's eyes lifted in surprise. Happy Jack was nought but a remote trading post. Mudlark Sullivan, the old prospector he had encountered while crossing the Mogollons, had led him to believe it was a place of some standing. Maybe it was just that to an old-timer used to living the solitary life in the wilderness.

The main log cabin was connected to another structure by a covered awning. It looked like a bunkhouse where travellers could stop over for the night. On the other side was a lodgepole enclosure holding a milk cow, a couple of dirty pigs and a few scrawny chickens.

The rider pushed down the gently shelving slope, cantering across the open spread of sagebrush. Drawing closer to the isolated settlement, it was clear that other travellers were inside. Three horses were tied up outside. Their heads hung down in the harsh noonday heat.

Happy Jack was named after Jackson Thorpe who had established the post some twenty years before. A toothy, good-natured grin had endeared him to miners and cowboys alike. It was a pack of renegade Apache bucks who had not appreciated the chatty proprietor's garrulous humour. Jack was found one day with a dozen arrows in his back. All that had been stolen was his stock of moonshine liquor and a couple of old flintlock rifles.

Since then, owners of the trading post had been much less jovial. Yet the place still retained its contrary name. Perhaps to raise a smile in an otherwise unforgiving landscape. It had certainly worked for Cole Rickard. He was more than ready to avail himself of the facilities on offer.

But as he neared the lonely outpost, the usual studied vigilance once again took control. Always the cautious operator, Cole moved across to tether his own mount to a lone palo verde tree on the blind side of the main building. The drooping branches, still cloaked in their array of golden flowers, provided some welcome shade for the tired animal. Before entering the trading post, he filled a bucket with water from the trough and allowed his cayuse to slake its thirst.

Then he loosened the revolver in its holster. A man in his position could never be too careful. That was how he had managed to survive so long in such a precarious calling. With due care, he pushed open the heavy wooden door. Before entering he gave the interior a panoramic scan that took in everything at a glance.

Two men sat at a table, their attention

focussed on plates of food. One was a Mexican. A wide heavily adorned sombrero oversaw the obligatory drooping moustache and flashing eyes. The latter now appraised the newcomer with a hint of the curious rather than any leaning towards animosity.

The other guy was older and of Anglo descent. Stout of girth as opposed to the Mexican's lithe build, his gaze was focussed wholly on the food, which he shovelled into a gaping maw with evident relish.

Satisfied they posed no threat, Cole gingerly took a step across the threshold.

'No need to be so jumpy, stranger,' said the man behind the counter. The proprietor poured a shot of whiskey and pushed it across the bar. 'Mosey on over here. First drink is on the house. I ain't got the same beaming grin as my predecessor, but that don't mean I can't make folks welcome at Happy Jack. The name's Amos Coolidge, but most folks call me Cowpat. Can't figure out why. But it don't matter none.'

The guy's square head with its circlet of dirty brown hair was a clear giveaway as to how he had acquired the derisory handle. Having the appearance of a dead polecat, it was a badly made wig. Cole suppressed a smile and the overwhelming desire to stare.

The moment quickly passed. Yet Cole still hung back. Three nags, two customers. So where was the third guy? Once again searching eyes flitted around the room, a cautious hand resting on the gun butt. Coolidge seemed genuine enough, but an innate caution born of an instinct for survival held him back.

'You sure are a nervous dude, ain't yuh?' snorted the proprietor.

Cole continued to scan the shadowy far recesses of the room as he replied, 'You ever heard the saying, 'There's always free cheese in a mousetrap'?'

'Can't say that I have,' said the proprietor creasing up his mousey features in thought. Then the nickel dropped along with the hospitable beam.

'Well, heeding that snippet of finely

honed piece of logic has kept me alive in a tough world.'

'That ees very good saying, *señor*,' the Mexican concurred with a judicious nod of approval. 'You are right to be *sospechoso*.' A wry smirk crossed the handsome profile while a finger jabbed at his chest. 'Fernando Estrela treat all *hombres* with same caution until he get to know them.'

Cole gave the poignant remark a justifiable bow of acknowledgement.

'Only trying to be friendly, is all,' grumbled the trader. 'You don't want a free drink? Ain't no skin off'n my nose.' Coolidge removed the glass and began pouring the contents back into the bottle. 'But there's no need to be —' He stopped in mid-flow. The beady eyes screwed up as he studied the newcomer more closely. 'Don't I know you from somewhere, mister?'

'Another bottle over here, Cowpat.' Mustang Charlie Bassett had suddenly discovered his own voice.

Cole now had a better look at him.

Stout and rather bullish and sporting a broken nose, Bassett ignored the newcomer. The request emerged as a blurry gabble. Shreds of food clung to his beard as Bassett continued forking a large *tortilla española* into his mouth. The jasper clearly enjoyed filling his ample belly.

His summons for more alcoholic sustenance had temporarily interrupted Cowpat's line of thought. Grabbing a full bottle off the back shelf, the proprietor sauntered over and set it down on the table. 'Where's Frank gone?' he asked pointing to the abandoned plate opposite broken nose.

A twitch of the bullet head indicated the back door. 'Out back taking a leak.'

Cowpat nodded before returning to his side of the counter. Cole joined him, having satisfied himself that no skulduggery was afoot. The guy's own features were now much more plainly delineated.

'So what is it to be, stranger?' the trader asked. 'Most guys who call here welcome a free drink. There again, maybe you've heard good things about my woman's special *tortillas*. Each one freshly made. That it?' He called across to the guzzling diner seeking confirmation. 'You enjoying those on your plate, Mustang?'

A grunted response was accompanied by a nondescript shrug. Cowpat took that as a positive reaction. He was about to restate his inquiry when his gaze was again drawn to the angular profile of the newcomer.

'Get me a jug of buttermilk. My throat's burning up,' Cole croaked out.

The trader raised a bushy eyebrow at the unusual request then called out to his wife in the back room. 'One jug of milk out here, woman!'

'Travelling far?' The inquiry was merely to fill in time until the beverage arrived.

'Some.' Cole's reply was curt and non-committal. 'Got me some unfinished business to take care of in Maverick.'

But the garrulous proprietor was not listening. The strange hairpiece appeared to shift on its balding support as Cowpat snapped a thumb and finger together.

'I remember now,' evinced the

animated trader, jabbing a finger at the newcomer. 'You're the Reno Kid. I was up in Denver when you brought in Black Dog Bowdrie. You came into the Occidental saloon for a drink after delivering the cuss to the marshal's office. I was chief bartender. That was one mean-eyed son-of-a-bitch you'd caught there. Guess he fetched a high bounty.'

Cole's back stiffened. This was the last thing he needed. Recognition this far south. He had not operated in Arizona for more than four years.

At that moment Cowpat's Indian wife appeared with the jug of buttermilk. The Apache squaw known as Ponkasante had been sold to Amos Coolidge by her tribe the previous fall. No consent from the woman was sought by the tribal elders. No discussion instigated, except over the final bill of sale. Apache law had spoken and Ponkasante had to obey, or face death by stoning.

And so she was given over to a grim life as little more than a slave to the trader.

The squaw gave the lone traveller more

than her usual surly regard. This man was different from the regular array of drifters who passed through Happy Jack. It was unusual for a white-eyes to order such a beverage. His bearing was alert, watchful and wary, but hinted of a deep sadness within. She stood a moment contemplating the torment that lay behind those doleful eyes.

The brief twinkling of introspection was abruptly curtailed.

'Back where you belong, woman,' rapped her husband. 'There's work to be done.'

The unintended interruption gave Cole time to think of a suitable response to Amos Coolidge's startling declaration. Pouring out a glass of the delicious beverage, Cole knocked it back in a single draught. His mouth crinkled into a half-smile as he wiped a hand across his mouth.

'Boy, that sure hit the spot and no mistake,' he sighed, pouring another glass. 'Much obliged, ma'am.'

Ponkasante returned the smile. It was

her first such display since arriving at the trading post all those months before. A man had actually acknowledged her existence. Returning to her chores, the woman's step was much lighter. She would remember the hard-boiled yet gently considerate stranger for many moons to come. His solicitude would elicit a glow of hope in the dark days that lay ahead, a splash of colour into her life of menial drudgery.

But Cowpat was not to be sidetracked. 'What you doing in these parts then, Reno? I thought your bailiwick was up north in Colorado.'

Cole quickly shook his head. 'You got the wrong fella, mister. My name is Cole Rickard. And I ain't never been to Denver.'

This time it was Coolidge who shook his head along with the precarious rug perched thereon. 'Don't cotton to that notion. Amos Coolidge never forgets a face. I'm just like the elephant that never forgets —'cept with me being a mite on the leaner side, of course.' He laughed at the witticism expecting the Kid to join in as confirmation of his claim.

'Well this time you're on the wrong trail, friend.' Cole's voice hardened as he held the other's gaze in a frosty grip. 'Like I just told you, the name is Cole Rickard. Now scarper and let me alone to enjoy my drink in peace.'

Cowpat shrugged then backed off. He could recognize the icy cut of a cold-eyed gunslinger from a hundred paces. Giving the newcomer a quizzical frown he moved across to join Fernando and Mustang Charlie.

Moments later they were joined by his partner.

'Could have sworn that guy was the Reno Kid,' Cowpat averred scratching his ear. He threw another surreptitious glance towards the milk drinker. 'In fact, I'm darn certain it's him. So why does he not want to be eyeballed?'

'I have never met thees *hombre* before, but he sure wears hees gun like he know how to use it.' The Mexican stuck a cheroot in his mouth and lit up.

The two other men looked at one another. Frank Quintel was a young punk who wore his own six-shooter low in a fancy tooled rig. On hearing the name of the legendary bounty hunter, his eyes lit up. Bassett, fifteen years his senior and far more circumspect, instantly perceived the gleam of fire in his partner's lurid smirk. He had seen it often enough before. And it spelled trouble.

'I reckon he's scared,' jeered the cocky braggart. 'Getting too old for gunplay.'

'Easy there, Frank,' Bassett cautioned laying a restrictive hand on the hothead's arm. 'The boss don't want no trouble. Remember what we're here for.'

'Charlie ees right, *muchacho*. It not good to draw attention to good selves.'

The three men were awaiting the arrival of Jeb Quintel; the boss of the notorious outlaw gang known as the Shadow Riders was also the elder brother of Frank Quintel. They were intending to rob the wagon carrying the monthly army payroll to Fort Defiance. Cowpat always received a cut for providing the gang with a hangout.

Jeb had sent the trio on ahead to brief Cowpat while he sussed out the bank in Globe for their next job. The rest of the gang were headed for Pima Pass where the stage was expected around noon in three days' time. They would camp out there until the boss and his three associates joined them.

'You hear me, boy?' pressed Mustang. 'Getting caught up in some showdown could spoil Jeb's plan.'

But Frank was not listening. He brushed off his buddies' caution with a surly grimace. 'You pair of boobies might be afraid of this dude, but I sure ain't. My betting is the yeller-belly don't want us knowing the truth cos he's lost his nerve. That'll give me the edge to take him out.'

'Don't be such a durned fool,' urged a suddenly much irritated Charlie Bassett. 'Guys like that eat young gunnies for breakfast. Jeb asked me to tag along to keep you out of trouble. Now heed my advice and let the guy drink his milk in peace.'

Such a churlish rebuke would have received Quintel's full ire had he not been so eager to challenge the renowned bounty hunter. But the young pretender was past any sort of dissuasion, no matter how vigorously espoused. All he could see was his name being spoken of in awe as the gunslinger who beat the Reno Kid to the draw.

Settling his rig comfortably, Frank Quintel rose from his seat and ambled over to the counter. The cracked smile held no levity. It was cold as a mountain stream. Here was an easy way to gain the reputation he had always craved. Move out of the shadow of his older brother. Cold eyes glittered at the thought of becoming famous throughout the Southwest.

'Over here, Cowpat,' he rasped. 'Give me a shot of whiskey. I need a real drink.'

The trader did as bid then hissed out a muted warning. 'I don't want no trouble in here. You listening to me, Frank?'

But the kid ignored him, knocking the

drink back in a single gulp. He slammed the glass down on the counter hoping to jerk a reaction from the other man. Cole remained immune to the intended provocation.

'Never figured a tough big shot like the Reno Kid would stoop to drinking baby juice.' His reedy voice was laced with acrimony. 'Guess that rep of your'n was all make-believe after all. You ain't no more than a mama's boy.'

Cole looked straight ahead ignoring the rancid jibe. The last thing he wanted was more trouble now that he was so close to his goal. He lifted the glass and slowly imbibed the white liquid.

Yet deep down, he was seething. Not on account of the blatant insult. That was like water off a duck's back. Cole knew exactly where this dilemma was heading. There was to be no easy way out. This young tough was intent on a showdown. And nothing was going to stay his hand.

A wolfhound raised its head over by the fireplace. The dog's low growl cut through the atmosphere like butter. Instinctively sensing the sudden tension in the room, its fur stood on end.

Again, a sweating Cowpat tried appealing to reason. 'No need for this, Frank,' he nervously implored the hothead. 'Reno here was just leaving. Ain't that so, Kid?'

Both men were deaf to the panic-stricken entreaty. Cole knew that the escalating confrontation had shuffled beyond any possibility of a climb-down by either party. Yet still he tried.

'Can't you corral this hot-headed greenhorn, fella? How am I supposed to enjoy my drink with him breathing down my neck?' Cole couldn't help himself, he was so annoyed. The entreaty was to Mustang Charlie, clearly the more mature of the trio.

But it was Fernando who spoke up. 'Now it has come down to thees, *señor*, I Fernando Estrela, am more than a leetle intrigued to see eef the great Reno Kid ees all they say he ees.' The Mexican casually pursed his lips and pushed a perfect smoke ring into the fetid air.

Rather than cooling the heated

53

exchange, the greaser's remark had only inflamed the situation. Charlie merely shrugged his shoulders. He turned aside, washing his hands of the whole fiasco, merely muttering, 'Jeb ain't gonna like it.'

Frank snarled out a rabid epithet, his pudgy face glistening with sweat. The kid's right hand flexed above the gun butt of a bone-handled Colt Frontier. 'Nobody speaks to me like that, old man,' he barked out. Legs akimbo and hunkering down, he adopted the hunched stance of a gunslick who was beyond the pale. 'Fernando is right. Let's see how good you really are. Now if'n your backbone ain't filled with that cow slop, make your play.'

Cole levered himself off the counter. He fastened a probing eye on to the challenger. His usual ploy in such situations was always to let his antagonist draw first. Intuition and experience had taught him the skill of studying a man's body language. And it never varied. A slight widening of the eyes, a lift of the shoulder.

And so it was with Frank Quintel. The

impatience of youth took its toll, the kid drawing first. His gun rose, hammer snapping back ready to deliver its lethal charge. The index finger tightened on the trigger. But it never managed the final hallelujah.

Cole's revolver bucked once only. It was enough. The gun appeared to have jumped into his right hand.

A plume of red blossomed on Frank's shirt. He looked down in shock. This was not how it should have been. Then his punctured body lurched backwards, tumbling over a chair. A final twitch of muscles and he lay still.

The smoking gun immediately swung to cover Mustang Charlie and the Mexican. Both outlaws raised their arms.

'Don't shoot, Reno. I ain't got no wish to stoke up the fiery furnace,' Bassett professed with vigour. 'Frank sure had it coming to him. But Jeb Quintel won't be so forgiving. And he's due here within the hour.'

In his mind's eye, Charlie could see the payroll snatch continuing on its merry way unimpeded. The leader of the Shadow Riders would want revenge before any more jobs were pulled. Frank was his only family. Then another thought entered his head. This would give Punk Adler the chance to muscle in and stir things up with the rest of the gang. But the steady six-shooter pointing at his belly quickly pushed the notion from his head.

Cole likewise knew that he would need to hit the trail and disappear into the wilds of Arizona before the gang boss could organize any pursuit. He resolutely cursed his bad luck in running into yet another reckless hotspur. But that was what his sorry life had become. One gunfight after another. Would it never end? Maybe there really was no way back.

Cole grabbed a fistful of jerked beef sticks along with the milk jug as he backed out of the trading post. Happy Jack's had suddenly lost any humour it had hoped to imbue in its most recent visitor. Downing the rest of the milk, he tossed the jug aside and mounted up. A wary eye was kept locked onto the windows of the post to ensure none of the occupants tried to delay his departure.

No sign of a gun barrel appeared as he spurred away. But he knew that Jeb Quintel was due in from his visit to Globe soon. As luck would have it, their paths were unlikely to cross, although the vengeful brother of Frank Quintel in company with Mustang Charlie and the greaser would not waste any time in dogging his trail.

There was only one way to deal with such a pursuit.

4

Cast Afoot

Cole eventually found a suitable cluster of boulders from which to set up an ambush. He concealed the sorrel in a clump of cottonwoods then clambered up onto the ledge overlooking the open trail. There, he settled down to await his pursuers. The beef jerky provided some much needed sustenance.

Ensconced beneath a convenient rocky overhang sheltered from the harsh sun, he had no idea how long his vigil would last. Would Quintel come straight after him? Or would he decide to stay over at Happy Jack and wait until the following day? One thing was beyond question: if Mustang Charlie's assertion was correct, follow he surely would to enact justice for his slain brother.

Had Cole still been an active bounty

hunter he would have sought to take the guy in. But those days were now in his past. At least, that was his sincere hope. Trouble in the disreputable form of the Devil unfortunately had a bad habit of popping up to burst your bubble.

The shooting of Frank Quintel was a melancholic example of the horned demon's conniving tactics.

His thoughts returned to the task in hand. All he could do now was to wait it out. He prayed that the inevitable confrontation would be sooner rather than later.

His morbid anticipation was to be rewarded. Two hours after establishing himself on the shelf of rock, the silence was broken by a dull yet regular thud of hoof beats. And they were coming from the direction of Happy Jack. Cole tossed away the half-eaten stick of jerky and crawled to the edge of the shelf.

Rifle at the ready, he removed his hat and peered over the lip. The open plain provided an unrestricted vista for miles. The rising plume of yellow dust was about half a mile back. He could make out three riders. It had to be Jeb Quintel and his two sidekicks. Within minutes they were approaching the ambush site. Cole gave a nod of satisfaction on recognizing the distinctively brutish features of Broken Nose.

He had never laid eyes on the elder Quintel before. However, his reputation, if not the name, as an effective outlaw leader of the Shadow Riders was well known. So was the knife scar he carried above his left eye. A white slash in contrast to the black brow opposite gave him a wolfish appearance. The gang had intimidated the territory for two years without capture, disappearing after each caper like shadows in the night.

Hence the name allotted by Sheriff Grant Souther of Prescott.

The guy sat tall in the saddle and carried himself with a confident ease. Cole knew he would have to be extra vigilant when handling the outlaw boss.

He waited until the trio were no more than fifty yards from the shelf before he despatched two bullets. Each ploughed into the hard-packed ground immediately ahead of the riders. Gouts of sand spurted into the air, startling the horses. The animals reared up on their hind legs and stumbled to a halt. Before the men could react, Cole was on his feet, the rifle at his shoulder.

'Hold it right there!'

The blunt order was measured and restrained, yet issued in a terse threat that could not be ignored. He had no wish to have any more deaths on his conscience. In the old days he would not have hesitated in blasting these critters out of their saddles. But his brash life as a ruthless manhunter and firebrand was over. Enough killing had been done to last him a half dozen lifetimes.

Indeed, he shivered at the notion that such a lifestyle had been his career of choice. Any terminal gunplay now would only be as a last resort. Earlier on this very day he had been forced into yet another fatal showdown; Frank Quintel had given him no room for manoeuvre.

But when he was offered an alternative, it had to be to give his adversaries an even break. This was such a moment.

His aim now was merely to prevent these jaspers from following him. And he knew just how that could be achieved without blood being spilled. It was now their choice to determine whether they would see another sunrise.

'OK, boys!' he hollered making sure to keep the pursuers covered. 'Raise your hands and step down. Any false moves and this long gun will finish the argument permanently.'

Quintel snarled. But the outlaw knew better than to resist. The men slid off their mounts.

'And keep them mitts high and wide.'

Maintaining his watch on the captives, Cole scuttled down from his lofty perch. Warily, he approached the three men. It was Quintel who spoke first.

'You could have prevented it being a killing shot, Reno,' came the rasping accusation. He was referring to his deceased kin.

'I wasn't given any choice,' responded Cole firmly.

Quintel's reaction was to be expected. A disdainful snort said it all. 'There's always a choice. You went for the wrong one. Frank was only a young kid. Sure, he was a tearaway. But he was my brother. I ain't about to forget that in a hurry. You best watch your back from now on.'

'A backshooter, is that it, Quintel?' Cole hawked a wad of chewing tobacco at the outlaw's feet. 'I might have known a lowlife of your ilk couldn't face a man down.'

Quintel's face turned a darker shade of purple. He was almost tempted to go for his gun. It was Mustang's restraining hand that prevented an early visit from the Reaper. 'Hold up, Jeb. He's only trying to goad you.'

'You'd do well to heed your buddy, mister,' advised Cole. 'He's got some sense. He'll also tell you that Frank knew what he was about.' Cole was vainly hoping to persuade the incensed outlaw to accept his claim that the shooting was unavoidable. It was a vain hope, but still he tried. 'All these young guns are the same. He wanted to be the one who bested the Reno Kid. It was self-defence. Frank drew first.'

Cole looked to the other man for confirmation. Mustang shrugged. It was not his call. And the Shadow leader was not about to heed any excuses. 'Frank stood no chance against a gunslick of your calibre. It was pure murder. Make no mistake, mister, I'm gonna seek you out and do the job properly. Then it'll be Jeb Quintel who can strutt his stuff. *I'll* be the jasper who outgunned the Reno Kid.'

'Well it ain't gonna be anytime soon.' Cole was becoming tired of the aimless chitchat. 'Enough of this jaw-jabbering. Now shuck them irons, pronto.'

Quintel ran his tongue along the length of his thin lips.

Cole recognized the signs. Yet another hint that a sly rat was working out the odds of beating his captor to the draw. Always alert for the cunning ploys practised by most experienced gunmen, he studied Jeb Quintel's reactions. He was no brazen tenderfoot like his brother and would require extra care.

Instead of untying his leg thongs, the outlaw hooked his thumbs into the gun-belt. A sigh of resignation hissed from the cruel mouth as if to admit he had been thwarted by a better man. To Cole's experienced eye it was a sure sign of an imminent challenge.

'Don't try it, mister.' Cole's voice had changed to a hard, brittle snap. He lifted the rifle meaningfully. 'Only a mug would figure the Reno Kid wasn't clued up on all the sneaky tricks critters like you go for.' An ugly leer challenged Jeb Quintel to make his move. The outlaw was left in no doubt that a dose of lead poisoning from Doctor Death would be his sure-fire remedy for such a reckless deed. 'Now, all you jerks, ditch them belts.'

Quintel scowled. But he was no fool. He knew it was going to take more than a one-to-one contest to crack this nut. The three men slowly did as ordered.

The chance of getting the better of the renowned bounty hunter had passed them by.

'Now it's the turn of your boots and socks.' The mirthless smirk remained pasted onto the gunfighter's leathery features. His order found the men protesting vigorously. Cole allowed them to voice their complaints without interruption.

'You can't cast us afoot in this god-forsaken wilderness,' Quintel griped. 'It ain't human. Our feet'll be cut to ribbons without socks.'

'Have a heart, Mister Reno,' pleaded Mustang trying to ingratiate himself. 'We've learned our lesson. You won't get no more trouble from us. Ain't that right, Jeb?'

The gang boss was forced to swallow his pride. 'Guess I was trying to overreach myself. And Frank always was a knuckle-headed mule. How are we gonna survive out here without boots?'

All the fight appeared to have drained out of the hard-nosed villain. But Cole was not moved by the feeble petitions. He had heard all these excuses many times before. None of it washed with him.

'I won't tell you again. Dump the footwear. All of it.'

His brusque mandate was sharp and to the point. And Quintel knew that Reno would have no compunction in carrying out the threat. Bullets would fly should more disputes be forthcoming. A series of suppressed grunts found the three wretched gunmen barefoot and unarmed.

'Now get to walking,' Cole snarled. 'You should make it back to Happy Jack in maybe three days … if'n you're lucky and don't step on no rattlers or scorpions. And then there's the gila monsters. Those fellas just don't know when to let go once they grab a hold of yuh. It sure would be a pity for that to happen. Now get moving!'

A flick of the rifle urged the glowering barefooted outlaws to set off back the way they had come.

'I'll get even with you, Reno, if'n it's the last thing I do,' growled Quintel. 'And don't think for a minute that showing us mercy will save you.' But it was an impotent throwaway lacking any teeth.

'Could be you're right, Quintel,' Cole tossed back. 'Maybe I have been too darned soft.' He loosed off a couple of slugs that found the three crooks dancing a merry jig. A hearty guffawing from their tormentor jarred in Quintel's ears. 'Watch where you put them feet, boys,' the chuckling subjugator shouted. 'Tarantulas are also known to inhabit these hills. And their bite ain't to be relished neither. Enjoy the walk.'

The three downcast ruffians immediately abandoned their simmering rancour and threw all their attention into avoiding any such denizens that might increase their suffering. Cole waited until they were well out of sight before continuing with his own journey south.

Again his brow furrowed in thought. Quintel and his boys were forgotten as he drew ever closer to his ultimate goal.

5

Luck of the Devil

For the first hour after being cast afoot, the sole aim of the owlhoots was to avoid any sharp protrusions. Apart from numerous grunts and curses when hidden snares dug into their soft skin, silence reigned. Fernando led the way. As a poverty-stricken child brought up in the slums of Nogales, shoes were a luxury only worn on Sundays. As a result his feet were tough as old leather.

Jeb and Mustang soon had to rest up. Already their feet were bleeding.

'We can't go on like this,' the older man mumbled. Removing his bandanna, he gently dabbed at the torn skin. 'What we gonna do, Jeb?'

The whinging voice held a note of panic that the gang boss was not slow in denigrating to conceal his own burgeoning fears. 'Cut your grousing, Mustang. We'll get out of this soon enough.' He did not elaborate. Nor did Bassett. A far more serious issue suddenly occurred to the old bronc-buster.

'What we gonna do for water out here?' He peered around mournfully.

Quintel silently cursed his stupidity. The hollow gaze that blankly scanned the arid terrain held no answer to such a basic problem. So intent had all three been on avoiding any mishaps, they had overlooked that most vital of elements.

It was Fernando who came to the rescue. He had walked on ahead and come upon a clump of beavertail cacti. Hacking off the sharp spines with a rock, he broke open one of the large green plates. Inside was a stringy mush. After peeling away the hard outer shell, he sucked on the damp flesh. It tasted bitter, but was better than nothing and would keep them going until they reached Happy Jack.

'Over this way, *muchachos*,' he called out. 'Here lies our salvation.' The other two hobbled over to join him. 'Do not expect vintage champagne. But cactus *agua* will stop our bodies from drying up.'

Seeing their buddy sucking on the green plate, Quintel and the ex-bronc-peeler immediately fell upon them. True, the moisture within tasted foul. But beggars can't be choosers, as the saying goes.

They were now able to fully appreciate the manner in which these bizarre desert dwellers were able to thrive and produce such a prized tonic. Both men promised themselves that when they escaped this torment, never again would either take the fruits of the desert for granted. With their thirst temporarily slaked, the three castaways continued their shambling journey. The pace slowed to little more than a stumbling plod. Bassett was getting on Quintel's nerves with his constant bleating. He gritted his teeth and closed his mind to the griping. Head down, he ploughed on.

The Mexican had again wandered ahead. Suddenly, another buoyant summons edged with hope found the two sorry *gringos* scurrying as best they could round to the far side of a rock stack. There they found Fernando beside the weathered bones of a long abandoned wagon. Much of it was buried in a sand drift. But it was the canvas cover the Mexican was ripping apart with a rusty knife that caught their attention.

As well as the knife, there was also an array of ragged clothing.

'Eh, boys,' he exclaimed gleefully. 'We are een luck again, *si?* With these things we make our own footwear.'

An hour later, they were back on the trail, and making better progress. The makeshift footwear was cumbersome, but offered some much appreciated protection. The mood suddenly lightened. Jeb Quintel was able to further add to the upbeat raising of spirits with a surprise announcement.

A couple of miles further on, he signalled a halt beside a large organ pipe cactus.

Bassett slumped to the ground. 'I'm plum tuckered out,' he groaned. 'You fellas go on. Come back for me when you reach Happy Jack.'

'No need for that, Mustang,' breezed a grinning Jeb Quintel. 'Ain't much further now.' Bassett gave him a lop-sided grimace of puzzlement.

'How you figure that?' asked the equally baffled Mexican.

Quintel was enjoying the subterfuge. 'This is where we swing off the trail, boys,' he declared with a sly grin.

'But this ees not thee way to Happy Jack,' evinced the puzzled Fernando. 'Why you go thees way, *patrón?*'

'Over the other side of that ridge is a ranch where we can get some fresh mounts.' Quintel pointed to a notch in the rocky skyline ahead. Winding between clumps of sagebrush and the now much revered beavertails, the track headed straight towards it.

'How you know thees?' asked Fernando.

'It was afore I met up with you, boys,' he said. 'I was running with a gang of roughriders on the border with Utah in Monument Valley. We used to come out the canyons to hold up passing stagecoaches. Trouble was, we got to be too darned cocky. Kept operating the same plan of attack. That was our downfall.'

'One day we tried it on with another coach at the same spot. But this time it was filled with bluecoats. Half the gang were cut down or captured. Me and a guy called Montana Jaxx were the only ones to escape unscathed. We split up. I headed south. Jaxx reckoned to have salted enough away to buy a piece of land in California. I ain't heard from him since. So I figure he must have made it and settled down.'

Quintel scratched his head at the recollection. 'Never stick to the same routine. That's my advice to you boys. And I've followed it ever since. Those army jaspers had us sussed out. We didn't stand a chance.'

'You never mentioned this before, boss,' Mustang interrupted. 'I always reckoned you were a Nevada guy.'

'It don't always pay for a man to advertise his past,' cautioned the outlaw, tapping his nose with meaning. 'Mouthing off too much has a habit of biting you on the ass.'

'That ees wise thinking, *patrón*. So how you come across thees ranch?' Fernando was eager to hear the finale seeing as it coincided with their current circumstances.

'I was heading south aiming to cross into Mexico.' Quintel was getting back into his stride. Hawking a sly wink at his Mexican buddy, he continued, 'Those *señoritas* down Sonora way sure know how to look after a guy, don't you think, Fern?'

The Mexican sighed. His eyes glazed over. 'You are indeed right there, *patrón*.'

'So what happened?' pressed Mustang, also eager to hear the rest of the story.

'I had a pesky suspicion that some dude was on my tail.' Red pokers glinted in Quintel's eyes. He spat on the ground. 'Might even have been that skunk Reno. Anyway, my cayuse was flagging badly. I needed a new one, and quick. Hoping to throw him off the scent, I turned off here. And just by chance, I came across this horse ranch.'

'The one over yonder?' Charlie pointed to the approaching ridgeline.

'One and the same. There was nobody about apart from a corral full of ready-made broncs. I just grabbed the nearest one, saddled up and left mine.' He shrugged as if this was the most natural thing in the world. 'After all, fellas, don't they say that fair exchange is no robbery?'

The adage brought roars of laughter from his two associates. 'You sure are right there, boss,' agreed Charlie.

'Only trouble was, the owner didn't cotton to my generosity.' Gaping mouths greeted this sudden change in fortune. They hung on Quintel's every word, silently urging him to reach the conclusion. 'He came out the cabin at the moment I was mounting up, a gun in his hand. The varmint must have spotted the exchange.'

'What happened? Did he shoot you?' exclaimed Charlie.

'Still here, ain't I? But that poor dupe is strumming with the angels.' He crossed himself in mock acknowledgement of the wrangler's demise.

Following these strange revelations from their leader, the three footsloggers made a left along the thin track. It had been stamped out by a family of coyotes. They soon passed the skeleton of a dead antelope, its bleached bones now all that remained. With Fernando's arm around the hobbling Bassett, they pressed on towards the notch on the horizon.

Around late afternoon, they staggered up the final rise and over the lip. And there below, a verdant sward opened up with the all-important horse ranch at its heart.

The three men slumped to the ground gasping for breath. It had been a tiring trudge, even with their supply of beaver-tail plates and the makeshift footwear. Bassett lay on his back sucking in air.

Quintel heaved a sigh of relief that the ranch was still operating as such. And judging by the activity taking place, it was a thriving concern.

'We sure are in luck, boys,' he averred

with gusto. 'It looks like they're doing good business down there.'

Mustang Charlie soon recovered from the arduous trek knowing they had reached what appeared to be their salvation. He was especially enthralled by the equine venture. Much of his life before taking to the owlhooter trail was on such enterprises. His practised gaze followed the skilled endeavour of the lone broncpeeler to bend the wild horse to his will.

'Those guys can earn good money at this business,' he declared. 'A top hand can tame eight broncs a day earning himself five bucks a head. But it's tough work.'

'That sure ees *bueno dinero*,' maintained Fernando, impressed. 'Why you stop?'

Charlie stretched his tired limbs and creaking bones. 'Busting nags is apt to age a fella before his time. It's gruelling work. And I got the bruises, sprains and badly set bones to prove it.' He stretched his stiff shoulders. 'Mustangs ain't the only things that get busted.'

They were studying the action down below. It was a mesmerizing sight to behold the skilled bronc man at work. Charlie avidly filled them in with a detailed resume of the wrangling task being enacted.

As one newly tamed cayuse was released into the holding pen another bounded into the fenced stockade. The bay gelding hammered around the enclosure trying to find a way out. The buster's first job was to throw a rope around its neck and lash it to a snubbing post. Gingerly, whispering sweet nothings, he slipped a hackamore bridle over the shaking head.

Bridled and hobbled but still full of fight, the toughest job was then to blanket and saddle the recalcitrant animal. The battle between man and beast can be a salutary lesson for both parties. Much as they wanted to cheer the guy on, the watchers were obliged to curb their passionate enthusiasm. Noise from the ridge could carry on the light desert zephyrs that scurried hither and thither up here.

Their breath was held in check as the rider failed in his first attempt to mount up. He would have been trampled underfoot by the stomping shoeless hoofs had he not jumped aside in the nick of time.

Approaching from a different angle, he used a slicker to divert the animal's attention long enough to successfully complete the intricate manoeuvre.

'That a boy,' hissed Charlie, slamming a bunched fist into the ground. 'You have him now. Get that cinch tightened pronto!'

The bronc-peeler seemed to hear the advice and instantly did as the old roustabout suggested. Charlie smiled. The horse began tossing and bucking, desperate to remove the irksome hindrance.

The buster was dragged around the stockade like a rag doll. Only by tugging and hauling on the rope was he able to maintain his footing. At the same time he drew closer to the crazed beast until he was near enough to grab the bay's ears. Squeezing hard, the animal whinnied. But the sudden pain was enough to distract the gelding, thus allowing the guy to swing aboard.

Now it was a question of teaching the cayuse the art of obedience. Gut-jarring hell broke out as the skittish gelding desperately tried to unseat the alien invader. Its back arched to an acute angle. But the man hung on. High above the mesmeric performance, the excited yells of glee from the buster could be clearly heard. Charlie Bassett almost joined in the frenetic cheering. Just in time he held back.

Clinging on to a short halter with his left hand, the buster began hazing the animal with the slicker. That and the judicious use of a quirt wrapped around his wrist were the principle means of persuasion as man and beast battled for supremacy. But there was only ever going to be one winner.

The man then rode the animal around the stockade, hauling up and dismounting on numerous occasions until he was satisfied the bay had gotten the message as to who was boss. As the tamed mount became used to its new master, soft words were spoken to show there were no hard feelings. And so another bronco was tamed.

The peeler wandered across to a water trough and removed his hat. Untying his necker, he dipped it into the scummy liquid. Without squeezing out the moisture, he dragged the cloth across his sweat-smeared face and neck. Arms stretched wide to ease the stiffness in his strained muscles.

'That surely was a fine sight,' Fernando concurred before adding a proviso. 'But no amount of dinero would persuade good self to engage in such work. It is now clear as fresh water, amigo, why you chose a life outside thee law.'

'We'll camp up here tonight,' said Quintel, 'and move down at daybreak to make our choice before those jaspers are awake.'

Mustang Charlie dragged his admiring thoughts away from the nostalgic sight below. All the excitement attached to the age-old contest betwixt man and beast was reflected in his wistful gaze. Having watched the scintillating performance, Charlie's eyes misted over as evocative thoughts of a past long since confined to history washed over him.

But that's all it was — an evocative longing for a way of life that had, in truth, only brought him aches and pains by the bucket load. And much as he had insisted that good money could be made by the top hands, there was no way such a brutal way of earning a crust could be sustained. Carry on like those guys below and he would have ended up kicked to death, or a helpless cripple. That notion was enough to persuade him that the right decision had been made.

You never clapped eyes on a bronc-peeler over the age of thirty. Most had either been forced to retire, or gone the way of Charlie Bassett.

The nostalgic yearning cast aside, the one-time buster took heed of the boss's take on the proceedings. And he was not impressed.

Making camp up here was not a good idea. Bassett was the only member of the Shadow Riders who had the nerve to voice his dissention. Age, and his having ridden with Quintel for more than two years, had given him a certain degree of authority. The gang leader heeded his advice.

So it was that the old bronc-rider now aired his views.

Yet even he always chose to be prudent and circumspect in any suggestions he made that did not concur with those of Jeb Quintel. Like all arrogant jaspers who led from the front, the guy balked against his decisions being brought into question. But these were unusual, if not desperate circumstances that the three outlaws now found themselves in.

'I was thinking, boss, that maybe staying up here all night ain't such a good idea.'

He paused, holding his breath, and waited for Quintel to listen, or blow his top.

The gang boss turned towards his associate. His face was blank, ambiguous. It had always been Jeb Quintel's policy to heed any suggestions made by his owlhooter associates. There were times, though, when under stress, or more likely the influence of the demon drink, that he shunned any dissention. Hence Bassett's reticence.

The response was measured and acquiescent. 'You gotten a better plan, Charlie, then let's hear it.'

'There's a couple of hours' daylight left,' Bassett remarked. 'The rider down there will be calling it quits soon. I figure there are maybe just two guys in the outfit. The other one has likely finished early to rustle up some chow.' He pointed to a twist of smoke rising from the stack of the cabin. 'Looks like he's stoking up already.'

As if on cue, a man emerged from the cabin and began hammering on an iron ring. The buster lifted an arm in acknowledgement.

He went on to explain the scheme he had in mind.

'So what d'yuh figure, boss?'

Quintel hummed and hawed to himself as he tossed over the various ramifications involved with what Bassett had outlined. Both men waited. It was Fernando who spoke first. 'Ees good plan, *amigo*. Although why good self to go down first?'

Charlie was ready for that objection. 'That's cos I might know some of those dudes. We bronc men travel around and get to know each other. The last thing we need is an extra burr to complicate matters. And another thing. My face is on that wanted dodger we saw pinned up outside of Snowflake.'

'I agree,' Quintel concurred. 'It's a good plan. Well done, Charlie. That ain't just an ugly mush a-sitting on your shoulders.' It was a back-handed compliment much appreciated by the old buster. 'So this is how we'll carry it through.'

6

Horsing Around

The Mexican was instructed to wait on the ridge until the others were in position.

Quintel led the way down the slope. It was a painful descent through a tangle of mesquite and thorn that had the two men grimacing as the rough ground tormented their lacerated feet. It seemed like half a lifetime before they reached the easier flat terrain. Keeping to the cover of the corral fence, they sidled up to the rear of the barn. Being on the blind side of the log cabin prevented them being spotted by the busters.

Silent as wraiths, the two outlaws entered through the rear door of the barn and slipped inside. A row of stalls occupied by horses lined both sides. The freshly disciplined animals ignored the newcomers, continuing to munch on their feed bags.

It was clearly chow-time all round.

The nearest was a fine Appaloosa stallion that Quintel immediately singled out for himself. 'Seems like you were right, Charlie,' he praised. 'Now all we have to do is wait on Fernando playing his part.'

He hobbled back to a corner of the barn and signalled to the Mexican through a window that they were in position. A raised arm was acknowledged from the ridge.

While they were waiting, Bassett's gazed focussed on the line of horse tack hanging on the wall. Lined up neatly was every kind of metal bit including spade, ring and curb, all well polished with no evident rust. Alongside were headstalls — the California, split and ever-popular hackamore, all in pristine condition as would be expected from a professionally efficient outfit as this clearly was.

As always, to a guy who had made his living with horses, it was the saddles that were of particular interest. One especially had caught his discerning eye. Not on account of its style — it was a standard Denver model — but this one had carvings on its cantle and rear skirt that he recognized.

Mustang Charlie frowned in concentration. Now where had he seen this saddle before? Unlike a wild bronc, a good saddle took much longer to break in. But once achieved to a rider's satisfaction, it was rarely changed. Horses came and went. But a good saddle was for life, or until it fell apart.

He was given no further time to cogitate on the baffling puzzle.

'On guard, Charlie,' Quintel whispered. 'Fernando has arrived.'

Fifteen minutes had passed when Estrela was seen approaching the log cabin from the front. The Mexican bandit's nerves were stretched tight as banjo strings. It took the greatest effort to espouse the casual demeanour of an innocent traveller in need of help. The forced smile glued to his visage was flat and cold.

He paused outside the cabin, drawing breath before calling out.

'*Hola, señors*! Anybody at home?'

Moments later the plank door opened a fraction and a gun barrel poked out. 'Who's there and what d'yuh want?' The gruff voice was laced with suspicion.

'My wagon has broken axle down thee trail. You help fix, *por favor, señor?* I haff money to pay.' He stepped forward.

'Hold it right there if'n you don't want a gutful of lead. How do I know you ain't some hoss thief?'

The blunt-edged challenge was immediately answered by the Mexican holding up his arms. 'Would I give warning if such were thee case? See, *señor*, I have no weapon. How can one lone *hombre* do you any harm?'

The bronc-peeler was still not convinced. Horse thieves were a constant hazard in this business. And nobody was above suspicion, especially a greaser. 'So why ain't you wearing any boots?' The query was spat out.

'*Caballos* attack me, which ees why I

walk here for over two hours. Boots old. They split and fall apart.' The woebegone expression was no veil of deception. His feet really were sore.

A grunt followed as the speaker turned to discuss the matter with his sidekick inside the cabin. 'OK, guess you're on the level.'

The door opened wider and a bow-legged jasper stepped out. He was on the short side but held the Loomis shotgun with confidence. Fernando was not about to buck such a lethal deterrent.

'But I ain't taking no chances,' the man rasped. 'We had some thievin' varmints try their luck only last month. They're occupying unhallowed land over yonder. You go first. Over to the barn. But try any sly moves and you get both barrels. Now move!' He jerked the gun, urging the Mexican to about face.

'*Sí, sí, señor*. I no pull any tricks.'

Fernando's crafty smirk was hidden from the buster who was following behind. The scheme hatched by Mustang Charlie was going according to plan.

The ex-buster had said that the newly broken horses would be housed inside the building. Clearly he was right.

Wild untamed cayuses could now be seen behind the buildings. They were securely caged in a strong pitch-pole corral. Such wild creatures would have kicked the plank structure to matchwood in no time. Newly tamed broncs were also kept separate to get them used to wearing a full saddle rig.

Inside the barn, the outlaw boss positioned himself and his sidekick on either side of the main door. 'You club him down with that jackpole soon as he comes through the door,' Quintel hissed, his voice a tremulous croak as the tension mounted. 'I'll cover you with this pitchfork.' The deadly prongs glinted in the sunlight beaming in through the window.

Mustang gripped the heavy wooden implement tightly.

The muffled sound of footsteps heralded the imminent arrival of their quarry. A brisk nod between the ambushers and the door was pushed open. Fernando moved inside and quickly stepped to one side. The buster followed but his eyes took some seconds to accustom themselves to the dark interior.

That was the moment Charlie Bassett stepped out from behind the door and cracked him over the head. The dull thud echoed round the stark interior of the barn. The man went down like a sack of flour. He was out for the count. The door creaked shut on rusty hinges. Inside their stalls, the tamed horses continued with their repast, unaware of the violent action taking place in their midst.

'The other guy will soon come out the cabin when his buddy fails to appear,' muttered Bassett.

Quintel nodded. He peered down at the guy on the floor. Satisfied that he was out of action, the gang boss grabbed up the shotgun and moved across to a window overlooking the cabin some fifty yards distant. Unlike a rifle, these weapons were only effective at short range. 'All I need is for him to move closer. This beauty will do the rest.' He stroked the long gun's shiny rosewood stock.

Mustang stared down at the man lying on the ground. His eyes rolled, a shiver of dread filling his whole being. Now he knew where he had seen that saddle before. This guy was Ike Crawley, his old partner.

And he, Charlie Bassett had laid him out cold. Shock stunned the Mustang Man, his muscles cramping up. It had been an instinctive reaction to chop down Ike Crawley that he now deeply regretted. Previously, his attitude had been detached. Suddenly it had become personal. The guy had been a friend as well as a colleague. They had busted broncs together for two seasons before Charlie quit.

This meant that the other guy in the cabin had to be his son, Will.

How could he go through with this any longer? It wasn't right. Up on the ridge when he had first proposed the scheme, everything seemed so simple, straight forward. They needed horses, boots and guns. They were down below.

Suddenly, his priorities had changed.

The man on the floor was coming to. Groaning, but at least he was still alive and would recover. A man facing a charge of buckshot would be cut to pieces. Charlie Bassett's mind was in a quandary. What should he do? Betrayal was hard to acknowledge. His current buddies, or old pals? He was stuck between a rock and hard place.

Sure, he had killed men before. But the cold-blooded murder of a man he had known and called a friend was all wrong. His mind was made up.

Go through with it and their blood would be on his hands. He was now sure that the guy on the floor would meet a similar fate. Could he live with that? Seconds were ticking by. The full attention of both the Mexican and Quintel was concentrated on the cabin door. Any minute it would open, and Will Crawley would step outside.

Crunch time had arrived like the angel of death. No matter what the outcome, he could not allow Quintel to shoot down Will Crawley.

Charlie heard himself voicing his opposition. The words sounded eerie, as if they were being spoken by someone else.

'Why don't we just grab the horses and ride out through the back door, boss? Ain't no need to shoot a man down like this. It don't sit right.'

Quintel spun on his heels. He glared at the speaker. 'And leave two guys eager and willing to chase us down? You crazy? Not only that, we need boots and guns. They ain't about to hand those over willingly.'

'What is thees, Charlie?' protested Fernando in support of the boss. 'It was you who propose plan. Why so against it now?'

'I can't let you kill those guys, Jeb. That must be Will Crawley inside the cabin. This guy's his father, Ike. I only just eyeballed him. We used to be good buddies.'

The decision made, Bassett hefted the jack pole above his head and launched himself at the gang leader.

Jeb Quinel was caught out by the sudden rush. But he was quick to recover. A sharp exclamation of anger gushed from the open mouth as he hauled back on the trigger. The Loomis barked. Fire and death burst forth in an ear-shattering blast of devastation. Bassett was flung back, his hands clawing at the ragged hole in his stomach. The result of both barrels at point blank range was not a pretty sight.

The Mexican finished the job by pinning the twitchy body to the dirt floor with the pitchfork. Charlie Bassett's frame was quivering like a skewered pig. Blood poured from the flapping mouth. Only another vicious jab from the lethal prongs managed to terminate the gruesome spectacle.

Inside their stalls, the horses trembled and whinnied with fear.

'You darned fool,' Quintel cursed at the bent and blooded torso. 'Why in thunderation did you have to be so goddamned loyal?' Smoke twined lazily from the barrels of the Loomis.

He was not bothered about the untimely demise of his lieutenant. It was the fact that the jigger inside the cabin had now been alerted. Getting rid of the critter had suddenly become that much more difficult.

'What in the name of hellfire are we gonna do now?' he railed helplessly.

Dismayed and alarmed by the sudden death of their sidekick, the two outlaws stood staring down at the speared effigy. It presented the macabre appearance of a giant butterfly pinned to a display board.

Moments later a shaky voice called out from the cabin. 'What's going on in there? You alright, Pa?' Fear was evident in Will Crawley's tremulous appeal. 'Is that greaser causing you trouble?'

All were questions that could only be answered if he himself went to investigate. But the young horse tamer was not about to step beyond the portals of the cabin until he knew the score. A gun poked out of the cabin window. Two shots were loosed at the upper section of the barn. More out of apprehensive frustration and ignorance than any hope of resolving the disturbing fate of his father, who was inside.

Quintel rummaged in the elder bronc-peeler's pockets, emitting a yip of satisfaction on extracting a couple of spare cartridges. He pressed them into the empty barrels. In those few minutes he had worked out a plan to give them the edge. It rested on the fact that Will Crawley figured there was only one man involved in the attack he now believed to have been perpetrated against his father.

The gang leader quickly outlined his ploy.

Fernando smiled. He moved across to the window addressing the man inside the cabin. The lyrical cadence floated across the open sward. 'Your *padre* ees a leetle groggy, *señor*.' He held his peace for a few seconds to allow the implications of his announcement to register. 'Come out with your hands high or he is dead buster for sure. I not greedy. A horse and boots is all I need.'

'What was the gunfire all about?' came

back the worried reply. 'Is Pa wounded?'

'Just a bump on head, *señor*. Nothing serious ... for now. We had thee scuffle and gun went off by accident.'

'Bring him out so I can see he's OK,' Crawley ordered after due consideration of the proposal. He did not trust the Mexican, but had little choice in the matter. His pa's welfare had to come first. 'And leave the gun behind.'

'You also come out, *señor*, without weapon,' replied Fernando aiming a wink at his hidden confederate. 'Then you saddle horse for me.'

The two parties emerged from their respective cover simultaneously. Unbeknown to his assailants, during the verbal exchange Ike Crawley had recovered his wits. Yet he still made out the pretence of being dazed and wobbly on his pins. Once outside in the open, he pushed the greaser to one side and hollered to his exposed son. 'Watch out, boy, there's another rat inside with the gun. He's gonna —'

Those were his final words. The deadly

blast of the Loomis took him out. The second barrel intended for Will Crawley fell short of its target, merely digging a hole in the sand three feet short of the scrambling peeler, who quickly disappeared back inside the cabin.

Quintel cursed aloud tossing the gun aside as Fernando rejoined him in the barn. He was beginning to wonder if they wouldn't have been better off continuing along the main trail back to Happy Jack. One man down, another dead outside. They were unarmed and still had to get rid of the young horse-tamer. Riding off through the back door on saddled mounts bootless, and without guns or water was not an option to be considered. Will Crawley had to be disposed of. But how?

This time it was Fernando who came up with a plan. And this one had to work.

7

Smokestack Lightning

Having mulled over the situation, it was now a question of which outlaw was up to the task. In bare feet, only the most resilient would be capable of pulling it off. Fernando's youth and early background in the slums of Nogales meant his feet were harder. He was tough and wiry; the obvious choice.

'You up for this, Fern?' Quintel fixed the Mexican with a firm eye. 'I'm putting all my trust in you being able to pull it off.'

'Fernando Estrela not take on jobs he cannot finish,' was the gritty resolve. 'That *hombre* ees already out of thee picture.'

Quintel nodded. 'It sure was my lucky day saving your hide down in Bisbee.'

'I the lucky one, *patrón.*'

That had been three months before. Estrela had run foul of a Mexican bandit going under the handle of *El Fogonero*. The Fireman had been the cause of a significant blaze that destroyed the house of Estrela's parents over the border in Nogales. Ostensibly, it was in retaliation for an unpaid land grant that had proved to be worthless. Fernando had tracked the bandit to the Arizona town of Bisbee.

The feisty *peón* unwisely challenged the arsonist in his own back yard, namely the Sunrise saloon. The bandit had scoffed at the threat made by this skinny no-account. His men had quickly disarmed the young hornet. He was taken outside and tethered to a wagon wheel. *El Fogonero* sauntered outside ready and eager to deliver a sound thrashing. The long bull whip snapped.

But the twitching serpent never got to spit its deadly venom, being smashed in two by a well-placed bullet. Jeb Quintel and his gang had arrived in town just as the brutal chastisement was about to be conducted. He quickly surrounded the bandit and his men. The leader of the infamous Shadow Riders had a loathing for whip-wielders having suffered a similar fate himself in his youth.

When The Fireman objected in his own language, Quintel wasted no time in fruitlessly requesting a translation. He shot the bandit straight through the heart. The others rapidly saw sense and backed off.

And that was how Fernando Estrela came to join the enigmatic company of owlhooters. And he had since proved to be a resourceful member of the gang. The young Mexican's most recent proposal was clear evidence of that.

All Quintel could do now was watch from the wings, trusting his confederate to carry through the plan of action he had explained. It was now time to play his part. The gang boss hustled over to the window and called to the man inside the cabin. His idea was to distract the buster in order for Fernando to do his bit.

'Looks like we've gotten ourselves a stand-off, fella,' he declared in a self-assured tone intended to display confidence of an outcome to his advantage. The fact that he had no means of repulsing any challenge was thrust aside. 'You in there, and us out here. Neither of us going any place fast. Why don't you just give us what we want and we can call it quits and depart on friendly terms.'

Will Crawley was distraught at the sudden violence and death of his father. He had been unable to hold back the tears. But the killer's carefree attitude and notion that he should surrender effectively cast off the downcast mood. He was filled with hate and anger. Moving across to the shuttered window, he poked the Henry repeater through the tiny shot hole and loosed off a couple of shots.

'That's your answer!' he hollered. 'I've gotten all I need in here. Sometime soon, you bastards are gonna have to come out. Then it'll be me that does the killing.' He backed up the threat with another two shots.

Quintel smiled to himself. The guy was now good and riled, his whole attention focussed on the barn. Another few jibes were tossed out to keep the dupe's mind concentrated. That allowed Estrela to sneak around to the rear of the cabin. There, he gingerly hauled himself on to the pitch-pine roof.

The greatest of care was needed as he inched his way across to the smoking stovepipe. The slightest creak might alert the guy down below.

Quintel followed his partner's every move as the lean young Mexican slowly crept into position. His heart was hammering nervously as he willed the guy onwards.

'Come on, boy,' he murmured to himself. 'You can do it. Just a little bit further.' In the course of urging his confederate onward, Quintel had unwittingly exposed himself through the barn window. A bullet chewed a large hunk of wood from the frame inches from his head. Sharp fragments sliced open his cheek, drawing blood.

He cried out, slapping a hand to the wound. 'Jeez! What the heck!' Quicker than a randy roadrunner, his head disappeared from view.

A raucous chortle from inside the cabin saw the irate gang boss berating himself for his folly. Unable to reply, he prayed that Will Crawley would not cotton to the fact that he had run out of ammunition as he followed Estrela's progress from a more discrete angle. Inch by inch, the Mexican drew closer to his objective. One false move and it could all be over. Half a dozen rifle bullets through the roof would soon dispose of the intended threat.

Finally, he reached the stovepipe.

Removing his shirt, he stuffed it down the metal tube thus choking off the escaping smoke. It was then a case of crawling to the edge of the roof where it overlooked the front door. With the shutters and doors all closed up, it would not be long before the inmate would be forced out into the open.

The cabin had been purposefully erected with its back against a near vertical rock wall four hundred feet high. With only one entrance and windows that were shuttered, it offered excellent protection against warring tribes of Mescalero Apaches. That protection was about to prove its undoing in the current stand-off.

Inside the cabin, the first Will Crawley knew that he was in danger was the sudden gush of smoke from the cooking fire. It took only seconds for the backdraft to fill the small room with choking and noxious fumes. Coughing and spluttering, he pressed a bandanna to his face.

How had that happened? It did not occur to the young bronc-peeler that skulduggery was taking place above his head. All he knew was that to remain inside the cabin was not an option. He would be overcome within minutes. Clutching the Henry to his chest, he hustled across to the door and dragged it open. A brief pause on the threshold, then he launched his lithe frame out into the open. His intention was to take cover behind the horse trough.

And he would have made it, had not Fernando Estrela been ready for just such a manoeuvre. As Crawley appeared,

Estrela launched himself on to his opponent's back. They both went down in a heap. But the Mexican had the advantage of surprise and emerged on top. He did not waste any time. Will Crawley did not know what hit him.

The rusty knife Estrela had secured from the abandoned wagon was driven hard into Crawley's back. Once, twice, three times it rose and fell.

The Mexican stood up. He leaned over the dead man, gasping in lungfuls of air, the knife raised. But there would be no further resistance from Will Crawley. The stand-off was over. He threw the gore-smeared blade away as if it was poison, then scrambled back onto the roof and removed the blockage.

Quintel emerged from the barn and walked across to the cabin. Exhibiting a cold disregard for the deceased, he retrieved the knife and wiped it clean on the dead man's shirt, then handed it back to his associate.

Ever the ruthless brigand, Quintel rapidly brushed off the violent confrontation, announcing with a cheery grin that he was hungry. 'There's grub awaiting us inside the cabin, Fern. Seems a pity to waste it. My stomach's rumbling louder than a herd of charging buffalo.'

He laughed. The raucous bellow was rather too loud. It was certainly no expression of amusement, rather a release of taut nerves and strained muscles. Much as he tried to make light of their recent foray, it had taken its toll.

But not enough to affect his appetite.

Not so the Mexican. At that moment, the last thing on Fernando Estrela's mind was filling his stomach. Exactly the opposite, in fact. The undigested beavertail remains were regurgitated in a spasm of lubberly wretching. Another ten minutes passed before he stumbled into the cabin.

Quintel had thrown open the windows to allow the smoke to dissipate.

'Mighty fine stew, Fern,' he commented without noticing his associate's drawn and haggard features. 'Get a plate and fill up. There's plenty left.'

'I theenk stomach need rest and plenty of water first,' he gurgled, hugging the offending portion of his anatomy.

Only then did Quintel heed the man's waxy look.

'You don't look too good, *hombre*,' he muttered pushing the jug of moonshine across the table. 'A hefty slug of this will soon fix you up.'

Fernando complied. He coughed and spluttered as the fiery tipple burned its way down his gullet. But it certainly appeared to do the trick, bringing some much needed colour to his cheeks. He took another swig and immediately felt better.

'What did I tell you?' breezed Quintel. 'Now ladle out some grub and eat up. We have work to do.'

A half hour later and both men were feeling like their old selves.

The first task was to hunt out some suitable footwear in the back room so recently occupied by the Crawleys. It was a strange experience for Estrela to delve through the personal possessions of the dead men. The very thought of the disposal of the three bodies down a convenient ravine was less harrowing now that he had recovered his composure, and he set about carrying out the task.

Quintel was more pragmatic. Guns, ammunition and fresh duds were his priorities, followed by another plate of rabbit stew from the cauldron simmering on the fire.

'Reckon we'll stay here the night, then set off in the morning,' he declared while forking the delicious repast into his mouth with one hand. The other reached for a glass of moonshine. 'By hokey, these guys sure knew a thing or two about living well out here in the wilds. This chow is a sight better than the slop served out at Happy Jack's.'

Fernando nodded in agreement. 'Ees lucky for us you knew about thees place, *patrón.*' His beaming smile dissolved as he thought back. 'Not so good for poor old Mustang, though.'

Quintel lifted his shoulders in a listless apathetic disinterest. 'You shouldn't feel so blue about it. His allegiance ought to have been with the Shadows, not some guys from way back.' To emphasize the point, he punched out the crown of the hat he had taken from Will Crawley. Quintel preferred to wear his headgear Texas fashion. It was a new Stetson. His old one had been shredded by the young horse-tamer following the unwise exposure in the barn. 'A Judas, that's all he turned out to be. The skunk don't deserve any sympathy.'

Once the meal was finished, smokes were lit as each man retreated into his own thoughts. Quintel was already plotting how to avenge his dead brother. That was now his number one priority. Although he also secretly aspired to the status his younger kin had failed to achieve.

8

Welcome to Maverick

The last two miles were taken at walking pace. Cole needed time to think, to absorb the terrain. Probing eyes lit upon memorable landmarks. Angel Rock over to his right with its distinctively coned summit; the elongated ridge of sandstone on the left where he had discovered the remains of an abandoned *pueblo* while out hunting; and the towering saguaros everywhere amidst the splay of mesquite, catclaw and tamarisk.

His first sighting of the town itself was the white spire of the church. A lump caught in the back of his throat as, slowly, the rest of the buildings resolved themselves into a familiar amalgam.

Ivor Seagrove's livery stable still occupied the lot beside Swiss Creek. But the town had grown to double its previous size. Buildings of all sizes stretched back from the main street. Some of them looked mighty smart. He drew the sorrel to a halt beneath the overhanging canopy of a cottonwood. Now that he had finally arrived, a nervous tension rippled through his tight frame. He felt like a kid on his first date.

Would Marcia be pleased to see him? A wide, loving smile of welcoming forgiveness lighting up that beautiful countenance. Or would it be a surly frown of disdain? And Joey. Would his son even recognize the sorry excuse of a father who had abandoned him? Now that the time had arrived for facing up to his failings, Cole was reluctant to take the final plunge.

He stepped down and lit up a cheroot. The smoke helped to calm his trembling nerves. At that moment, a wagon trundled across the creek bridge and headed his way. It drew to a halt. The bed of the wagon was filled with farming supplies.

A young guy clad in faded dungarees and a slouch hat called out a cheery greeting. 'Hi there, stranger. Ain't seen you around here before. New to these parts?'

'Guess you could say that,' replied the wary newcomer. He was hedging his bets. No need to disclose any past associations.

'Well you ain't likely to enter a more friendly town in the whole of the territory.' He pointed to a signboard pinned up on another tree. It read *Welcome to Maverick: elevation — 3,226 feet — population 1,257.* This latter had been crossed out and been replaced by 1,259.

The man elaborated. 'A neighbour of mine has just had twins. My wife is expecting our first child in the fall. We sure are looking forward to being a true family.' He held out a hand. Cole took it. The guy's grip was firm and sincere. 'The name's Harvey Cumstick.'

'I'm the Re — Cole Rickard,' the newcomer quickly corrected. He had become so used to being addressed as the Reno Kid that he almost forgot. This chirpy dude had caused his guard to drop, the natural caution to slip. He coughed to hide the lapse in concentration. 'I'm thinking of settling down here myself.'

The hesitancy passed unnoticed. The name clearly meant nothing to Cumstick. The guy must have moved into the valley some time after Cole had left.

'You've made a wise choice, Mr Rickard. Maverick is going places. There's plenty of land for everybody if'n you're into farming or ranching. And there's no animosity between the various factions. We all get along fine. There's even a sheep herder in one of the branch draws to the north. I run a small spread down the valley apiece. The Smiling Face.' He pointed to the brand etched onto his wagon. It matched the guy's beaming grin. 'We're doing pretty well. Got a hundred head of prime Herefords. And I also breed pigs and chickens. Lucy, my wife, grows all our own vegetables in her garden.'

Cumstick was more garrulous than a snake-oil salesman. Cole couldn't resist a smile. But he liked the guy. The rancher was a good advert for the town. Though if truth be told, the listener was a mite jealous. It was more than that. He envied the guy. This young farmer appeared to have the perfect life. Everything that Cole Rickard aspired to but had so far been unable to hold down.

Once again, the questions loomed.

Would it ever come about? Was he ever going to be permitted to finally bury the Reno Kid? Or was his destiny already predetermined? Forever fated to be a wandering gunfighter, awaiting that inevitable final showdown.

He struggled to maintain a sanguine outlook to keep the gloom from his reply.

'You sure give a good account of the place,' Cole averred, pasting on his best effort at a positive response. 'Let's hope things turn out right for me as well.'

'All you need is an optimistic outlook. It sure has served me well. Nice meeting you, Cole,' replied Cumstick. 'If'n you stick around, we're bound to meet up at the monthly hoedown in the Buckeye saloon.'

Cole's face registered surprise on hearing the name of his old business interest. He covered the slack jawbone with a quick rejoinder. 'This place serve cold beer? My throat's drier than the desert wind.'

'Flush Harry keeps a fine cellar. Best saloon in Maverick. No cardsharps either. Any tinhorns that figure he's an easy touch soon get a burr up their asses.' He chuckled at his indelicacy before slapping the leathers and moving off with a final, 'See you around.'

Cole stubbed out the cheroot and mounted up. So his old partner was still in charge and keeping everyone in line. Cole was still in the dark regarding Donovan's use of his nickname. He had no inkling that it had been his notoriety that had maintained the peace for so long before that final ignominious confrontation with Wesco Doyle.

His number one priority now was to call in at the Buckeye and seek Harry's help in contacting Marcia and his son. Walking the sorrel down the middle of the main street was an edifying yet disturbing experience. Many things had changed.

The town now had street lighting, and all the stores were connected by boardwalks with verandas.

But some things never changed. The name of Chalk Fenton was still emblazoned on the law office signboard. The starpacker was slouching in his chair outside as was his usual custom around midday. Cole pulled his hat low to shade out his features. He had no wish to court attention this early on.

He urged the sorrel quickly past the law office. But the sheriff paid him no heed. Just another itinerant traveller passing through.

Further down was the Buckeye. A much larger sign than previously now graced the two buildings. Donovan had patently acquired the adjoining empty property. Cole wondered if perhaps he had acquired a new partner as well to help fund the enterprise. According to the sign, it now incorporated a dance hall and theatre in addition to the regular saloon.

And it even looked as if a fresh coat of paint had recently been applied. Perhaps

Flush Harry had somehow been expecting a visit? Wishful thinking on Cole's part. There was no chance of anybody knowing about his current appearance. He moved across to the hitch rail and dismounted.

Stepping up onto the boardwalk, he paused before entering the saloon and lit up another cheroot. He needed the smoke to settle his nerves, give him chance to figure out a line of approach. After readying himself, he took a step forward and almost collided with a woman hurrying the other way.

'Pardon me, ma'am,' he apologized doffing his hat.

The woman looked up. It was Miss Aveline Beddows. So astounded was she at seeing this disquieting memory from the past, that she dropped the bolts of cloth she was carrying. Cole quickly retrieved the fallen items. The starchy dame had made no secret of her distaste for the infamous bounty hunter when he had begun courting her friend all those years ago. Clearly she was still running up dresses for the local women. And time hadn't softened that austere demeanour. Her beaky snout was still stuck in the clouds. Some things never changed.

But Cole didn't hold a grudge. 'Allow me to help you carry your things…' But he was given no chance to deliver the gallant gesture.

'Wh-what are y-you doing h-here …?' the pedantic spinster blurted out, shocked by this man's abrupt and unexpected appearance. The stammered reaction became more pronounced. 'You're … you're … It can't be…You should be… '

'How is Marcia?' Cole interrupted without thought for the woman's bewilderment. He assumed it was just a natural surprise at meeting him after five long years. He was more concerned about other matters than this woman's disbelief at his unannounced return to Maverick. 'Is she in good health? And Joey, how's he?'

He wasn't afforded the opportunity to proffer any more questions. Nor did he receive an answer. The startled woman shook her head, staring at him as if he were some kind of ghost, a macabre denizen impossible to comprehend. She couldn't escape quickly enough. Cole was mystified. The woman appeared to be terrified of him. Scared out of her wits. Surely he hadn't been that much of an ogre.

He launched a puzzled frown at the woman's back. It didn't make any sense.

Shoulders lifted in acceptance. Women were a law unto themselves; it was best for a guy not to even try figuring out their motives. He quickly turned his attention to a more pressing matter.

The front window afforded a panoramic view of the saloon's interior. There he was, standing behind the bar: Flush Harry Donovan, as large as life. He looked much the same, a few extra grey hairs, and that belly was protruding more than it ought. A glass of beer was under close scrutiny. Cole smiled. His old partner always had been a stickler when it came to dispensing the finest quality beverage.

He pushed through the door and gave the room a closer inspection. As expected, the back mirror was highly polished. The gaudy painting of a somewhat scantily clad female now graced the wall above. Otherwise everything appeared the same. It was as if he had only been away a couple of days. He sauntered over to the bar.

'Be with you in a moment,' the saloon owner said without taking his eye off the foaming brew. 'Just checking this delivery is up to standard. The Buckeye takes pride in always serving its customers nothing but the best.'

'Glad to see you're keeping up the high standards,' muttered the newcomer.

The beer checker froze. For a moment he just stood there, stiff as a pikestaff. Then his eyes slowly shifted to regard the speaker. So stunned was he at the vision now before him, that the glass slipped from his hand and smashed on the bar top. The contents spilled across the polished surface, but went unheeded. Those staring peepers maintained their hypnotic fixation on the newcomer.

Then his mouth began flapping. But nothing emerged.

Cole blinked. His brow furrowed. This was the same reaction as that from Aveline Beddows. Surely he wasn't that much of an unwelcome pariah?

At last, Donovan found his voice. 'Is it really you, Cole? But it can't be.'

Cole was becoming a mite exasperated by this bizarre behaviour. He grabbed Flush Harry's hand and touched it to his stubbly face. 'Feel that, Harry. Whiskers and flesh. It ain't no ghost you're touching.'

'But it can't be... You're supposed to be —'

'What in thunder is going on around here?' Cole's frustration was bubbling over. 'First I have Aveline Beddows figuring I'm some kind of apparition. Now you. What gives, Harry?'

The saloon owner shook off the torpor that had gripped his innards. He called across to a bartender who was clearing some tables. 'Hey, Digweed! Clear up this mess, will you? I got some business

125

to discuss with this gentleman in the back office.'

'Sure thing, boss,' came the drawled reply.

Without another word, Donovan led the way. Once in the privacy of his office, he poured two glasses of whiskey, handed one to his guest and downed the other in a single draught. 'You best do the same, Cole. You're gonna need it.'

'I don't like the sound of this, Harry.' The reply was faltering, hesitant. The drink remained untouched. 'What's been happening here that's so all-fired unsavoury?'

'You ain't gonna like it.'

'Just tell me!' Cole's voice had risen to a barely controlled bark.

'Fact is ... we all thought you were dead.'

'Dead! How come?'

'And that ain't all.' Donovan swallowed nervously. 'Marcia has remarried. Joey now has a new stepfather that he calls Pa.'

This time it was Cole's turn to display stunned shock. It was total and absolute.

He slumped into a chair. The whiskey disappeared down his throat. He held out the glass for a refill. That vanished at an equally fast rate. Only then did Cole Rickard turn back to face his old friend. His face was a blank mask behind which all manner of disparate thoughts were churning.

'You best spill the beans, Harry.'

Donovan sat down behind his desk. He folded his arms thinking how best to explain away such a screwball disclosure.

'The guy's name is Luther Duggan. He arrived in Maverick about a year after you left claiming that the Reno Kid was dead. Everyone was shocked at this announcement. Not least Marcia. Duggan gave the impression of having been in business with you up north in a place called St Elmo, Colorado.'

Cole's body stiffened. His eyes narrowed to thin slivers of blue ice. It had to be his old partner. 'Did this jigger have a broad Irish accent and a lazy squint that gave his face a lobsided appearance?' he shot back. 'Made him look kind of shifty?'

'That's him,' replied Donovan.

Cole bit down on his lower lip. 'I knew the pesky rat as Lex Dooley. He's even had the gall to keep the same initials.'

'He sure had the gift of the gab,' Donovan continued. 'Still does. Before I knew what was happening he had bought into the saloon. Had all these ideas about expanding the business. Then it was Marcia's turn. He charmed her with all that blarney. She was soon hooked like the rest of us. The guy seemed genuine enough. Had the dough to invest, not to mention a bucket full of charisma that included having young Joey hanging on his every word. Marriage soon followed. After all, as far as everybody here was concerned, the guy was telling the truth. Why should we think otherwise? You were dead, so she was no longer committed.'

'I see you've bought old Jackson's place next door. Was that his idea as well?' The cutting remark was laced with irony.

Donovan shrugged. 'You and me had intended doing that anyway. And it sure was a good move. We run dances and the monthly hoedown. And the top acts from around the country have been booked in.'

This was not what Cole wanted to hear. 'You two seem to have hit it off big time.' The remark emerged as a scathing hit of sarcasm. 'Reckon all that Irish hooey didn't need to talk you around.'

'Now that ain't fair, Cole,' protested Donovan. 'If'n I'd known what the skunk was up to, I'd never have gone along with making him a partner, or letting him go anywhere near Marcia. You know me better than that.'

Cole knew he had overstepped the mark. He apologized, acknowledging that it was his anger that was getting the better of his mouth.

'Sorry about that, Harry. I ain't thinking straight. This varmint has really done the dirty on me. Did he say how I happened to meet this unfortunate end?'

'One gunfight too many.' Donovan's eyes lifted as if to imply it couldn't have been anything else, knowing Cole as he did.

'Guess I asked for that,' came back the sheepish reply.

Donovan smiled to show there were no hard feelings, then continued. 'He reckoned you'd been drinking and got into a fracas with some cowhands. The booze slowed you down when they called you out. Duggan claimed to have tried pacifying the punchers, but their leader wanted to acquire that all-important reputation. Far as we were concerned he had succeeded. The Reno Kid was no more.'

A heavy silence descended over the two old partners. Each was cocooned in his own mind warp.

It was Donovan who broke into the tense atmosphere. The saloon boss was coming to realize how easily he and the rest of the town had been hoodwinked by this charlatan. They had all been taken in by his smooth charm, made to look like naive fools, simple-minded dupes.

He gripped the side of the desk, knuckles blanching with an inner fury.

'It was all a load of flimflam to wheedle his way into our confidence. The guy's a no-good trickster, a fraud. It makes me ashamed of my Irish roots to have believed all that hogwash. I'm beginning to wonder when he intended pulling the plug on me. Vanishing in the night with all our profits.'

Tight features hardened as he concluded the bleak account. 'And to cap it all, he reckoned that your final choking request allegedly urged him to visit Maverick and smooth things over with your wife. Well he's sure done that while ingratiating himself fully into her confidence.'

'Not to mention her bed,' Cole snarled, downing another shot of whiskey.

9

Shake Hands with the Devil

Cole lurched to his feet and paced the room. The truth bore no resemblance whatsoever to this lurid charade.

It was time to set the record straight.

By the time the Reno Kid arrived in St Elmo, six months had passed following his ignominious flight from Maverick. Surprisingly, he had slotted back into his old profession without much effort. That wasn't to say that he did not regret the fateful actions that had led to that sorry affair.

The question as to whether he would have done anything different was one that had no answer. The die was cast and he had to accept the consequences. For now, at least. Perhaps at some point in the none too distant future he could return and hopefully smooth over troubled waters. But he knew deep down that it would take a long time for the dust to settle.

Reno booked into the Comfort Hotel. Having sampled the bed in his room, he had to agree with the owner's claim that the premises possessed the softest mattresses in Colorado. A solid night's sleep and a hearty breakfast now behind him, he ventured outside. An early mist hung around the tops of the mountains and the air was cool and crisp. St Elmo was high up in the San Isobel Range. Even in summer it was an effort for the sun to drag itself above the rimrock and make its presence felt.

The town was just another gold mining settlement. It had only been in existence for a few years but already it had become the hub of the local area. Supplying mining equipment, the town also acted as the jumping off point for prospectors heading into the surrounding hills.

It had originally been given the prosaic name of Forest City due its being surrounded by dense stands of pine and aspen. The more imaginative appendage stemmed from a council member who had read a popular novel of the day back in 1866 entitled *St Elmo*. It was about the patron saint of sailors. The guy had once been a ship's captain and the name stuck.

In the meantime, another piece of lawless endeavour was beckoning. Reno breathed in the crystal clear ozone then headed across the street for the marshal's office. That was the place where wanted notices were always to be found. Judging by the date on the one he was now studying, it had only just been pinned up. A jasper sporting the flamboyant title of Dirty Dan Pickersgill was wanted for robbery. Reno had never heard the name before.

He scanned the description which indicated that the outlaw had carried out his latest caper only two days before. A regular practice appeared to have served the outlaw well regarding the manner of his skulduggery. Hence, five similar robberies had been ascribed to the same perpetrator.

Removing the notice, Reno knocked on the office door. A muted voice invited him to enter. Marshal Line Satcher was pouring himself a cup of coffee. He recognized the newcomer immediately.

'Ain't seen you around these parts for a spell, Kid.'

His greeting was even. Not exactly friendly, but neither was it hostile as with many of his contemporaries in other towns. Bounty hunters never quite knew how their search for paid work would be received. A working relationship existed between these two stalwarts that had served both men well in the past.

Their last encounter had resulted in Reno sharing his reward with Satcher due to help given in apprehending Gentleman Jim Swinburn — a shifty gambler and confidence trickster.

'Fancy a cup of my finest Arbuckles?' The marshal didn't wait for a reply. He levered himself out of his chair and wandered across to the ever-bubbling pot on the stove. Pouring a mug of the steaming brew, he passed it across. 'Guess you're here about Dirty Dan.'

The manhunter laid the notice down on the marshal's desk. 'Got any extra information you can give me, Linc?' he asked sipping at the scalding drink. The brew was thick, strong and sweet, just as he liked it.

'Last sighting of the critter was from Lex Dooley. The guy runs the mining equipment store down the street. Pickersgill robbed him in broad daylight three days ago. A couple of bullets chased him out of town, but the critter escaped unhurt. Dooley reckons the cocky braggart stupidly let slip he was heading for Leadville. So like as not he'll go over Woodstock Pass by way of the Sherrod Loop.'

Reno scratched his head. 'I ain't never been that way before. Any help you can give to catch up with this dude would be much appreciated.' The inference was clear. Help given by Linc Satcher would be rewarded. And with the marshal possessing an intimate knowledge of local terrain, his assistance would be vital.

'He's got a three day start,' the lawman averred, handing over a large Havana. 'I reckon your best bet is to take the old Indian trail over the Devil's Horseback.'

The two men lit up, imbibing the aroma and taste of the renowned cigars. Satcher went on to explain the prospective short cut. Both men then went outside and the marshal pointed to a distinctive mountain peak.

'There's a narrow trail up through the trees. But it's clear enough to follow. Always make sure to keep Mount Princeton on your right. By travelling light and replenishing your supplies at Tin Cup and Winfield, you should easily get ahead of him. He'll have to go by Twin Lakes before dropping down into Leadville. That's the ideal spot to nail the bastard.'

'Best if'n I hit the trail perty soon then,' Reno concluded. 'Three days is a good start. The only problem is my horse is plum tuckered out. He needs a rest.'

Satcher had the answer. 'Hang on here a minute.'

He went back inside the office and quickly scribbled out a note of authorization.

'Give this to Jake Harlow who runs the Turret livery barn. Tell him that you're doing some work for me.' He offered the bounty hunter a knowing wink. 'Ain't so far from the truth, is it?' As Reno turned away, the starpacker offered a whimsical piece of advice. 'Keep well up wind of Pickersgill. That moniker wasn't granted lightly. The guy has a distinct aversion to soap.'

Reno laughed. 'So it says on the dodger. Do you reckon the knucklehead realized he was leaving his calling card when he pulled all those jobs?'

Satcher shrugged. 'At least it should give you fair warning of his approach.'

Before heading down to the livery, Reno decided to call in at the mining store and find out some more information about the robbery.

Dooley was a bluff rangy Irishman

with a brogue to match. A profusion of unruly red hair cascaded from beneath the brown derby perched askew his head. A twitchy right eye gave his face an odd lilt. The other twinkled evocatively and spoke of hidden depths that would only be revealed to his most trusted confidents.

A born salesman, Dooley was eager to draw the newcomer into his confidence. The lyrical cadence was a distinct help in gaining people's trust. He was pleased to meet the renowned bounty hunter. They shook hands. Reno was well versed in the vagaries of human nature, but the Irishman's jovial and affable manner had him hooked.

Dooley explained that he had started out in mining but quickly discovered that serving the needs of others was far more lucrative. 'And to be sure it was a sight less hard on the body.' The hearty guffaw exuded a jaunty humour that did not quite reach his eyes. Reno joined in. He liked the guy. But had he paid more attention to the veiled signs, perhaps history would have followed a different course.

'You catch this varmint, me fine fella, and return the goods,' Dooley promised in a low, conspiratorial manner, 'and you'll find that Lex Dooley will be very grateful.' He did not elaborate, but the hint was that an extra reward on top of the official bounty would be forthcoming.

The manhunter left soon after with a positive impression of the man who was to become his partner ... and stinger.

Following Marshal Satcher's instructions, Reno managed to reach Twin Lakes in two days. He reckoned that he must now be a good half day ahead of the outlaw. That was always presupposing that Dirty Dan followed an expected route. He had no reason to think otherwise.

Unless, of course, the heist man remembered dropping himself in the mire by mentioning Leadville to the robbed storekeeper. The next few hours would resolve that issue. If'n the guy had deliberately laid a false trail, Reno would be up the creek without a paddle.

All he could do now was lay the trap he had figured out, then wait and hope.

It was around four in the afternoon that the steady drub of hoof beats assailed his acute hearing. Could this be his man?

He peered out from behind a tall aspen to view the open track to the south. The lone rider was wearing a red checked shirt and black leather vest. His wide-brimmed plainsman hid the face, but Reno knew from the description given by the St Elmo lawman, as well as Lex Dooley, that this was his man.

Reno tugged on the rope he had stretched across the trail between two tree trunks. It was tied at chest height, the intention being to unseat a horseman. A watchful rider might just spot the impedance in time. But Pickersgill was likely too sure of himself now to warrant any extra caution. Leadville was over the next ridge, no more than two hours' ride distant. He would be there before nightfall.

Reno hid behind the broad trunk and waited. The pace of the approaching horse never faltered. The danger had not been spotted. Seconds later, a burbled cry of anguish was followed by a dull thud as the upended rider hit the dirt. The ambusher rushed out from cover, six-gun at the ready, but he had no need for any concern. The guy had been knocked out cold.

Quickly, he dragged Dirty Dan into the shelter of the camp he had set up in a small glade some one hundred yards off the main trail. It was a tough task. Pickersgill was a burly dude who clearly didn't believe in skimping his grub. He also exuded a sour aroma redolent of stale booze and sweat. Line Satcher had not exaggerated; this guy needed the attentions of carbolic and a hot tub.

And Reno would likewise require the deluxe treatment following this caper.

He tied the outlaw securely to a thin trunk, then went in search of the guy's horse. Luckily it had not wandered far, having discovered some succulent grasses beside one of the lakes.

Back in camp Reno searched the saddle-bags for the stolen items but found nothing. Dirty Dan must have stashed them away. Probably, he was amassing a stockpile until such time as he could head for the bright lights of California and live the high life for a spell. Reno would soon find out. A mug of ice-cold water was tossed into the bearded mush of his prisoner.

'What in the name of blue blazes is going on here?' Pickersgill railed as he coughed and spluttered, shaking his head. Only then did the realization dawn that he was fastened up tighter than a calico queen's corsets. 'Who in hell's teeth are you?' he demanded, struggling to get free. It was a fruitless exercise.

'I'm the Reno Kid, the guy that's taking you back to St Elmo to stand trial and earn me a good payoff,' Reno smiled, extracting the Wanted dodger from his pocket. He held it up in front of the scowling captive. The icy grin was instantly replaced by a menacing grimace that augured badly for Pickersgill should his answer be in the negative. 'Now where are all the goods you've stolen?'

'A damned bounty hunter!' rasped the captive. 'Well you can go to hell, mister. It'll be me that sees you facing a jury. I ain't done nothing wrong. You have the wrong man. Now set me free. Then I might decide to forget this ever happened.'

'Wrong answer, Dirty Dan.' Reno smiled when the prisoner's eyes bulged. A pinched nose emitted a lurid sniff of distaste. 'And the name sure fits. Now we can make this easy. Or you and me are gonna fall out big time. Which is it to be?'

'Stuff you, Reno,' snarled the brash outlaw. 'You've got nothing on me. I ain't carrying no stolen goods.'

'That's cos you've hidden the loot. Cough up now and I'll make sure the law hears about your co-operation.'

But still Dirty Dan maintained a stoical disdain and refused to co-operate. 'I've heard all about you, Reno. But it don't scare me none.'

'So what have you heard?'

'That you're a no-good yeller backshooter.'

The sneering insult saw the Kid grabbing a hold of the outlaw's shirt. His revolver snapped to half cock and jammed into Pickersgill's neck. His verbal response was a barely controlled hiss. 'And you'll also have heard that guys like me have the choice of how we deliver up scum like you. Now figure out which it's gonna be for you if'n that loot don't come my way.' The gun went to full cock, its hard barrel matching the cold, merciless gaze.

The outlaw was staring death in the face.

'OK, OK!' he croaked, his heart racing at fifty to the dozen. The brigand perceived that there was no mercy in the flinty regard. Refuse to co-operate now and he would assuredly be strumming with the Devil. 'OK, OK, y-you win,' he stuttered. 'I'll take you to where I've buried the loot.'

The hideaway proved to be a cave up a side gulch that had once been home to a grizzly bear. And there was a considerable amount of gold, paper money and various pink-tied documents stashed away. It was one of these latter that was to draw the Reno Kid into the underhanded machinations of Lex Dooley.

Pickersgill revealed that he had been planning one last job in Leadville before heading for California. So Reno's assessment of the guy's plans had been correct.

No problems were encountered on the ride back to St Elmo. At the first night's camp Reno cleaned himself up in a creek. Dirty Dan was kept securely trussed up then forced to endure the same treatment under the watchful eye of his captor.

Once his prisoner had been delivered to the marshal's office, Reno called in at the bank to collect his reward, a portion of which found its way into the marshal's pocket. Both of them then moseyed across to the saloon to celebrate their windfall.

Reno later went to visit Lex Dooley, who was overjoyed to retrieve his stolen goods. The storekeeper was as voluble as before. And he kept to his word. One of the documents was the filing claim to a gold mine he had won in a poker game. And it was this that found the Reno Kid enmeshed within the spider's web.

'I've had it assessed and transferred into my name,' Dooley enthused, prodding the affidavit. 'And I'm giving you the chance to invest in what is already a lucrative prospect. With your input, we'll be able to buy the heavy drilling equipment to really make this mine pay big bucks.' He looked at the somewhat bewildered potential new partner. 'It's a sure-fire winner. But it needs added capital that I don't have. So what do you say?'

Reno's furrowed brow indicated he was tossing over the pros and cons of the proposed joint venture. His head was rather thick after one too many at the saloon. Perhaps if he had been more alert, Dooley's persuasive eloquence would have been subject to greater scrutiny. He merely skimmed over it. A few peremptory nods of understanding and he was more than happy to give his consent.

'Sounds good to me, Lex,' Reno declared rather diffidently. There was only one thing that was bothering him. 'Only problem is, I don't know a thing about mining.'

The Irishman hawked out a jaunty guffaw. 'You don't need to. We hire in the labour to do all the hard work. All we have to do is sit back and rake in the profits.'

The Kid thought for a moment trying to gather his thoughts. It would make life a lot easier. And this guy seemed genuine enough.

Everything would be above board and legal. How could he lose?

Prophetic last words that were to cost him dear.

Nevertheless, he signed on the dotted line confirming the deal.

10

Snake Bite

Everything went smoothly for the first six months of their association. Reno had taken to overseeing work carried on at the mine. Ore samples had indeed proven their worth. And the seam was highly productive. The money in the bank was mounting up and all seemed well with the world.

With Reno away from civilization for substantial periods of time, the opportunities for young guns to challenge his reputation were scant. He had reverted to calling himself Cole Rickard. Another six months and there would be enough dough stashed away in the company safe to enable him to sell his share of the mine. That would let him move away and start up afresh where nobody would recognize the name of the Reno Kid.

Maybe he would head back East to Chicago, or New York. Perhaps even a trip over to Europe would be forthcoming. The options were unlimited for a man of visible means. He still thought about his wife and son, though less and less as time passed. Dreams filled his head. But like all bubbles, they were bound to burst eventually.

It happened one Sunday morning.

Dooley wanted him to make a personal inspection of the mine. A new territorial ruling had been issued that stated all mines operating above a certain threshold had to receive an annual inspection to determine safety procedures. Apparently, too many unwarranted accidents had been reported and the authorities needed to act. A wire had been received from the Colorado Mining Legislature stating that a surprise visit was planned for the coming week.

Urgent attention was, therefore, necessary to ensure their operation complied with the rules.

'Just make certain there are no loose

props, or rotten beams. Anything you find, let me know and I'll arrange for them to be replaced before the inspectors arrive.'

The urgency in Dooley's voice and his stoic regard were at odds to the normally light-hearted banter. The serious tone was a convincing enough argument for Cole. His partner's final declaration was the catalyst that spurred him to abandon his day off. 'Should those inspectors find anything, we could be closed down for months. All our profits will be used up complying with their durned regulations. I'm counting on you to make sure that don't happen.'

During that last six months the mine had been operating at full capacity thanks to the new equipment. And Cole had become well versed in the industry and its operation. So he felt well able to spot any safety hazards that might be present.

Dooley's choice of days had been deliberate. The workers always headed into town on Saturday night and slept off their carousal during the day of rest on Sunday.

As a result, the mine would be devoid of any potential witnesses to what he had in mind for his gullible partner.

Cole set off first thing on Sunday morning. The mine was a two hour ride up into the hills behind St Elmo. There was a steady climb through the stands of pine before he branched left along Staghorn Gulch. At the top end was the Exchequer Mine. Cole had no reason to figure there was any skulduggery afoot. His partner was a more than credible charlatan. All that was on his mind was checking the mine out for any abnormalities.

Had he been thus disposed, perhaps he would have spotted Dooley dogging his trail. But Cole had grown lax in such matters. He had no reason to suspect that anything untoward was afoot. And the trickster made certain to stay well back to prevent such an occurrence. He knew exactly where his unsuspecting partner was headed.

Cole tethered his mount outside the wooden shack that served as an office and cantina. Taking a tallow brand he hurried across to the entrance, first checking the stanchions for firmness and wear. A match was applied to the torch after which he moved into the main body of the diggings. He followed the narrow-gauge horse-drawn railroad, carefully checking every post, roof support and anchoring cable.

They had even installed a steam pump to extract the water that dribbled through cracks in the rock to prevent flooding at the lower levels.

His estimate was that a thorough search should occupy no more than a couple of hours. There were plenty of spare torches scattered throughout the galleries so spotting any unsafe sections should pose no problems. A pot of paint and a brush were held in the other hand to mark those areas needing attention.

Dooley arrived fifteen minutes later. A crafty smirk broke the stern look as he spotted the tethered sorrel. A quick look around informed him that his associate was inside the mine.

'This is where you and me part

company, sucker,' he muttered to himself. 'Permanently. Then I can go pick up where you left off.'

One night in a moment of drunken petulance, Cole had disclosed his innermost regrets concerning his past life in Maverick. The whole sorry episode had come pouring out. The perfect wife and son, a half share in a saloon with a trustworthy partner, a respected position in a town that was going places. In short, the ideal life, the epitome of everything a man of his dubious reputation could desire.

And it had all been destroyed by an arrogant need to prove his machismo. Tears had welled up in his eyes.

But the next day, there was no recollection of the piteous outpouring of grief. Nursing a sore head he mumbled, 'Did I make a fool of myself last night, Lex? Always was too darned talkative after a few drinks.'

'Like what?' asked Dooley nonchalantly.

'Oh! You know, things about my past?'

'To be sure, nothing at all, pard,'

replied the breezy Irishman. 'It was mostly about all those young turks who have tried to outgun you.'

Cole sighed. 'Some'n a guy struggles to live down. Be glad you ain't so burdened, Lex. It's a damn blasted yoke around my neck, to be sure.' He chuckled at the inept effort to copy his partner's lyrical brogue.

Lex Dooley chuckled along with him. But his eyes remained flat and cold as a dead fish. He had remembered every last word. And now he intended to capitalize on that private exposé. Dooley had always hankered after such a life himself. Now he had the chance. By relating a plausible sob story, he was confident of being able to ingratiate himself into Maverick society.

The key to carrying out the dastardly ploy was dynamite. Dooley had read up on its safe use and obtained practical advice from miners purchasing the explosives from the store. He carried the sticks over to the mine entrance and proceeded to secure them to the appropriate beams and cracks in the rock.

Peering inside the dark recess, he listened intently for any sound that would betray his partner's presence. Apart from the constant drip, drip from overhead, silence pervaded. Reno was well inside.

A mirthless smirk cracked the macabre Irish facade. 'This is going to be one showdown from which there will be no escape for the Reno Kid,' he muttered under his breath.

Sufficient fuse wire was attached to the sticks of dynamite, which he fed back across the open ground to a safe haven behind a tailings heap. A match was applied to the fuse. Then he settled back and watched it fizzle and spit, chewing away like a hungry rat scuttling across the sandy shelf towards the final denouement.

'So long, Kid.'

Moments later a series of cataclysmic explosions ripped apart the entrance to the Exchequer Mine. Rumbling and growling like an angry giant, the mountain shuddered in protest. There was no denying the brutal efficiency of high explosives. Broken rock tumbled down, completely blocking the mouth. A huge dust cloud bubbled and fermented out of the shattered entrance to the once vibrant mine.

Dooley was mesmerized, stunned at the wholesale destruction he had wrought. But it was only a temporary aberration. He punched the air and cheered at the total success of his heinous endeavour. Nobody could survive that. Not even the legendary Reno Kid. He spat on the ground.

'You were just too trusting, Kid,' he sighed, almost feeling sorry for the poor sap. 'But a man has to take his chance where he can in this tough life. Winner takes all.'

There was no remorse in the callous indifference to his partner's fate. It was merely a question of the survival of the most devious. And Lex Dooley had hit the jackpot in that respect. He wasted no more time in contemplating his future. That would come on the long ride south to Arizona. First he needed to empty the safe and make a swift departure before the alarm was raised the following day.

But Dooley had made a fatal error of judgement when luring the Reno Kid into his sticky tentacles. By giving the entire running of the mining enterprise over to his new partner, the Irishman had shown little interest in its daily operation. No questions were asked just so long as the profits kept rolling in.

As a result he knew nothing about the safety procedures that Reno had installed on the advice of his new foreman. Hardrock Harris had suggested that a couple of narrow air ducts be driven down from the hillside above the mine to provide fresh air and a means of escape, primarily for noxious gases. But also for men as a last resort should there be a cave-in.

That oversight on Dooley's part was to be his Achilles heel.

The first Cole knew that something was wrong was the rumble of shifting rock. It was preceded by a muted roar that sounded suspiciously like an explosion. He had heard enough of those over the last six months. But how could that be happening? Being a Sunday morning, the mine site was empty.

The groaning and shaking rapidly grew more pronounced. Could it be an earthquake? Dust funnelled down the shaft in which he was working. His blood froze. A mining collapse was not something he had experienced before. It felt and sounded terrifying. All around him the wooden beams were cracking under the strain. Rocks came tumbling down from the fractured roof.

Panic threatened to overwhelm him, freezing his muscles. But the human survival instinct kicked in and found him scrambling towards an upturned ore wagon. Death stared Cole Rickard in the face. He was convinced it had arrived in force when he blacked out.

Sitting in the back office of the Buckeye saloon, Cole paused to light up a cheroot. During the lucidly eloquent description of his adventures since leaving Maverick, Flush Harry Donovan had listened intently. The bottle of whiskey was almost empty. With the grim revelation reaching the point where his old friend was about to enter the welcoming arms of the Reaper, he felt compelled to interject.

'How in thunder did you manage to get out of that scrape? Even the irrepressible Reno Kid must have assumed that his end had arrived.'

'You sure ain't wrong there, buddy,' Cole declared emptying the rest of the whiskey into a glass and imbibing a liberal slug. 'Those rocks were coming down every which way. I had no chance of avoiding them. I ended up with a dislocated shoulder.' He gingerly flexed the injured appendage. 'It still gives me jip in cold weather.'

Then he removed his hat. Donovan couldn't restrain a startled grunt. A livid purple scar was etched into his friend's head above the left ear where hair now refused to grow. Cole ran a finger across the dent in his skull.

'How I survived that is anybody's guess. The Good Lord must have been on my side that day.'

'So how did you get out of that hell hole?'

Stunned by the sudden thump on the head, Reno managed to crawl under the wagon before he passed out. Some time later he came round with a stinking headache. But at least he was still alive. It could have been minutes, hours, or even days. The blackness was complete. All the torches had been extinguished. The only thing that the victim recalled was that he was close to one of the air shafts.

And that was how he managed to escape from the jaws of certain death. He was only able to use one hand due to the dislocation but metal rungs had been inserted for just such an eventuality. With no light, the assent of the narrow flue was literally a matter of touch and go. It was still daylight when he reached the plateau above. The bone-jarring ordeal had taken the better part of two hours.

He pulled his bruised and battered frame out onto the hard rock surface. And there he lay, gulping down lungfuls of oxygen that tasted like pure nectar. Feeling faint and light-headed, the pain in his shoulder throbbed abominably. Rheumy eyes slowly opened, trying to absorb the near-death experience.

According to the sun's position in the azure sky it was around three in the afternoon. He had faced down gunslingers and not batted an eyelid. But almost getting buried alive under a collapsing mine was enough to frighten the Devil himself. His stomach wretched at the thought.

There came a time when he knew that remaining on the exposed plateau was not an option. Scavenging buzzards were circling overhead. He had to reach civilization, or death would surely claim him. After the mind-boggling ascent of the airshaft, there was no way he intended that happening without a fight.

A descent back to ground level was impossible. The acclivitous face of the rock wall precluded any such attempt. The only alternative was to head north and hope to join the main Leadville-Salida trail.

He found a rock pool to slake his thirst and clean up his wounds, of which there were numerous. Then he set off. The trail was fifteen miles as the crow flies. It ought to take no more than a couple of days in this terrain.

In effect, it took him five days of gruelling toil, living off berries and the odd rabbit shot with his revolver. He finally stumbled out onto the trail just as a team of freight wagons was passing. Exhaustion had claimed his tormented body. He finally came round some three days later in the hospital at Salida.

The dislocated shoulder had been re-set but ached abominably. And the head wound had needed a dozen stitches. Apart from that he had come through the ordeal surprisingly well. The doctor in charge released him after two weeks under the proviso that a period of convalescence was needed for another two weeks. Following three days of inactivity, Reno was edging for a return to St Elmo.

The question uppermost in his mind concerned the cause of the mine collapse.

11

Defanged

The shock hit Reno like an express train on learning that his partner had scarpered and taken all their savings. The safe lay wide open. It was completely empty. Nobody knew where Dooley had gone. Reno's sudden re-appearance in the mining town merely compounded the puzzling enigma. The unpaid mine workers were disgruntled, but nobody else in St Elmo had been affected. Sympathy was expressed but little else.

He reported the gruesome incident to the town marshal, but there was little that could be done with the perpetrator having disappeared.

A trip up to the mine enabled him to piece together the macabre course of events. Remnants of the dynamiting told their own story. Reno cursed his folly at being duped by the silver-tongue blackguard. How could he have been so easy to fool, so gullible?

It was the Irish blarney. The guy sure knew how to spin a tale.

And he had exercised the same slick glibness upon the citizens of Maverick.

But it was worse than that. Dooley had been prepared to kill his partner in a most hideous manner to attain his loathsome goal.

The recollection made Cole see red. He hammered a bunched fist on Flush Harry's desk. Donovan's green parrot, a reminder of his Irish heritage, squawked loudly in protest at being roused. That was one of the reasons the saloon owner had accepted the charlatan Dooley's explanation without too much effort; the shared culture had a lot to answer for.

Cole ignored the tetchy bird as another slug of whiskey slid effortlessly down his gullet. It helped to calm his wrangled nerves.

So what to do now?

'Duggan is due here' — Harry looked

at his watch, checking it with the ticking timepiece on the wall — 'in thirty minutes. We have a meeting to discuss changing our supplier of beer.'

Cole smiled. 'Well it's sure gonna be a meeting he never expected.'

'How do you figure on playing this, Cole?' Donovan's voice was edged with an uncertain waver. He took it for granted this guy was itching for a showdown where gunplay was likely to be involved. That was the last thing Flush Harry wanted. 'I sure don't cotton to a shootout in the Buckeye.'

Cole's reply was unexpected and initiated a sigh of relief.

'Neither do I, Harry. Much as I'd like to fill the critter with a gut full of lead, those days are over. I intend doing everything according to the letter of the law.' His insistence that the infamous Reno Kid's past was buried seemed heartfelt and genuine. 'Sure, I'll confront him. Then I'll march the bastard over to the sheriff's office. Let Fenton sort it out. Attempted murder ought to merit a long stretch in the pen. Not to mention bigamy. Last I heard this territory had no plans to go the way of Utah with those wife-collecting Mormons.'

Over the next few minutes they quickly thrashed out a ploy to catch Lex Dooley, or Luther Duggan as he now called himself, on the wrong foot.

The parrot seemed to agree with their plan. 'That's the way to do it! That's the way to do it!' came the effusive chuckle as the two men returned to the barroom.

It was agreed that Cole should conceal himself behind a velvet drape on the upper veranda. Donovan, meanwhile, would greet his new partner from behind the bar. The saloon man was adamant that the use of a gun would be from him alone, and only to get the drop on the blackguard. Shooting would be a last resort should he resist.

The hollow sound of the wall clock chiming the half hour brought the participants of the confrontation to a height of acute tension. All eyes focused on the Buckeye's front door. The regular patrons were kept in the dark about the coming showdown. It would only have heightened tensions and given the game away.

A long minute passed before a measured tread heralded the arrival of the trickster. Cole peered from behind the heavy drape. He was surprised on suddenly being confronted by the snake. Dooley was wearing a smart tailor-made suit with white linen shirt and black necktie secured by a diamond stickpin. And all purchased with stolen money. Cole was seething.

He now regretted having left his guns in Flush Harry's office.

Then again, perhaps that was a wise decision.

Dooley strolled across to the bar acting as if he owned the place. The cocky strut was no idle performance. He had taken over from Cole Rickard, assuming his role in every respect. The skunk had every reason to sport the beaming smile of greeting.

Bestirring himself, Cole struggled to control his temper as he emerged from cover. Slowly he began to descend the stairs. Dooley was facing away from his cheated one-time partner.

'You seem to be doing mighty well for a no-good thief and fraudster, Lex.' The remark was delivered in a flat monotone making its impact all the more effective. The general babble of conversation was stilled as all eyes turned towards the speaker as he descended the stairs. 'I'm kinda wondering how you came by that good fortune. Care to enlighten these good folks?'

Dooley froze. There was no mistaking that evenly measured voice. In the flick of a sidewinder's tongue the question flashed across his brain as to how the Reno Kid had managed to extricate himself from that death-dealing explosion. But it was only momentary.

Any normal dude would have been transfixed by the sudden challenge. But not Lex Dooley. The cat was well and truly out of the bag. His odious trickery had been uncovered. There was only one option left. And he took it.

Unaware that momentous events were unfolding around her, Polkadot Sal, one of the show girls, had wandered into the bar. Rehearsals for a forthcoming performance had just finished in the theatre next door.

'Pull me a jar of beer, Digweed,' she said in a croaky voice. 'My throat is dry as dust after all that warbling.'

The girl was not given the opportunity to assuage her thirst. Dooley saw his chance and took it. He hauled out a Colt Lighting hidden in a purpose-made shoulder holster and pumped a couple of shots at the unarmed man on the stairs.

Luckily for Cole his accuracy was awry. The bullets chewed slivers of wood from the banister rail inches from where Cole was standing. He dropped to the floor.

Without waiting for a reaction to his gunplay, Dooley grabbed the singer and jabbed the barrel of the pistol into her swanlike neck. He then backed away towards the door. 'Any of you critters follow, and the dame is dead meat.' Another bullet encouraged the saloon occupants to stay well back.

'The rat means it,' Cole shouted. 'He's capable of anything.'

Outside on the street, there was only one other horse beside his own. Dooley recognized it as the sorrel owned by Reno. He slugged the girl over the head and tossed her to one side like a discarded rag doll. After mounting his own cayuse, he hauled off with the gun through the saloon window until it clicked on empty.

Then, leading the sorrel behind, he dug in the spurs and galloped out of town, only abandoning the animal when he was well clear.

All hell had broken loose in the Buckeye. Men emerged from cover. All attempts to calm things down were ignored as they struggled to come to terms with the sudden violence that had erupted in their quiet town. Only the raised voice of Flush Harry announcing that drinks were on the house brought the panicking throng to order.

Cole pushed his way through the dense mass of humanity surging over to the bar.

On the street, he helped the injured girl to her feet and sat her down on a chair. Harry soon joined him. He called for the swamper to go fetch the doctor.

'Boy, I never reckoned on him acting that way,' he stuttered out, still bemused by the sudden turnaround of their plan.

'He sure had me fooled as well,' agreed Cole, who had been equally startled by the braggart's quick-witted reactions.

'Did you see which way he went, Sal?' Donovan asked the still woozy songstress. She groaned but managed to point a wavering hand in the direction of the setting sun.

'The guy even had the quick-wittedness to take my horse so I couldn't follow,' Cole railed angrily, having being caught out once again.

'Take my horse,' Donovan offered. 'He's well rested in the corral out back. And you bring that skunk back. I don't care how you do it. The rat's gonna pay dear for making idiots of us all.'

Cole wasted no further words on fruitlessly berating himself. He thanked his friend and hustled round to the rear of the Buckeye to find a large bay mare munching on a nosebag. The horse needed saddling, which wasted more time. Swinging the animal around he pounded off in the direction indicated by Polkadot Sal.

Unlike Dooley, Cole was well acquainted with the local terrain. He quickly figured out that the fleeing Judas would stick to the main Tucson highway. There was a little-used back trail that led over Turkey Flats that would bring him out ahead of the charlatan. He was pretty certain that Dooley would not be aware of it. Half a mile west of Maverick, he branched off down a shallow arroyo.

Pushing the strong bay to its limits, he kept up a punishing pace. All he could do now was hope that his supposition was correct. After an hour of hard riding, Cole rejoined the main trail. The only trouble was he was unarmed. In the heat of the moment the legendary gunfighter had forgotten to pack his hardware.

A desperate search along the edge of the rutted highway soon provided the luck he sought. A rocky ledge above the roadway offered the perfect spot for an ambush. He concealed the bay behind some boulders then scrambled up on to the lofty perch. It afforded a fine view back along the trail.

But Lady Luck has a habit of removing her favours. A sandstorm was brewing from the east. Swirling dust devils danced and cavorted, becoming ever more frenetic in their antics as the storm gathered strength. If it continued directly toward Cole's position, he would be overwhelmed and Lex Dooley could easily escape in the enveloping blizzard.

The fleeing Irishman must also have sensed that he might be caught out and forced to hunker down. He spurred the horse onward, trying to outrun the storm. It was a bold yet reckless manoeuvre. Unseen obstacles could easily cause a fall.

Cole's narrowed gaze struggled to pierce the increasingly opaque gloom. The growing howl of the wind-ravaged sandstorm made it near impossible to see anything else. An approaching rider's hoof beats would be muffled and incoherent.

Cole only became aware of his adversary's close proximity when he saw Dooley's horse tear a hole in the ochre wall. He was no more than fifty yards away and due to pass directly beneath Cole's crouched situation.

The storm now came to his rescue. Dooley had taken heed of the high possibility that he might take a tumble and slowed accordingly to a steady trot.

Cole prepared himself for the leap of a lifetime. His whole body tensed. Judging the moment right was essential. As the rider passed by, he dropped onto the cantle behind him, at the same time swinging a punch at his head. Both men were thrown to the ground in a heap of tangled arms and legs. Having the advantage of surprise, Cole was first on his feet. He dragged Dooley up and delivered a couple of short jabs to his jaw.

The guy staggered back, but he soon recovered. Shaking off the sudden attack, he threw himself at his attacker and bore him down. Both men rolled about in the swirling maelstrom hammering at each other's bodies. Fists flew before Dooley managed to scramble out of reach. He drew his pistol and aimed point blank at his advancing opponent. Once again Cole Rickard stared death in the face.

And once again he was able to thwart the Reaper's invitation.

Dooley had forgotten to reload his revolver. He threw the useless hunk of metal at Cole's head but it was easily evaded. This time it was Cole's turn to gain the upper hand. He sunk a right fist into Dooley's midriff finishing with an uppercut that snapped the critter's head back. A final solid drive and the scheming toad was laid out cold.

Cole sank to the ground. But this was no time to linger. The sandstorm was increasing in force. He quickly tethered the unconscious man with his own lariat and dragged him under a rocky overhang. There they hunkered down to await the storm's passing. Sandstorms can last for days, or blow themselves out in a matter of minutes. This one lasted about half an hour before veering away to the south.

They had been lucky. The sun once again made its presence felt.

Securing Dooley to his saddle, Cole led him back along the main highway on the return trip to Maverick.

Lex Dooley had little to say for himself. He had been caught out bang to rights. No excuses were offered; no regrets expressed. But worst of all, he felt no remorse for the heinous actions he had perpetrated, the lives he had tainted with his abject chicanery. Cole felt only contempt for the guy.

He delivered him to the sheriff, who was more than a mite surprised to witness his prisoner walking into the jailhouse.

'Guess I've lost that bet I had with Harry,' he muttered in a rather glum voice that was accompanied by a cheery smile as he locked Dooley in a cell. Cole gave the remark a quizzical frown. 'Reckon I had you all wrong, Cole. Once a gunslinger always ... as they say.' He held out a hand. Cole gladly accepted it.

'I was wrong and Harry was right. My betting was that you'd bring this jasper back strapped over his horse. You sure appear to have changed your ways.'

12

Bad News Travels Fast

Harry Donovan insisted that his old buddy should have the best room on the top floor of the saloon. Once he had settled in, the two friends went downstairs and sat at one of the tables.

'Much obliged, Harry,' Cole said. 'I hadn't figured on the guy being such a slippery fish. He almost caught me out again.'

'It's the least I can do for an old friend,' Harry enthused, pushing a full bottle of five star brandy across the table. 'You've brought back that conniving weasel without a shot being fired. I don't know how you managed it, but the town is grateful. If'n there's anything else you need, just say the word.'

Cole's manner was subdued. He did not feel the same elation as that exuded by Flush Harry. The saloon owner quickly picked up on the tight atmosphere. He frowned. 'Some'n else bothering you, Cole?'

'I need to see Marcia,' he murmured. 'Do you think you could arrange a meeting? It will allow me to explain. Persuade her that I'm a changed man. Then, if'n she still can't see a future for us, I'll leave town straight away.'

Donovan protested. 'There's no need for that, Cole. Now that Dooley is out of the frame, we could join up as partners again. Why not stick around and see how things go? She's a headstrong woman. And you never know. She might change her mind.'

'If'n she don't,' sighed the downcast man, 'I couldn't stay knowing Marcia was so near yet so far.' Then he bucked up some. 'But that's only if'n she rejects me again. As you say, she might have softened towards me. So how about that meeting?'

'Leave it to me,' Donovan promised getting to his feet. 'I'll go see her right now.'

While he was awaiting the all-important liaison, Cole's nerves twanged and jerked. He was on tenterhooks, unable to settle.

The saloon door opened. His eyes immediately swung expectantly towards the sound of creaking hinges. But it was only a young boy of around eight years of age. He rushed in brandishing a wooden pistol. Hunched down, he adopted the stance of a gun-fighter on the prod. Peering around he hustled over to the nearest table, which so happened to be that occupied by Cole.

'Stick 'em up, mister,' the boy ordered. 'I've got you covered. Move a muscle and I'll drill you.' His stern look brought a smile to Cole's face, which he attempted to wipe off by obeying the brisk command.

'Don't shoot, partner,' he blubbed effecting the cowed recoil of a beaten villain. 'You've sure gotten the drop on me. I'll come quietly.'

'OK, let's go.' The toy gun wagged. 'I'm taking you over to the sheriff and claiming the reward. I'm a bounty hunter.' He squared his narrow shoulders, preening as if it was the most noble of professions.

'What's your name, mister?' Cole asked. 'Guess I need to know who it is that's arrested me.'

'I'm Joey and —'

But that was as far as it went. At that moment, a woman entered the saloon. Cole sucked in his breath. It was Marcia.

She called across to the boy. 'How many times have I told you not to come in here?' she admonished the youngster. 'This is no place for a boy to be playing. Now come outside this minute.' Her strict tone left Joey in no doubt as to who was calling the shots now.

'Oh, Ma,' he grumbled. 'I wasn't doing no harm. Ain't that right, mister?' He turned, appealing for this man's support.

Cole's gaze met that of his wife. Marcia flinched on recognizing the familiar profile of the man she had long since thought was dead. But her face remained impassive, giving nothing away.

'Do as your mother says, Joey,' he

counselled in a measured way. 'She's right. You shouldn't be playing in a saloon.'

Head hanging on his chest, the boy turned to shuffle away. Cole ruffled his hair. 'And don't worry. I'll make sure to give myself up to the sheriff and tell him it was you that made me see the error of my ways.'

That brought a smile to the boy's face. Perking up, he strutted out the door to resume his hunt for outlaws and brigands elsewhere.

Marcia cautiously approached the table. 'And have you seen the error of your ways, Cole?' she posited, sitting opposite this man who had once meant so much to her. 'Or, like Joey, is it just a charade?'

'I came back specially to try and sort things out between us,' Cole averred, reaching across to hold her hand. She did not remove it. 'He seems like a fine boy. You've brought him up good. I never for one minute reckoned on my ex-partner taking over my life. It came as just as much a shock to me as everybody else around here.'

'Harry told me all about it on the way over here.' She went on to explain how Dooley had ingratiated himself into her affections. 'I would never have succumbed to his odious charms if I'd known for one minute that you were still alive. But you never contacted me. So what was I to think?'

'I don't blame you,' Cole replied. 'But once I'd left Maverick under that cloud, the only way to handle it was go back to my old ways. Then I met Lex Dooley. He had been robbed by one of the wanted villains I delivered up to the law. Going into partnership with him helped me shuck the bounty hunter reputation.'

His head drooped. 'Although it never really goes away.' He was thinking about his most recent encounter and the unforeseen demise of Frank Quintel. 'I can only hope that with your help, I can settle down again. And this time I'll make every effort to be a proper husband and father. That is if'n you can see it in your heart to forgive me. Harry wants me to resume our partnership in the Buckeye. No guns. Just an accounts book and pen. Those will be the tools of my trade from here on if you'll have me back.'

Marcia needed time to think about what he had said. He certainly appeared genuinely contrite. 'That's good news, Cole. I heard how you brought in Luther and I believe what you say. If I agree to make a fresh start, don't let me down again.'

Cole did not enlighten her that he would have used his guns to their full effect had he been so armed. Such a confession was best left unspoken, as were the other unsavoury elements blighting the last five years. He had no wish to rebuild bridges that had not been broken.

The relaxing sound of his wife's voice was a mellifluous lullaby to his ears. The ardent look spoke of a love rekindled. Her touch, the squeezing of a hand, caused his heart to beat faster. Could it really be true that all was forgiven? It appeared so. His whole being buzzed with elation.

This called for a celebration.

But it was not to be.

Just when it appeared that he had his future mapped out, the Devil once again stepped in to stir up the dregs of his past.

A cowboy burst through the doors of the saloon. The guy looked as if he'd been riding at a hell-for-leather pace. His clothes were caked in trail dust, which he attempted to brush off with his hat.

'Looks like you have a hornet up your ass, Buzz,' remarked one onlooker.

Buzz Fetterman had just delivered a couple of prized bulls to Hawk Tamblin who operated the Tumbling T ranch near Safford. He had ridden hard back to Maverick to deliver some extremely disquieting news.

'Give the guy a drink,' suggested someone else. 'Looks like he could use one.'

'Make it a cold beer,' said Fetterman stumbling over to the bar. 'You ain't gonna like what I have to say.'

Digweed quickly pulled the drink, which was downed in a single draught. 'So what's this bad news that's so all-fired important?' demanded the bartender.

The whole saloon had swung to face the newcomer. Mordant curiosity and outright fear were stamped across staring faces. Everybody was on tenterhooks when it was revealed that what he had to impart was allegedly bad for them all.

'After delivering the bulls to the Tumbling T, I called in at the Wayfarer saloon in Safford,' Fetterman began taking a pull at his refilled jug. 'Only intended to stay for a couple, but I met up with some old pals I hadn't seen for a spell. We got to jawing. You know how it is.'

'Just get to the point, Buzz,' interjected Digweed. 'We ain't interested in an account of your idle chin-wagging.'

Fetterman huffed some. 'Only setting the scene for what I have to say,' countered the irked cowpoke.

Then he launched into the meat of what he had witnessed.

13

Jeb Quintel's Promise

The cowpuncher was standing at the bar in the Wayfarer saloon when two drifters walked in. His pals from the Tumbling T had left and Buzz was finishing off his beer and minding his own business. The sale of the bulls had gone as planned. The few drinks had been well earned. Perhaps he would stay over in a hotel. The boss couldn't begrudge him that before returning to the home ranch.

He had no wish to get into any more conversations. The two jaspers sauntered over and stood next to him, quickly stymying that notion.

One was a hard-nosed jasper sporting a scar above his left eye. His sidekick was a greaser. The two men quickly reduced the level of the bottle of whiskey they had bought. Scarface was clearly the boss.

And he was intent on regaling anyone in the immediate vicinity about how he was going to make some dude pay for killing his brother. Fetterman tried to ignore the drunken harangue.

It was only when the name of the Reno Kid cropped up that he took any notice.

'That son-of-the-Devil killed Frank,' the heavily soused bruiser spat out. 'The poor sap stood no chance against a top gun hand like Reno. But he made a big mistake getting involved with a Quintel.' The outlaw wagged a finger and nodded. 'Yep he sure did. And he let slip where he was headed. Maverick. So that's where we're headed. Me and my buddy Fernando here.' A casual arm was draped around his partner's shoulders. 'Then I'll finish the skunk off. And Jeb Quintel will become the dude who bested the Reno Kid.'

A satisfied smirk graced the hard features as he tossed down another slug of hooch. Having finished his slurred delivery, Quintel turned back to the bar and ordered another bottle. Fetterman was thinking hard. His brow furrowed in puzzled concentration. The Reno Kid was supposed to be dead. Some guy had ridden into Maverick over six months before claiming that he had witnessed the renowned bounty hunter's demise at the hands of a cowpoke in St Elmo.

Yet here was a guy squashing all that alleging Reno had shot his brother only days before at the Happy Jack Trading Post. It didn't make no sense. Somebody had to be wrong. The burly cowboy turned to address Jeb Quintel.

'I thought the Reno Kid was dead,' he said, careful not to appear bellicose. 'Some guy has been spreading the rumour that he was shot up in St Elmo.'

'You calling me a liar, mister?' Quintel's tone was aggressive and challenging.

'No, of course not.' Fetterman backtracked hurriedly in an effort to calm the fractious drinker. 'Just saying what I'd heard, is all.'

'Well I can tell you, fella,' Quintel jabbed a finger into the cowboy's chest, 'the Reno Kid is alive and well.

Too darned well. And he's heading for Maverick. But not for long.' An ugly snort meant to be a laugh rumbled up from his throat. 'Ain't that right, Fern?'

'Sure ees, *patrón*,' the Mexican agreed. 'Reno. He not know yet. But his time ees running short.'

Fetterman was stunned. So who was this guy Luther Duggan? And why had he claimed the Reno Kid was dead?'

To make certain he had all the facts correct, Fetterman asked his neighbour to explain what had happened. Quintel was more than willing to expand on the recent incident at the Happy Jack — although he conveniently brushed over the killings at the horse ranch and the humiliating loss of footwear.

'That jasper is gonna rue the day he went up against my kin,' he boasted. 'Next time any of you turkeys hear the name of the Reno Kid, it will be how Jeb Quintel took him down.'

The name of the infamous bounty hunter had brought a gasp from the assembled throng. Quintel smiled. He revelled in the notoriety that his self-assured claim had produced.

'How you gonna do it Jeb?' asked one interested spectator. 'I heard the Reno Kid is faster than a bolt of lightning.'

Quintel sniggered, then tapped his bulbous snout. 'I've said too much already, boys. It don't pay to divulge trade secrets. But what I can say is…'

Buzz Fetterman was not listening. Any thoughts he had harboured about spending some time in Safford were ditched. This was startling news that had to be delivered forthwith. And only he was privy to the showdown that was surely looming. Without further ado, he tossed down the remains of his drink and hurriedly departed.

The ride back to Maverick was undertaken in double-quick time. Only stopping for calls of nature, the cowboy pushed his mount to the limit. It was well lathered and almost fit to drop when he finally stumbled to a halt outside the Buckeye. Leaping from the saddle, he hustled into the saloon.

Fetterman was enjoying the attention that his outpouring had engendered. Another drink came his way, which was downed with relish. All eyes were focused on the speaker. It was a rare event for a humble cowhand to be the centre of attention. And he was making the most of it.

Then slowly, one or two eyes gingerly swung towards the man sitting at the back of the room. Most were aware that he had just brought back Luther Duggan, who was now languishing in the jail.

But not everybody was aware of Cole Rickard's infamous past. Five years had passed and there were many newcomers who had chosen to settle in the locality in and around Maverick. Henry Cumstick was not the only one to recognize its potential as a fine place in which to live and raise a family.

But all that could be put in jeopardy when Jeb Quintel arrived seeking revenge.

Buzz Fetterman gulped as his gaze followed that of the other patrons. He had not realized the object of his excited outpouring was in the saloon. His face assumed a rosy hue. 'I . . I didn't know you was...'

'Ain't your doing, Buzz,' Digweed placated the contrite cowboy. 'But if'n I was you, I'd drink up and head back to the ranch.'

Fetterman nodded and quickly left.

Cole ignored the cowboy's mumbled apology. He had more important matters to consider. Somehow, Quintel and his buddy must have found some horses. So what had happened to the third outlaw? More important, though, how had he known to head for Maverick? Then he remembered, cursing his overactive mouth. Once again the Reno Kid's reputation for violent gunplay was harrying his trail.

Seemed like he was stuck with it like fleas on a dog's back.

And that is what Marcia clearly felt also. She leapt to her feet glaring at the man her disdainful gaze now accused of duplicity.

'Nothing has changed, has it?' To Cole's ears the leaden charge, flat and lacking any venom sounded worse than any virulent outburst. 'The same old Cole Rickard, the same old reputation following you about like a bad cough.' But it was the next snipe that really cut to the chase. 'You're no better than the deceitful fraud who sought to replace you.'

'But Marcia, I —'

A raised hand chopped off any denial on his part. 'There's nothing can change the way you are. It seems that there will always be somebody willing and eager to challenge the Reno Kid. What Buzz Fetterman said is ample proof of that. I am going now. And I don't want anything more to do with you. Try to contact me or Joey and I will report you to the sheriff for harassment.'

Once again he tried explaining. 'My reasons for coming here are genuine, Marcia. I truly have changed.' He spread his arms apart. 'No guns. Those days are over.'

'But they're not, are they?' The stinging rebuttal struck him in the face, such was its venomous outcome. Marcia's eyes now blazed with fury. 'And they never will be. If that was the case, this man Quintel would not be after you for killing his brother. Are you saying he's mistaken?'

'No, but it wasn't my fault, he —'

'It never is your fault, Cole.' She made to turn her back on this man to whom she had once given her heart. 'There is nothing more to be said. So don't try and follow me. It's over. Goodbye, Cole.'

Tears welled in her eyes. In the course of little over an hour, the two men in her life had let her down badly. One a lowlife fraud, the other a bounty hunter who was destined to live and die by the gun no matter what.

Cole was stunned. His eyes followed Marcia as she left the saloon, in essence disappearing out of his life. He was sorely tempted to rush out and plead his case.

'Not now, Cole.' It was the calmly logical voice of Harry Donovan. 'Give her time. Perhaps she'll come round having slept on it. This isn't your fault. I know that. But women always did let their hearts rule their actions.'

'Trouble is, Harry, time ain't on my side.' Cole was staring at the clock on the wall, the measured swing of the pendulum a constant reminder of the imminent showdown. 'If what that cowboy said is true, those jaspers will be here tomorrow and I'll have to face them down.' He poured out a glass of whiskey and knocked it back. The bite of hard spirit did nothing to assuage his gloom.

Cole's assessment of his adversary's arrival would have been correct had not Jeb Quintel made a detour to Pima Pass. His intention had been to forget about the intended robbery and head directly for Maverick. It was Fernando who urged caution regarding such a provocative action.

'Thee boys will not be pleased that you forsake thees job,' he warned as they left the Wayfarer in Safford.

'Who cares what those goons think?' Quintel bristled indignantly, fixing his sidekick with a caustic glower. 'I'm bossing this outfit. They'll do as I think fit.

197

Anyway, there'll be another payroll along next month. We can do that one. Getting the Reno Kid out of my hair has to take priority.'

The Mexican knew that he had to tread carefully when contradicting Quintel. He might easily treat it as a personal affront, which would be an unhealthy move. Mustang Charlie would have harboured no such qualms, but he was dead. Even so, Estrela decided to push his luck.

'They might well decide to pull job on ownsome,' he speculated. The idea had been broached by Charlie Bassett while they were waiting for Quintel at Happy Jack. Only now had it resurfaced. 'Punk Adler ees not likely to just walk away. And he will persuade the others that they can go it alone. That hombre has always wanted to boss hees own gang. Thees would be chance he has been waiting for.'

Quintel's brain was tossing over the implications of what Estrela had suggested. And it made sense. Adler was a big mouth. Worse than that, he had ambitions. A top gun hand when the chips were down, but not a jigger to cold shoulder. Fernando was right. And so a detour over to Pima Pass was made.

The gang were told that the payroll had been delayed. He softened the grumbling discontent by dipping into his own stash of funds. It was an uncharacteristic gesture, but nobody was about to complain when a few nights of carousel in Benson were in the offing. The gang parted. Even Punk Adler was smiling.

So here they were on the outskirts of Maverick in the San Carlos Valley. A sleepy town where not much was likely to disturb the tranquil ambience. Quintel smiled at the notion. Well, that was about to change big time.

During the ride over from Pima Pass, Quintel had come to realize that in taking on the Reno Kid man-to-man, there was no certainty he would come out on top. The outlaw boss was a competent gun hand. But there were better. Punk Adler for one, and probably Fernando as well.

Quintel smiled to himself. A coyote's bark displayed more levity. There was always more than one way to skin a cat. Booking a one-way ticket for the bounty man on Boot Hill would require the cunning of a successful owlhooter. Somebody with guile and ingenuity.

That person was Jeb Quintel.

Frank had stood even less chance than he, but hadn't the sense to back off. Although his younger brother had come off worse in the confrontation at Happy Jack, Quintel was secretly glad. Of course he would never confess to such an admission, even to himself; kinship pride demanded an eye for an eye.

But with Frank out of the running, the road was left wide open for him to step in and claim the prize. In his own devious way.

'I'm going in alone,' he informed his sidekick. 'You stay here while I take care of things.' Quintel had expected Fernando to object but had his reply ready. 'I have to face him alone. Folks need to see that Jeb Quintel has made his play in time honoured fashion and come out the winner.'

'*Sí, patrón*. I understand.' The need to prove one's *masculinidad* was a powerful force in every Mexican male. There was no more to be said.

Jeb Quintel nudged his horse towards the town.

Cole was idly playing patience in the Buckeye. Any attempt at conversation was brusquely rebuffed. He was becoming ever more tetchy as the time passed with no sign of Quintel. He had no doubt that the guy would show. Perhaps he was playing the waiting game to unnerve and demoralize his opponent. Well, it was working.

Each resonant hourly toll of the clock set his nerves on edge. And his mouth felt sour like there was something dead inside.

He called across to the barman. 'Hey, Digweed, you got some buttermilk around?'

The tapster's heavy brows lifted at the unusual request. 'Reckon I can run some to earth, Mr Rickard,' he replied. He disappeared out back returning

201

moments later with a jug and glass, which he deposited in front of Cole. A glass was poured but the contents left untouched.

A down-at-heel prospector had just shambled through the door and called out. 'Anybody in here by the name of Rickard?'

Cole instantly threw off his inertia and stood up. 'Over here, mister.'

The milk was forgotten as the old dude wandered over and handed him a note. 'Fella said you'd give me some'n for my trouble.'

'Did this guy have a scar above his left eye?' snapped Cole before reading the note.

'That's him. A right shifty character,' snorted the oldster. 'And he was packing a brace of pistols in a fancy rig as well.'

Cole flipped a silver dollar in the air, which the prospector caught with nonchalant ease. A quick bite to check it was genuine, then he moved across to the bar.

Opening the note, Cole read the scrawled words to himself.

'Is it from this guy Jeb Quintel?'

inquired Flush Harry, who had sidled up behind his buddy. Cole nodded. He handed the note across. It read: *At end of China Alley. Come alone. And bring a gun.* It was not signed. There was no need.

'You keep out of this, Harry. It's between me and destiny.' He gripped his old pal's hand firmly. Then, in words barely above a whisper, avowed, 'It's gonna be the last time. Of that I can promise you. And tell Marcia that I'll always love her and little Joey, no matter what.'

14

No Way Back

Strange words. Almost like an epitaph. Harry Donovan frowned in puzzlement as his friend left the saloon.

Settling the belt and holster on his hip, Cole Rickard, the Reno Kid, headed for China Alley. There was nobody on the street. It was as if the whole town sensed that trouble of a violent nature was brewing. Cole moved into the centre of the thoroughfare and slowly began the walk of providence.

China Alley was a narrow passage between a Chinese laundry and the Lotus Flower Oriental Eatery. The name was depicted in Chinese characters with its English equivalent underneath. Cole paused at the entrance. The sun failed to penetrate the gloomy passageway.

Loosening his six-shooter, Cole started

down the narrow opening. A cat squealed, then darted out beneath his feet.

Halfway down, he stopped and called out. 'Show yourself, Quintel, and let's get this business settled once and for all.'

'It's already settled, Reno.' The gruff declaration was punched out from a dim recess. It was followed by a loud report and a flash of orange. Two bullets struck Cole high up in the chest. 'And I'm the winner.' A surly chortle followed the downed man as he slumped to the ground.

Quintel stepped out of the shadows and walked across to the crumpled form. An ugly grin split the harsh features. A thin beam of sunlight glanced off the bushwacker's taut features as he stared down at the man he had shot.

The victim of the cowardly ambush groaned. Quintel stepped back, fleetingly nonplussed. He pointed his gun at the dying man ready to deliver the coup de grace. But another voice stayed the Reaper's hand.

'Pull that trigger and it'll be the last thing you do, mister.' The blunt promise came from the lips of Sheriff Chalk Fenton. 'You're under arrest for murder. Now drop the gun.'

'It was a fair fight, Sheriff. Me and this dude had things to settle.' Quintel was sweating in the cool of China Alley. 'I didn't force him down here. He came of his own accord.'

Quintel was taken aback by the lawman's unexpected appearance. Fenton had been checking on a mundane complaint about rubbish left behind the Chinese laundry when the shooting started. He ignored the plea of innocence. His own gun rose menacingly. 'Drop the hogleg. I won't tell you again.'

The shooter hit the ground with a dull thud. It was then that the fallen man pushed himself up on one elbow. 'It's true what he said, Sheriff,' Cole blurted out gasping for breath. He was clearly far gone.

'Easy there, mister. You need a doctor.'

'No time for that. We did have things to settle. And he beat me fair and square. But it was me that drew first.' Cole coughed out a plume of blood. The final curtain was about to fall. All three of them knew it.

'I don't need your help, Reno,' growled the killer.

Cole forced a smile. 'This ain't help, Quintel. It's a curse that's gonna haunt you for what little time you have left. You're now the gunnie who shot the Reno Kid.' He stopped to get his breath back. 'And it's a heavy burden to tote around. Young punks like Frank are gonna be out to test you and claim the crown…' A macabre guffaw rattled in his throat. More blood issued from the open mouth. 'A crown of thorns, more like. Look at me good, mister. And see yourself in a month or two, maybe even a year if'n you're lucky.'

He sank back. The effort of his final denouement too much. His eyes blinked once then closed. Cole Rickard and the Reno Kid were no more.

At that moment, Flush Harry dashed down the alley. 'What's happened?' he demanded. Then seeing his friend on the ground, he hurried across and bent down.

'Is he …?'

'Afraid so, Harry,' the lawman replied. 'And apparently it was a fair fight. This guy beat the Reno Kid to the draw.' He pointed to the revolver clutched in the dead man's hand. At some point following the shooting, Cole had drawn his pistol to add credence to his interpretation that it had been a fair showdown.

Witnessing Quintel's unctuous smirk, Harry slammed a bunched fist into the killer's face. The outlaw was caught unawares by the sudden move and went down. A brutal kick in the ribs followed it up. Harry was fuming and ready to administer more of the same. Quintel rolled away to escape the furious assault.

'Get him off'n me, Sheriff. I ain't done nothing wrong,' he whined.

Fenton sensed that all was not as it appeared. But he had no proof that the Kid's version of events was not the truth.

'OK, Harry, let him alone,' the sheriff ordered laying a firm hand on the assailant's arm. 'I'll deal with this. Before passing away, Reno admitted to me that he drew first. So there's nothing I can do if'n this guy ain't broken the law.'

'You can't hold him. Is that what you're saying?' exclaimed the outraged saloon owner. 'It ain't right. He's a durned murderer.'

Fenton shrugged. 'That ain't what the law says. My hands are tied. And until an ordnance is passed prohibiting the wearing of firearms within the town limits, all I can do is make sure the critter leaves town.'

Like numerous other lawmen throughout Arizona, Chalk Fenton had warrants for the arrest of the gang known as the Shadow Riders. But the name of Jeb Quintel and a solid and reliable description were distinctly lacking. He had no idea, therefore, of the true identity of this unsavoury character.

He then turned to address the alleged winner of the contest, who was wiping blood from a pulped mouth. 'There'll be no more gunplay in Maverick while I'm in charge, mister. So I advise you to get out while you can. News of this nature gets around mighty fast. And I can think of two young hotheads hereabouts who'd love to go up agin the slick gunhand who bested the Reno Kid.'

Quintel scrambled to his feet and snatched up his hat. He was about to retrieve his revolver when the lawman snapped. 'Leave it! You can make do with the other one. Now git afore I change my mind.'

A thoroughly chastened Jeb Quintel mounted up and swung away. He had much to think on before returning to his waiting buddy on the edge of town. A story had to be hastily concocted to ensure he emerged from the fracas in a good light. The bleeding mouth could be explained away easily enough.

The gunfire in China Alley had attracted a host of onlookers. Craning necks sought to peer into the gloomy passage.

'What was all the gunplay about?' posed one jigger.

'Seems like there's been a shoot-out.'

'Who between?'

One boastful strutter who seemed to know more than others provided enlightenment. 'The Reno Kid's been shot dead.' Gasps of awed shock at this momentous news rustled through the gathering throng.

'I thought he was dead already,' said a grizzled war veteran.

'He came back here after five years away up north.'

'What about that Irish jasper who ingratiated himself into Marcia Rickard's bed? Guess he wasn't too happy.'

And so it went on. Numerous theories were latched onto and discarded as the crowd surged back and forth. Each neck-stretcher hoping to discover the truth and pass it on. Information like that was always worth a few free drinks for the informant.

A wagon driven by Harvey Cumstick pulled up at the edge of the crowd. 'What's all the fuss?' he inquired of the nearest bystander.

'There's been a gunfight.'

'Anyone killed?'

'They say that the Reno Kid has been

bested by some tearaway,' was the know-ledgeable reply.

'I thought he was dead,' said a bewildered Cumstick.

'So did everybody else. Guess we were wrong. And it also seems like his real name was Rickard. Cole Rickard.'

Cumstick gasped aloud. 'I was only talking to that guy a few days past. Reckoned he was fixing to settle down here.'

The informant responded with an ironic chortle. 'He's sure done that but in a place he never expected.' Cumstick gave the remark a quizzical frown. 'The graveyard, where else?'

The tit-for-tat discourse was cut short when the crowd parted to allow a solitary female to pass down the alley. Knowing elbows nudged into ribs as Marcia Rickard gingerly neared the scene of sudden and violent death. She came to a halt on seeing the bloodstained body of her husband. Overcome by grief, she clutched at an iron downspout. And would have collapsed had not Harry Donovan quickly stepped forward to hold her upright.

'I'm sorry, Marcia,' he mumbled inanely. 'Guess his time had come. He knew it would one day.'

The woman remained silent. Her face a white mask. A single teardrop chased a path down a smooth cheek. She quickly brushed it away. Why had she not stuck by him? Other questions filtered through her distraught brain, all encompassed by the guilt that now assailed her whole being.

This was the only man she had ever loved. Or ever would. Life had dealt them both a poor hand. She watched as the undertaker carefully loaded the shattered corpse onto a wagon, and covered it with a black cloth. It slowly moved away. Assisted by Harry Donovan, she followed behind, head bowed. Pain and anguish were written indelibly across her ashen face.

Aveline Beddows joined her, murmuring endearments.

It was three days later that the funeral cortege made its way to the small graveyard on a hill overlooking Maverick. A couple of limp palo verde trees and some wild roses attempted to break the austere nature of the bleak site. A grave had already been dug at one end where the preacher stood, Bible in hand.

A light breeze wafted across the open sward rippling leaves on the trees. Cactus wrens chirped and swooped about, unconcerned by the sober occasion taking place in their midst. There was a surprisingly large turnout. Those who had known the deceased took frontal positions around the empty hole. Others were merely curious, eager to follow the final moments of the infamous bounty hunter.

The low babble of conversation faded as the preacher began intoning the funeral dirge. His flat delivery was awkward and strained for a man who had never personally known the coffin's incumbent.

Following the burial, most of the gathering departed. There was food and drink available at the Buckeye that nobody wanted to miss.

Left behind were the nearest and dearest. Marcia had reverted to her true married name. Her marriage to Lex Dooley, or was it Luther Duggan, had been a sham. Young Joey clutched her hand. He had never really known his father. So the man in the grave was a stranger.

'Your pa loved you, Joey,' his mother intoned struggling to keep the grief from her voice. 'He wanted only the best for you. Promise me that you'll always look on Cole Rickard as your true father.' For the last few years, the charlatan known as Luther Duggan had played that part surprisingly well. Now he was in jail awaiting collection for trial in Colorado.

The boy's response was a brief nod. His whole world had been turned upside down.

'He will live on in our memories.' Marcia gripped his hand firmly. 'And this grave is a reminder of all he meant to us both. Make sure that you visit it often.'

Even though there was no way back for the Reno Kid in this life, perhaps he would now be reconciled with his loved ones in their hearts as well as the hereafter.

15

Finale

Three weeks after the burial of the Reno Kid in Maverick, the Shadow Riders led by Jeb Quintel were concealed behind some rocks at Pima Pass. The monthly payroll to Fort Defiance was due any minute. Tension gripped the participants. The gang boss had gained added celebrity amongst his men after relating his own version of the events leading to the shoot-out at Maverick.

Being the man who had taken down the Reno Kid and satisfied family honour sat well on his shoulders. The robbery would cement his reputation amongst others of like mind.

The only burr in the ointment was Punk Adler. The guy had not made any overtly disparaging comments, but the sour looks when he thought the boss was not watching had made Quintel suspicious of his intentions. He pledged to chop the guy down to size once this caper was over and they were in the clear.

The wagon containing the strongbox was escorted by four troopers. Moments later it appeared in the mouth of the pass. A deep rift in the Swisshelm Mountains, this was the only feasible route for a wagon travelling from Tucson to the army fort.

The Shadows were well hidden amongst the rocks on either side of the trail. Quintel was always the one to set the ball rolling. He waited until the wagon was well into the pass. A raised hand signalled the onset of the heist.

His rifle instantly belched flame and death. One of the troopers was lifted from the saddle. The rest of the gang opened up. In no time the three other guards quickly followed. At the top end of the pass, three more men jumped out in front of the careering wagon. The driver and his associate knew better than to resist. They drew the rig to a stumbling halt.

Quintel smiled to himself as he emerged from cover. Easy as falling off a log.

'Glad you boys saw sense,' he praised the two survivors. Then to his men. 'Throw that box down and let's see what we have here.'

Two bullets smashed the iron lock. Inside were stacked wads of greenbacks, ten thousand dollars in total according to his informant — the company payroll clerk. Quintel riffled through a pack of notes and peeled off a handful, which he handed to the driver. 'Your reward for not causing us any trouble. Don't spend it all in the same saloon, boys.'

Then he slapped the lead cayuse on the rump. The animal jerked forward. The eight Shadows chuckled uproariously as the driver struggled to get his rig back under control. Neither of the two men looked back. The money they had been given was more than three months' wages for each of them. And they intended keeping it.

As with other previously successful raids in the vicinity, the gang retired to

Happy Jack for the all-important share out. A couple of days spent at the trading post then the gang split up to go their separate ways. There was enough dough for each man to enjoy a fine spree in the flesh pots of Mexico for a few months.

'We'll meet up back here in November,' said Quintel.

'Where you headed, boss?' Punk Adler asked casually.

'Figure I'll trail down to Nogales where gals are cheap and the booze is even cheaper.' He chuckled at the notion. 'You up for that, Fernando?'

'That ees good thinking, *patrón*. I introduce you to my *parientes*. They make you very welcome.'

Adler joined in. 'Sounds good. Maybe I'll join you. I can't allow the guy who shot the Reno Kid to get himself into bother.' The smile seemed genuine, but the eyes remained cold and granite hard.

Quintel gave nothing away but he knew what game Adler was playing and would be ready when the skunk made his move.

The expected confrontation came

sooner than expected. They were camped out that same night beside Boulder Creek en route to the silver boomtown of Tombstone. Quintel was poking at a rabbit that was being spit roasted over the fire. Fernando had gone down to the creek for water. The two men were alone.

'Me and the boys have been talking,' Adler growled. 'We figure you're past it, Jeb. Toting that Reno reputation around ain't good for business. It will attract too much attention, which the Shadows don't need.'

Quintel maintained a calm head. Without looking up his reply was icy cool and measured. 'And I suppose you're the guy that thinks he can take over.'

'Why not? I can out gun you anytime.'

Slowly, Quintel rose to his feet and turned to face his adversary. 'Then let's not waste any time. You want to boss this outfit? Then you'll have to get rid of me first. And I ain't volunteering. So you best put up, or shut up.'

Punk Adler was puzzled. His broad forehead crinkled. He knew for a fact that he could beat Quintel to the draw. Only the guy's talent for nosing out good jobs had stayed his hand thus far. But now ruthless ambition to lead and ride up front had propelled him to take this decisive action.

He hesitated. Quintel sneered. 'Scared that you ain't as good as you figured. Is that it, Punk?'

The pretender to the outlaw throne growled. His hand dropped to the gun on his hip. But it never lifted. His mouth opened wide in shock, then looked down at the tip of a large knife protruding from his belly.

'There ees only one leader of thee Shadows and it ees not you, hombre.' Fernando had known all along of Adler's surreptitious intentions. The pair had deliberately engineered this situation to draw him out.

'Well that sure worked to perfection, Fern,' Quintel gushed as Adler slumped to the floor. 'A guy doesn't always have to be the fastest draw in the West to gain an enviable reputation.'

'You are right there, *patrón.*' A sinister twinkle burned in the Mexican's eyes. 'A man needs brains and cunning. Plus a ruthless streak, I theenk.' His gun rose and pumped two bullets into the smiling face of Jeb Quintel. 'Now I, Fernando Estrela, can finally return to my homeland, head held high and with a reputation to match.'

Quintel lurched forward, unable to comprehend what was happening. The rictus of death stared him in the face. A groping hand clutched at thin air. Suddenly a light dawned in the dying man's watery eyes.

But it was too late for Jeb Quintel, who tried to speak but couldn't. His killer looked askance, unable to comprehend what the dying man was trying to say.

A year had passed since the morose burial of Cole Rickard. Life in Maverick had settled down to much as it was before. Flush Harry Donovan was sitting in the Palace Hotel awaiting the afternoon stagecoach from Tucson. He was expecting the arrival of a leading lady who had been booked for a two week performance at the Buckeye.

The stage was due in ten minutes. Sipping at his coffee, he idly perused the latest edition of the *Bisbee Herald*. It had been left by a travelling salesman in barbershop accoutrements. A heading at the bottom of the page caught his eye.

Slowly he read the article. Eyes bulged wide as the import of the news struck home.

FAMOUS GUNFIGHTER SHOT RESISTING ARREST

Yesterday, the renowned Mexican gunslinger, Fernando Estrela, was shot dead on the main street of Bisbee when he refused to surrender his guns. An ordnance recently enacted to combat lawless brigands from south of the border forbade the wearing of firearms within the town limits. Estrela had objected, taunting

Marshal Sam Grover to remove them if he had the nerve.

Estrela had been drinking. The marshal gave the gunslinger ample opportunity to obey the order, but the gunman refused, claiming the man who held the reputation for killing the infamous Reno Kid had every right to bear arms where and whenever he chose. A further attempt to defuse the rapidly escalating showdown proved fruitless. Estrela was intent on enhancing his infamous reputation at any cost. Even if it meant going up against a lawman.

He went to draw his gun, but drink had slowed his reactions. Marshal Grover was given no option but to draw his own pistol and shoot the man. Before he passed away, the gunman was heard to mutter the words:

'Now I understand what you mean about the curse, Jeb.' Everybody was mystified regarding this strange dying announcement. If any readers can provide enlightenment, the editor of the *Bisbee Herald* would be eager to hear from them.

Numerous reports had come down the grapevine of gunslingers allegedly claiming to have shot the Reno Kid. All had proved to be fictitious. But this one appeared to be genuine. Jeb Quintel had done the actual shooting but he was known to have a Mexican sidekick. Mention of a curse further added credence to the report. Estrela must have got rid of the outlaw leader and assumed the mantle himself.

Perhaps now the curse of the fast gun could finally be laid to rest. Like all the others before him, Fernando Estrela had learned too late that for those who live by the gun there can indeed be *No Way Back*.

(W)hole

(W)hole

by
Ruth Madison

iUniverse, Inc.
New York   Bloomington

iUniverse books may be ordered through booksellers or by contacting:

iUniverse
1663 Liberty Drive
Bloomington, IN 47403
www.iuniverse.com
1-800-Authors (1-800-288-4677)

Because of the dynamic nature of the Internet, any Web addresses or
links contained in this book may have changed since publication and
may no longer be valid. The views expressed in this work are solely those
of the author and do not necessarily reflect the views of the publisher,
and the publisher hereby disclaims any responsibility for them.
ISBN: 978-1-4401-3541-5 (sc)
ISBN: 978-1-4401-3542-2 (ebook)

Printed in the United States of America

iUniverse rev. date: 04/08/2009

1

Looking out toward the Charles River, Elizabeth stopped
short at the sight of an unexpected figure. At first all her
eye caught was the glint of sun against metal. As was
her habit, her head darted quickly to confirm that it was
round metal, that it was the spokes of a wheel. Usually
when this happened to Elizabeth, the wheel turned out
to be attached to a bicycle. This time it wasn't a bicycle,
but the very thing Elizabeth's mind kept a constant watch
for.

Across the water she could see a young man in a red
wheelchair. He was sitting close to the edge and watching
the swirling, dark water. His hands sat folded in his lap
and he didn't seem to notice the wind dancing with stray
bits of his loosely tied black hair. He wore a brown coat,
and jeans covered his compact legs. His feet were tucked
neatly below him.

Time may have slowed. Though she was across the
river, Elizabeth felt as though she stood just in front of

him and they two were the only breathing creatures in the world. There was nothing else. *I want you.*

Elizabeth's body threatened to wrench itself from her control. She could feel her skin flushing. Her gut ached and cried out. She didn't know who he was, but she wished that she could. The longing started in her stomach and stretched up to her lungs and throat. Though she didn't often see disabled men in the harsh New England climate, whenever she did see a wheelchair, the same reaction overtook her body.

For a moment she allowed herself to imagine being close to this man; brushing her fingers through his black hair, touching the muscles in his arms, and watching him adjust his lifeless legs. Even from here she could tell he was paraplegic and there was nothing temporary about the wheelchair.

"Hey, Elizabeth! What are you looking at?"

Elizabeth snapped out of her daze and saw her friends several yards ahead, waiting for her. "The water," she said, "It's so beautiful this time of year."

She rushed ahead and dragged them with her so they would not have the chance to see the man. Just before they turned the corner, Elizabeth snuck one last glance back. He hadn't moved, and his eyes remained locked on the rushing water.

The girls continued to walk through Cambridge for the rest of the afternoon. The air was mildly cold and whenever the wind picked up it felt like tiny bites on the skin. Occasional leaves from the carpet of yellow, red, and orange above their heads would suddenly be released and drift to the ground. The girls looked in shop windows and commented on what they liked and didn't like. They planned for the days when they had money of their own.

"Is there a Gap around here?" Becky asked.

"There are other stores in the world, you know," Amy said, "Look at that dress."

She was pointing to a sweeping black ball gown with a halter top and no back.

"Where would you wear that?" Becky said.

"When I'm rich," Amy said, "I'm going to wear things like that every day."

Maureen said, "Look at that sweet little sundress next to it."

It was white with little rosebuds. A smudge on the glass in front of it showed its popularity with window shoppers.

"Yeah, if you wore something like that people might think you're innocent and nice," Amy joked.

Maureen elbowed her, and Amy was about to say something else when Becky ran ahead and pointed at a home decorating store. "Oh," she cried, "I can't wait until I have a place all my own and I can decorate every room."

Amy and Maureen looked at each other. "Housewife-in-training," they said at the same time and laughed. It was their favorite way to tease Becky.

Elizabeth was in the back, thinking about the man she had seen. If only there was some way to find out who he was. It wasn't fair. She almost wished that she hadn't seen him so she wouldn't have her desire awakened with no way to release it. She closed her eyes and enjoyed the feel of the air on her face, cooling the flush on her skin. She loved the sense fall gave that things were changing, but in predictable ways. As soon as the leaves turned colors and the temperature of the air dropped, winter was an inevitability beginning its journey to them.

As the sun began to set, Elizabeth and her friends made their way back to the subway. The girls' feet pounded down the grimy steps into the depths of the building. They waited for the train in the deep and dimly lit station, and watched crumpled napkins and bits of newspapers get caught on the benches.

The train arrived rattling and whining. It ground to a halt and the doors swooshed open, air from the station rushing into the bright interior. Elizabeth sat on the seat, bouncing along with the train, while Becky and Maureen gossiped together about boys from their school, and Amy started conversations with strangers. The train sped toward Alewife station.

Her friends no longer bothered to ask Elizabeth what she had been up to. They saw each other every day at school, and by now everyone knew exactly how boring Elizabeth's days were. At seventeen years old she already had well-formed routines that she rarely deviated from. Her friends thought she liked it that way. They had no way of knowing that habits kept her strong and able to withhold parts of herself from even them, her closest friends.

That night Elizabeth couldn't sleep. She had put on her purple pajama pants and her white camisole pajama top, and she had brushed her teeth, done her physics homework, turned out the lights, and lay in bed. The night was thick and vast around her. The shade was pulled to within one inch of the ledge and she could see a sliver of darkness.

She heard a faint scratching that she took to be her mother's pencil. Her parents, in the next room, were not asleep either. In all the years of her life Elizabeth had never managed to catch them asleep. Even as a little child with nightmares, whenever she ran to her parents' room, she found her mother sitting at the dresser making lists and her father reading a book in bed. They were always so calm. Her father would pat the bed and little Elizabeth would climb up to hear a part of his book. She used to love those evenings listening to Plato and Marsilio Ficino.

What would he do if he knew the truth about his daughter? Would he look at her with disgust? Would he be unable to recognize her? In her nightmares Elizabeth often watched variations of her father's face as he was let in on her secret. Whether he looked at her with anger, with pity, with fear, or with confusion, the end of the dream was always the same; he would turn from her and disappear.

Elizabeth had tried many times to forget the desires that haunted the back of her mind. Now that she was finishing high school and facing the choices of the rest of her life, she was trying even harder than before. For weeks she had tried to keep her mind away from disability. She moved her secret notebook out from under her bureau and hid it in the basement. What was the point though? As soon as she saw the man at the river, all those weeks of work meant nothing. Her body responded to him whether she wanted it to or not.

The house creaked as Elizabeth tiptoed out of her room, down the stairs, and into the living room. It was an old, solid house and every once in a while would give a little groan and settle itself. Elizabeth pulled open the door to the basement and musty air hit her. She felt dust on her bare feet as she stepped carefully down the stairs. The concrete floor was cold and Elizabeth walked carefully so as not to step on anything sharp that could be on the floor.

She went straight for the ironing room where they stored all the out-of-season clothing. As it was the beginning of September, the winter coats, scarves, and mittens were still there. The sweaters had already been brought up for the start of fall.

In the back corner, behind the garment bag that stored her mother's wedding dress, was a cardboard box that claimed to contain a computer printer. Elizabeth knelt and felt the cold of the floor on her knees, even through the material of her pajama pants.

Slowly she pulled open the sides. On top was a stack of books that looked innocent enough. Should anyone happen to open the box it would just look like some old books of Elizabeth's. However, the books had something in common. From *Treasure Island* to *The Westing Game*, they all had male characters with disabilities. Biting her lip, Elizabeth spread them out on the floor beside her.

Next she unpacked the videos. *Dr. Strangelove, Born on the Fourth of July, Daredevil, Scent of a Woman,* and *George Wallace*; all movies with disabled male characters. Under those were some loose pictures and then the prize: her notebook. Elizabeth lifted it out with trembling hands.

She had created the notebook thinking that she could move the sickness out of herself and contain it within the pages. Now she knew the foolishness of that plan. When she thought of the images in these pages her head felt hot and heavy and her stomach wrenched. It had somehow made her sickness more real, instead.

She packed the rest of the materials back into the box and opened the notebook's cover. Inside were photographs she had taken, and pictures from magazines, or off the Internet. Wheelchairs, crutches, casts, paraplegics, amputees... The familiar tingling began between her legs.

Pressing the notebook closed against her chest, and wrapping her arms over it, she crept quietly back up to her room. After going through the familiar pictures again, savoring each, Elizabeth slid the notebook under her bureau, where it seemed to pulse with its black secret.

Back in her bed Elizabeth closed her eyes and let her hand creep down under the covers. In her mind she saw Long John Silver. He was fighting a storm at night, pacing the deck of the ship furiously with his one crutch pounding down with each step. His empty pant leg swung wildly in the wind. He maneuvered, turned, and wielded the crutch.

Elizabeth's hand was inside her pajamas now, cool fingers touching skin that was rapidly heating up. An itch within her body had begun and she used her thoughts to make it stronger. Her body now begged for pressure.

Elizabeth gave it, pressing rhythmically. This was familiar to her. After all these years, she knew the effect that thoughts of disabled men would have on her and now she also knew how to satisfy the desire that came with those thoughts. It wasn't until she took sex-ed in sixth grade that she figured out what that tingling sensation was. Many times in her childhood she felt it, but never dared give in to the urge to press. After that class, she let herself satisfy the itch.

Suddenly she saw the man from the Charles River in her thoughts. His hands were touching her bare arms and her skin became covered in goose bumps. In her imagination she leaned down and pressed her lips against his. Elizabeth curled her hands around his bicep muscles and she felt her hips try to press themselves against his lean body.

On her bed, Elizabeth's body quaked. She pushed her fingers harder and harder. Her toes curled around the baseboard of her bed and she squeezed all the muscles in her legs. With a tiny sigh, only just barely released through her lips, a shudder went through her and she was limp.

She breathed deeply and pushed the hair that was sticking to her forehead off her face. Then she opened her eyes and looked at the ceiling. Though her body had relaxed, her mind was still tense. How had someone else's pain and her pleasure become so closely linked?

Pleasure and guilt had always gone hand in hand for Elizabeth. Her first memory of these feelings was when she was four years old, but she knew they had begun long before that. Her four-year-old self recognized the desire as a familiar feeling. Just as she knew then that looking at disabled men felt good, she also knew she could never let anyone find out that she thought so. Secrecy wrapped itself around Elizabeth's heart even in her most intimate moments.

Inside Elizabeth was a voice that told her terrible things. *There's something wrong with you.* Sometimes for days she wallowed in the sick seduction of that voice.

Her parents thought she was just being a teenager when she closed herself in her room. Often she sat on the floor and stared at nothing, listening to an endless tirade of her faults and she pinched herself to draw the pain out of her mind, to the outside of her body.

Though she believed this desire for disability was wrong, something to be destroyed, she couldn't seem to do it. The desire was stronger than she was. Despite her best efforts, when a character in a book went to the hospital, she became excited. Deep inside she always hoped for an injury in stories. She was the only girl she knew who liked to watch war movies, and she did because the odds of injuries were better in those movies than others. Like any addiction, it seemed to be impossible to get rid of the thing that brought the greatest pleasure to her body.

2

"Come on, come on, today is the big day," Elizabeth's mother said, dumping a handful of make-up on Elizabeth's bureau. Susan was tall and slender with sleek blonde hair brushing her shoulders. She was always poised and perfect and Elizabeth felt like a clumsy fool next to her.

"Not for me," Elizabeth groaned. She pulled the bed covers over her face, but quickly felt the air disappearing and uncovered her head again. "Cousin Libby's the one getting married."

"Weddings are always a big occasion," Susan said, "Besides, you can get some ideas for the future. It's never too early to start thinking about your own wedding."

Susan rushed out of the room, high heels thumbing against the carpet, and Elizabeth sat up slowly, muttering about her first day for sleeping in for a week. Then her eyes fell on the camera sitting beside her mother's make-up and she felt better. Maybe, since she could take pictures, the wedding wouldn't be too boring.

Elizabeth quickly slipped into the dress her mother had picked out for her and began gently cleaning the camera.

"You could have at least put on the lipstick I gave you," her mother said as Elizabeth arrived at the car.

"Yeah, yeah, yeah," Elizabeth said as she pulled her dress out of the way of the door. The side of the road seemed aflame with the colors of the trees. Elizabeth squinted her eyes until all the colors blended together and their car was navigating the narrow strip between the sheets of fire.

They pulled up at a curb and Elizabeth stood watching the groups of people disappearing through the church doorway. It was a simple white church, nestled among trees and bushes. Elizabeth snapped a picture, and then followed her parents inside.

Elizabeth's grandmother, her mother's mother, was already waiting for them. Elizabeth's father, David, bypassed her with a quick, "Hello, Margaret," and went to find a seat. Elizabeth followed, feeling her grandmother's critical eyes on her back.

She looked around to see who had come. Her mother's family wasn't very large, and Elizabeth didn't think Libby had many friends, so most of these people must be with the groom. Twisting herself entirely in her seat, Elizabeth suddenly lost her breath when she saw the man sitting at the back of the sanctuary.

"What is it?" David said.

"Nothing," Elizabeth said when she recovered her voice.

It was him. The man from the river. Same black hair, tied neatly in a ponytail against the nape of his neck, same steady eyes, and same red wheelchair. The coincidence so stunned Elizabeth that she was staring openly. In the entire throng of people he seemed to be the only one sitting perfectly still.

Then a friend was beside him, leaning over, touching his shoulder. The man smiled easily and hit the pew in front of him with his hand. The friend sat and the man from the river leaned closer to that last row. He was by himself in the space behind the pews.

The man must know the groom. Elizabeth had certainly never seen him before that Saturday morning in Cambridge. What did it mean that she was seeing him again? What should she do now that this man, who seemed to have rolled straight out of her fantasies, had appeared in her life again? She had to be cool around him, and show him that she wasn't as ignorant as other able-bodied people. Not staring might be a good start.

Elizabeth turned forward in her seat. All through the ceremony she didn't see what was in front of her, but thought of the man sitting several rows behind her. Was he staring at the back of her head? Sometimes she thought he was taking her in with his even gaze. She fluffed at her mass of yellowish brown hair and hoped it looked nice.

After the bride and groom had kissed and run down the aisle, everyone slowly stood up and gathered their things from on the seats or under the pews. They moved in a mass to the stairs leading down to the church basement. While Elizabeth shuffled along behind cousin Libby's mother, she looked over to the elevator at the end of the corridor they were passing. The man in the wheelchair and his friend were there alone.

The man wore a dress shirt that puffed out behind

the low back of his wheelchair. His arms hung at his sides, the fingers gently grazing the slim metal rails of his wheels. Elizabeth pressed her fingers into the palms of her hands and felt her fingernails driving marks into her flesh. Then she was on the stairs and he disappeared from her view.

At the reception, Elizabeth sat between her mother and father. Even while eating she kept her camera around her neck. Every so often she would lift it up and take a picture: of the ring bearer chasing the flower girl across the dance floor, of Libby's mother trying to be charming to the groom's mother, and whenever she could get away with it, she pointed her camera at the man from the river and took his picture too. Those she would save for herself.

Please God, she begged, let my obsession have a reason, let this man be someone I can be close to. She could almost imagine that she had been born and created to be in this man's life. Maybe there was a purpose in all things, as her grandmother always said.

"Elizabeth," Susan said, "You've hardly touched your food. Put down that camera and eat."

One thing Elizabeth did like about weddings was the routine. There was a script that was always closely followed and you knew what would come after what. When the food was finished, the bride and groom had their first dance, and then people were up and out of their seats. Elizabeth stayed put at the table, but her parents went to dance, and most of the other people got up and stood in clusters around the room talking with the people they already knew.

Her camera lay in front of her and she sat rubbing

her bare arms to keep them warm. Not wanting anyone to notice her interest, she was trying to avoid looking directly at the man from the river. Strange how her reaction to disability appeared to be the same as anyone else's; no one would ever be able to tell that she was uncomfortable around it for a completely different reason.

He was now sitting next to the band on the edge of the dance floor, watching the people move. His friend stood next to him and they laughed frequently. Into her view came her mother. Susan was walking directly up to the pair. What was she doing? Elizabeth wondered in horror. Her mother was about to humiliate her and there was nothing Elizabeth could do to stop her.

Susan wasn't interested in the man in the wheelchair. In fact, she stood directly in front of him, blocking his view as she spoke to his friend. Then she pointed in Elizabeth's direction and Elizabeth immediately cast her eyes in another direction and pretended she hadn't been watching them.

Elizabeth picked up her camera and peered through its lens. What else could she photograph? What would Libby want to remember? She moved the camera around randomly. A tie appeared in the viewfinder. Slowly she lowered the camera and found the friend standing in front of her.

"Hello," he said.

"Hi," she said. Already she could feel her face flush. What had her mother said to him to make him come over here and talk to her?

"What's your name?"

"I'm Elizabeth."

"I'm Robert, it's nice to meet you."

"You too," she said. He had nice, soft-looking, brown hair and a neat, clean-cut appearance; his eyes were friendly, his jaw was strong. Her friends would call him cute. She would too. She knew he was. Her mind accepted the fact that he was attractive, but her body was not responding to him. If he was just…for an instant she pictured him in a wheelchair, but she felt uneasy doing this, as though her thoughts might cause something awful to happen to this innocent man.

"Would you like to dance?" he asked.

Elizabeth was surprised. "Um, sure," she said.

Robert held out his hand. Elizabeth put down her camera and took it. On the dance floor there were only two other pairs shuffling back and forth, clinging to their partners so close it seemed they were about to bolt for the bedroom. This made Elizabeth uncomfortable and she didn't quite know how to hold Robert. He took the lead and brought her into a traditional dance hold. They began to shuffle too. The music was slow and boring.

Afraid to look directly into his eyes, Elizabeth mostly let her eyes drift over his shoulder. As they slowly turned, she saw that her parents were watching her closely.

They turned again and suddenly Elizabeth found herself looking at the man she had been secretly observing all evening. He had a beautiful wheelchair. It was small and sporty, with wheels that turned in slightly, and a red tube tucking his feet underneath the body of the chair. He was wearing sneakers with his suit. His pant legs were loose. One of his hands lay in his lap and the other held a glass of champagne.

Just before Robert and Elizabeth turned again,

her eyes drifted up to his face and their gazes locked. Electricity seemed to shoot through all the veins of her body. She turned her head to stay with his eyes for as long as possible before her partner turned her around.

"Are you all right?" Robert asked.

"Hmm?"

"You don't seem like you're really here."

"Sorry. I don't care much for weddings."

Robert laughed. "I thought all girls loved weddings."

They turned and Elizabeth was looking at her parents again. She saw her mother frown at the same moment that she heard a voice on the other side of her.

"May I cut in?"

They both stopped moving and broke apart. Elizabeth turned and saw the man from the river and her stomach seized up. He was even more beautiful close up.

"Are you serious?" Robert said, but the man wasn't looking at him. He held out his hands to Elizabeth.

She felt as though she was in a dream. She saw her hands stretch out to touch his and she saw her fingers trembling. The skin of his hands was thick and rough when she tightened her slender fingers around them. She didn't notice Robert stumbling to the side of the dance floor and sitting down in the chair she had been occupying.

Suddenly, for the first time, the man seemed very short. Elizabeth was acutely aware of how tall she stood above him. From a distance he had seemed larger than life and now he only came up to her waist. She stepped slowly forward and back and the man holding her hands was rolled back and forth with her. She could feel the heat in her face and knew she was blushing. Hopefully he would think she was just flushed from the lights and the dancing.

How could she know this wasn't a dream? Pinching herself did not seem like a practical test; instead she tried to open her eyes very wide. If she were asleep, perhaps her real eyes would pop awake if she could get her dream eyes open enough.

The man in front of her raised an eyebrow. It wasn't a dream. She was so nervous that she could not find a place to rest her eyes. It was too intense to look into his hazel eyes, it was too rude to look at his legs, so she tried to focus on his nose.

"My name is Stewart," he said.

She couldn't seem to make her voice function. It was as though she had forgotten how. At last she whispered, "I'm Elizabeth."

"Do you know the bride or groom?" Stewart said.

"The bride is my cousin. You?"

"Robert is the groom's older brother and I'm Robert's roommate."

Elizabeth tightened her fingers on his callused hands. Now she was aware of nothing else going on in the room. She was looking directly at his face and he was looking up at hers.

"You're a photographer?" he said.

"I hope to be," Elizabeth said, "I'm working on it, but I can never find good topics."

"You don't want to take event pictures?"

"I want to be an artist, but when I find an artistic subject, I don't know what it means." Elizabeth's blush deepened. She had never really talked about her concerns about her photography. Her friend, Amy, often laughed at her attempts to take pictures of playground equipment upside-down, but here she was telling a stranger that she had no idea what she was doing. Time to get the focus off of herself. "What do you like to do?" she asked.

"I'm in college and I find it takes up a lot of my time."

"Really? What are you studying?"

"I'm getting a physics degree."

"Oh wow. Smart."

He smiled and Elizabeth's stomach turned over. He had a great smile that relaxed his whole face.

"Are you going to discover great things?" Elizabeth asked.

"I'm going to help other people discover great things. I want to teach high school."

"Can't you just get a teaching degree?"

"I could, but I love practical physics and I want to know as much as I can about it before I start teaching other people."

"That's really cool."

"I'm glad you approve."

The song ended, but Elizabeth did not let go of him. Lights around the room dimmed and the club music started. Suddenly there were more people crowding in. Stewart and Elizabeth were pushed toward the center of the floor. People grooved and bounced, paying no attention to the two still figures.

Stewart released her hands and began to move again, pushing his wheels back and forth in sharp motions, approximating dancing. Elizabeth started bobbing in front of him. She laughed.

"I don't really know how to dance," she confessed.

"I've always been a terrible dancer," Stewart said, "You move well, though."

"Thanks," Elizabeth said, scrunching into herself, and crossing her arms.

"I didn't mean to embarrass you."

Elizabeth shook her head. Embarrassment wasn't what she was feeling. There was a strong urge in her to leap on Stewart; to scratch him with her nails, to bite his skin, to grab his flesh. Here in front of her was the man she had hoped for all her life.

"Stewart?"

"Mmm?"

"I saw you before. A couple weeks ago. At the river."

Another song started, but Elizabeth couldn't hear much difference between it and the previous song. The lights had gotten even darker and the people around Elizabeth were nothing more than shadows walling her into this space with Stewart.

He looked up at her. "I spend a lot of time there," he said.

"You really love the water, don't you?"

"Yes, I do," Stewart said.

"Me too," Elizabeth said, "My mom and I go to Cape Cod all the time and I love to just stand in the ocean and let it lap around me."

Stewart smiled. "That brings back memories," he said, "Do you participate in any water sports?"

"No," Elizabeth said. "I can barely do the breast stroke. What about you?"

"I used to surf a little."

"Wow!" Elizabeth said, "I've never met anyone who surfed before. That is really cool. Do you still boogie board or anything like that?"

"No," Stewart said, "I just swim laps at the school gym."

Elizabeth frowned. "Must be hard to go from surfing to swimming laps."

"Yes." Stewart laughed. "Thanks for bringing it up."

"I'm sorry," Elizabeth said.

"I appreciate a person who speaks her mind."

While they spoke, Elizabeth was scheming. She was a woman and she decided it was finally time to put her manipulative instincts to the test. It was up to her to get this man permanently into her life. He was not only paralyzed, but also handsome, young, and charming. She couldn't let him slip away.

First step was getting him to see her as different from the other able-bodied people he encountered every day, but she didn't want to give away too much of her knowledge about disability or he would be suspicious and might figure out her secret.

In the dim room Elizabeth caught sight of her mother's yellow hair. Susan was pushing her way through the crowd. There was no time left to make an impression on Stewart.

"Elizabeth!" she said, "You have school tomorrow. Come on, we have to get home."

Elizabeth smiled apologetically at Stewart. "See you around?" she said.

"Sure," he said.

"Thanks for the dancing," she said. As she moved toward her mother, she kept her eyes on Stewart for as long as she could. Remember me, she thought with all her might, you haven't seen the last of me.

3

The day after the wedding Elizabeth was back in school and back to her normal routine. She met up with Amy before classes started and they stood outside the school in the entranceway.

"I love weddings," Amy said, "Was it romantic?"

Elizabeth shrugged. "I guess it was good for a wedding. It was kind of weird, really."

"What do you mean?"

"Libby isn't a grownup, she's only like four years older than us. There's nothing about her that seems wife-like, but here she is married. It's really strange."

"Sounds great to me. Used to be that you had to know something to be a wife, now you just have to be pretty," she said while fluffing her hair.

"I don't think you have anything to worry about," Elizabeth said.

"Aw, thanks," Amy said. "Were there any cute guys

there? Weddings are a great place to meet men, you know."

Elizabeth felt the heat coming to the surface of her skin again as her mind flashed to Stewart. She suppressed it and focused on the concrete stairs beside them. "Actually," she said, "Yeah, there were one or two."

"Wow, is my little Lizzie growing up?" Amy glowed with excitement.

"Oh, shut up," Elizabeth said. It was at moments like this that Elizabeth felt a veil go up between herself and the rest of the world; between herself and the friends who would never know the forces that motivated Elizabeth. *How can I ever tell you the truth?*

The bell rang. Amy sighed. "Ah, school," she said tragically.

"Come on," Elizabeth said, and dragged Amy a little harder than necessary toward class.

After an uneventful day at school Elizabeth walked home. It was a long walk and she was supposed to take the bus, but it was embarrassing to be a senior on the bus. And Elizabeth liked the walk. The pounding of her feet and the fast breath of her quick pace helped her mind focus. She could think about things and answers rose to the surface, as though churned to the top of her body.

Today was a particularly beautiful walk. The air was heavy with moisture. Elizabeth took the bike path through the orange and yellow trees that seemed to burn through the heavy mist obscuring the path ahead. Her backpack grew heavy on her shoulders. She watched her feet and felt almost disconnected from her body.

What was she going to do about Stewart? He was way too cool for her. She was an awkward, slightly geeky kid and he was athletic and confident and gorgeous. What could she hope to offer him? What would they even have to talk about? But the logical side of Elizabeth's brain had long since given up. Her heart was too far ahead for her mind to catch up. She had to at least try.

Arriving back at the house, she took the key from the bottom of the mailbox and walked in. Rather than do homework, as her parents always tried to convince her to take up her afternoons, she went straight to the computer in the den.

Elizabeth didn't have a computer in her room because her mother was afraid it was sending out deadly rays at all times. Rays apparently blocked by walls. There was one computer for the family and it was kept in a closable closet in a corner of the den.

Though her parents were still at work, Elizabeth closed the door just in case. She loaded up the Internet and sat down. She was going to find Stewart. She couldn't pretend to herself that she just happened to stumble across him. No, she would have to hunt. Sometimes you just had to take things into your own hands. There was a shortage of disabled men in Massachusetts and Stewart was so much more than that. Thank goodness for the Internet.

Elizabeth didn't have much to go on. She wasn't even sure how he spelled his name. The only piece of luck was that it wasn't as common a name as, say, Robert. She was fairly sure that as a first name it was spelled "Stuart", so she searched for that, along with "college" and "Boston." There were a few promising hits, but as she pursued them, nothing seemed to quite match the man she had met.

Next she tried pairing the name with the word "surfing." Again, there were a few hits, but the people were too young or too old to be him. In desperation she tried spelling his name "Stewart" along with "surfing." The top hit was titled "Where is Stewart Masterson?"

Clicking it brought her to a fan page. The photo in the biography was him beyond any doubt. He was standing on a beach, wearing a wet suit, and holding a board that was a few feet taller than himself. He was laughing toward the camera and holding up a large gold trophy. His black hair was wet and flattened against his head.

Elizabeth crossed her legs on her chair and leaned forward. The article on the page spoke of all his accomplishments and Elizabeth was astounded by the list. She knew nothing about surfing contests, but the names of those Stewart had won took up most of the page.

At the bottom were the words the search engine had found: Where is Stewart Masterson? The paragraph mentioned that Stewart had been taken to a hospital after an incident during a tropical storm in California six years ago, and no one had seen him since.

As Elizabeth perused the other web pages she discovered that no one knew what had become of him. A large crowd saw him go into an ambulance, but after that he disappeared.

"Why is the door closed?" Susan said as she stepped into the den.

Elizabeth scrambled to minimize the windows. "Oh my God, Mom, you scared me!"

Susan walked to the window and pulled open the

blinds. "You're very jumpy today," she commented. Then she walked down the hallway to the kitchen to stare at the cabinets.

Cautiously, Elizabeth pulled the Internet windows back up. If no one could find him, how was she going to? She had an advantage over these people, though, she knew he was living in Boston and going to college. Now that she had his first and last name, she started going to college directories for every school she knew in the city.

There were no results until she found University of Boston. "Bingo," she breathed. There was his name and a phone number and email address.

"Elizabeth! Come help me find something for supper," Susan called.

Elizabeth wrote down the email and phone number, and then shut down the computer. "Don't we still have some pasta left over?" she said as she walked into the kitchen.

"Yes," Susan said, "That's perfect."

Throughout supper Elizabeth wondered how to best get in touch with Stewart again. There was no way to avoid embarrassing herself. She was going to have to be very direct. Was it best to call him or email him? What exactly would she say? *Please let me touch your wheelchair?*

She pondered for several days, but the longer she waited the more chance that she would lose this opportunity. At school she asked Amy, "Is it better for a guy to ask you out or do you do the asking if you don't think he will?"

Amy got serious. This was her area of study. "Traditionally, of course," she said, "The girl always had to wait around for the guy to get off his lazy bum and ask her. Now girls are empowered to do the asking."

"Yeah, but does that scare men off?"

"Look at it this way, Liz, no one likes to be rejected. Why would men want to have the responsibility of always being the one getting rejected? They like girls doing the asking because then they don't have to take any risk. You should go for it. You're getting too old to have not been on a single date."

"Thanks, Amy, that's real nice."

"You know it as well as I do, darling. Talk about scaring guys away; you're smart, mature, and serious. All the boys are terrified of you."

"That makes me feel a lot better," Elizabeth said glumly.

"So now you're ready to do the asking, that's good."

"Yeah, I'm ready."

With Amy's words echoing in her ears, Elizabeth ran up the stairs to her house after school, pushed open the door, and ran straight for her room. She whipped out the cell phone her mother made her carry for emergencies and punched in Stewart's number. She pushed the send button before she could stop and think about what she was doing.

"Yeah?" the voice on the other end said and waited.

Elizabeth dropped to the floor, sitting with her back against her bed. She started to speak, discovered that she had no voice, and coughed. "May I speak to Stewart, please?" she said.

Her heart was pounding so hard in her ears that she could hardly hear his reply. "This is Stewart, who are you?"

"Elizabeth. We met at the wedding."

"Oh. How are you?"

"I'm good."

"Was I drunk enough to forget giving you my phone number?"

"No, not at all. I, um, you know, Robert is part of the family now, so it's not that hard to track you down."

"Okay," he said slowly. "Was there a reason you wanted to track me down?"

"I was hoping you'd come to a movie with me on Friday," Elizabeth said. Then she held her breath and scrunched her eyes closed.

"Are you asking me on a date?"

"Yes," she whispered.

A laugh filled her ear. "That's a first," he said. "What time on Friday?"

"7:00?"

"Okay, I'll pick you up then. Plan to tell me where you live?"

"Actually, could I meet you there?"

Elizabeth heard hesitation, but he said, "Sure." She named the theater and gave him directions to it.

"See you there," he said.

Elizabeth clicked the off button and then felt a surge of energy run through her. She threw the cell phone across the room and then crumpled papers into specks in her hands until the excitement drained out a little and Elizabeth was left with a glowing satisfaction in her throat. She had done it. For the first time in her life she had taken a step towards what she wanted and she had not been struck by lightning. Not yet, anyway.

The days went by too slowly. On Friday Elizabeth

developed pictures in order to relax and distract herself from thinking of what might happen that evening. She had converted the first floor bathroom into her own dark room.

With the pictures done, Elizabeth squinted at them hanging in the red light. Upside-down playground equipment. It had to mean something, right? It seemed like a meaningful subject, but Elizabeth didn't know why. Maybe she didn't have to know. She could fake it: send a portfolio to a magazine and just let other people come up with what the meaning was. Did artists really know the true meaning of their work? If they did then there would be no need for critics and reviewers.

As she cleaned up her equipment, she saw a stray picture corner hiding under a box of chemicals. She pulled it out and, when she saw what it was, pressed it against her chest and looked behind her, even though she was alone in the room and the door was closed. It was an image of a disabled boy she had seen at school. If her mother had come in here to clean up, she could have seen this. Elizabeth had taken the picture with her zoom lens of just his paralyzed feet on his wheelchair's pedals.

Now she had a date with an actual flesh-and-blood disabled man. First she wondered how she'd gotten so lucky, and then she remembered that no matter what happened with this man, she could never be fully honest with him. If he found out that she was attracted to his disability, he would certainly hate her. *You're sick. There's something wrong with you.*

She sat on the edge of the bathtub with the photograph in her hand. She hung her head. Maybe she should go to therapy for this. No one in her family went to therapy; they would want to know why she needed it. Besides, she didn't think she could tell even a psychiatrist that when she was little she had torn the legs off her Ken doll and built him a wheelchair made out of Duplos. Once, she threw him off her grandmother's balcony, called it a hiking accident, and wrapped his arms in wet toilet paper that hardened into casts.

Elizabeth realized that it was getting late and she needed to get ready for her date. She started to tear up the photograph, then stopped and put it on the bottom of the box, under all her other supplies. Just in case.

Elizabeth put everything else away and closed the door behind her. She went up to her room to get ready and found herself presented with the traditional female dilemma: what to wear. Stewart was by far the most attractive man she had ever met. Possibly the most attractive she had ever even seen and she was intimidated.

Her closet was divided into two halves: the clothes she bought and wore, and the clothes her mother liked on her. This might be an event for the clothes that fashion-forward Susan liked. On the other hand, Elizabeth wanted him to know her and like her. It was stupid to worry about things like that. This was just one date.

Like a lightning bolt, her mind flashed an image of her kneeling in front of him, stretching her arms and running her hands over his bare chest. Elizabeth closed her eyes and focused on her breath. She let the image pass. Was this what everyone felt? For normal guys or girls? Elizabeth could never know for sure, but she hoped it was. She hoped that she was feeling something normal at last.

There had been no incident in her childhood to trigger a connection between lust and disability. There was no reason for it; it was just there and always had been. Elizabeth had no experience of what it felt like to have these feelings for a man that she could actually express them to. Or for a man that she could tell her friends or family about. She could envision herself in the future married to an able-bodied man, and she could imagine companionship, preparing meals, or even raising children, but she could not picture desire, lust, or sex with such a man.

With Stewart she was trying to stop her mind from visualizing all the way. So far she'd kept it under control—except for those little images that leapt into her mind too suddenly for Elizabeth to censor. Yes, tonight was a night for a Susan outfit. Elizabeth pulled things roughly from that side of the closet.

She tried on a black dress, but it was far too short on her. Elizabeth was tall for a woman, so she didn't often find dresses that she liked the length of. A red skirt and black top ensemble made her feel too bold. A white sundress with a sweater made her look like a child. She looked over the wild shirts. Susan believed that the best way for Elizabeth to overcome her flat chest was to wear tops with lots of details on them, or fun patterns, or 3-D bits sewn on.

Finally Elizabeth settled on a tan shirt with brown cardigan patterned with fall leaves and jeans. Now she was going to be late and she was never late. She hopped down the stairs and into the kitchen.

David and Susan were both there. They had been arguing over what to do for supper for the past several minutes and when Elizabeth came in David said, "Come on, we're going out."

"Actually," Elizabeth said, "I was going to catch a movie with my friends, do you think you could drop me off?"

"You never go out at night," David said.

Susan said, "She finally starts to get a life, and you discourage her! Do you know how hard I've worked to get her to go out with her friends instead of having sleepovers and watching videos like they were ten?"

Elizabeth shrugged, as though she was just doing this as a favor to her mother. All three got in the car and David drove to the center of town. Elizabeth peered out the window from the backseat long before they got to the theater, trying to see if Stewart was waiting outside for her.

"Actually," she said, "We're meeting up at the coffee shop first, can you drop me there?"

David complied and Elizabeth got out.

"I don't see Amy and Maureen," David said, "Should we wait for them?"

"Come on, this is the safest town on the planet," Elizabeth said. It was true, so her parents drove away to find a restaurant they liked. Elizabeth waited until their car was out of sight, and then walked back to the theater.

The cool fall air danced under her nose and carried the smell of popcorn to her a couple blocks before she arrived at the little theater. It was after dark now, but the street was well lit with streetlamps.

Elizabeth saw him before he saw her. Her stomach tightened a few more notches. He was absently watching the cars go by. The closest street lamp cast shadows over his face. He was sitting perfectly still, his elbows on the small tubular arm rests covered in black grippy material, and his hands lay on his lap. He wore jeans, with a tear on the knee, and a black sweater that was too baggy. The excess cloth was dripping over the sides of his seat and threatening to get caught in the wheels.

Then he looked over and saw her. His face instantly lifted into the smile that Elizabeth found so charming. His wheels squeaked against the stone path as he turned.

"I'm not too late, am I?" she said when she got to him.

"Not a bit," he said. He took her hand. She smiled and squeezed it, but Stewart tugged on it until she leaned over and he kissed her cheek. "Come on," he said.

Though the entryway to the theater was steep, there weren't any stairs. The concession counter was about the level of Stewart's forehead. Elizabeth volunteered to get popcorn. Stewart gave her money for it.

"You don't have to do that," she said, trying to hand it back.

"This is a date, right?" he said, handing her the bills. He went to get the tickets.

Elizabeth watched him. His shoulders rose as he pushed the rails on his wheels, and his knees shook slightly as he moved. Elizabeth may have started down a path that could lead to disaster, but right now she decided to just enjoy the events that she had set in motion.

Together they went into the theater. They sat in the very front row, where there were cut-away seats for wheelchairs. Elizabeth leaned back and tried to put her neck on the back of her seat, but she was too tall. She didn't pay much attention to the movie; she kept stealing glances at Stewart beside her.

Once in a while he would look at her at the same moment that she looked at him and they both laughed. It wasn't a funny movie. She looked down at his lap and saw the tear in his jeans. Through the hole she could see a piece of the flesh that he couldn't feel. It fascinated her and she longed to touch it. She knew it would feel normal to her fingers, but she couldn't imagine what it must be like to see someone touching your body, and not feel the touch.

Stewart reached over and put his hand on her thigh. She was afraid to breathe for the rest of the movie, afraid to move and disturb his hand or cause him to lift it from her body. Stewart probably didn't know that this was Elizabeth's first real date— as long as you don't count going to a Middle School dance and talking to a boy most of the night, or being invited to the after party for an eighth grade production of *Cats*.

She wondered if they would have time to talk after the movie, or if he would bring her straight home. She hoped there would be a chance for learning more about him. And she wondered how to signal to him that she would want a second date. The next step of her plan to keep him in her life was to be a fantastic date so that he would want to ask her out again. He was confident enough to do it if he wanted to.

4

The movie ended and Stewart did not move. He was going to wait for all the other people to clear the way and be the last out. Elizabeth rocked her feet back and forth on the concrete floor, and twisted her head around to watch all the people leaving.

"Would you like to get some dinner?" Stewart asked.

Elizabeth smiled. "Yeah," she said, "I haven't eaten."

"This is your town, so tell me what's good."

Elizabeth named a restaurant that she knew to be wheelchair accessible. When everyone else had left, they emerged from the theater. Elizabeth walked with her hand on his shoulder, feeling the thick, solid muscle across his upper back. She had expected that she would want to show off being with him. In fact, she had worried that her motivations might not have been pure. Perhaps part of her attraction was wanting to look cool and interesting to other people. Yet at this moment she thought of none of that. She was unaware of any other person. She had been curious to see how people responded to Stewart in public, but she didn't have a chance to find out because she was completely oblivious to anyone else in the world.

"Did you enjoy the movie?" Stewart asked.

"Oh yes," Elizabeth said with enthusiasm, though it was being with him that had her so flushed, and not the movie.

The night had become cold while they were inside. The knitting of Elizabeth's sweater was loose enough that cold air could wiggle its way to the flesh of her arms. She took her hand away from Stewart's shoulder and crossed her arms tightly over her chest, pulling her neck down as much as she could.

"Are you cold?" Stewart said.

"Yeah," she said sheepishly.

He laughed. "You grew up here, didn't you?"

"Yeah," Elizabeth repeated, smiling.

Stewart stopped moving. "Here," he said, "Take my sweater, I'll keep warm by wheeling."

"That's okay, I'll be fine. The restaurant is just up there." After a moment she added, "Thanks, though."

"No problem," he said.

Elizabeth headed straight for the ramp around the back and she saw Stewart give her a strange look. She knew he was wondering how she had known where the ramp was. Hopefully he would pass it off as luck and in the future Elizabeth could be more careful about hiding her knowledge. She couldn't have Stewart asking questions about why she knew what she knew.

Once they were seated, Elizabeth relaxed her arms

and leaned her elbows on the table. "So when are you going to teach me to surf?"

"Not going to happen."

"Why not?" She smiled in what she hoped was a charming manner.

"They have schools for that, you know."

She leaned closer to him. "I want to learn from the best."

"You Googled me," he said, "Is that how you got my number?"

Elizabeth sat back and frowned, her attempt at charming seduction ruined. "More or less," she said, "How did you know that?"

"I never said anything about being good at surfing. It's okay, I Googled you too. Discovered that you played lead angel in your church's nativity pageant when you were ten."

"I live a very exciting life."

"Clearly."

The waitress came over to take their order. Elizabeth moved her foot against the edge of his wheelchair, and touched his sneakers under the table. He had no idea and just continued ordering. Elizabeth slipped her shoe off and wrapped her toes around the metal tube that held his legs off the floor.

The waitress didn't notice either. Elizabeth felt her secret being fed. It was a very hungry secret, always needing new stimuli. The waitress turned to Elizabeth and she ordered a salad. She was too nervous to eat. Her stomach felt tiny.

As soon as the waitress had walked away, Stewart said, "Now you aren't one of those girls who says she isn't hungry and orders a salad to be dainty, but actually goes hungry, are you?"

"I'm really not that hungry. Really," she said.

"If you change your mind, remember that you can order something else, okay?"

Elizabeth nodded.

After dinner they went around the town together. Nothing was open anymore. The shops they passed were all dark and the streetlamps gave only small circles of yellow light.

"Do you feel safe here at night?" Stewart asked.

"Oh, definitely. This is a very good neighborhood. I wouldn't do this in the city. Is the school you go to right in Boston?"

"Yes," Stewart said. "It's a charming city."

Elizabeth glowed with pride. She loved her home and she liked being able to show it off to him. "Where are you from?" she said.

"Don't you already know everything about me?"

"Hardly. The Internet had a lot to say about where your competitions were and how you placed, but not much about your actual life."

"I live in South Carolina," he said.

"Really? Is surfing big there?"

"It's not bad. I was born in California."

"Ah, that explains it."

"Believe it or not, not everyone in California surfs."

"Yeah they do," Elizabeth said. "What made you leave California?"

"I went to live with my aunt and uncle. I didn't have a lot of choice."

"Oh," Elizabeth said, "What happened to your parents?"

Stewart laughed. "Not exactly first date material."

"Think of the wedding as the first date."

"Oh, okay, so the second date is the time to bare our souls? You don't have much tact, do you?"

"Sorry," Elizabeth said. "My friend Becky says I don't beat around the bush. Amy says I don't even know there's a bush there."

She had no qualms about asking him personal questions. The only thing she wouldn't ask was how he broke his back. She had studied disability and read many people's stories. They all said that people were always bothering them for the details of their accidents. So Elizabeth didn't want to seem like your average, ignorant, able-bodied person.

She also couldn't talk about disability for the same reason she couldn't talk about her own desire for it. If she said the words, the truth might be written across her face plainly for anyone to read.

"You're not going to answer that, are you?" Elizabeth said.

"I don't like to talk about myself," he said, "There's a reason none of those websites has any information about my personal life."

"What made you want to come to Massachusetts?"

"Experience something different," he said. It was a quick, smooth answer, and she suspected that he had been answering that question a lot.

"Just wait until it snows, then you'll see why we don't have any disabled people here." She turned red. Her mouth had gotten away from her and she looked nervously at Stewart. She hadn't meant to say anything about his disability or say anything that suggested that she had even noticed it.

He laughed. "You may be right, but I hate to take the easy way. Come on, I'm parked out behind the theater."

Elizabeth liked the look of his car when they got to it. Though she didn't know much about brands and types, she could tell that Stewart's car wasn't stuffy or pretentious. It was small and blue and had some bumps and bruises. Stewart leaned back to reach in his pocket and pull out keys.

Elizabeth wasn't sure whether to watch Stewart get in or not. She desperately wanted to, but she also wanted to seem cool to him. She wanted him to think that his disability didn't factor in for her, that she was hardly even aware of it. Sadly she was hyper aware of it, maybe more so than the average person.

He was concentrating on the car, though, not looking at her, so she stood behind him and watched as he grabbed the driver's seat of his car with one hand and maneuvered his body as close to the edge of the wheelchair as he could. He grabbed the steering wheel with his other hand and held his breath while he pulled his butt to the seat. One at a time he grabbed each knee and lifted his legs into place.

Elizabeth looked at the empty wheelchair. Without him in it, it seemed very small. "You can get in, you know," Stewart said.

She nodded and went around to her side. Through the window she saw that he had turned the chair upside down and pulled off the two larger wheels. As she got in Stewart said, "Watch your head" and wheelchair components went by her into the back seat. She frowned and tried to figure out how it could be so easy to pull the wheels off and yet they stayed on while he was using the chair. Elizabeth had never seen anything like it before.

"Ready?" he said, grabbing the gas/brake lever with one hand and putting the car in reverse with the other. She nodded.

"You'll have to direct me to your house."

Elizabeth did so, but finished up at the last crossroad before her house. "You can let me out here," she said, "It's not too much further."

Stewart frowned, but he stopped the car. Elizabeth started to get out. "Wait a minute," Stewart said, "This is a date, right?"

Elizabeth wasn't certain what he meant. She wanted to lean over and kiss him, but what if that wasn't what he was talking about? Was she about to make a complete fool of herself? She looked into his face and it wore an expression of waiting. She slid closer to him along the bench seat, her knees bent under her, until she was almost touching his legs. She pressed her lips to his.

Even if she was wrong about what he wanted, this was worth it. Her lips parted and she tasted the heat of his breath. As though her body had stopped obeying her commands for restraint, she found herself touching his face, with her hands cupping his jaw. His lips moved, changed pressure and, ever so gently, his tongue touched the tips of her teeth. He took her arms in his hands and lifted her onto his lap. Her arms suddenly wanted to be filled with him and she grasped him as tightly as a lifesaver.

When they separated to breathe for a moment,

Elizabeth looked into his hazel eyes, but found that she couldn't go deep. She looked at his eyes and knew immediately that no one had ever penetrated to see the real Stewart.

"I have to go," she whispered.

He nodded.

She straightened herself and got out of the car.

"I'll call you," Stewart said. Elizabeth stood in the cold night and, for the first time, didn't feel cold. Her body was burning up as though she had a fever. She watched Stewart drive away. A minute later she was still standing on the side of the road in the dark and she was wondering if she had imagined the whole thing.

Elizabeth walked back to her house and opened the door slowly and cautiously. She peered her head in first. The living room was dark and no one was up. She tiptoed in and up the stairs. She tiptoed as fast as she could to get to her room and close the door behind her. She didn't want her mother to see her. Susan would know somehow what Elizabeth had been up to.

She leaned against the back of her door and looked at her childhood room. It hadn't changed in the last several hours, but she had. Everything looked small to her and she felt a distance, as though she was seeing everything after she had been away from it for many months.

In the morning Elizabeth was afraid to go downstairs. She was sure that Susan had the ability to look at her and know. Not that she had done anything bad. She just kissed him. It felt wrong only because such a fire had been set in her body because of it.

She did go downstairs eventually. "Are you ready to go?" Susan said.

Elizabeth grabbed an apple. "Yeah," she said.

David was packing exams into his bag. "I'll meet you down there," he said, since Elizabeth was already bouncing on her toes at the top of the stairs to the basement. She hopped down the stairs and through the door to the garage. She pressed the button to raise the garage door and sat in her dad's car waiting. Behind her she could see the colorful leaves gathering on the driveway. The tree branches were almost bare already.

That could mean only one thing. Elizabeth knew what she was going to be doing that weekend: raking leaves.

David got in the car. "Your mother wants to know if you need a coat," he said.

"I have a sweater," Elizabeth said, holding up her sleeve to demonstrate the presence of her sweater. It was a bit long in the arm, but her Bubby, her Dad's mother, had knit it for her a year ago and it had a pretty design of mystical sea creatures.

Once they were on the road David asked Elizabeth how school was going.

"It's going," Elizabeth said simply.

"Good classes?"

"Yeah, senior year is great. I can slack off and finally take pottery class."

"And here I thought pottery classes were for mental institutions," David said.

Elizabeth rolled her eyes. Her father was always trying to be funny, but he wasn't.

He dropped her off in front of the school and Amy was waiting outside near the stairs. Elizabeth walked over and they exchanged pleasantries while walking to

Maureen's locker. It was the same everyday. Maureen's parents didn't let her wear makeup, so every morning the girls gathered while Maureen applied makeup with a mirror in her locker.

"Did you see what George was wearing at the parent dinner?" Maureen said.

That had been the night of the wedding, so Elizabeth had missed it. "I wasn't there," Elizabeth said.

"He was absolutely flaming," Amy said.

Maureen, tilting her head while she brushed on mascara, said, "He just doesn't usually dress like a gay guy. We all know and he knows we all know, so he just dresses normal. But then his parents were there, the people he hasn't told, the people who would have the biggest problem with it, and he was dressed in these tight pants and a pastel turtleneck. It was bizarre. I couldn't stop staring."

"They make pastel turtlenecks?" Becky said.

Amy shrugged. Ignoring Becky, she said, "I don't get it."

"Makes sense to me," Elizabeth said. They all turned to her. Maureen paused with her lipstick on the way toward her mouth.

"Okay," Amy said, "Do you want to explain it to us?"

Elizabeth felt her face turning red. Why did her skin have to be so sensitive to embarrassment? The slightest thing could bring a flush to her face. "Well," she stumbled, "It's just that they're his parents and he really wants them to know. He wants to end the secrecy, and be close to them again. But he's still afraid of them knowing. So he's trying to get them to figure it out on their own, so that he doesn't have to tell them. Then when they ask, he can be on the defensive and not the offensive."

"Huh," Maureen said.

"It makes some sense," Amy said, "That psychology elective must be paying off."

The bell rang and they dispersed to their classes. Elizabeth didn't have any friends in her psychology class. She watched the other students. She looked at Ted and Sarah, of whom she had always been jealous. They had been a couple since the fifth grade. Today they were sitting next to each other and Sarah kept flicking tiny pieces of paper onto Ted's desk. She'd giggle and twist her hair. The teacher didn't seem to notice.

Now Elizabeth didn't feel jealous of them anymore. It no longer looked like what she wanted. She had the chance to be with a guy that she was attracted to and to be with an adult, outside the sphere of grades, tests, and football games. What would all these children think if they knew that she had been on a date with a college student?

Stewart was the most amazing opportunity of her life. She had never dreamed it would ever be possible for her to date someone she found attractive. Now desire was overwhelming her and she could hardly focus for thinking about the feel of his lips on hers and his strong fingers against her flesh. This was exactly the way it was supposed to be and Elizabeth glowed with the joy of finding that she was capable of that kind of attraction.

After school Elizabeth actually did her homework first thing. She was using it to distract herself from thinking about Stewart and wondering when he might call. He had made it clear that if they were going to have a relationship, he intended to be in the driver's seat. Elizabeth felt she had done all she could and now the ball was in his court.

She sat at the dining room table and saw her father's car drive by the window before he pulled into the garage. When he got up the stairs and put down his things, he came into the dining room and said, "It's about time we got the storm windows up. I'm going upstairs to change and then you can help me."

Elizabeth put her books away. She loved helping change the window screens. Seasons in New England were always an adventure and each change was marked by activities and procedures. There was a time for apple picking and cider and then there was a time for leaf raking, and a time for snow shoveling, sledding and hot chocolate; a time for planting in the garden and pressing flowers and a time for lemonade and the clinking of the metal tags for the community pool. The weather was inescapable, it accosted you, and all you could do was find strategies to deal with it. The changing of the screens into storm windows was a momentous occasion, signaling the coming of winter.

David came back downstairs a few minutes later wearing his pants with white paint stains and a Brandeis sweatshirt. One by one he and Elizabeth went around to all the windows. They pulled down the screens and removed them, then took the solid plates of glass and slid them up behind the window. Susan came home part way through the operation. She went to the kitchen and started warming up some apple cider for when it was finished. Elizabeth's hair stuck to her sweaty forehead. She was wearing her "artist" outfit of overalls and a little white T-shirt underneath. The smell of warm apples and cinnamon reached them upstairs.

"Okay," David said, as they finished the last one, "We are ready for the snow."

Elizabeth and her father raced down the stairs and grabbed the mugs of cider with cinnamon sticks. The house was already warmer. Susan went to the hall closet and took down some more blankets to put around the living room.

The phone rang and Elizabeth was the closest, so she reached for it, even though it was never for her.

"Hello," she said, "Foster residence." As she had been taught to say when she answered the phone at six years old.

"Elizabeth? Is that you?"

It was Stewart. "Oh,' she said, "Hi." She was going to ask where he got this number from, since she had called him from her cell, but she thought better of it. They were even.

"You busy?" he said.

"No, just hanging around with my parents."

"I won't interrupt your rocking good time, then. I just called to say that our suite is having a Halloween party. Do you want to come?"

"Absolutely," she said, "Count me in."

"Okay, great," he said. "Can I pick you up?"

"I guess so," Elizabeth said.

"Or better yet, I'll be getting into my costume, so I'll have Robert pick you up."

"Perfect," Elizabeth said.

When Elizabeth hung up the phone and returned to the living room, her mother said, "Who was that?"

"Becky," Elizabeth said smoothly.

"Are you two getting together?"

"Not for a while. You know how she loves to plan ahead," Elizabeth said. She hated to lie to her parents, but they would never understand why she had to see Stewart.

Susan nodded and looked over David's shoulder to help him with a crossword puzzle.

5

Halloween night Susan and David were going to a party. They had invited Elizabeth, but she turned them down. She said she intended to stay home and give the trick-or-treaters their candy. As soon as the car drove down the street, Elizabeth took her costume out and put it on. She was a ladybug, with a tight red T-shirt decorated with black dots, black jeans, and cheap fairy wings. She stood on her bed at her window and waited for Robert.

She looked over to the bureau and, after only a moment's hesitation, she pulled the notebook out. She leaned against the wall and felt the double-edged sword of pleasure and shame enter her heart. It felt even worse now that she knew Stewart. She had to consider how it would make him feel if he knew about these pictures. She could imagine his accusation with every image of a wheelchair. *You're sick. There's something wrong with you.*

Elizabeth didn't want to be dirty. She didn't want to touch herself when she looked at these pictures, but she wasn't strong enough not to. It wasn't as though she had ever been given a choice. If someone had asked her when she was in the womb what kind of man she would like to be attracted to, this is not what she would pick. As far as Elizabeth knew, no one had asked. The decision had been made by the time she was born because she had been carrying the weight of her secret since before her earliest memory.

And then the little blue car was there. Elizabeth breathed, composed herself, and ran out of her bedroom. On the way down the hall she stopped at her parent's room and grabbed her mother's mascara, taking a moment to smear some on her light colored lashes. That done, she dashed out of the house, grabbing the spare key from the little dish next to the door.

It was colder than she had anticipated and she went back into the house for a coat. Then off down the walkway and into the little blue car.

"Hi," she said to Robert and realized how awkward this moment was. He had been dancing with her and then she had abandoned him in favor of Stewart and now he was running errands for Stewart too.

"Hi," Robert said cheerfully. He had on a dress shirt and slacks with fake glasses, nose, and mustache.

"Nice costume," Elizabeth said.

"You too," he said, "Very cute. I think Stewart will like it."

The other thing that made this awkward was that Robert knew Stewart so much better than she did. Even if they had only just started to be roommates, Elizabeth had only had the one date. She had also never been to a college campus, much less a college party. She wanted to be accepted by these people and not give away her ignorance.

The drive into the city took several minutes and they were both quiet. Neither one was good at conversation. Elizabeth saw all her favorite parts of the city go by. There was Harvard Square, and Commons, and they followed the Charles River over the salt and peppershaker bridge. Finally Robert parked in Stewart's designated place and they got out. Elizabeth tried to shrink into herself a little, but with her height it was impossible. She wondered if other people on the campus were dressed up.

She followed behind Robert as they walked up to a building. He held open the door for her and a pair of girls who were leaving obviously thought they were a couple. No, Elizabeth thought, I've got someone much more exciting to connect with. Robert passed the elevators and opened the stairwell door.

"You don't mind, do you?" he said, "It's only on the second floor."

"Oh, no problem," Elizabeth said, happily following him up the stairs.

As soon as they opened the door it was clear that there was a party. In the hallway between suites, the lights were out and fake candles were plugged in. A pumpkin with a jack-o-lantern face drawn on in Sharpie sat on the floor and cotton "spider web" was hanging limply on the walls.

Elizabeth looked around immediately for Stewart. She suddenly didn't feel safe here. Her mother was always saying that college parties were full of brutish men and stupid women and that they were just rapes waiting to happen.

Elizabeth was caught between the adult world and the child's world. She wanted to be grown up and independent, but she was still finding her footing in the world. She thought she was ready to handle a real party full of semi-adults, but now that she was here she wanted to run home and hide under the covers and have Susan rubbing her back. She didn't know yet that this is what it meant to be an adult; always seeing yourself as a child and then being expected to handle things, to know things, to take responsibility for things.

Elizabeth thought she saw a wheelchair in the corner of her eye and turned in that direction. She hadn't been wrong, it was a sleek red wheelchair, but Stewart wasn't the man in it. This man was wearing a black wig and a white T-shirt with a necklace of shells. He was too bulky for the chair, and also too drunk. He kept bumping it into people or walls.

Then Stewart walked into the hall from his room. And he was walking. He wore long leg braces over his pants and pulled the full weight of his body with forearm crutches. He was dressed unlike himself. He had on a football jersey and a blonde wig balancing on top of his black hair.

"Hey, Elizabeth," he said, "I'm glad you made it."

The first thing she noticed about him was that he was taller than she had expected. Somehow seeing him seated all the time made it difficult to envision what he would look like standing up. Even though he was leaning forward at an angle, she could see the full extension of his legs for the first time. "What are you?" she asked.

"I'm Travis," he said.

"And I'm Stewart," the man in Stewart's wheelchair said.

"Oh," Elizabeth said.

A slender blonde girl wearing a white mini dress with a nurse's hat walked over and kissed Robert. Robert nodded at her and said to Elizabeth, "My girlfriend, Courtney."

"Nice to meet you," Elizabeth said politely.

Several people then tried to introduce her at once.

Stewart said, "This is my date." At the same time that Robert said, "This is Stewart's girl," and Travis said, "But who are you?"

Elizabeth looked at them all, looked at Courtney, and said, "I'm Elizabeth."

They shook hands.

"Don't mind them," Courtney said, "Come on, let me get you a drink."

As Courtney took her arm and led her toward the common kitchen, Elizabeth looked back over her shoulder at Stewart. Even with the ridiculous outfit, he looked cool and confident as ever.

"What are you having?" Courtney said.

Elizabeth looked at all the bottles and colors. "I don't know," she said, not wanting to admit that she had never gone out partying with the other high schoolers and had not tried to locate her parents' liquor cabinet.

"In that case, try this," Courtney said. She handed Elizabeth a tiny shot glass and Elizabeth sipped the contents. Courtney laughed.

"What is it?" Elizabeth said.

"A buttery nipple."

If she had had any left in her mouth, she would have spit it out. "A what?" she sputtered.

"You're adorable," Courtney declared.

Elizabeth looked at Courtney's cleavage and super-high heels. She looked around her and realized that all the girls were similarly dressed. Many looked like hookers, there was a genie, another nurse, a fairy all in black, and even a girl in a plaid mini skirt and a white shirt tied over her breasts with Mary Jane shoes. Was she trying to look Elizabeth's age? Illegal? Was that sexy?

Elizabeth had dressed totally wrong for this party. She wasn't sexy; she was just sort of cute. Courtney handed her another drink and then they got back to the boys. Elizabeth thought she would stop feeling out of place when she found Stewart, but she still felt she stood out. Everyone could see she didn't belong here.

Music was playing loudly and people were bobbing and moving. Elizabeth was getting jostled and pushed. She eventually almost knocked Stewart over. "Sorry," she said.

"Why don't we go sit down? My arms are getting tired. Fifteen minutes is about my limit with these things."

She followed him to the common room of his suite. His movement was very precarious. He moved his right crutch, then his left, then used the trunk of his body to pull the legs forward. For one moment in each step he fell forward onto the crutches and looked like he was going to go crashing down. He never did though. His amazing sense of balance reminded her that he had been a surfer.

As Stewart came into the room a girl dressed as a devil called out, "What happened to you, Travis?"

"You know how it is," Stewart said, "I was playing football and got tackled by a cheerleader."

The people in the room laughed.

"Just temporary, right?" An angel said.

"I'm sure I'll be back to myself tomorrow."

Stewart stopped in front of the couch and carefully maneuvered around until his back was to it.

"Do you need help?" the angel asked.

Elizabeth felt even more invisible. If he needed help, he could turn to his date. She would have liked to give the angel a dirty look, but the girl hadn't really done anything wrong.

"No thanks," Stewart said, dropping onto the couch. He pulled his arms out of the handles and laid the crutches on the floor. He held a hand out to Elizabeth and she stepped over his legs and sat down beside him.

"How have you been?" Stewart asked.

"Good," she said, "I'm good." She put her arm over his shoulders and snuggled close. "Do you know all these people?" she asked.

"Not all," he said.

"With all these people around," Elizabeth murmured, "How could you ever have noticed me?"

"You noticed me first," he said.

"Oh yeah," she said. "You're very noticeable."

"I suppose I am. Noticeable and invisible at the same time, some trick, huh?"

"You? Invisible?"

"Sure," Stewart said, "Didn't anyone ever tell you you're not supposed to acknowledge the guy in a wheelchair?"

"I guess I missed the memo."

Stewart laughed. "Clearly," he said.

"Do you like my costume?"

"Very much," he said. He reached over and scooped her up, pulling her onto his lap. The tops of the leg braces were uncomfortable under Elizabeth's butt, yet she didn't move. The pounding music and chattering voices faded into the background as they looked at each other.

"You're staring at me," she whispered. She couldn't look away from his beautiful eyes, which were too light in shade for his dark hair.

"Sorry," he said, but he didn't move his gaze.

She was the one who initiated the kiss, and then they were making out on the couch in full view of everyone. The lighting was dim, but it only took a few seconds before people noticed and they all began hooting and cheering. Of all the people to hook up at a party, they hadn't expected it to be Stewart. Most of them knew and liked him, but hadn't ever considered the guy in the wheelchair dating or kissing or...other things.

Elizabeth stopped to breathe, but kept her forehead pressed against his. He smiled and she felt a reflection of his smile spread over her own face.

"What are beaches in California like?" she asked.

"Colder than beaches in South Carolina, actually."

"Really? That's so unexpected."

"It was a pleasant surprise for me after I moved. The waves are not as big, though."

"What's the most amazing place you ever surfed?"

Stewart looked blankly at the black and gray tiled floor while he thought. "It's hard to pick between South Africa and Hawaii."

"Someday I'm going to travel to exotic places like

that," Elizabeth said, dropping her head to his shoulder and imagining the oceans he had seen.

"All you have to do is get some sponsorships and people will pay you to go."

"Oh is that all?" Elizabeth laughed. "And how am I going to learn how to surf?"

"You'll think of a way." He paused and, realizing the direction she was going, added, "Other than me."

"You're no fun."

"It's about to be winter. There's no way I'm taking you out to a beach at this time of year."

"Does that mean you'll take me when it gets warmer?"

"No. Just trying to put you off."

Elizabeth laughed again and ran her fingers over his head, pulling off the wig, and shaking his hair to muss it up. He grabbed her arms and held her down.

"Hey, Stewart," Robert said and they both stopped laughing to look up at him. "Here, I brought you this." Robert handed him a beer.

"Thanks, man."

"Yeah."

Elizabeth watched Robert walk back to Courtney in the hallway, where most of the party was happening.

"He really takes care of you, doesn't he?" she said.

"It's his job," Stewart said with a sigh.

"As your roommate?"

"He's not exactly just a roommate. My aunt hired him to keep an eye on me."

"Are you serious? That's crazy."

"Par for the course with my aunt."

"Robert's a PCA?"

"That's right."

"You don't seem like you need much help."

"You haven't seen me do laundry."

"What did you do to the laundry?" She giggled.

He held one of her hands in his and massaged the fingers as he spoke. "Let's just say they don't have front loading washers here."

"Oh no!"

Stewart shrugged. "I do whatever I can to make Aunt Claire nuts."

"I bet you're good at it."

"Thank you, I am."

Across the room, Travis fell straight off the wheelchair and onto the floor. Hearing the crash, Elizabeth looked around and discovered that the music had stopped and almost everyone had gone home; except for a few people fast asleep on the couches nearby.

"Did you like the party?" Stewart said.

"It was excellent," Elizabeth said, "Now I know what college is like."

Stewart laughed. "Exactly," he said, "College is just like this."

"My Dad's a professor," Elizabeth said, "At Brandeis."

"What does he teach?"

"Philosophy. You're going to be a teacher too, aren't you?"

"There's a big difference between college philosophy and high school physics."

"I'm in physics now," Elizabeth said.

"Weird, isn't it? I'm going to be teaching people your age."

"How old are you?"

"A quarter of a century."

"Yeah, that's old."

Stewart laughed. He looked behind him to the hallway, "Care to see my room?"

"Would I? Let's go."

"It's been a long time since someone was that enthusiastic," he said, "Will you go grab my chair from off of Travis?"

Elizabeth went to get it while Stewart unstrapped the braces from his legs and smoothed his pants. When Elizabeth brought the chair back she put the hand brake on just as he was saying, "Could you…yeah, the brake, that's it. Okay." He left the crutches and braces and transferred back onto his chair, then led Elizabeth down the hall to his room.

She was surprised, when she stepped through the door, at how neat it was. She always thought college boys would be messy. The floor was completely clear, and that Elizabeth had expected because of the wheelchair. She could see which side of the room belonged to Stewart immediately and it hardly looked lived in at all. The walls were bare, the sheets were white, and a stack of books was the only thing on the floor.

"Home sweet home," Stewart said, "You can close the door, Robert will be with Courtney until I call."

Elizabeth smiled and went over to lock the door. On her way back Elizabeth noticed a picture framed beside his computer. She nodded at it and said, "Your aunt and uncle?"

He shook his head. "My parents."

She picked it up and looked at it. The two figures

were standing on some rocks, a waterfall behind them. His father, round and average with brown hair and eyes and his mother, sparkling, with hair as black as his own.

After a moment Stewart rolled forward, took the picture from her hands, and placed it back on his desk. "Tonight is not for the past," he said.

She stood in front of him and he took hold of her hips with his hands, pulling her toward him. She climbed onto the wheelchair, wrapping her legs around the back and relishing his kisses. His hands moved up and down her back, unhooked the ladybug wings and untucked her red shirt from her black pants. In his arms, she felt comfortable. She was exactly the right shape, and fit perfectly in his grasp.

Elizabeth was getting hot and she pushed the sleeves of her shirt back. Stewart stopped and frowned. She followed his gaze to her arms. There were two small bruises on the side of her elbow where she had pinched herself to try to draw the sickness out of her body. Stewart grabbed her wrist and pulled her arm out straight, examining a few other bruises scattered over her skin.

"Did I do this?" he asked.

"No, of course not."

"Then, how did it happen?"

"I'm just, you know, clumsy."

"That's the worst excuse I've ever heard."

Elizabeth didn't know what to say. The frown did not leave Stewart's face. "Sometimes," she said, "Stuff just builds up inside you, you know? It helps to pull the pain out." Elizabeth waited for Stewart's response.

He bent his head and kissed each bruise. "Don't ever do that again," he said, "Promise me."

Elizabeth nodded, surprised that he cared so much about her stupid little bruises.

They moved to the bed and sat beside each other, leaning against the wall.

"Do you use those braces a lot?" she asked.

"No," he said, "Not much. Just for parties, when I don't want to be staring at belt buckles all night." He held out his arm and showed her where one of the crutches rubbed his skin raw. "My uncle bought them for me for Christmas the year after I got out of rehab."

"Your uncle is really like a father to you?"

"He likes to think he is. My Dad is more than enough to handle, though, I don't need another one."

"My Dad is great. My Mom too. But sometimes I wonder…" Elizabeth stopped.

"What do you wonder?"

"Well, I just wonder if their love is really as unconditional as they think it is. Does that sound dumb?"

"No. What makes you say that?"

"I've never tested the limits of their love. Not that I want to, but I think if I did I might find the end of it."

Stewart was quiet for a moment, and then he said, "I don't think there could be anything in you that would make them reject you, Elizabeth."

She looked at him. She saw a hint of pain on the edges of his face and she knew he recognized the fears that she spoke of. "Thank you," she said, "That's nice of you to say."

"I mean it," he said.

Elizabeth smiled. Then she caught sight of the

glowing red numbers on his alarm clock. It was 1:30 a.m.

"What's wrong?" Stewart said, seeing her face suddenly drop.

She bolted for her cell phone. She had turned the ringer off. There were six missed messages from her parents. She wasn't used to having the phone, since she was almost never away from home. It was something her mother insisted she have.

"Oh no, I'm in big trouble. I have to get home."

He frowned, but only for an instant. Elizabeth wondered if she had imagined it. "Why the big rush?" He was back to his unreadable face.

"It's not you, it's just my parents. I lied to them." She bit her lip and hoped Stewart's opinion of her wasn't lowered.

"What is this, the first time?" he said with a laugh.

Elizabeth shrugged. "I'm not a big rebel."

Stewart sighed, shrugged, and said, "Okay, calm down, I'll drive you."

"Thanks."

Elizabeth ran to the car and hopped up and down until Stewart got there.

"Step on it!" Elizabeth said when they were settled in the car. Stewart laughed and pulled the hand lever.

"You're not supposed to be out this late?" Stewart said, navigating the Boston streets.

"My parents went to a party and I said I was staying home."

Stewart said, "Yeah, you're going to have to work on those lying skills."

Fifteen minutes later they were nearing Elizabeth's street.

"Drop me off here," she said.

"I'm not going to leave you to walk back in the dark. Just let me drop you off at the house." He paused, and then added without looking at her, "Your parents won't be able to see me from the car."

Elizabeth thought about it. "Okay," she said.

He pulled over and she got out and ran up the walkway, not even watching Stewart's car. He stayed on the side of the road to make sure she got in.

Elizabeth opened the door as slowly and softly as she could, cringing against the squeak. She tiptoed into the living room and took long steps toward the stairs.

"Don't even try it, Elizabeth," her mother's voice said. She emerged from the top of the staircase and walked slowly down to the living room. Seeing Elizabeth's outfit, she said, "You could have told us you were going out. Why did you want to worry us?"

"I'm really sorry, Mom, I just forgot."

"David!" Her mother called up the stairs. "She's home."

A moment later her father came down.

"I'm sorry, daddy," she whispered.

"What's going on with you?" he said.

"I think she's finally being a teenager," her mother said.

"I didn't agree to that. This teenage business has to stop now. Come here." David held out his arms and Elizabeth ran to hug him. She had never been disobedient or tried to stretch the rules. He would let this one go.

"Go on to bed," he said.

She passed her parents on the stairs and went around the corner.

"Where do you think she went?" Susan said.

"She only has three friends, it must have been something they dreamed up," David said.

"She could have been with a boy."

"Keep dreaming, sweetheart," David said.

6

"I'm sorry," Elizabeth said. "I just mean, I didn't want to leave like that. I was having a good time." She was sitting on the floor in her darkroom with her cell phone. Her back was pressed against the porcelain tub and she was looking up at the ceiling.

"So was I," Stewart said.

"We should work out a system or something," Elizabeth said.

"For what?" Traces of a Southern accent in his voice were easier to hear when he spoke on the phone.

"For seeing each other. If you're still interested in seeing me, that is."

She paused and waited, holding her breath until he said, "I'm interested."

Elizabeth breathed out slowly and sank down onto the rug on the floor. Her hair spread around her head. "I like to have a plan," she said.

"Okay," he said slowly, "Again, what kind of plan?"

"Once a week, maybe."

"You are a strange one, Elizabeth," he said.

"I'm sorry, I'm new at this."

"Just come to the city next Friday night and don't lie to your parents."

"I'll tell them I'm sleeping over Becky's house. Once the winter starts, we do that every Friday."

"And how would that be not lying?"

"Stewart, be reasonable. I can't tell them I'm going to a college campus to sleep in a boy's room."

"I'm not used to hiding."

"Don't take it that way, please. Give it time, that's all. My parents don't need to be involved."

"You're very young," Stewart said, "I think they're automatically involved. I would rather be upfront and have their approval."

Elizabeth couldn't think of anything to say. She couldn't tell him that if her parents saw him they might realize the truth about Elizabeth's interest in the handicapped. *You're a pervert.* Finally she said, "Let me do it in my own way, okay?"

"Fine," Stewart said, "Just come on Friday."

"I'll catch the subway after school."

Elizabeth had never taken the subway by herself before. Without her friends, she never had a reason to. They were the ones who thought of things to do and went out to do them. Elizabeth had always followed along. Now for the first time she had a reason to get out of the house.

She told her parents that she was sleeping over with her friends. Her parents were not surprised. Even though Elizabeth and her friends were almost eighteen years old they still had a good time by spreading sleeping bags on the floor and talking late into the night. Elizabeth packed her backpack and carried her sleeping bag.

"Do you want a ride?" her father asked.

"No, I'm going to walk," Elizabeth said. Becky's house was about a mile from their house.

"With all that stuff?"

"It's good exercise," Elizabeth said. "Besides, I want to enjoy the fall weather before winter comes."

"Okay, let us know if you want to be picked up in the morning," he said.

It was a further walk to Alewife station than to Becky's house. It was still early in the afternoon and the sun was out. There was a nip to the air, and Elizabeth reluctantly zipped up her jacket. As she walked and her legs got tired, she thought about what it would be like if Stewart could show up at her house to pick her up. How great it would be if her parents knew and were supportive.

Maybe if Elizabeth had done an even better job hiding her secret she would be able to tell them about Stewart without dire consequences. There had been too many years, though. Elizabeth had not always been successful at hiding her interest in the disabled. To her it seemed obvious.

She thought that anyone looking at her would be able to see the secret written all over her life. That was why she wondered if her friends and family really did know, and were just afraid to say anything. It was the proverbial elephant in the room, no one was willing to bring up the subject.

They had to have noticed what all her favorite movies had in common. Becky was the one who had told her about *Born on the Fourth of July*, with its paraplegic main character. She had known that Elizabeth would enjoy that, but did she know the reason? They had to have realized why Elizabeth had adored Long John Silver from the moment she read *Treasure Island* at nine years old. If her friends and family did know, there would be no way to keep avoiding the subject if they met Stewart. If they didn't know, they would figure it out fast. He was the biggest clue to her sickness that there could be.

The subway was a lonely place when you were by yourself. Elizabeth didn't feel the same rush of excitement about going into the city that she felt when she and her friends did it together. Now she just saw all the empty faces around her and she was sitting by herself, one of them. Was this the fate of people whose love failed them? Was it Elizabeth's destiny to sit in the subway, slouched and defeated, as though she would never move from the seat? People looked at her, but no one smiled. Even if she caught their eye, the faces were grim and deflated.

At the station near Stewart's school, he was waiting for her. When she got off the subway she almost didn't see him. People were rushing on and off the train and Stewart was buried in the crowd. Elizabeth's body was well attuned to picking out wheelchairs in any setting, though. She smiled, delighted that he had come to meet the train.

"Hey," she said with a shy smile.

"Hi," he said. He was wearing a sweater and a scarf.

"You're looking almost preppy today," Elizabeth commented.

"I'm starting to learn that in Massachusetts, you do whatever works," Stewart replied.

They made their way toward the elevator, over filthy concrete floors, and surrounded by larger-than-life people in ads on all the walls. Stewart stopped to wipe his wrist on his jeans. He had accidentally let it touch one of his wheels, which were picking up a lot of the dirt on the floor.

Out on the street little dry brown leaves were gathering against the sides of buildings and against the curb. The leaves rustled as they crowded closer together and were swept up in the wind.

They crossed over some painted lines on the sidewalk that represented the path to follow the freedom trail. Elizabeth put her hand on Stewart's shoulder and it rode up and down with the strokes of his arms.

"Look!" she cried, "Socks!" She pointed to the store display of knee-high socks in bright stripes. Stewart stopped and looked at the store, then looked up at her, waiting until she added, "...And other things" when she noticed the corsets and crotch-less underwear in the same window.

Stewart laughed heartily and Elizabeth smacked his shoulder because she was embarrassed. He kept laughing. "Hang on a minute," he said, and he crossed the street without Elizabeth. She stood on the sidewalk and watched him go in.

When he came back to her, she raised an eyebrow. "What did you buy in there?"

"Never mind that," he said and continued wheeling toward campus.

At the dorm, they found Travis and a few other guys sitting in Stewart's common room.

"There you are," Travis said, "We're going clubbing, you coming?"

"Can't," Stewart said, "Elizabeth's too young."

"Oh man, Stewart, we need you."

Stewart shrugged. "Maybe we could sneak her in."

Travis was standing in the doorway, leaving Stewart sitting in the hallway and Elizabeth standing behind him. Travis threw his hands in the air. "You can't bring a girl," he said, "We need you as a wingman." He turned his attention to Elizabeth. "You should see this guy, the girls go nuts for him."

"That's comforting," Elizabeth said, smiling down at Stewart. "I'll be sure to talk him into going now."

Travis imitated a girl's voice and said in squeaky tones, " 'What happened to your legs?' 'Oh my God, that's so sad.'"

Stewart shook his head. "Have fun," he said, and pushed past Travis into the common room.

"Sorry guys," Elizabeth said as she walked in.

Travis and his friends headed for the elevator. "Next time, Stewart," he called back.

A few hours later Stewart and Elizabeth were lounging in the common room wondering what to do. The TV was on in front of them, but they weren't watching it.

"Well," Stewart said, "if we want a really good time, we could go rent *Born the Fourth of July* and eat popcorn." He laughed.

Elizabeth rolled her eyes. She wished she hadn't told him that it was her favorite movie. Although he hadn't seemed to make anything of it.

"We could play a board game," she said.

"Did you bring any with you?" he asked.

"No."

Elizabeth pulled out her camera and focused it playfully on him. He reached forward and snatched it out of her hands. "Hey!" Elizabeth said. He tried to hold it out of her reach, but she had the height advantage and grabbed it back. That gave her an idea. "I know what we can do, I bet you have pictures you could show me," she said.

"That's true, I suppose I do. Hang on a minute."

When he came back, he was holding a small stack of photographs in his mouth because he needed his hands to move.

Elizabeth took the pictures and wiped them off on her shirt. There were only three. "This is all you have?"

He shrugged. "Yeah. You want to look at them or not?"

Elizabeth looked down at the first picture. It was a picture of the ocean. He came all this way away from home and instead of pictures of friends and family, he had a picture of the ocean.

"That's me," Stewart said.

Elizabeth frowned. "I don't see you, I see a wave."

"I'm inside the wave."

"Oh." She squinted and held the photograph closer, but she couldn't see anything but a solid wall of water. She turned to the next photograph. It showed a young boy who was clearly Stewart; his dark hair almost touched his shoulders, even then.

"That's me," Stewart said, "When I was nine. I still lived with my father then."

In the other room the telephone rang, but Robert picked it up. Elizabeth was about to ask Stewart about his family again, but Robert poked his head around the door and said, "Stewart, telephone. It's your uncle."

Stewart left Elizabeth where she sat and went over to the doorway where Robert was holding the phone out to him. Elizabeth looked down at the last picture. It was another of Stewart's mother. Elizabeth recognized the woman from the picture on his desk. Here she didn't look as vibrant: she was thin and her cheekbones were sticking out under her tight skin. But she was still smiling in the same warm way Stewart did.

Stewart stayed in the doorway with his back turned, not far from Elizabeth. The dorm phone was cheap and she could just hear his uncle's voice crackling through the line.

"Hey, Uncle John, it's Stewart. Is something wrong?"

"No, no, I just haven't talked to you in a while. Whenever you call the house Claire doesn't let me talk to you."

Elizabeth turned down the volume on the TV a few degrees and slid a little closer to the doorway.

"Are you really okay at school or do you just say that to keep Claire happy?" Stewart's uncle continued.

"I'm okay."

"I always knew you were a smart kid."

"I tried my best to hide it."

"Not studying all the time, are you? Did you join any clubs?"

"No, no clubs, but I socialize, don't worry."

"I met your aunt at college, you know. We were both taking the curriculum required science class at the same time. If not for core curriculum we might never have met,

since she was an education major and I was business."
John sighed. Then he said, "Ms. Morris called."

"What did she say?"

"It was one of her bad days. I didn't tell her where
you were."

"You can give her my phone number next time."

"You don't owe her anything, Stewart."

"You can still give her my number."

"Okay, next time. So, what are you up to tonight?"

"I have a friend over at the moment."

"Oh, okay then. Guess I better go. We'll be seeing
you for Christmas, then."

"Yep."

John said good-bye and Stewart hung up. Elizabeth
quickly looked back to the television.

"What's on?" Stewart said as he came back over to
the couch.

"Interview with someone or other," she said.

"Not so interesting then?"

"Not really," Elizabeth said.

Stewart sat in his wheelchair in front of her and she
tried not to look at his pants. His jeans were frayed at the
bottoms and his socks had fallen down around his thin
ankles. One foot was crooked, making him pigeon toed.

She circled her own legs with her arms because her
hands had to hold onto something. Just looking at that
one crooked foot, she felt the itch on the inside of her
body.

"What's the matter?" Stewart said.

"Nothing," Elizabeth whispered. Would she ever
understand why the sight of his feet being out of his own
control stirred such longing in her? Suddenly she wanted

to cry, and felt the sting of the tears on the edges of her eyes.

Stewart moved from his wheelchair onto the couch beside her, lifting his legs up onto the large box they were using as a coffee table. Elizabeth snuggled up against him.

"Are you sure you're okay?" he said.

She nodded with her head pressed against his shirt. "Just hold me," she said. He pulled his arm tighter around her shoulder. While she was here, close to him, she almost felt justified in her perverted desires. As long as he was with her, she had a reason. In this last month Elizabeth had not been as self-loathing as she was used to being.

"I know what will cheer you up," Stewart said.

He grabbed his wheelchair and pulled it closer, reaching down into a pocket that hung below the seat and lifting out a bag. "Here, I got you this."

Elizabeth frowned. "What is this?" she said.

"Well the sooner you open it, the sooner you'll know."

Inside the bag was a pair of knee-high black and red-striped socks.

"These are the best!"

Stewart laughed. "From the store we saw," he said.

Elizabeth dangled her legs off the edge of the couch and peeled off her green frog socks to replace them with her new ones.

"What a great birthday present," Elizabeth sighed, resting her head on his shoulder.

"It's your birthday today?" Stewart said.

"Tomorrow," Elizabeth said, "I'm eighteen tomorrow."

"Oh, so you'll be legal," he said, laughing and kissing her neck. She squealed.

Robert walked by. "Hey you two, I'm going to the library, okay?"

"Yeah, okay," Stewart said and Robert continued, shaking his head.

Stewart reached around Elizabeth and grabbed her camera from the cardboard box coffee table.

"What are you doing?" she said, jumping off his lap.

He focused the camera on her and snapped a picture. "I can see why you like this," he said, "Capturing a moment, what control."

"That's delicate, be careful!"

"What are you doing for your birthday?"

"Oh, my friends are coming over and we're going to watch a movie and eat cake."

"I guess I'm not invited, then."

"You wouldn't want to go, it'll be a girl movie."

"Aren't your friends curious to meet me?"

"Um, no, not really."

Stewart took a picture of her guilty face.

"You haven't told them," he said.

She shook her head. She waited for him to say something, to complain, to get angry, but he said nothing. He put the camera back down and turned away from Elizabeth.

He got back on the wheelchair and turned to his room. Elizabeth picked up her camera and followed. In the room Stewart went to Robert's computer and turned it toward his bed.

Elizabeth didn't know what to say. A movie came on the computer and Stewart went to his bed. Elizabeth stood in the doorway, watching as he pushed himself to the edge of the wheelchair, grabbed the bed and yanked his body onto it. He didn't look at her, just watched the movie.

Elizabeth held the camera up to her eye. Through the viewfinder she saw Stewart turn to look at her. He shook his head.

"Don't," he said.

She snapped a picture. She put the strap around her neck and walked closer to him. The look on his face was confused. He didn't know what she was going to do next.

She lifted his shirt off his body and took a picture of his bare chest: wide and strong. She touched the long, white scars that ran horizontally around his body, and traced each one with the tip of her finger. Another picture, and Stewart tried to reach over to swat her. He was unbalanced and fell onto his side. Elizabeth came close again and focused on the black and white tattoo of a tiger's head on Stewart's bicep.

"What are you doing?" Stewart said.

"Making you mine."

"Put the camera away and come here," he said. As she laid the camera aside and climbed onto his bed she wondered what it was about him that made her want to do what he said. He gave directions with a kind of authority that she wasn't used to. Was it a skill he had learned from being disabled and getting the kind of help he wanted from people? Had he learned to expect people to do what he said? Or was it something about her personality, some weakness in her that inspired him to give her orders? Perhaps this was what he had always been like. She couldn't know how his personality might have changed or not changed after his injury.

Lying beside him, she looked at his empty wheelchair. There was a cushion on the seat that had the impression of his butt in it. She touched his hands, the rough surface. These were the hands that grasped that rail, or grabbed that seat, moved that brake.

Stewart pulled her until she was facing him. She looked at his eyes and now, while she lay facing him and the wall, she couldn't see his disability at all. He was like a perfectly average man, but no, there was still something special about him.

The image of his disability was comforting to her. She had immersed herself in images of paralysis and scars since she was a child, and now they made her feel safe. Even without those things, she still felt drawn to Stewart.

Then the phone rang.

"You're popular today," Elizabeth said.

"Shit," Stewart said, craning his neck in the direction of the phone. "I can't get over there in time," he said, "Will you pick it up for me?"

"Sure," Elizabeth said. She hopped off the bed and grabbed the phone. "Hello, Stewart and Robert's room," she said.

The voice on the other end was confused. "Stewart, please," the male voice said.

"Okay, hang on." Elizabeth pulled the phone toward Stewart and he had meantime been negotiating his body closer to the side of his bed that the desk was on. Stewart reached out and got the phone.

"Hello?"

"What, do you have a secretary now?"

"Jeff," Stewart said.

"Who was that?" Jeff said.

"A friend."

"Uh-huh. I'm sure."

"I'll fill you in later. Were you just calling to catch up?"

"Chuck called me the other day."

"Now that I don't want to talk about."

"Really, Stewart, you should think about it. He isn't trying to exploit you. You wouldn't have to go in the water or anything. He just wants you to talk. Lend us some of that charm and inspiration you're known for."

"Flattery is not going to help your cause."

"Just think about it, okay? Chuck's offer is a good one and the people miss you. We all miss you."

"That's sweet."

"Even Lee. None of us meant for things to turn out the way they did."

"I'll talk to you later, okay?"

"Okay. Do you have my new number?"

"Uh, no, what is it?" Stewart waved his hand so Elizabeth got a piece of paper and pen and Stewart said it out loud while she wrote it down. "Okay," Stewart said, "Thanks, I'll talk to you later."

Stewart held the phone out to Elizabeth. "Put that back for me?"

"What was that about?" she said.

"My friend Jeff is trying to convince me to get back into the surfing world."

"Really? That's cool."

"The person who organizes the competition in California wants me to speak there."

"Are you going to do it?"

"No." Stewart said it as though it was already obvious.

Elizabeth frowned. "Why not?"

"I have my reasons."

"That's always been a convincing one. Every time my mother says that, I stop pestering her right away. Come on, Stewart, I've seen the websites. Those people adore you." She flopped back onto the bed beside him.

Stewart sighed. "I don't have the energy anymore."

"I know you miss the ocean. I know you want to go back to it."

He turned his head and frowned at her. "How do you know that?"

"It's written all over you. The sea is a part of you."

"Can't fool you."

"Were you trying to?"

"You're too inquisitive. Yes, I feel empty without the ocean. But I can't go back, and that's just how it is."

"Why?"

"See? Inquisitive."

"It's for your own good. Just tell me why you can't do it and I'll tell you why your reasons are crap."

"I just can't. Let it go, Elizabeth."

Elizabeth started to say something else, but Stewart said, "Let's talk about how you think you can hide me.

That's what I don't get. You asked me out, you wanted to be here, but you don't want anyone to know about it."

"You're reading too much into this. The birthday party is just something I always do with the girls."

"I don't like feeling used."

"Stewart, come on," Elizabeth said. She touched the side of his face. "I just want you all to myself for a little while."

"If we're going to keep doing this, I'm bound to meet them. So get your friends and family used to the idea of me now."

"Yeah, yeah, yeah," she said.

"Okay," he said. He kissed the tip of her nose. She jumped on top of him, straddling his body, and pressed her lips on his.

When they grew tired of kissing, Stewart instructed Elizabeth on how to play the DVD on Robert's computer so they could start the movie over again.

Elizabeth didn't notice falling asleep, but the room was dark and they were lying on his bed. She woke up when Stewart nudged her.

"Is it time for bed?" he whispered.

Elizabeth nodded and closed her eyes again.

"Not so fast," Stewart said. "You brought your sleeping bag, and Robert will get you set up on the couch."

"In the common room? Why?"

"I'll see you in the morning," Stewart said.

Robert was waiting for her in the common room. Elizabeth pouted at him. "Why do I have to sleep out here?"

Robert shrugged. "I would guess that Stewart

doesn't want you to see his whole getting ready for bed routine."

"I don't mind," Elizabeth said.

"He does. Just be patient. It takes Stewart a long time to feel comfortable being vulnerable in front of someone."

Elizabeth didn't say anything else. She lay down on the couch and snuggled into her sleeping bag. Elizabeth fell asleep easily and in the morning Stewart drove her home. He stopped at the street corner, but before he pulled away he said, "Tell them the truth."

That night, back at home, Elizabeth had supper with her mother and father, but was quiet. She was thinking about Stewart. It was hard not to tell her parents about him; she wanted to tell everyone and show him off. But she knew she couldn't and over the years she had developed a quiet and introspective nature. She was used to keeping things from her parents.

There were always hints; of course, she couldn't cover over all the clues that pointed directly at her secret. And lately she hadn't been trying as hard to cover it up. Some part of her wanted to be found out, and the rest of her was horrified at the mere possibility.

At school Elizabeth was also keeping Stewart a secret from her friends. Of course, Stewart was becoming a big part of her life now and if she didn't talk about him, she no longer had anything to say. Stewart wanted her to tell her friends about him. He wanted them to know. Could she tell them without revealing any details that would make them suspicious?

All day she was distracted and had trouble concentrating on her teachers. Her friends noticed that something was different. At lunch they demanded to know what was up.

"Nothing," she insisted.

"Oh really?" Amy said, "Do you know how long I've known you? I can read you like a book."

"Is that so?" Elizabeth said, trying not to sound too defensive.

"Yes," Amy said, "You, my dear, are a creature of habit and we haven't seen you for a Saturday movie in four weeks."

"That's true!" Maureen said.

"I've been busy," Elizabeth said.

Expectant silence. Eventually Amy said, "That's it?"

"Come on, Liz," Maureen moaned, "You're killing us!"

"Okay," Elizabeth sighed at last. Her heart pounded surprisingly hard. "I have a boyfriend."

She couldn't say anything else, being drowned out by both girls screeching.

"Okay," Amy gasped, "Tell us everything. And I do mean everything."

Elizabeth smiled. "Well, I met him at my cousin's wedding. He's a college student—"

"Oh my God," Amy interrupted, "Liz has a college guy! I'm so impressed."

"Um, thanks?" Elizabeth said.

"What's his name? How old is he? Is he cute? How long have you been together? How did he ask you out?" Maureen said.

"What was the first question again?"

"Name."

"Oh, Stewart."

"Huh. That's an odd name."

"He's really handsome, though."

"Thank goodness," Amy said, and without pause continued, "When do we meet him?"

This was the question Elizabeth had been afraid of. "I don't know…he's a busy man. He's got school and jobs and everything."

"I know you'll squeeze us in."

"I'll talk to him about it."

"Good."

The bell rang and they were off to their afternoon classes. The energy that lunch may have given Elizabeth soon evaporated. She was staring at her notebook and ignoring the teacher when someone yelled, "First snow!"

All the students leapt from their seats and ran to the windows. The teacher's words trailed off and he too went to the window. The flakes were so small they could hardly be seen and some student must have been staring very intently out the window to notice the start of the new season.

As they watched, the miniscule drops of white began to gather along the ground, covering dirt, or broken glass on the pavement, or cracks in the sidewalk.

No matter how tired they might get of the snow, every year the first snowfall was heralded with delight and joy. Elizabeth loved it. Now she could go home and take out all her winter clothes, the heavy shirts that she had been thinking about and missing during the summer and fall. She could start doing all her favorite winter activities, like sledding in the park, or down her front steps (would her mother again tell her she was too old for that?), the neighbors would pull out their cross-country skis to take their dogs for walks, and her kitchen at home would take on the permanent smell of hot chocolate. Pine wreaths on the doors and the sound of shovels scraping against walkways. The groaning plow truck and sitting at the kitchen table in the mornings listening to the radio for school cancellations.

"Okay, okay," the teacher said, "Back to your seats."

But no matter how much he talked, their concentration was broken for the rest of the day by dreams of snowmen better than the neighbor's and carving forts from the pile of snow at the ends of the driveways. Those that were too old to get away with it would either use the excuse of their young siblings or find some nearby children to baby-sit or play with. Hard snowballs with ice in them would be thrown at the smokers at the corner of the high school.

After supper that night Elizabeth went up to her room and closed the door. She was tense from admitting Stewart's existence to her friends and she knew of only one way to relax. There wasn't a lock on her door, so when she pulled her secret notebook out from under the bureau she opened her closet door and hid herself behind it just in case. She flipped through the notebook in the dim light.

She didn't need to be able to see the images. Even the fast glimpse of a shadowy picture called it to her mind. The notebook was almost full because Elizabeth's secret needed new stories of pain to excite Elizabeth's senses with. Yet some of the older pictures were as familiar to her as the curling shape of her headboard, whose smooth grooves she used to run her fingers along when, as a child, she was too frightened to sleep.

Some things she had been unable to put into her notebook, and in the closet she rested her head against the wall, closed her eyes, and tried to recall the movement of the wheelchair in *Gattaca*.

She soon returned to the physical pictures in front of her, cradling the notebook in her lap. With one finger she traced the circle of a wheel, her fingernail scratching the paper. Her other hand rubbed gently and slowly against her underwear.

Now that she had Stewart she shouldn't need this. Why couldn't she stop? She had spent so many secret hours sitting on the floor of her closet, the legs of her clothes hiding her face. Here she almost felt hidden from herself as well. As though the actions that took place in this closet were outside of time and did not count.

Suddenly the door to her room opened and her mother was saying, "Lizzie? Where are you?"

Elizabeth slammed the notebook shut as fast as she could and stood up from inside the closet, trying to compose her face.

"Hey, Mom, what's up?"

Her mother frowned. She looked like she was about to ask what Elizabeth was doing in the closet, but she didn't.

"How is school going?" she asked instead and sat down on Elizabeth's bed. Elizabeth came and sat beside her. "Just fine."

"You don't talk to us much these days, I wanted to know if something was on your mind."

"Oh no, I'm fine, Mom."

Susan stroked Elizabeth's hair fondly and said, "This is going to be a big year for you. High school is ending and you'll be applying to colleges. Have you thought at all about where you want to go?"

"I think I might want to stay in the area, actually. We are in Boston where there are great schools every mile or so."

"That's true. And we'd like to have you nearby. Just think, you could go to Brandeis and take classes with Dad."

"That's a little too close, Mom. I'm thinking of schools actually in the city, like UBoston for instance," she said, casually mentioning Stewart's school.

"That's a good school, sweetie. You know you'll have to apply to six or seven though. Make sure you pick one that is easy to get into and one that you think is too hard to get into."

"How do I know?"

"You can look at the average SAT scores and such, the schools will send you that information. Start looking at some of those college brochures we're getting in the mail."

"Okay, Mom."

Susan smiled. "All right, I just wanted to check on you." She kissed Elizabeth's forehead and left. Elizabeth got up and closed the door again. Then she slid her notebook back underneath the bureau and took out her homework.

7

That **Friday Elizabeth met** up with Stewart two blocks from her house and he drove them to the mall. Stewart pulled into the parking lot and slowly they drove past the handicapped parking spaces. They all seemed to be full.

"Damn old people," Stewart muttered and Elizabeth almost laughed. She thought she was the only one who got annoyed that most of the cars marked with handicap plates and placards belonged to old people. Every time she saw the little wheelchair logo, her heart lifted with excitement. Then it just turned out to be some old lady.

Finally they found a space and got out of the car. Together they entered the mall.

"What kind of shoes are you looking for?" Elizabeth said.

"Something not sneakers that won't slip off my foot pedals."

"I like your sneakers. They're appropriate for any occasion."

"Well, I don't know if they're appropriate or not, but I do wear them for every occasion. I'd like to have some choices."

"You really think you can find nice shoes that aren't slippery?"

"I'll try. Might have to just get some moleskin to stick on them."

"Or if worse comes to worse, Velcro."

Stewart laughed. "That would be perfect," he said.

"So shoes first and then what?"

"A new dress for my grandmother's Christmas party."

"Oh right. Okay."

"Where are you going to be for Christmas?"

"I've already got a plane ticket to South Carolina."

"That's good," Elizabeth said.

"It depends," Stewart said, "But sometimes you have to go home."

Elizabeth nodded. "Family is a trap," she said, "You have to be nice to them, you have to listen to what they say, you have to be afraid not to be who they want you to be."

"Well put," Stewart said.

They were wandering the bright corridors of the mall, their eyes being led astray by the colors as they spoke. Elizabeth knew the mall well. Every Thursday she and her friends took a bus there after school. Or at least they used to. Now it was more like whatever day they were all free. Elizabeth led Stewart toward a shoe store.

He said, "What are you doing the Saturday after Thanksgiving?"

"Actually, I'm supposed to see my friends. They've noticed I've been gone over the weekends."

He pushed his wheels harder and quickly got ahead of Elizabeth. She could see his anger in the short, sharp pushes.

"I told them," Elizabeth said.

Stewart stopped but didn't turn around. "About me?"

"Yes."

"Okay, so what are we doing the Saturday after Thanksgiving?"

Elizabeth caught up with him. "You want to meet my friends, fine. I'm not responsible for what happens."

"I want to meet your parents too."

"You met them at the wedding."

"They didn't even see me at the wedding. I want you to tell them that I'm your man."

"I can't. You don't understand."

"What don't I understand? I'm serious about dating you and I'm not going to do it behind your parents' backs."

"God! Okay, you can meet everybody! Do it your way, do whatever you want!"

"Elizabeth, it is not at all unreasonable for me to meet your parents and your friends. Don't make it sound like it is."

"Here's the shoe store," she said, walking ahead.

"So what are we doing with your friends?"

"Sledding," Elizabeth said, not looking back.

"Oh good, I've never been sledding before."

They entered the store and the clerk asked how he could help.

"I need shoes," Stewart said.

There was a pause, the clerk looking down at Stewart's body, looking confused. "Shoes?" he said.

"Yes," Stewart said. "You sell shoes here. I have feet, you see, and they need shoes."

"Right, okay," he said, "I'll be right back."

Stewart looked up at Elizabeth and said, "I don't know why this is such a hard concept."

She shrugged. While Stewart tried on shoes, Elizabeth stood by the glass wall. Mostly she watched the people going by. She was very close to home now and she wondered if anyone she knew would catch her here with this man. Part of her wanted to show him off, but she knew she couldn't risk the consequences. She glanced back to Stewart and he was focused on the shoes, so she was able to watch him squeezing his lifeless feet into them. Sometimes she thought she could just look at his feet all day long.

When Stewart was satisfied, they left the shoe store and headed for the dress shop upstairs. On the glass elevator, Stewart said, "Maybe you can start with trying on swimsuits and work your way up to evening gowns."

Elizabeth laughed. "You don't really want to be here all day, do you? Let's get in, find a dress, and get out fast."

"You're my kind of girl."

Even though it was a joking remark, it filled Elizabeth with warmth. She hoped she really was his kind of girl.

With the dresses, Elizabeth had no idea where to start, so she did what she did every year. Stewart rolled ahead, not realizing she wasn't beside him anymore. He looked back and saw her standing in the entrance with her eyes closed. When she opened them, she headed for the dress her gaze landed on and picked through the hangers with the tips of her fingers.

"What are you doing?" Stewart said.

"Finding my size."

Stewart shrugged. "Okay," he said.

They left the shop, she with a dress bag over one arm and he with a box of shoes in the mesh basket below his chair.

"You want to see anything else while we're here?" Elizabeth asked.

"No, I have work this afternoon and I need to get back."

"Oh," she said, trying not to make a disappointed face. She had been planning to spend the evening with him as they had been doing most Fridays.

"You can come if you want to."

Elizabeth smiled. "Absolutely. I've got nothing to do today but homework."

"On a Friday?"

"My mother." Elizabeth rolled her eyes.

"It won't be too exciting at the gym with me, but I do usually go swimming afterwards. We'll stop at your house so you can get a swimsuit."

As they spoke, Elizabeth had been so focused on him that she didn't notice her mother's friend approaching.

"Elizabeth?" the woman said, "Is that you?"

Elizabeth looked up and stopped walking abruptly. "Mrs. Mills. Hi."

"What a surprise, although where else would I find you but a mall? Teenagers are all the same!"

While Mrs. Mills spoke, Elizabeth tried to edge her

way in front of Stewart. She felt a sharp poke to the backs of her legs as he hit her with his knees.

"And who is your little friend?" Mrs. Mills said.

"I'm Stewart." He smiled and held out his hand.

"Oh my," she said, ignoring the offered hand, "Are you a friend of the family? Susan never mentioned…"

"He's a friend of Libby's husband," Elizabeth cut in before her mother's friend could say that Susan had never mentioned knowing a cripple. As Mrs. Mills tried to figure out how that explained why the two of them were shopping together in the mall, Elizabeth said, "It was great to run into you. I'll say hi to my Mom for you. Okay, great."

Elizabeth hurried on and Stewart followed her more slowly. Mrs. Mills continued to stand and watch them leave. When they got outside, Stewart said, "Has anyone ever told you that you're a terrible liar?"

"I never really tried," Elizabeth called back to him.

"Could have fooled me."

She stopped at the car and waited for him to catch up. "Look," she said, "If I'm going to tell my parents, it better be me telling them and not some gossip."

"Forget it," Stewart said.

"Don't be angry. I will tell them."

"Did you know that people used to be proud to be seen with me?" He parked his chair in the space beside his car and got in. Elizabeth walked around to her side and got in.

"You don't understand," Elizabeth said, "You always take things the wrong way."

"It's insulting, Elizabeth, what other way is there to take it?"

"It's not because," she fumbled. "I mean, it isn't because of you."

"I don't really want to hear your excuses."

Elizabeth reached over and touched his hand where it rested on the steering wheel. "Don't give up on me," she said, "I like being with you. I'm proud to be with you."

"Prove it," he said.

Elizabeth turned to the window. "I will," she said.

They stopped at her house and she ran inside to get a swimsuit. Since her parents weren't home, Stewart parked in the driveway while he waited.

Elizabeth ran back down the stairs and the walkway.

"Did you get it?" Stewart said when she burst back into the car.

Elizabeth lifted her shirt, revealing the black one-piece underneath.

"Okay," Stewart said, "We're off."

At the campus, Stewart stopped at his room, and then they both headed for the gym. Elizabeth had never been farther than his dorm before. Stewart pulled the heavy front door open and Elizabeth held it.

"Am I allowed to be in here?" Elizabeth whispered.

"I'm the front door guard and I'm sneaking you in. There's a chair behind the desk you can use, since I brought my own."

Elizabeth followed him behind the counter. She sat on the extra chair and kicked her legs. Stewart slid his legs under the desk that bordered the turnstiles, and Elizabeth sat behind him. The lobby was empty when they came in, but after a moment a couple of tall men walked in.

"Hey, Stewart," one of them said as they handed him their ID cards.

"Work hard," Stewart said, "I'll be watching the game."

When they walked on and disappeared into the weight room, Elizabeth said, "Do you know them?"

"They play on the basketball team."

"Oh," she said. "So, what else do you do around here?"

"Not much," Stewart said.

The door banged open and Travis walked in. "My man!" he said, "I'm going to beat your pull up record today."

"Get a witness," Stewart called after him.

"You really do know everyone," Elizabeth said. Stewart looked back at her. "People know me," he said with a shrug.

Elizabeth laughed. "No one knows you," she said. "What you mean is they think they know you, but really they only know the image you put up."

"That's deep," Stewart said. He held her gaze, but after a moment he burst out laughing. "You're such a teenager," he said.

"Yeah, I am. So?"

"You must be actually looking into applying to colleges now."

Elizabeth nodded.

"Any ideas?" Stewart said.

"This place seems nice."

"You're looking to do photography still?"

"Absolutely," Elizabeth said.

Stewart spun around to face her. "So does this school have a good photography department?"

"I don't know," Elizabeth admitted.

"Do not apply to this school just because I'm here. You need to do what's best for you."

Four girls came into the gym next. They greeted Stewart with casual ease. It was clear to Elizabeth that he had become a fixture in the lives of the gym regulars.

"I'm serious," Stewart said when they were gone, "Find the school with the best program for what you want to do."

"Yeah, yeah, yeah," Elizabeth said.

Stewart's replacement came not long after. "Okay," the new boy said, "Time for the pool, Lisa's waiting."

"Am I getting that predictable?" Stewart said as he pushed his chair out from behind the desk.

"I'll be worried the day I can't find you at the pool," the boy said.

Elizabeth followed Stewart down the hallway. Seeing him from behind, Elizabeth was again struck by how short the wheelchair made him and the way the chair moved was so unlike any other way of moving. She had begun to forget about the wheelchair when looking at his face, but now the memory of it was refreshed. They passed the stairs and took an elevator down a floor. At the girl's changing room, Stewart said, "See you in there."

After stripping off her clothes, Elizabeth stopped at the mirror. There were other girls there, most of them putting clothes back on and getting ready to leave. They peeled off swimsuits and walked through the room naked. Elizabeth sighed at her own reflection.

Her hair hung in limp waves to her shoulders. She

tied it back, but then she could see the stick figure that was her body. Unlike the women around her, Elizabeth was all bones and angles. She crossed her arms over her chest and walked into the pool area.

From across the room she saw Stewart talking to a student lifeguard. He was wearing red and black swim shorts and nothing else while sitting in his chair at the side of the pool. His naked feet were balanced on the foot rest and his lean, muscular arms hung at his sides, with only the tattooed tiger's eyes staring at Elizabeth. The long, white scars wrapped around Stewart's stomach and across his back.

The woman he was talking to was laughing and leaning forward. She was short, with a red swimsuit, and brown hair in a perky ponytail. Her eyes sparkled as they met Stewart's.

Elizabeth walked over slowly. She felt as though she was about to interrupt a moment. Her bare toe touched the bottom edge of Stewart's tire before they noticed her.

"Elizabeth," Stewart said, "This is Lisa."

"Hi," Lisa said.

"Hi," Elizabeth said.

Stewart seemed completely unaware of the tension as the two girls looked at one another.

"Well," Lisa said after a moment, "The water is waiting."

Stewart nodded. He pulled up to the deep end and put the brake on his chair. He leaned forward until he fell head first into the water.

Elizabeth and Lisa stood together on the side. Elizabeth saw the way Stewart smiled as his head emerged, dripping. He pumped his arms and started swimming laps. His legs dangled behind, but it didn't seem to hinder him.

"I used to get so nervous," Lisa said and Elizabeth looked around to make sure she was talking to her. With her eyes still fixed on Stewart, Lisa continued, "We have this special equipment for handicapped people, but he never used it. I was afraid something would happen and I wouldn't know how to help." She looked at Elizabeth. "But just look at him. It always amazes me how capable he is."

Stewart swam up to the side. "Are you coming in?" he said to Elizabeth. She nodded and slipped into the water. Together they played childhood games of tea parties under water and splash contests. Elizabeth had an advantage in splashing since Stewart was using his arms to stay above water. In races he beat her because she had only had one year of swimming lessons when she was a kid and she had forgotten most of what she knew. She was surprised by how the water games children played were the same across the country. She had done these things with Amy, Becky, and Maureen in the summers.

"Let me see your standard stroke," Stewart said as he grabbed onto the wall and hung to the edge.

"My what?"

"Your crawl."

"Oh." Elizabeth put her face in the water and started beating her arms and legs. Within minutes she was pulled upright and Stewart had one arm around her.

"That was terrible," he said.

"Thank you, I try." She tickled his stomach to get him to let go, but it had no effect. Elizabeth kept moving her fingers up until she found the spot where he could feel the tickling.

"Okay! I'm letting go." He released her and pulled back to the wall again. "Try it again, but this time think about sliding your fingers into the water first. And come over here and do it right beside me because I'm going to fix your kick."

Following Stewart's instructions, Elizabeth's swimming began to get smoother. "Am I ready to learn to surf yet?" she said.

"Not even close," he said.

The people around them in the other lanes began to leave. Elizabeth saw them glance at the vacant wheelchair as they went by. It probably wasn't beautiful to them the way it was to her.

When the rest of the pool was empty, Lisa came back over and lay down on the concrete, resting her chin on her hands right by the edge of the water.

"Is it closed?" Elizabeth asked Stewart.

"Lisa and I always stay late and have the pool to ourselves," he answered. He swam over to Lisa and Elizabeth followed. She had never before thought about these many moments Stewart spent without her, in the presence of other girls. Not only other girls, but girls who were maybe prettier or more talented. Elizabeth swallowed back her jealousy.

"Hey, Stewart," Lisa said, "Do people call you Stew?"

"Some people have tried."

"You don't have a nickname at all?"

"Nope. Stewart is the name my mother gave me, so that's the one I'll keep."

"It's a strange one," Lisa said.

"Sticks in the memory," Stewart said.

Lisa joined them in the water. Elizabeth hung back because she could see Lisa was as good as Stewart at swimming. The two of them decided to race and Elizabeth was supposed to referee. As they came swimming towards her, though, she noticed they both slowed down. Both Stewart and Lisa got slower and slower until it was like a contest to see who could be last. When they finally reached Elizabeth, Lisa asked Stewart if he was all right.

"I don't think you were doing your best," he said.

"Oh," she said and looked away.

"You don't have to let me win," he said.

As Lisa's face turned red, Elizabeth broke in. "Are you sure you can handle losing?" she said.

"Hey!" Stewart said, "Aren't you on my side?" He laughed.

"I think it's about time to lock up," Lisa said.

Stewart nodded. He swam to the edge, put his hands on the ledge and heaved his body out of the pool, landing lying down on the tiled side. The girls got out nearby, giving him space.

"Throw me my towel?" Stewart said after resting a moment.

Elizabeth grabbed it from his gear and tossed it over. He dried off, threw his towel over the back of the chair, and pulled himself up onto it. Then he arranged his feet and put his knees in place.

"My father sent me an interesting article, Stewart," Lisa said, while locking the door behind them. "It said there's a new treatment where paralyzed people are getting sensation back." She looked at him.

"You told your father about me?" he said, but he was looking at Elizabeth as he said it.

"Yeah, it stood out as something to mention, you know, that a quadriplegic is working at the gym. Wait, that's not wrong to say, is it?"

He smiled. "Actually, I'm paraplegic."

"Sorry."

"It's all right."

"What's the difference again?"

"Just think of 'para' meaning 'two' and 'quad' meaning 'four.' Only two of my limbs are affected by paralysis."

"Oh. I see."

"I've heard about that treatment too," Stewart continued, "but it only works for people with a particular type of injury."

"Not your kind?"

"No."

"So it'll be a lot longer before there's a cure for you."

"If by cure you mean walking, then yes, I'm not holding my breath. My life isn't broken and I'm getting by just fine without my legs."

"I didn't mean to offend."

"I'm just telling you because I don't expect you to know."

"I never knew a disabled person before you."

"I'm just me. I can't speak for anyone else."

She smiled. "I'm glad I met you," she said, "I'm glad you work here."

"Well, thank you. I'll see you on Monday."

"Yeah," she said, to Elizabeth she said, "It was nice to meet you."

After Lisa walked away, Stewart said, "Ready to get home?"

"I suppose so."

"I'll see you for sledding, if not before."

"Yeah, yeah, yeah," Elizabeth said.

8

Elizabeth and her friends arrived at the hill before Stewart, so they began without him. There were lots of small children taking advantage of the first major snowfall, and parents standing in a line at the top of the hill beside the street. People Elizabeth's age apparently had better things to be doing with their winters.

All the girls went down the hill a few times, trading sleds in between. Each of them had a different style sled, so they shared. Elizabeth climbed up the hill again after her third run and saw Stewart's car parked across the street. Her friends caught up behind her and stopped short. They saw Stewart crossing the street, coming in their direction and immediately Elizabeth's friends knew that he was the one they were waiting for.

He stopped on the shoveled sidewalk and looked at the foot high wall of snow in front of him.

Elizabeth said, "Well, this is Stewart."

Amy said, "Oh." The other two were silent. Elizabeth

continued, saying, "Stewart, this is Amy, Becky, and Maureen."

Smiling broadly Stewart offered his hand to each in turn. They shyly greeted him.

"Let's get started," Stewart said. "This is one sport I've never tried, but it looks fun." He nodded behind them to where small children were shrieking as they hurtled down the hill.

"You've never been sledding?" Amy said. The look on her face suggested that she thought sledding might still be too dangerous an activity for him to try.

"I grew up on the beach," he said, "No snow."

"No more talking," Elizabeth said, "let's get sledding." She walked behind Stewart, grabbed his chair, and tipped him right onto the snow bank.

He used his arms to turn his body right side up again and for a moment Elizabeth saw a flash in his eyes and she thought he was angry. Had she gone too far? But then it was gone. He laughed and wiped snow out of his hair. He gathered a snowball and threw it up at Elizabeth's head. She ducked and the snow hit a small child just being helped into the car by his mother. Stewart's eyes opened wide as the mother turned on her heel.

"Sorry," Stewart said, "Mistake." The mother looked at him, then at the overturned wheelchair and said nothing. She brushed her son off, got him in the car and drove off without looking back.

"Oops," Maureen said, holding a hand over her mouth to hide her grin.

"Okay, back to the serious endeavor of teaching Stewart to sled," Elizabeth said.

"It doesn't look so hard," he said.

"Yeah, it's really not," Amy said. She and Maureen held a plastic sled steady while Elizabeth helped him on. Elizabeth sat down behind him and wrapped her legs and arms around his waist and chest, so he could lean back against her. She took the ropes and the others pushed them off.

For five seconds they were flying. The cold wind prickled Elizabeth's lips and eyes as she looked out over Stewart's shoulder. Her cheeks were glowing. At the bottom, Elizabeth turned the sled around to show Stewart where the path of their sled was marked in the snow.

"That's it?" he said.

"Now we do it again," she said.

Before she could stand up and grab the rope, he said, "Elizabeth, while we have a moment, will you tell me what's going on?"

"What do you mean?" She tried to act innocent, though she knew what he was talking about.

"Why didn't you tell them I was in a wheelchair before they met me?"

Yes, that was the question. Why couldn't she? Somehow she was never able to get the words out. In her fear of being discovered, she had actually never said the word "wheelchair" out loud. "It shouldn't matter, right?" she said.

"But it does, you know it does."

At that point Becky's sled banged right into theirs, knocking all three of them into the snow.

"I'm so sorry," Becky cried, "Oh, I was trying to steer, but I'm all out of practice. You're not hurt are you?"

"We're fine," Stewart said.

"I really didn't mean it, Liz."

"Calm down," Elizabeth said, "It's part of the fun of sledding." Her friend seemed to think Stewart was made out of glass. "Come on," Elizabeth continued, "help me get him back up this hill."

The next ride, Stewart went down on his own. He was lying back and couldn't see where he was going at all. Elizabeth followed in her own sled, but when they both reached the bottom, Stewart wouldn't let her haul him back up. He stayed and threw snowballs at kids as they arrived beside him.

Elizabeth and the other girls watched from the top of the hill. One little girl Stewart threw a snowball at started crying. They saw him drag himself over to her on his sled and gently wipe snow from her face until her mother arrived and snatched the girl up.

Becky said, "He's great with kids, isn't he?"

"Yeah," Elizabeth said, "They love him. He used to teach swim lessons before he moved here."

Then Amy sighed and said, "Liz, you never cease to amaze me. I know you've always been interested in this stuff, but dating a handicapped guy? I must admit I didn't know you'd go so far. Doesn't it bother you? Being around someone who can't walk?"

All the words to answer the question were there inside Elizabeth, but she couldn't choke them out. She had studied the politics of disability, she knew the arguments to use against people who saw physical disability as depressing. Yet, none of it came to her now. Now she could only stammer and turn red. Why couldn't she talk to her closest friends about these things?

Then she noticed that Stewart was no longer at the bottom of the hill. "Where did he go?" she said.

Her friends all began looking around and then Maureen spotted him coming up the hill by himself. He had tied the rope of his sled to his boot and was inching slowly up with the help of rocks and tree roots buried under only a light layer of snow.

As he reached them, Maureen said, "How did you do that?"

"I think it's time for ice cream," Elizabeth interrupted.

"Ice cream?" Stewart said in disbelief.

"It's a tradition," Becky explained. She pointed down the road and said, "See that shop? They sell ice cream and other stuff there. We always go there after sledding. It started because Elizabeth's dad used to make fun of her for putting ice cubes in her hot chocolate after sledding."

"Okay, I don't exactly see the connection, but I'm game," Stewart said.

He got back onto his chair and they all went into the ice cream store. All the girls got sundaes with whipped cream and cherries on top. Stewart got a coffee. They sat around one table and as soon as they sat down Amy turned to Stewart and asked, "How long have you been in a wheelchair?"

Elizabeth stopped eating. Why was that the very first thing anyone wanted to know about him? Of course, Elizabeth wanted to know the details of how he broke his spine, but she also knew that it was wrong to be curious. What did it matter how Stewart was injured? It was in the past, he was over it. It seemed impolite to bring it up again now. Her plan was to ignore his disability as much as possible and never bring the subject up.

"Six years," he answered.

"That's a long time," Amy said, "How old were you?"

"Nineteen."

"I'm so sorry. Do you mind if I ask what happened?"

He shrugged and said, "Just a surfing accident."

"You surfed!" Maureen jumped in, "So cool!"

"I did, yes."

"Were you good?" Amy asked coyly.

He smiled and, gesturing to his legs, said, "I guess not."

Amy looked like she wanted to laugh, but she stopped and composed her face. "That's really tragic. I'm sorry," she said.

Elizabeth cringed slightly at the word "tragic." That's right, that was what it was supposed to be. Did it make her a total monster that she couldn't feel the tragedy of it? Paralysis didn't seem terrible to her; it was beautiful. How could she be so callous? How could she dismiss this thing that to him had been tragic? She couldn't help being glad that he had been paralyzed.

"Nothing to be sorry for," Stewart said, "It's not your fault."

Becky, across the table, spit out onto her palm a cherry stem tied into a knot.

"Congratulations," Stewart said, "That's hard to do."

After the ice cream was finished, Elizabeth rode home with the girls and Stewart got in his own car. When Elizabeth got back to her house and Amy let her out, there was a honk and she looked up to find Stewart's car parked across the street from her house. She waved goodbye to her friends and ran over to his car, getting into his passenger seat.

"Did you have a good time?" she said.

"I like surfing better."

Elizabeth shrugged. "I've never tried it because someone won't teach me, so I don't know."

Stewart reached across the seat for her hand and rubbed her palm with his thumb as he said, "I think that went fairly well, although it might have helped if you had prepared them for the chair."

"Have you done it before?" Elizabeth asked, ignoring the last part. She wouldn't be able to explain to him why she couldn't tell people.

"What? Meet people who need to approve of me? No. No one approves of me, for whatever reason. I've never needed to be accepted before."

"The opinion of my friends matters that much to you?"

"It matters to you, doesn't it?"

She didn't answer. Elizabeth still didn't know what her friends' reactions really were. On the ride home they had been quiet. Even Amy had not brought up the subject they were probably all thinking about.

Looking over at Stewart she saw that he was also lost in thought. Elizabeth wanted to forget about what other people thought. She slid over and straddled him, kissing his lips.

He laughed, took hold of her shoulders and held her back for a moment. Then he let her go and she fell against his body. The steering wheel was pressed against her back and she was afraid that if she moved too much the horn would beep. Grabbing the seat control lever she pushed his seat as far back as it would go. Stewart took hold of her shirt and pulled it over her head. He pressed it against the window, so no one would see in. The little car heaters blasted air onto tiny strips of her back. She took both their coats and pressed them against the windshield. Inside the car was like a small tent, a cocoon for the two of them.

Soon her bra also went and Stewart was kissing the flesh between her small breasts. It was while he was distracted that she went for his pants. She had already unzipped them and pulled them down to his knees before he noticed. He grabbed hold of her arms with a vice grip, but it was too late. They both looked down at the little tube coming out of his boxers and disappearing down his pant leg.

She knew what it was and was surprised that she hadn't anticipated it. Of course he didn't have bladder control. On some level she had known that he probably wore a catheter, but she hadn't thought about it. Here was a reality of paralysis that had never come into her fantasies. She was a little surprised to realize that it didn't bother her at all. He was more than worth something like this. Anyway, it was just a part of life.

"Elizabeth, please," he said, looking at her with a stony expression.

Elizabeth realized that he couldn't move his hips to get his pants back up. She pulled them up for him and redid the zipper.

"I'm sorry," she said. She hadn't meant to humiliate him. Then she realized that he was going to try to explain.

Probably he had gotten this far with girls before and they had not understood exactly what his injury was, what complete paralysis from the waist down entailed. She knew something about intimacy with a paraplegic.

When she was younger she had gone to the public library and done various searches with words like "disabled," "wheelchair," and "paraplegic," while compulsively looking over her shoulder to make sure no one was watching. Then she went through the library, found each book, and sat in the dark back corners of the stacks, pressing the covers against her legs so any passersby wouldn't see what book it was. One of those books was on the subject of sex and disability. She memorized its corner in the library and crept down there many days, not daring to ever try to check out these books.

"I can still—" he began, but she stopped his words by leaning down and kissing his lips.

"I know," she said with a smile.

"Do you?" he said, but didn't pursue it. He pulled her back down on top of him and wrapped his arms around her tightly.

"Stewart?" she said, her face pressed against his chest, her forehead against his collarbone.

"What?"

"I know you were good."

"What are you talking about?"

"It wasn't a surfing accident, was it?"

He loosened his grip and she sat on his lap, leaning her head against his window. He looked at her. "You could say it was a surfing accident," he said, "I just wasn't the one surfing."

As he told the story, he found himself being

transported back there. The day opened the same as any other. The only indication that something would change was the hurricane force winds beating on the balcony's glass doors. Stewart was in California, a few days before the biggest competition of the year there. He and Lee were staying in Jeff's apartment.

That day Stewart woke up on the couch. Jeff got the bed and Lee and Stewart traded couch and floor depending on who had surfed the best during the day. What woke him wasn't the wind, but the weatherman on the TV. Lee had woken up earlier and turned it on. A tropical storm was on the way.

Lee turned around and saw that Stewart was awake.

"Hurry up," he said, "The surf is amazing right now."

Stewart got up and walked onto the balcony, still in his boxers. They could see the ocean from Jeff's apartment if they turned sideways and leaned over the edge. Lee was right; the wind was creating much larger waves than usual.

Stewart turned back inside and began suiting up. Lee had gone into Jeff's room to rouse him. They all got their boards and didn't bother with breakfast. On the way down the street toward the water, all three of them carrying long boards under their arms, Pete Morris joined along beside them.

"What do you want?" Lee said.

"Are you practicing today? I'll carry your board for you, Stewart," Pete said, ignoring the other two. Pete had been bugging him since he arrived in California a week before. Pete barely knew how to surf, but he idolized Stewart and followed him around where ever he went.

"Go play in the kiddie's pool and leave us alone," Stewart said without looking at him.

Pete fell back and stood on the street watching his hero walk away. Stewart didn't give him a second glance. It was this moment that Stewart would regret for the rest of his life. In that one sentence he could have changed both of their lives.

After surfing the whole morning, Jeff, Lee, and Stewart went back to Jeff's for lunch. They left their boards on Jeff's balcony, which was only a few feet above street level. The winds had gotten worse throughout the day and the rain had started pelting the beach. People were being advised to stay indoors.

Lunch was sandwiches and not the average peanut butter and jelly, either. Jeff had thrown whatever he had left in his cabinets onto slices of bread. Stewart got a mac and cheese with olives sandwich and Lee had a honey and apple one. There wasn't a table, or anywhere other than the couch to sit. Stewart sat on one end of it and Jeff on the other. Lee sat on the coffee table.

They didn't talk, but listened to the rattling of the balcony door and the windows in the bedroom. After he finished his sandwich, Lee got up and opened the glass doors, walking onto the balcony.

"Watch it," Jeff said, "All my stuff is going to blow away."

"What stuff?" Stewart said. Jeff was barely able to afford the apartment, let alone anything to put into it.

"There's someone out there," Lee said from the balcony. Stewart and Jeff both got up, curious to see who was braving even fiercer elements than they had that morning. All three leaned over the side and squinted toward the water.

"Can you see who it is?" Jeff said.

"No," Stewart said, "I don't recognize the style. It seems a little raw."

"Stewart," Lee said.

"What?" He turned around and saw that Lee was looking at their surfboards. Stewart's was gone.

At the same moment that Stewart realized what had happened, Jeff said it. "Oh my God, that's Pete out there."

They watched, riveted. Stewart realized that Pete was trying to prove himself worthy of respect and a stab of guilt tore through the parts of his body where he would soon lose the ability to feel.

Before he could think about what he was doing, he had grabbed the railing of the balcony and leapt over it onto the ground. He was running down the street, seeing nothing but the tiny figure on the edge of an endless ocean.

"Were you scared?" Elizabeth asked, breathless.

Stewart was slammed back to the cold little car many miles away from the warm, dangerous beach. "Do you want me to tell the story or not?" he said. He discovered that he was breathing hard and took a moment to regain control. "I didn't have time to be scared," he continued, "I ran down the street, straight onto the sand and into the water without pausing."

The water was rough and dark. Stewart plunged ahead, desperately parting the water with his hands.

"Pete!" he screamed, even though he knew Pete couldn't hear him. Stewart was without a board or any safety equipment. He was swept up into the water and fought it with all his strength. From the time he was a small child he had always been afraid of the ocean. He had loved it, as his mother had, but he also recognized its terrible power and that he was helpless under its whim.

He felt it moving him and could not gain control. Soon he was sucked under the surface. All the roaring of the waves and wind became muted. He was in another world and he felt a sudden desire to surrender to it. His limbs became weak and blackness covered his vision.

He wasn't even aware of what was happening as his body was thrown against the underwater rocks. He didn't regain consciousness until after he had washed ashore. He became aware of people surrounding him. He was choking on the salt water and trying to vomit it up, but he was on his back and, for some reason, couldn't turn or sit up. Some strange hands grabbed him and turned him onto his stomach. He retched up the water and tried to see around him. They were strapping something constraining around his neck. Then he saw Jeff and tried to reach out. His fingers were weak and couldn't grip his friend's hand. Jeff's face was leaning over him, frightened, the lips were moving, but Stewart didn't know what he was saying.

They had him on a stretcher and he blacked out again as they lifted it and began carrying him up the beach toward the ambulance. He didn't see Pete's lifeless body, also spat up on the shore.

"Pete lost his life over something I said," Stewart finished. "I don't deserve the joy of surfing anymore."

"But," Elizabeth said, trying to process the entire story, "You're a hero."

Stewart laughed a hollow laugh. "No," he said, "Heroes are the people who succeed."

"You're awfully hard on yourself."

"Didn't you hear me? Someone died."

"You did everything you could. You not going into the ocean isn't going to give him his life back."

"Thanks, Elizabeth, that really helps," he snapped.

"It's a part of you and I don't know how you can stand to be without it."

Stewart touched the edge of her shirt where it was pressed against his window. "You want to know the truth? It's killing me."

"I know it's important to you."

"My aunt told me once that my mother took me with her to the beach three days after I was born, the very day that she was bringing me home from the hospital. I'm certain that I smelled salt water on her skin from the first moment she held me." Stewart paused and gazed absently over Elizabeth's shoulder. After a moment he said, "For so long I defined myself in terms of the sea. I was a surfer and that was all that I was. I lived only for the waves. When I lost the use of my legs it took me years to readjust my image of myself. Now I put all that energy into being a paraplegic and defining myself that way."

"I think you could let go a little. I mean, you're always going to be paraplegic, that's not something you have to hold onto. It isn't going anywhere. Why don't you let yourself explore the possibility of other identities?"

"That's when I'll lose my mind completely. Right now I have control over myself and my emotions. If I let that go for a single instant, my desire for the ocean will consume me."

"So go back to it. I know you can. And don't try to tell me that you're afraid."

"No. I mean, yes. I was always afraid. The danger is what makes it so powerful."

"So go to California, go back to that competition thing. I bet you're good at inspiring people."

"They won't listen." Stewart wasn't looking at her anymore. "People just want to stare and say 'isn't it too bad about the Masterson boy?'"

"That's very cynical. I think people will be happy to see you. When you go back—"

"I just can't." His voice was as sharp as glass. Elizabeth looked into his eyes and for the first time she saw pain there. His face was always so neutral that Elizabeth could rarely read his emotions. Now they were etched across every line. It frightened her to see the full force of his pain.

"I'm sorry I brought it up," she whispered. They left it at that, but Elizabeth knew that she wasn't going to give up on getting him back to the water. All that emotion was with him all the time and she couldn't stand to know that he suffered so much. She would find a way to give him back the ocean.

9

At school on Monday no one said anything to Elizabeth about Stewart, but she sensed a kind of awe from her friends. Some kind of distance had come between them, Elizabeth felt alone and removed. They treated her like she was some kind of saint. Did everyone really think that dating Stewart was a chore? He was no different from… All right, he was different. But she liked him, she wasn't dating him out of pity. Didn't anyone else see his power? Did they see what she saw? Or were her friends and family seeing a broken man?

Finally Elizabeth got up the courage to say to Amy, "So, what did you think."

She paused. "Well, you and he come from very different worlds."

"I guess," Elizabeth said, "But we have some kind of connection."

"I hate to say this, but are you sure he isn't just taking what he can get?"

"What are you talking about?"

"Let's be honest, sweetheart, I don't think girls are lined up around the block to go out with him. He might be kind-of desperate."

"Is that what you think of me?"

"No, of course not. But I'm trying to understand his perspective. I mean, he doesn't seem like the type of guy I would expect to be interested in you."

"You think only geeks like me, is that it? He's too cool for me?"

"I'm not trying to say that it's true, but have you considered that he might not be thinking about what you have in common or what kind of future you could have? He might just be thinking, here's a girl who'll have me."

"That's the most cynical thing I've ever heard."

"Just be careful, Lizzie. I don't want to see you get hurt."

The conversation left her uncomfortable and distracted for the rest of the day, but she knew the truth and Amy didn't. Elizabeth knew that she and Stewart had a real connection, she just hoped she hadn't ruined her chances with him after what happened on Saturday. It was hard to imagine Stewart being embarrassed, and in fact the next weekend when she was back in his room, nothing seemed to have changed.

"I have to do homework," she said.

"Go ahead," he said and he watched her unpack her backpack onto his bed. For a few minutes he stayed at his desk and also worked on homework.

At the finish of her first problem, Elizabeth looked

up and realized that Stewart was right next to her. He touched her leg. She smiled.

While he got onto the bed, Elizabeth pushed her books onto the floor and made room. Soon they were pulling each other's clothes off. Stewart was ahead. He got her panties off and tossed them aside at the same time Elizabeth got his shirt off over his head.

Just then the doorknob rattled. It was locked, but someone was trying to come in. They both heard the key being put into the lock. Elizabeth's eyes opened wide. She grabbed Stewart's blanket and pulled it all the way over her head.

Robert walked in, looked over at the lumpy bed, the half naked Stewart, and the pair of panties on the floor. He frowned.

"Am I disturbing something here?" he said.

"You could say that," Stewart said.

"But," Robert said and stopped.

"Would you mind going to the library or something?" Stewart said.

"I guess I could do that," Robert said slowly. He took his books from his desk, and gave another frown in the direction of Stewart's bed, and then he scurried out and closed and locked the door behind him.

"It's safe to come out now," Stewart said to his covers.

"Are you sure?" Elizabeth replied, lifting them back just from her head.

"Robert has been traumatized for life, but other than that, no harm done."

"I'm so embarrassed," Elizabeth moaned. She left the covers over her and covered her face with her hands.

"Don't be silly," Stewart said, "We didn't do anything wrong."

"I'm sorry," Elizabeth said, "I can't do this now. All I can think about is the look on Robert's face."

Stewart started laughing and soon Elizabeth was giggling too. She snuggled her head against his shoulder and they lay side by side.

"There's still homework over there," Stewart said.

"Yeah," Elizabeth said, but she didn't move.

Stewart laughed again.

Elizabeth crinkled her nose at him. The mood had passed, and neither said anything about what had almost happened. Elizabeth had never before understood even the desire for sex. She didn't know how her peers could have a hard time controlling themselves. It hadn't really appealed to her. Now she understood. Now she knew the feel of desire sizzling through veins, unable to be contained.

"Do you like me?" Elizabeth said, breaking into the silence with Amy's words still humming in the back of her mind.

"Sure."

"No, like really."

"Why would I still be here if I didn't?"

"Well…"

"Oh, I see," Stewart said, "You think I'm desperate. You think I have to settle for whatever girl is willing to go out with me."

"No. I mean, I don't think that, but I thought maybe you thought…"

"I'd rather be alone than be in a relationship with just anyone. I'm good at being alone."

"You do make a good point there," Elizabeth said.

Stewart laughed. "Don't be insecure," he said, "It's not an attractive quality."

The door opened a crack and Robert's head slowly appeared. Once he saw that they were clothed, he came into the room and started putting his books away.

"About time to get you home," Stewart said to Elizabeth. He reached for his chair, but he stopped suddenly and fell back. Elizabeth jumped off the bed in alarm when she saw that his legs were twitching. Robert glanced over, but didn't move. The twitch traveled up Stewart's body until he was shaking all over. He closed his eyes and after a moment his body was still again.

"You're pushing yourself too hard," Robert said, not looking up from his desk.

"Shut-up," Stewart said. Then he opened his eyes and saw Elizabeth's ashen face. "Hey, hey," he said, "It's okay. You look terrified. Come here."

She went to him and he held her close.

"Are you okay?" she said.

"Yes. It's just something my body does when it's tired."

"Okay," she said, getting up again.

"I'll walk you to the subway station," Robert offered.

"Thanks," Elizabeth said, as she put her long arms through her heavy winter coat.

"I can take her," Stewart said.

"You need to rest," Robert said, "Don't even think about getting up until tomorrow."

Elizabeth looked at Stewart and shrugged a little, as if to say: I guess it doesn't matter who takes me.

"All right," Stewart said. "Come give me a kiss."

"Okay," Robert said.

Stewart rolled his eyes. Elizabeth leaned over and kissed his lips, then followed Robert out of the room.

As soon as the stairwell door closed, Robert said, "Look, Elizabeth, I like you, I really do."

Elizabeth frowned. "Okay," she said, unable to figure out what he was leading into. He didn't look at her. A blast of cold wind hit them as they left the dorm building.

Robert continued, "I would love to pretend that it's totally normal for a beautiful young girl to throw herself at a paraplegic man, but we both know that it's not usual."

"What are you saying?" Elizabeth said. Throw herself at him? She felt the heat of embarrassment creeping over her face, but there was anger too. Just what was he accusing her of?

"Don't be dense here," Robert said, "There's something else going on that you aren't telling Stewart. There's some reason you're going after him and I want to know what it is."

Had Robert guessed the truth or did he think something else completely? There was no way she was going to have this conversation with him. He would not be the first person in the world that she told her secret to. She said, "My motives are really not your business."

"I protect Stewart, got it? Anything that could hurt him is my business."

Elizabeth stopped walking and turned to Robert with her hands on her hips. How could he think that she wanted to hurt Stewart? "He's a remarkable man and I am able to appreciate that," she said, "I'm sorry if other girls are too stupid to. I'll walk the rest of the way by myself, thank you."

Back at home her parents were in the living room watching TV. When she opened the door her mother said, "You've been spending a lot of time out and about."

Elizabeth's habit had always been to come straight home after school and not go out after that. Except for winter Thursday afternoons at the mall, she didn't see friends in the evenings, just at school and on the weekends. Now she had broken that pattern and her parents were suspicious.

She shrugged and sat down on the couch between them. "Just a lot going on, I guess," she said.

Her mother rubbed her sweater sleeve. "We're watching the news," she said.

They watched the news every night without fail. "How exciting," Elizabeth said. "Who's trying to destroy the world today?"

"When did you get so cynical?" her father said, "You're supposed to be the idealistic youth."

"I'm going upstairs," Elizabeth said, pulling herself up and leaving her mother's hand behind.

"So soon?" Susan said. "You could stay and talk for a while."

"You guys enjoy your news."

Elizabeth went to bed early that night and spent the morning doing homework. She didn't want to think about the night before, but somehow she couldn't think about anything else. Was she really ready to give her body over to him? In health class the teachers were always saying that you had to wait. What was she waiting for, though? Could any more perfect opportunity ever present itself? Was it wrong to have sex with him when she hadn't been entirely honest with him? Did guys care about that kind of thing?

Her English paper was quickly turning into a treatise on the subject of thwarted desire. She recognized Stewart in Ethan Frome, in the way he simply did what he had to do without daring to go for the things he wanted. She saw herself also and wrote passionately about the feelings Ethan Frome must have had when he thought he had finally found someone to love.

From there Elizabeth thought about the promise she had made to herself to give back to Stewart the thing he missed with all his heart. While she pondered what to do, she worked at cleaning out her school backpack. What could she possibly do? She was just a child with no connections to anything in Stewart's world. At the bottom of the bag she came across a piece of paper she didn't recognize. There was a phone number on it with the name "Jeff." That was Stewart's friend, how had she ended up with his number? She had written it down, but she thought she left the paper on Stewart's desk. Then an idea came into her mind. With her cell phone she dialed the number without giving herself the chance to think about what she was doing.

"Hello," the voice crackled over the phone lines.

"Hello, is this Jeff?"

"Sure is, what can I do for you?"

"My name's Elizabeth and I'm a friend of Stewart's."

"Are you the secretary?"

"Yes, that's me." Elizabeth climbed onto her bed and lay back, looking up through her skylight.

"This is a surprise. Is Stewart there?"

"No, I'm calling you because I want to help you get him back to the surfing competition."

"But you haven't told him that?"

"You know how he is. He won't listen, but trust me I know that he really does want to be there."

"Listen, Elizabeth, I don't want to push him. He's not in very good shape these days."

"Have you seen him since it happened?"

"Well, no. Not since he left the hospital in Santa Monica for the rehab place in South Carolina."

"Then trust me, he's in great shape."

"But he's still, you know, crippled."

Elizabeth cringed at the word. "Yes," she said, "But I know something about paraplegia and you have to believe me that there's nothing physical keeping him out of the water. It's only guilt."

There was a pause on the line and Elizabeth glanced down at her phone to see if she was still connected. Then Jeff said, "Now why would you say a thing like that?"

"He told me what happened. He told me about Pete Morris."

"Wow, he must really trust you. Him, me, and Lee are the only ones who know the truth about that. Now I guess you too."

"Stewart is longing for the ocean and it's eating him up inside."

"I've been trying to convince him for months."

"I have a plan."

"Ah, a devious mind. I see why Stewart likes you."

"I think you should talk to him in person. Because

you've been his friend for so long I know you'll be able to gauge the situation and see how to push him."

"Are you going to talk him into coming to see me? I mean we've been friends since we were fourteen, but I haven't seen him in six years. I figured he doesn't want me to see him in that condition, stuck in a wheelchair and all."

"I don't think that's it," Elizabeth said, "He seems completely adjusted to being disabled. In fact, I don't think he would consider it being stuck."

"I don't know anything about these things."

"I think you should see him for Christmas. He'll be at his aunt's house in South Carolina and I'd like to pay for you to go as my Christmas present to him."

"That's very generous."

"That's how certain I am that he'll be glad to see you."

"Okay, I'll do it."

"Jeff, can I ask you something?"

"Shoot."

"Why does Stewart live with his aunt and uncle? What happened to his parents?"

"I don't know if I should be telling you about that."

"You know how he doesn't like to talk about himself. Please tell me."

"I suppose I owe you something for giving me the chance to see my buddy again. Stewart's mother died when he was a little kid, and his dad never showed much interest. I never met either of them. His aunt is hilarious, though. I only met her once. She traveled all the way to California to watch him compete the year he got sent to live with her. His father lives less than an hour from the beach and he never came. Not once. He didn't even come to the hospital after it happened. Stewart never told me this, but I heard a rumor that his father kicked him out because he got in a fight with his stepmother. Some people even said that he hit her. Anyway, once Aunt Claire saw what surfing was all about she was satisfied and let him do his thing. It was a big adjustment from having no one in his family care what he did to living with Aunt Claire. That year she came she asked me all kinds of questions about surfing. I assured her that it was safe."

The line was quiet again and Elizabeth said, "Surfing wasn't what hurt him."

"You said he's okay, right?"

"He's great, in fact."

Jeff laughed. "He always was a charmer," he said.

At school the next day Elizabeth's friends were talking about movies and Elizabeth was barely listening. She was thinking about how to buy a plane ticket for Jeff without her parents finding out about it. She didn't have a job, but she still had a lot of money saved from her bat mitzvah. If she touched it her parents would almost certainly find out. Christmas was coming up fast so she decided to tell her parents sort-of the truth. She would tell them that she needed to take out money for Christmas presents and hopefully they would never realize how much. Soon Elizabeth's friends were on the topic of their favorite movie, *Top Gun*. All Elizabeth's friends loved it and she didn't get it.

Finally she interrupted, saying, "Why is it that everyone loves that movie? I can understand guys liking it, but what's in it for us?"

"Have you really forgotten The Volleyball Scene?"

"The what?"

"You should watch it again, Elizabeth, you must have been too small the first time. The men play volleyball, with their shirts off, all sweaty. Best part of the movie."

Elizabeth had seen it only two months ago. She remembered them in a bar, she remembered one guy dying, she remembered motorcycles and sex. She could not remember them playing volleyball at all.

"Gotta love a guy in uniform," Maureen piped up.

"Exactly," said Amy with a noble nod of her head, "It's a universal truth."

"Oh," said Elizabeth, "Yeah." She had liked some men in uniforms before. The ones in *Born on the Fourth of July* or *Coming Home*. The vets who had been shot and it showed.

She had a sudden urge to tell them how hot Lt. Dan from *Forrest Gump* made her. What would they say? Would there ever be a time that she could be honest with her friends?

10

When she got home Elizabeth developed new pictures she had taken of her friends at school and tried to study at the same time. This was her last year of high school and it was beginning to sink in that she was not going to be seeing much of her friends anymore. None of them were even applying to any of the same schools as each other.

The pictures were frozen and lifeless. Her friends' smiles seemed trapped behind the paper. The next set of pictures startled her as they developed. It was like she was a ghost, looking at her own living body. It took her a moment to remember that Stewart had grabbed her camera and taken pictures of her. She was always the one behind the camera, but here she was looking at herself as though through Stewart's eyes.

Her stomach felt tight and she switched to reading her Physics textbook. The problems soon swam in front of her eyes. She felt around her for a bookmark and remembered the extra picture buried in her spare-parts box. Pulling it out, she stuck the paralyzed feet deep in her Physics book and went back to the pictures again.

With the pictures hanging to dry, Elizabeth heard the front door open and her mother's heels clicking on the wood hallway toward the kitchen. Elizabeth took a deep breath. Today was the day she was going to tell her mother about Stewart. She put her supplies away and then opened the door.

Susan was standing in high heels and a skirt suit at the kitchen counter, looking through the cabinets. When Elizabeth came in her mother asked without turning around, "What do you think we should have for supper?"

"I don't know," Elizabeth said.

"Here's some canned soup, "Susan said, "We'll have that. Your father is getting home late tonight, he called me at work, so he'll fend for himself."

"Okay." Elizabeth had learned years ago that her mother might sound like she was talking to herself, but she wanted a response. Even for a statement like that, which didn't seem to need a response, Susan wanted to hear something from the person she was talking to. Unlike people who want the last word, her main concern was to make sure people were listening to her.

Susan got out a can opener and dumped the soup into a pot. Elizabeth walked over and hopped up onto the counter beside her.

"Do you have something to tell me, Liz?"

Mothers always knew. "Actually, yeah, I do."

Susan stopped stirring and fixed her eyes on Elizabeth. That made it much harder.

"I'm fine," Elizabeth began, "No problems, just some news."

"You're going to kill me with nerves, for God's sake just say what it is."

"I have a boyfriend."

From deep, worried creases her mother's face suddenly stretched out and expanded into a grin. "Oh, sweetheart, that's wonderful. What's his name?"

Elizabeth looked down at her sneaker as her foot scuffed at the cabinet she was sitting on. "Uh, Stewart."

"So, tell me all about him!"

"He, uh, wants to take you and Dad to dinner tomorrow night."

"How sweet of him. Sounds like you've got a winner, Liz."

That night after her father got home Elizabeth heard their voices drifting from their room. She wondered if they were talking about her and slipped quietly out of her own room to find out.

"So our little Liz has a boyfriend?" her father's voice said.

"That's what she said."

"Wonder who he is."

"Oh, I know Liz. He'll be a cute little guy with glasses she met in her math class."

"Is that so?"

"His name is Stewart."

"I hate to be the one to burst your bubble, my dear, but parents don't know when they name their child whether he'll be good at math. 'What's in a name?'"

"Don't quote Shakespeare at me, Professor Foster, I know my daughter."

"I suspect you're right, but you never know, Lizzie may surprise us. Care to lay down some money on it, Susan?"

"Don't be so crude."

Elizabeth left then. Now she knew what they were expecting, and how different their expectation was from the reality. That never led to good things. She should tell them, she should warn them. But already she knew that she wouldn't be able to get the words out. She would never be able to say it. And when they saw him they would look at her and wonder why she didn't say anything. She would lie and pretend that she thought she already told them, but they would know she knew she hadn't.

The next night Susan and David started getting ready as soon as they got home. Since the question of what was for supper was an argument they had every night, they were glad to know for once what they were doing for food.

"What a thoughtful young man, taking us to dinner," Susan said as she examined herself in the mirror. She fluffed at her blond waves and moved the hair of her bangs around until no white hairs showed.

"Strange idea for a high schooler to get in his head, where is he going to take us? Friendly's?" her husband said. He was putting his tie on.

"He's obviously very mature. Do try not to interrogate him too much. This is just what Lizzie needs to get out of her shell. She's too quiet, too withdrawn. Socializing is good for her."

"All right, Susan, does my tie match my shirt match my jacket?"

She looked at him through the mirror with her

mouth scrunched critically. "Yes, you've done a fine job, dear."

"Good, let's go. He's meeting us at the restaurant?"

Susan nodded. She fastened pearls around her neck, took her jacket and they both walked down the stairs.

"Don't you look nice," Susan said as she saw her daughter.

Elizabeth had her wavy hair half up and half down. She wore a knee length blue skirt and a blue-flowered white top with matching cardigan. She wore no jewelry and no makeup, but her face shone with youth. Her fingers tapped against her knee nervously.

They got in the car and everyone was silent the whole way to the restaurant. Stewart had picked a very fancy place, trying to impress the Fosters. As they walked toward the front door Elizabeth saw Stewart's car parked in one of the handicapped spaces.

At the front podium Elizabeth said they were with the "Masterson" party and the Maitre D ushered them in. Elizabeth saw Stewart across the room, but didn't smile. She walked over with her parents, seeing that he was sitting on the far side of the table so that he was facing the door and could see them coming. She didn't know if he had planned it or not, but the tablecloth hid his wheelchair from view.

As they arrived at the table, Elizabeth's parents glanced at each other and stood, uncertain what to do next.

Elizabeth sat down next to Stewart at the round table and he smiled broadly at her parents. "Hello," he said, offering his hand to her father, "I'm Stewart. Please have a seat, forgive me if I don't stand." That's when her father looked down and saw the wheelchair. His grip on Stewart's hand tightened for a moment.

"I'm David Foster," he said with a guarded smile. "How did you hurt your foot?"

Stewart took a deep breath. "It's not my foot," he said, "I broke my back several years ago."

"Oh. I'm sorry." He sat down.

"I'm Susan," Elizabeth's mother took Stewart's hand. She too sat down. "Weren't you at Libby's wedding?"

"I was actually. Robert is my roommate."

"I see."

Elizabeth picked up a menu and tried to look preoccupied. Stewart looked at her, but she didn't respond.

"What do you do, Stewart?" Susan asked.

"I'm majoring in Physics at UBoston."

"Oh. College." Her brow wrinkled, she glanced at her husband.

Again silence. Elizabeth said, "The chicken looks good." She got no response.

Their waiter arrived to take the drink orders. Elizabeth got a Coke, her parents a glass of wine each and Stewart stuck with water.

"Tell us more about yourself, Stewart," Susan said.

"What do you want to know?"

"Liz was a little unclear on the details, you're how old?"

"Twenty-five," he admitted.

"I see."

The waiter came to take their orders. Elizabeth's parents ordered hurriedly, still distracted by wondering how they had ended up here.

The waiter gone, it was time to get serious again.

"What do you plan to do with your Physics major?" David asked.

Stewart hesitated before saying, "I hope to teach high school."

"You believe you'll make a good teacher?"

"I have some experience with it. I've tutored kids in physics, taught swimming, and coached surfing."

Elizabeth spent a lot of time looking at her plate, and glancing at people at other tables. Her father stopped asking questions, lapsing into an unhappy silence. The minutes ticking by before the food arrived were excruciating. Stewart tried to change to lighter conversation, but for any questions he asked he got a one or two word answer. Everyone pounced on the food when it arrived, it gave them something to do, a reason not to talk.

After dinner Stewart paid and again there was silence while he waited for his credit card to come back.

Finally Susan said, "It was lovely to meet you, Stewart. Good luck with your studies."

"Thank you," he said. He looked over at Elizabeth, but he said nothing to her.

The car ride home was utterly silent. Elizabeth put her feet up in front of her on the back seat, so her knees were pressed into her chest. From there she wrapped her arms around her legs until she was as close to a fetal position as she could get. The silence from the front of the car was palpable. Her mother's usual yammering was gone and her father's jovial smiles too. Elizabeth wondered what they were thinking. Had they guessed the truth or were they stuck in some less frightening possibility? Would they ask her about it or would everything soon settle back to the way it had been before? Instead, would there always be tension between she and her parents from now on, both of them knowing and neither one willing to say it? Was the silence really as hostile as it felt? At last her mother turned in her seat to look back at Elizabeth and said, "Why didn't you tell us?"

"I don't know," Elizabeth whispered. She looked out the window, avoiding her mother's gaze. Her father said nothing until they got home.

Elizabeth was about to go straight to her room, but her mother stopped her.

"Elizabeth, hang on a second. Come back here and talk with us for a minute, okay?"

Obediently she sat in the brown over-stuffed easy chair and fiddled with the edge of the decorative pillow she had moved aside.

"So, did you like him?" she ventured.

"Elizabeth," her father said. Both he and her mother sat down on the couch and faced her, their knees together and their hands clasped over their knees. They just looked at her. "Elizabeth," her father began again, "We know that you have always wanted to help the handicapped. It seems to be your calling in some way. However, we think that you may have taken it too far this time."

"What is he making you do?" Susan burst in, "Are you taking care of him? Helping him? Did you get trapped because you're too nice to say no?"

"Oh God," Elizabeth said, "Nothing like that. He's a nice guy. You should give him a chance."

"You can't just date this man," Susan said, "Think of your future."

"I'm only eighteen."

"You have to make careful choices from the start," her mother insisted. "If you invest too much in this relationship, it could scar you for future relationships."

"Future relationships?"

"Elizabeth, you should be using this time to meet nice, young, Jewish men," her father argued. She heard her mother snort at the "Jewish" part. Susan said, "Wouldn't it be easier to date a normal boy?"

"No," Elizabeth said, "It's easiest to date someone I'm in love with."

"Elizabeth," her father tried to curtail her. Susan sank back against the couch. "Love?" she said. To herself she muttered, "I should have done something sooner. I should have discouraged her interest from the start. This is my fault."

David said, "You're still young. Your feelings are strong and you think you know what you want. Just go slow and be cautious, please. Someday you will understand why."

"What happens when you want to have children?" Susan said, again ignoring David.

David took her arm and said to her, "Let's not get ahead of ourselves. Elizabeth is right, she's only eighteen."

"Are you going to let her keep seeing him?" Susan said.

"I don't know what else to do," David said. "I can't forbid her. She's old enough to make these kinds of choices. Look at the bright side, at least she won't be having sex and getting pregnant."

Sometimes her parents' ignorance shocked Elizabeth.

Now was not the time to tell them that paraplegic men were still sexual beings and many could still father children. The activist in her wanted to protest. Now was not the time. Someday she would prove to them that Stewart was a man capable of all the aspects of manhood.

"You don't understand," her mother said, "Did we teach you emotions wrong? What you feel isn't love, you're too young for that, it is pity. Feeling sorry for the man is not a reason to attach yourself to him."

"Susan, she isn't that serious yet. Are you, Elizabeth?"

Elizabeth was beginning to feel very self-righteous. She knew about paraplegia and they never would. They wouldn't see everything that was possible. They would never understand the beauty of wheels turning, of limp limbs, of hands pressed against metal, of physical effort.

"No," she whispered.

Back in her room she lay down on her bed and thought about all that had changed in the last few months. Usually in her fantasies she enjoyed the men's pain. She liked to see them fall, and recover; suffer and get over it. She tried for a moment to integrate Stewart into that kind of fantasy, but her mind wouldn't go there.

He was different from her fantasies. Knowing him as a real person, she didn't want him to hurt. Could it be that, despite his injury, he wasn't a part of her secret any longer? She really didn't want to see him struggle or suffer. She was proud of being with him because she was proud of all the overcoming of difficulties he had done.

The next weekend Elizabeth went back to lying to her parents. She said she was going to movies and the park with the girls, but actually she went to the park and then the movies with Stewart.

They left the park quickly because of the cold and sat in the lobby of the theater waiting for their movie.

"Dinner didn't go so well," Stewart said.

"I told you it wouldn't."

"You could have warned them."

"How come I have to do that? I don't want to be the one bringing the bad news."

"I'm bad news, am I?"

"Come on, don't be like that, you know what I mean. You have to admit that it isn't any parent's dream for their daughter to bring home an older, tattooed surfer in a wheelchair."

Absently he rubbed her arm. "It's hard to argue with that. What are we going to do now that we know your parents don't like me?"

"My friends like you," she said, "And parents aren't supposed to like boyfriends."

"Come on," he said, "The movie is starting."

Elizabeth loved the movie. She came out of the theater jumping around in her excitement and gesturing wildly. Stewart rolled along calmly beside her.

New snowflakes were tentatively drifting down on the street and they glowed for a moment as they passed under streetlamps.

In the car on the way to his dorm Elizabeth said, "This time I really have to study, no fair distracting me."

"Fine," Stewart said, "Two can do that."

"I'm sure a little studying won't hurt you either."

Elizabeth climbed onto his bed and pulled out her

books and notebooks. Stewart sat at his desk. He opened up Solitaire on his computer and played for a while.

"What are you studying?" he said.

"History," she said, "Then physics, then math."

"I can help with the physics, why don't you skip to that?"

"Okay," Elizabeth said, "Just let me finish the questions I'm working on."

While she wrote, Stewart went to his window and looked out at the winter world. In the last few weeks the campus had been transformed and very few people ventured out to destroy the pristine beauty of the snow-covered landscape. There was a hill outside his building and some people had already stolen cafeteria trays to sled down it. But on the other side was an undisturbed football field where the snow was piling up in drifts.

"I'm ready," Elizabeth said.

Stewart turned and moved to the edge of the bed.

"Wouldn't you rather study at a desk?" he said.

"No," she said, "You sound like my mother."

"Okay, let's not go there. Just show me the problem." She slid her book around to face him and he read the physics problem.

"There should be a reference chart somewhere in the book that gives you all the formulas, then you just have to put in the numbers," Stewart said.

Elizabeth began to flip through the book, looking for the formulas. As she did something came loose from within the pages and drifted to the floor at Stewart's feet. Elizabeth didn't notice. Stewart looked down and frowned at what he saw.

The photograph lay half under the bed and seemed

to look up at Stewart with utter calm. In a strange kind of mirror effect, he was looking at his own feet and a photograph of feet that looked like his. He stooped down and picked up the picture.

"What is this?" he said.

Elizabeth looked up and as soon as she saw what was in his hand, her face turned crimson. "It's nothing," she whispered, but her reaction had already betrayed her.

"Nothing? Why on earth would you have a photograph of paralyzed feet?"

Elizabeth shrugged.

Stewart looked at her and suddenly Elizabeth saw on his face all the clues falling into place. He backed away without noticing he was doing it.

"Really," she pleaded, "It's nothing. I'll take it back, you can forget about it." She was sitting up on her knees now, biting her lip and pressing her hands under her legs. She frowned.

"How do you know so much about disability?" Stewart said.

"I don't know," Elizabeth ventured, "It just interests me."

"Bullshit," he said, "Don't lie to me."

"It isn't how you think, really it isn't," she said, leaning forward, her eyes opened earnestly.

"So you know what I'm thinking?"

Elizabeth nodded.

"You have a fetish," he said.

"A what?"

Stewart sighed. "Never heard that word before?"

"No," Elizabeth said defiantly, but even as she said it a memory came to her. It had been one of her vocabulary words in English class this year. The teacher read the definition as having a strong proclivity toward. Some of the kids had giggled and the teacher had been braced for the giggling. Elizabeth had not understood why, but suddenly it was clear. It meant a sexual proclivity.

Stewart continued, "You more than didn't mind my wheelchair when you went out with me. You're attracted to it. You have disability devoteeism."

The words hung in the air between them. She wanted to reach forward and brush them aside like a cobweb, but it was too late. Stewart had finally noticed the elephant in his room.

"You use this picture, don't you?" he said, dropping it back to the floor as though it had burned his hand. "It's like pornography to you."

Elizabeth cringed at the ugly word, but she couldn't deny it. No matter what she felt while looking at it, there could be only one way to describe what she had it for.

"Just because I've always... well, fantasized differently from other people, it doesn't mean that I don't have... real feelings for you."

"You expect me to believe that," Stewart said. "All this time you knew and you hid it from me because you were just using me."

"No," Elizabeth said, "No, it's not like that."

"What is it like? Tell me."

"I just liked you," she said, "And you're sexy. It doesn't change anything. Even if there is a name for what I have. Why is it wrong?"

"Because my paralysis is not me. Who I am is something different from my body."

"You talk as though it isn't a part of you."

"Would you not have gone out with me if we met a few years earlier, or if I had never been injured at all?"

"I met you exactly as you are now, and I am in love with you."

He didn't say anything else. She wanted to explain to Stewart, make him understand, but he clearly didn't want to talk to her right now. What was he going to do? Was she going to lose him over this? It was that fear that had compelled her to keep it a secret. Maybe she shouldn't have been deceptive, but if she had told him right away he wouldn't have even given her a chance. In the months they had been together would he be able to remember the redeeming moments, or would this new knowledge trump everything she had done, every way she had shown she loved him?

"I need to think about this," Stewart said.

"I'm sorry," Elizabeth whispered.

Stewart didn't say anything more to her. He left the room and Elizabeth sat there alone, watching everything she had wanted being sucked away.

It was bound to happen. She had known from the start that she couldn't hide the truth from him forever. She had known from the start that this day was inevitable. If only she could have been honest, maybe if she had explained it to him he would have taken it better. At least she wouldn't have hurt him as badly if she had been up front. But how do you tell someone that you get wet between the legs at the sight of his twisted and malfunctioning body?

Elizabeth was destined to be alone in her life because of something that wasn't her fault and she couldn't seem to control. How had this destiny been given to her? Was there nothing she could do or say to change it? She got up. She packed her bag with all her books and notebooks again. She picked the photograph up off the floor and looked at it for a few moments. Then she packed that too.

She left the room and closed the door. She walked down the hallway to the stairs and left without seeing Stewart again. The painful cold felt good on her skin. It pricked and the wind tugged on her scarf and hair. She made the familiar walk to the subway station and sat to wait for the next train.

There were other people around her waiting too. A group of kids around her age with backpacks, a goth girl dressed in black from head to toe, with dark black hair and six piercings on her face, a homeless man cocooned in dirty blankets, and a girl with a guitar singing with the case open in front of her.

The rush of the train could be heard long before they saw it. Elizabeth looked down the dark tunnel and felt the gush of stale air being pushed out at her. Then the single tiny light appeared and got bigger and closer until the whole shiny silver train was speeding into the station. It stopped and the doors opened. People got off and people got in. It wasn't crowded and Elizabeth found a seat next to the empty space reserved for wheelchairs. She looked at the little icon that showed a wheelchair and an old person with a cane and a crutch. No, in diagrams like this there wasn't much room for the possibility of sexuality.

Her body shook back and forth as the train dashed through the darkness. Inside everything was bright and the ads screamed out at her. The people stood and sat around grim faced and silent. She felt her heart pounding, but she told herself to hold off, to wait to feel the impact of what had just happened. She just watched the darkness outside the window and the slight changes in its texture and shape.

At the end of the line Elizabeth stood up and got off the train. Everyone else was also getting off and spreading and flowing up the stairs into Alewife station. Elizabeth now had to get on the bus, so she sat outside on the concrete bench. Did he not care about her, here alone in the dark, cold station? Had he ever really cared about her? It was hard to think that the last several months could have been nothing important. Those feelings she had had looking into his eyes could have meant nothing. Where would her life go from here? The world seemed so small and closed in.

Yet at the same time something was opening. There was a word for what she felt. If there was already a word for it, then other people felt it also. In all these years it had never occurred to her that there were other people struggling with the same demon. How stupid of her to think she was the only one.

11

When the phone rang Elizabeth knew it was him. She stood in the hallway and watched it ring. Her parents weren't home from work yet. It was Stewart and he was going to tell her he never wanted to see her again. She picked up the receiver.

"Elizabeth?" he said.

"Yes."

"I'm sorry." His voice was dead and heavy. It was the sound of a door closing.

"Please don't do this," she whispered.

"You aren't who I thought you were."

"But—"

"No," he interrupted, "It's over."

Elizabeth ran up the stairs and closed the door to her room. She didn't make it to her bed, but collapsed on the floor. She cried so hard she felt that there wasn't any liquid left in her body. When her eyes ran out of tears would they begin to cry blood?

Parents came by and knocked on her door once in a while, but Elizabeth made no response to them. She couldn't talk, and there was nothing either of her parents could do. The pain in Elizabeth's stomach doubled when she thought of all Stewart's friends knowing that she wasn't good enough for him. He thought she was a freak.

Elizabeth remembered now why she never told anyone about her... interest in disability. Because they would react as he had. He was far too good to be true. That wasn't how the world worked. Ask Stewart, tragedy was far more likely than good. Good didn't last, but pain did. She felt that she stood at the edge of a black void. She was tumbling into it and her future was nothing but empty darkness.

Elizabeth was not surprised by Stewart's reaction. She knew it would be the response of anyone finding out. Just most people wouldn't react so personally. Elizabeth was sure that if she asked people randomly on the street what they thought of the existence of a fetish for physical disability their reaction would be: oh that's sick; what a pervert; there are people like that? And they would be right. It was twisted, deviant, different, and frightening.

For the weekend Elizabeth did not leave her room. But on Monday she put on a brave face and opened the door. She was polite and friendly at breakfast with her parents and then sat attentively in class. All her energy was focused on the outside. Through out the day she refused to look inside herself at all. In classes she worked with gusto, but then lunch arrived.

There wasn't much outside herself to focus on at lunch. In fact, all her friends descended on her table and wanted to gossip. She tried not to listen. For the first time she saw the grains of the bread of her sandwich, there were so many shades of brown and shapes of the grains. Vibrant yellow cheese poked out of a corner, the density of the bread got tighter toward the edge just before the crust.

"Liz," Amy said, "What are you doing?"

Elizabeth looked up and saw that all her friends had stopped eating and were looking at her. She was still holding her sandwich, but had not yet taken a bite. She wondered if she was supposed to say something related to whatever they were talking about.

"Are you okay?" Maureen said.

Elizabeth put her hands down on the table for support. It was fake wood— cold and smooth, dark eddies swirled along the tan surface.

"No, "Elizabeth said, "Stewart left me."

The rest of the air was sucked out of her lungs and she couldn't say anything more. She let her head drop to the table and closed her eyes, hearing her friends begin their shocked gasps, and sympathetic clucks. Elizabeth could only handle one sense at a time, five was far too many. Taste was a nice sense, making few demands and easily pleased. But right now even that was ruined. All weekend her food had been like cardboard and a taste she could only describe as bitter disappointment filled her mouth.

The bell rang for lunch to end. Elizabeth didn't move. Maureen and Becky gathered together their books and bolted from the cafeteria. But Amy stood and walked over to Elizabeth, laying a hand on her shoulder.

"Let's take a walk," Amy said. "Some things are more important than class."

Elizabeth looked back at her. Though her friend was standing less than two feet away, Elizabeth felt a huge distance between them, as though she was looking up from the bottom of the ocean to Amy on the surface. Slowly Elizabeth nodded. She stood up and put her sandwich back in her bag. They took their coats and Amy led her outside. They wandered the grounds of the school as they talked.

Amy's boldness, which so often caused problems, now allowed her to attack the subject at hand straight on. She touched Elizabeth's arm affectionately and said, "I know you really care about him, but you have to realize that he was your first boyfriend. It's really rare that first relationships last. You have to go through the learning process. Besides which, you two are very different. You come from different places, have different experiences of the world, and you are much younger."

"This isn't what I want to hear."

"You just need some time to adjust. I know how empty you feel right now, I've been there."

"It's worse for me," Elizabeth said. The trees above them rustled as a wind sprang up. The sky was dark, a storm was on its way.

"It feels that way, but everyone goes through that pain at one point or another."

"It's different. You can't understand."

"Why don't you explain it to me then, Liz!"

Elizabeth had heard that the reason secrets had such a powerful hold on a person was the secrecy itself. That if one could just break the silence, the spell would be broken. Words and thoughts inside her head could sweep her away with their power, but supposedly words once spoken lost their magic. Her History teacher told stories about the power of the true name in mythology. Like the Egyptian god Ra. He had another secret name and if anyone found out what it was that person would have complete control of him.

"Elizabeth?"

She took a deep breath, "Stewart only proved that I can never be with a man I'm attracted to. Something is wrong with me."

"What are you talking about?" Amy was frowning, but suddenly her expression lifted and her eyes opened wide. "Wait a minute, is that what…oh wow."

"It's sexual, I'm attracted to disability." Her face was hot, her heart was beating absurdly fast, she could feel her whole body trembling. She had said it, was its power over?

"Oh, Elizabeth, I had no idea!"

The snow began to fall. Amy led Elizabeth under some trees where they were sheltered.

As they watched the snow drifting to the ground, Amy said, "I knew you were interested in the handicapped, but I never guessed why. How long have you had this?"

"All my life. I can't remember a time when it wasn't true. As a little child I didn't know it was sexual, but the feelings didn't change as I grew up and my understanding of them did." Her voice was coming out funny, it was shaking. "Do you hate me now?" she said softly.

"Why would you say that? Was Stewart mean to you about this?"

"He reacted the way I expected he would."

"I assume you didn't tell him."

"No, he figured it out. I'm so ashamed, Amy."

"Don't be. It isn't shameful. I think it's a little unusual, but what's so bad about it? I'd think he'd be glad you were able to see past his disability."

"I'm not seeing past it."

"All right, I think he'd be glad you were able to appreciate all of him."

"I wish he saw it that way. But I think of it like a curse that will forever keep me from being with a man completely. I can have an intellectual attraction to able-bodied men, but I've never felt lust for them."

"I'm sorry, Liz, I wish I could fix it for you."

"I think life is just a process of settling for less and pretending you never wanted more."

She curled up her knees, laid her arms across them and buried her face in her arms, crying quietly and listening to the wind.

How could she have known at four years old how evil it was? She couldn't know that it was sexual, she didn't know what sex was. But something in her knew how people would respond. Something in her knew that it was weird and an inappropriate reaction to the sight of disability. Even that young she must have known that the proper response was pity, not desire.

She was surrounded by darkness, sinking into the abyss, into the darkest part of herself. Did other people have these black holes, hidden deep within? Did something vile radiate through their bodies? Did they feel shame at their own thoughts? Was she normal? She knew that the things her mind thought about were unusual, but she wondered what it looked like inside someone else's mind. Did everyone have something to hide? She wanted to believe so. It was hard to continue to believe that something dark grew inside her without her consent and no one else felt anything like it.

Love was much harder than Elizabeth expected. She and Stewart had not flowed easily into unity. It was strange, but in the months they were together she had forgotten how to be alone. Stewart, though, had never learned how not to be alone.

You can destroy your feeling, her mind whispered to her, *cut it off, let it wither away on its own. If you truly love him, you'll stop. Stop noticing wheelchairs, stop your ears from picking up the sound of crutches. Live your life as an ascetic. Lots of people do it. It will purify you if you can live simply for pure and unrequited love.* Rather a romantic life, wouldn't it be? People would think well of her as long as they never knew the reason for it.

Back at home she dragged her finger down the pane of glass in the living room window, watching the dark mist turn to droplets of water just in the line her finger made. She pressed her face against the window and looked through the line she had drawn with her finger. Soon her nose was cold and wet. Outside she saw the little boy who lived in the house behind them creating an army of snow people. With unending patience he rolled the balls and stacked them. When he had seven or so done he made more balls that he piled in a corner of his yard. As Elizabeth watched, a war began. The little boy pelted his snowmen with more snow, knocking them over and killing them with the very substance they were made from.

Elizabeth wanted to go down there and repair the

chaos, rebuild homes for the snowmen. Their race was destined to end with the spring, but in the meantime they should be treated well. It was silly of her to think like this. It was just snow, more and more and more snow that stuck together or changed form into something new, but it didn't die, it didn't end. She didn't need to fear for it. Those snowmen would eventually become new snowmen the next year. The beauty of New England is that it teaches the body to sense the circular nature in everything. Things that die are reborn; and things that fade are renewed. Each thing happens in its time.

The little boy got tired of his game, went over and kicked down the two remaining snowmen. He jumped on their remains and soon there was no trace that they had ever been. Then he rubbed his mitten under his nose, pushed back his hat to reveal hair that was plastered to his forehead with moisture and ran up to his house, sliding open the glass door that was almost too big for him.

Elizabeth stayed against the window watching a little longer, even though everything was still and quiet in the yard. Her back yard was still fresh and smooth, but next door all the snow had been trampled and mushed. She could see the light on in the neighbor's kitchen and the little boy's snow gear drying on the radiator next to the back door: hat, mittens, snowpants, boots, scarf, and big fluffy coat. She remembered when she used to get bundled up like that to go outside. She remembered too how hot it got inside all that clothing when she was running around and playing in the snow. Snow itself could almost be warm if you were young and knew how to play. That was a skill forgotten when one grew older.

Then snow might become just a nuisance, or better

yet, something to brag about. Adults loved to gather and talk about how many inches of snow, how much ice was on the road, what they had driven through or what they had walked through. They were like war stories, each one topping the last. Going out of one's home was an adventure. In fact, staying in was sometimes an adventure too. After the radio announced that the roads were too dangerous, you might stand in the kitchen with a mug of coffee in your hand and watch the snow come down out the window. It seemed to be trying to bury you, to cut you off from everyone. The telephone lines would ice over and go down. Wherever you were, there you would stay, with only the company of a fire and a book.

Elizabeth liked to walk on the ice, particularly the ice on the edge of the road, where water might have run underneath and cleared a path, so that the ice was hovering above the ground, waiting to be stepped on and sunk back down to the earth with a satisfying crackle. Susan hated when Elizabeth did this, but Elizabeth knew she was clumsy and was going to slip and fall no matter what she did.

She used to brush the snow off the railing on the stairs up to the front door by running her gloved hand up it. The snow fell off in powdery billows and some got underneath the band of her glove and onto the bare skin of her wrist where it melted and itched.

As soon as she got in, she would peel off the wet gloves and lay them on top of the radiator. She would rub her wrists that were already wet, red, and itching. Those were the experiences of childhood. Now she was on the other side of the glass, staying safe and dry.

12

"Elizabeth," her mother knocked on the door, "your grandmother's Christmas party is tonight and you must go, so pull yourself together."

Elizabeth was lying on her bed. Since school had ended for Christmas break she hadn't even showered. It was as though she was creating a cocoon of grime over her body and that would somehow protect her from the hurt. The problem was the hurt was inside and maybe the dirt was holding it in. Though she still went through the motions of life she didn't register what she saw in front of her. She felt like the living dead. Every few moments a flashback would hit her and she would remember the feel of Stewart's shoulders or the way he looked moving ahead of her. Each time this happened, Elizabeth paused and closed her eyes, breathing slowly until it passed. At first she hated these moments and the additional pain they brought. Eventually she was glad for them because it was all she had left of him.

Elizabeth wished that there were nothing obligating her to interact with the world. If she could only just disappear forever and feel the peace of oblivion…but her mother was right, she had to go to the party. They only got together with her grandmother once a year and during that time everyone had to look and act perfectly. So, it was time to shower.

She walked absently to the bathroom, put her T-shirt and shorts in the hamper and turned on the water. The pressure of it hitting her was almost enough to knock her over. She wondered when the last time she ate was. She willed herself to be strong and the water ran down her body like fingers. Though she thought there was no liquid left inside her body, soon her tears were mingling with the shower, falling over her skin and burning. On and on she stood with water pouring down until there was a knock on the door and her mother's voice said, "Elizabeth? Are you all right in there?"

"I'm fine," she called and hurried to soap up and shampoo her hair. She turned off the water and wrapped a towel around her.

Back in her room she opened the closet and looked at the long plastic bag that held the dress she had bought. There was nothing to do but put it on. So she did. Then walked down the stairs where her father was searching for his car keys and her mother was saying, "You always lose them right before going to see my mother, I think you do it on purpose."

When they heard Elizabeth's feet on the stairs they both stopped and looked over. For a moment no one said anything, then her mother said, "Wow, Liz." And her father said, "You look all grown up."

"Thanks, "she murmured. It was more than the dress that made her look grown up; she had entered the world of adulthood when her heart broke. The pieces were never going to go back together the same way again. And that was what gave someone maturity.

"You two get in the car," her father said, "I'll be there as soon as I find the keys."

A few minutes later they were off. They drove the hour-long car ride with classical music playing. No one spoke. Elizabeth's mother had been Christian and her father Jewish, Elizabeth herself had been raised nothing in particular. Both families were still resentful about it. So Grandma often gave Elizabeth's father the cold shoulder. Bubby, her father's mother, was a bit more forgiving, but was in denial, telling everyone at her nursing home that Elizabeth was Jewish.

"Hello, David," Elizabeth's grandmother said with a curt nod as they walked in.

"Hello, Margaret," Elizabeth's father said and walked away to find the few people he knew.

"Elizabeth!" her grandmother gushed, "You're so grown up. Look, Susan, she has that pale beauty."

Elizabeth guessed she probably was pale, she couldn't feel any blood in her face at all. What would have happened if Stewart had come with her? Her grandmother would probably tell him how she always thought Elizabeth would grow up to be a nurse because as a child she played with dolls by wrapping them in bandages made of toilet paper. She had been a baby then, and a little less stringent about hiding her secret, though even then she had closed the door.

"You'll be off to college next year, then?" Grandma was saying.

Elizabeth nodded.

"She sent in her applications just a couple weeks ago," her mother said, "We won't know until April where she got in."

The two women talked about Elizabeth a little longer, Elizabeth not contributing anything herself. Eventually they began to talk about Susan's life and Elizabeth wandered away. She was not at a point where she felt she could deal with crowds, but there were people everywhere. Constantly people stopped her, asked about school and her future. She gave them a rote line about a science major with an art minor.

Everyone expected her to have plans, all of them pretending that their lives weren't a series of chaotic and unpredictable moments, spinning out of control. Stewart knew first hand that he was not in control and was not afraid to admit it. She sat down in a corner, hunched over, ruining the effect of her beautiful dress. She closed her eyes and willed everyone away. While she was suffering through this she wondered if Stewart was in pain. What was he up to right now home in South Carolina?

"Stewart is here!" Stewart heard as soon as he opened the door. Three children came barreling down the hallway and straight at him. The two girls arrived first and stopped short. They were seven and ten and suddenly, in the last three steps to him, they became shy. Their little four-year-old brother simply launched himself right onto Stewart's lap.

Uncle John, who had picked Stewart up from the

airport, was trying to get into the house behind him, but there wasn't space to get around.

"Hi, guys," Stewart said, "Let's move into the house a little."

"I get to ride," Joey said.

"Absolutely," Stewart said. He moved them further into the house. The wheelchair he was using was an old, folding one that John brought to the airport. Stewart could have taken his main chair with him, but then he'd have to let the airline stow it for him and he hated for strangers to touch it, so Robert had dropped him off and taken that chair back with him while Stewart used the airport chair until he got to South Carolina and John arrived with this one. It was a little heavier and bulkier than he was used to and his arms always ached after just a day of using it.

Aunt Claire came bursting out of the kitchen door at the far end of the living room. She was wearing an apron, but still had flour on her face and in her hair. She held a long wooden spoon.

"Stewart! Come in, come in, kids leave him alone now."

"That's all right," Stewart said.

The Christmas tree was set up in the corner of the living room, but hadn't been decorated yet. Most of Claire's other decorations were up: the fake candles in the windows, the giant swag of holly over the front door, the ball of mistletoe in the stairwell, and the Santa statue that Stewart almost knocked over as he turned toward the living room. He was out of practice maneuvering this chair.

"Hold on tight," he said to Joey. The girls ran over to

the sofa and watched from there. Stewart rolled over to where they sat. The kids clustered around him and Aunt Claire came over and sat down.

"Tell me about school," she said.

"Why don't you tell me about the plans?" Stewart said. He knew Aunt Claire loved to talk about all the things he didn't like to talk about.

"Tonight we'll be decorating the tree and then for Christmas Eve everyone will be over here, grandma and grandpa, and your dad is flying in from California." The timer in the kitchen went off. "John!" she shouted, "Will you turn off the oven for me?"

Joey was still sitting in Stewart's lap and Julia was inching closer. "I think there's room for one more," Stewart whispered to her. He shifted Joey to one leg and pulled Julia up onto his other leg.

"You really can't feel us?" she said.

"Nope," he said.

Aunt Claire interrupted. "I'm trying to talk to cousin Stewart."

Stewart and the children exchanged looks that said, you know how she is. These kids were the reason Stewart kept going back to South Carolina.

Uncle John had brought three-year-old Joyce to the hospital in California after Stewart's injury. Claire was heavily pregnant with Julia and couldn't fly. Stewart had been drifting in and out of consciousness, but his first memory of being in the hospital was waking up with Joyce's tiny face and big eyes looking down at him.

When he figured out how to move again, he held her loosely in his sore arms. She was not afraid. Despite all the machinery and metal and the things that frightened

Stewart himself, Joyce was not scared of it or of him. She was the only person who responded to him naturally in those first months.

Jeff and his uncle came to see him and they acted strangely, afraid of what he was feeling or thinking and guilty that they had come through without a physical mark. No one else had even come at all. Joyce had held him, had kissed him, and had laughed. He shared his Jell-o with her and she fell asleep snuggled against his body.

The other two just grew up with him in a wheelchair and it seemed totally normal to them.

"I made you a present," Julia said, "You'll never guess what it is."

"Then I won't even try," Stewart said.

Julia protested. "You're not being any fun."

"Okay, let me see. Is it a horse?"

"I can't make a horse! Be real, Stewart."

"How about a hair grabber? So I can pull your hair from across the room."

"I wouldn't help you pull my hair," Julia said, giggling.

Claire placed her hands on her thick knees and pulled herself up. "I have a lot of work to do in the kitchen."

As she left, Stewart whispered to Joyce, "Do you think we should go help?"

She shook her head. "Don't volunteer for work, that's what I always say."

"I see," Stewart said, "In that case, I won't ask if you want to help me unpack."

"I can help," Julia said.

"Me too," Joey said.

"Oh, they're just kids," Joyce said, "I'll go get your bag."

They all proceeded through the kitchen to Stewart's room. He had lived here for the last six years, and in a room upstairs for five before that, but neither one had ever looked lived in. There were no touches of personality. Beige sheets, navy blue comforter, and fluffy floral curtains that Claire had picked out. No posters or other decorations. The trophies were the only things he had that were his and Claire kept those lined up on the bookcase in the living room.

Joyce dropped his duffle bag on the floor. There was nothing but clothes and a few medicines in it. This room, having been built specifically for him, was well designed for a disabled person. Claire worked with special needs kids, so she had every device he could possibly use. He never needed to bring back any of his disability's supplies.

All three kids started pulling his clothes from the bag and grabbing hangers from the closet. This closet had a bar they could reach, since it was at waist height to a standing adult. Putting Stewart's clothes away had become a race.

"I'm finished, I'm finished," screamed Joey when he got back to the empty duffle.

Claire knocked on the open door. "Tree decorating time," she said. The two youngest children bolted past her, while Joyce walked calmly. Claire smiled after them.

"Come on, Stewart," she said. As he passed, she lay a hand on the back of his neck for a moment. Back in the living room boxes of ornaments were sitting waiting on the floor.

By the time they were finished the tree was bottom heavy. John was the only person who could reach the top half of the tree. Claire was short and reached only a little past where Stewart and the kids were hanging ornaments. Toward the end Stewart pushed his legs to the side and picked Joey up, so he could stand on the wheelchair and reach a little higher.

Stepping back to survey the result, John said, "Well, it certainly reflects our family."

Claire smiled and took his arm. "That it does," she said.

They brought their dinner plates into the living room, so they could keep enjoying the tree. John put The Messiah on the stereo.

"You know one more is always welcome," John said to Stewart while they ate, "Did you invite your girlfriend to come?"

"Actually, that's over," Stewart said, "We're not going out anymore."

"You poor thing," Claire said, "Are you all right?"

"Yeah, I'm fine," Stewart said.

"How could she? You've been hurt enough," Claire said.

"Yeah, yeah, yeah," Stewart said, just like Elizabeth. There was no point in trying to explain to Aunt Claire that the world wasn't out to get him and sometimes things happened that were not anyone's fault.

The next morning Stewart got dressed and went out into the kitchen. He found a breakfast laid out on the table for him: orange juice, toast, bacon, eggs.

Claire was standing at the sink with a pleased look on her face. Stewart didn't have the heart to tell her that he never ate breakfast. John still had his bathrobe on and his white hair was sticking up in all directions. Stewart waited until Claire left the room to ask him for a cup of coffee.

John brought him a mug and sat down in front of the newspaper. It was the day before Christmas Eve.

"What's the plan for today?" John asked.

"I was thinking of going to the barber shop," Stewart said.

"I'm sure Charlie would love to see you."

Claire came back with her arms full of wrapping paper and scissors. "Cleaning first," she said, "Then you can do what you like with the rest of the day."

She sent John upstairs and Stewart to the living room with a dust rag. Company was coming. It was only family, but maybe the grandparents were the most important people to impress.

Stewart had to watch carefully where he was going, or he might bump into something. Every time he went by the porcelain rabbit he nearly knocked it into the potted plant. And some days he considered purposely hitting it with his wheel. Aunt Claire would never blame him, just fuss over the broken pieces. Maybe she made her house difficult for him on purpose, a kind of obstacle course to test his dexterity and his patience.

In the living room he picked up the cloth rag from his lap and began wiping it over things: the coffee table, the piano bench, the window sills, the bottom half of the book shelves.

He was swiping the rag quickly over an old letter desk when he paused and wondered what Claire used it for. He pulled open the top drawer to find out.

There was a framed picture closed into the drawer. Lifting it up, he remembered the day it was taken. It was the day after he had won top honors at the Florida surfing competition the second year in a row. He had been goofing off and having fun; the picture showed him doing a handstand on his board while a wave carried him towards shore. In another couple seconds he was going to fall sideways into the waves and surface with seaweed on his shoulders.

What was this picture doing closed in a drawer? He looked around him, at the mantle piece and the piano and all the other places Claire put pictures. There were none of Stewart. He looked at the bookshelf and all his trophies were gone. Why hadn't he noticed that before? Years ago this picture used to be on the piano. He remembered Claire would point it out to her friends when they came to visit.

She used to be proud of him. Had she hidden the picture for fear of hurting him or because she couldn't stand to see how he used to be? Stewart put the picture back and closed the drawer.

After the dusting was done, he maneuvered his chair out of the living room and into the front hall. He stopped at the bottom of the stairs and called, "Hey, Uncle John!"

When John appeared, Stewart asked for a ride to the barbershop. This was why Stewart liked to have his car with him when he went back to Carolina. Not having a car he could drive made him too dependent on his relatives. They all already enjoyed helping him way too much.

John went to get clearance from Claire while Stewart

rolled out onto the porch and down the ramp toward the driveway. It hadn't yet snowed in South Carolina and some years it never did.

The drive to town was only five minutes. When they got there, John got the chair out of the back and unfolded it, then put on the brake and stood back to let Stewart get out without getting in the way. "Should I wait for you?" John asked.

"No," Stewart said, "I'll get a ride back from one of the guys."

John nodded and drove away. Back in a part of the country where traditions mattered, Stewart was going to the same barbershop he had been going to ever since he first moved to South Carolina. One of the old men sitting in the waiting area got up and held the door open for Stewart.

Charlie nodded at him as he came in. Stewart took up a place beside the magazine table. A man with white stubble over his chin and a baseball cap pulled down over his eyebrows nodded at him and said, "Haven't seen you around here in a while, Stewart."

"I've been in college up North."

A muttering went around the waiting area.

"Your aunt misses you," someone else said, "She tells everyone what you're up to."

"Good thing I don't tell her everything, then," Stewart said, laughing.

"Okay, Stewart, what are we doing for you today?" Charlie said, walking over, "Looks like you've gone a while without a trim."

"Actually, I'm ready to lose the ponytail."

"Woah," Charlie said loudly, and turned to the other men in the small shop. "Did you hear that?"

Some laughs and jokes circled.

"Bobby," Charlie said, "Help Stewart to this chair."

Stewart was used to this place and these men and the small town south had a way of helping anyone and everyone whether they wanted it or not. So Stewart was prepared for the way Bobby came over and, without a word, scooped him up, and carried him to a barbershop seat.

"Ready to stop being a girl and start being a man," Charlie said as he looked at Stewart in the mirror. After a chuckle he picked up his scissors and began to snip.

Stewart tried not to flinch as chunks of black hair fell to the ground. He had begun to let his hair grow starting when he was six years old and refused to get a haircut for his mother's funeral. The hair had never been past his shoulders, but having a ponytail had been an important way to rebel against his father.

Stewart watched his face transform. This was a new Stewart, one he had never seen before.

"What do you think?" Charlie said.

"I'll get used to it," Stewart said.

Bobby lifted him down and back to his chair.

"Need a ride home?" Charlie asked.

Stewart nodded. Charlie looked at Bobby, who took hold of Stewart's shoulders and started to push him to the door. The ride back to Claire's was narrated only by the voice on the radio.

"You can come in," Stewart said when they got there, "I'm sure Claire has some sweet tea in the fridge."

Bobby just shook his head and drove off in his truck.

When she saw Stewart coming in the door, Claire put a hand over her heart.

"You're the spitting image of your mother," she said.

The few people who had known his mother told him that often as he grew up. Claire had told him, when he first arrived at her house, that it was for this reason his father didn't want to have him around. He had wanted to erase the traces of Sharon. What had been the reason behind his mother's life, Stewart wondered. She had done little more than bring Stewart into the world and here he was, doing no one any good.

He passed Claire and went into his room. Each time he moved his head he felt the absence of his hair. It had been twenty years since he refused to do anything for his mother's funeral. He had almost believed that her death would never be real as long as he didn't acknowledge it by wearing a suit and getting his hair cut. This year it was finally time to give up and admit that Sharon Masterson was gone.

On Christmas Eve the rest of the relatives arrived. The grandparents were parked on the sofa, facing the tree. Stewart's father grunted a greeting to everyone and sat in the rocking chair in the far corner of the room. He and Stewart did not look at each other.

"I've been praying for you, Stewart."

"Thanks, Grandma."

"Jesus will heal you."

"Yup."

"Ah, you leave him alone," Grandpa said. "You fit right in with us, Stewart."

"Sure, Grandpa."

Stewart looked over at his father. He tried to think of a way to turn the attention to Richard.

"Where is Ellen?" Stewart said, "Surely she wouldn't have wanted to miss this nice family gathering?"

Richard was sitting closest to the dazzling tree. The lights reflected blue, red, and green on his glasses.

"She has her own family," he said.

"I was hoping for good news. No hope of a divorce then?" Stewart said.

"Stewart, hush," Claire said, swatting his shoulder.

"You just love to start trouble, don't you boy?" Richard said.

"It's not too late," Grandma said, "Lots of nice women out there. You should give Stewart a good mother. With a good mother, he'll have the courage to walk again."

"I have news for you," Richard said, standing and advancing on his mother, "Stewart is never going to walk again, no matter what he does. He will never give you great-grandchildren, so you better start pestering Claire's kids about that."

"Dad," Stewart said, but his father was paying no attention. As Richard got close to his parents, Stewart reached out and grabbed hold of Richard's belt. "What are you doing?" Stewart said.

"You haven't changed a bit," Richard said, turning on him, "Every time I see you I hope that you've grown up, but you never do."

Claire interrupted. "Rich, come and help me get the turkey out of the oven."

"Ellen is your stepmother and she deserves your respect," Richard said to Stewart before he left.

"Yeah," Stewart muttered to himself, "Like you do."

"Don't you listen to him, Stewart," Grandma started again, "You can read in the Bible about all the miracles Jesus performed. You just put your trust in him and he'll heal you."

"Okay, I will, Grandma."

"Is she right?"

Stewart turned his neck and saw Julia standing beside him in a peach colored nightgown that dragged on the ground. Julia continued, "I'll pray for you too if you want."

"That's a good girl," Grandma said, nodding with satisfaction.

"I'm going to go put on the porch light," Stewart said, "Why don't you keep me company?" He patted his lap and Julia climbed up. "Be right back," Stewart said with a forced smile at the grandparents.

He wheeled to the door, grabbed two coats from the rack, bumped down the one step onto the porch and closed the door behind them. He wrapped Julia in one of the coats.

How could Stewart tell her the truth? This fresh and hopeful face still believed in justice in the world. Stewart knew there was no such thing. He had known that from the moment he was her age, and his mother had died. But he didn't want her childhood to be as sad as his.

"Your grandma is very smart about a lot of things," Stewart began, "But she's wrong about this. I can't walk because the signals my brain sends to my body don't get there. Nothing is going to fix me."

"Are you sad?"

"No," Stewart said. He reached off the side of the

porch and snapped a twig from the rhododendron bush. "How could I be sad when there are such beautiful things in the world?" He tickled the side of her face with it. "People are going to say things about me in front of you. They are going to say things like 'it's such a tragedy' and 'his life isn't worth anything anymore' and 'thank God that's not me or anyone in my family.' But you'll know those things aren't true. You'll know in your heart, cousin Stewart loves his life and doesn't think there's anything wrong with him. You'll remember that, won't you?"

Julia nodded. She laid her head on his shoulder and curled her legs up on his lap. He could feel her breath slow against his chest. He stayed outside for a while. It was very quiet and still. Behind him was the window to the living room, but only the glow of the Christmas tree showed through it. Vaguely he could hear the sounds of his grandparents' voices, but here on the porch everything was at rest.

It was such a beautiful vision of home. He looked down at Julia asleep on his chest and smiled. His grandparents didn't have to give up on great-grandchildren yet.

As he considered his own future, the woman he imagined in his life wasn't Lee's twin sister, whom he had spent a summer romancing when they were sixteen, or any of the other girls he had known on the beach. They were hard, their bodies tight and their hair stiffened with salt. Elizabeth was all round edges and she seemed to need him in some way, as though he could shield her from the world. He could easily picture her walking through that door, carrying two cups of eggnog. She would sit on the porch steps and look at the stars and ask questions that he knew the answers to.

Reluctantly, Stewart went back inside. He rolled smoothly and gently to the kitchen. In the doorway he stopped and witnessed his aunt and his father bickering.

"Ellen refusing to see him isn't doing anything to help the situation," Claire said.

"Can you really blame her? The step-son that she cared for as her own hit her."

Stewart looked away. Another of his many regrets was the fight with Ellen that had gotten him sent away. Claire, as always, rushed to Stewart's defense.

"She doesn't bear any responsibility in that? Children are a reflection of their parents, Rich. You should have been more sensitive to him."

"Yeah, your sensitivity worked real well. It didn't stop him from turning out the way he did."

"Claire," Stewart whispered.

They both looked over and Claire's angry face melted into joy. "They're never so beautiful as when they're asleep, eh?"

Richard had a different reaction. "Be careful," he admonished Stewart, "You could drop her; you could hurt her."

Claire was on her way to get John, but she turned and hissed, "You could at least learn something about his condition instead of spewing your ignorance."

John came in a moment later and picked Julia up, carrying her up the stairs to her bed. "Don't listen to your father, Stewart," Claire said.

"I never have," Stewart said.

Then the doorbell rang. "Oh, that must be my surprise," Claire said.

"You're having a surprise delivered?" Stewart said. "Awfully late, isn't it?"

"Stewart, you can get the door."

He shrugged. "Okay," he said. He pushed his wheels, changed directions, and let the metal rails slip by under his fingers. Stewart swung the door open and looked up at the well-bundled figure in the doorway.

"Fuck, it's cold," the figure said.

"Jeff," Stewart said.

"Still recognize me, eh? I guess I haven't changed. You have. Did you notice that someone took a pair of scissors to your head?"

"What are you doing here?"

"You could at least invite me in. You never told me it got this cold in South Carolina."

"It never came up," Stewart said, "Come in." He rolled back out of the way.

"Your aunt invited me," Jeff said. He took off his hat, then his scarf, gloves, jacket, sweatshirt, sweater, and boots.

"No ear muffs?" Stewart said.

"Shut up," Jeff said, "Don't make fun of people less fortunate."

"Less fortunate?"

"Those of us who can feel how cold it is."

Stewart laughed. "Thank God you're here," he said, "My relatives are about to murder me with pity."

"I've arrived just in time. Don't want you to get a swelled head. Let's see if we can get some of that tender loving care directed my way."

"This way to the kitchen."

"Ah, you read my mind," Jeff said.

In the living room they passed the grandparents having the same argument they had had the first day of their marriage.

"You have to preheat the oven. That's what the word means, that's why it's in the directions."

"Then how come every time I bake it turns out fine? I have never preheated in my life."

"How do you know your cooking is so good? Maybe I'm just nice and don't say anything."

Stewart smiled up at Jeff. "Welcome to Christmas with the Mastersons."

"Hey, better than Christmas alone."

They entered the kitchen and Claire beamed. "Eat," she commanded, and Stewart saw that she had pulled all the leftovers from the fridge and arranged them on the Formica kitchen table.

After Jeff had eaten, with Claire hovering over him, Stewart said, "Get all that gear back on and let's go outside."

On the way out the door, Jeff said, "Chuck won't quit. Just get him off my back, will you?"

"I'm not much good these days."

"He wants you to talk and inspire. I know you're still good at that."

Stewart gave Jeff a look. A look that said, you know me better than that. "I'm not going to be their inspiration," Stewart said, "I don't feel like pretending to be heroic."

Jeff dropped onto the porch swing and it creaked under his weight. "Why do you always take things so badly? They don't need a flawed human being, they need someone to believe in. All you have to do is play the part."

"I'm tired of lying."

"It's not about you, Stewart, it's about what they need."

"Hey. You're supposed to be on my side."

"It's called tough love, baby."

Stewart rolled his eyes.

"You used to be reckless, you used to be the Tiger. Now you're Mr. Responsible College Guy."

"Maybe I grew up."

"You forget, Stewart, I know you. I've known you since before."

"That doesn't mean you know what it's like for me now." He turned his chair away from Jeff and rested his elbows on the porch railing.

"You still feel it. I know you do."

"So what?"

Jeff leaned forward, grabbed the chair and whipped it back to face him.

"Get your hands off me," Stewart said.

"This isn't you!" Jeff said, shaking the wheelchair.

Stewart shoved Jeff back against the swing. Jeff stood up, grabbed Stewart by the shirt, lifted him up and shook him hard. Stewart looked down to where his sneakers dangled several inches from the porch.

Jeff said, "How come now that you're in a wheelchair, you have to be a cripple?"

Stewart's fist flew at Jeff's face and connected with a loud smack. Grunting in pain, Jeff reeled back and dropped his hold on Stewart's shirt. Stewart fell hard on his back against the porch. He didn't lie still, but reached over and grabbed Jeff's ankles, pulling his friend to the ground with him. Jeff hit the porch with another groan and shoved Stewart away from him.

"Damn," he said.

Stewart started laughing. After a minute Jeff joined him and they lay side by side laughing.

"You're pathetic," Stewart said, "You just got your ass beat by a cripple."

They heard Aunt Claire's voice from inside coming toward them. "It's getting late, boys," she was saying.

Jeff scrambled to his feet and was about to help Stewart up when Claire opened the door and saw them.

"Oh my God," she said, rushing over, "What happened? Did he fall? Are you all right, Stewart?" She stopped and looked at Jeff. A black bruise was forming under his eye where Stewart had punched him. "What happened?" she said again, now confused and suspicious.

"I'm fine," Stewart said. He grabbed his chair and lifted his body up onto it.

"Well, come inside and get cleaned up," Claire said with an unhappy sigh.

The grandparents were staying in Stewart's room, so Stewart and Jeff got ready for bed and stretched out on the living room sofas. The house was dark and quiet, though the Christmas tree still glowed.

"You were the one who called the paramedics, weren't you?" Stewart said.

"Yeah," Jeff said. He knew immediately what Stewart was talking about. Being together again for the first time since it happened, they both had the awareness of that day hanging in the backs of their minds. The knowledge they shared of that moment brought them close in an unspoken way.

Yet, Stewart had never told Jeff about being under the water, about hitting the rocks, about what he was thinking as he ran and ran and ran toward that water and the hopeless task ahead of him. And Jeff had never told Stewart what happened to the rest of them, what they thought as they watched him, what actions they took to fix the disaster unfolding. Stewart was about to end that silence. He wanted to know what had gone on at the other side of the beach.

"What about Lee?"

"Just stood there. I guess he was stunned or something."

"Sometimes I think I should have held back, saved my own career and my own life."

"You've got your life."

"I know. But you don't know what it's like."

"You're okay and you know it."

"This girl," he started to say, but then he didn't know where to go from there. This girl had made him feel like an object. More than all the other people who stared or pointed or questioned, or referred to him by his wheelchair or called him a cripple, it was Elizabeth who had made him feel like nothing more than a chunk of metal. But he couldn't say those things to Jeff. Stewart hated to be weak and Elizabeth had made him weak. She had made a fool of him.

"This is all about a girl? That's fucked up, Stewart."

"Thanks for the insight, Jeff."

"I was wondering what happened to that secretary of yours," Jeff said.

"That's great, you're making this so much better," Stewart said.

"She really was different, huh?"

"More than you know."

Jeff looked like he wanted to keep pushing, so Stewart threw a pillow at him and said, "Go to sleep already, the kids will be in here first thing tomorrow."

Soon they both drifted to sleep and Stewart dreamed. The water was holding him up, carrying him, lifting him toward heaven. And then it was fighting him, pulling him down under the surface into a netherworld. All that had been familiar became dangerous. Rocks and crags were coming at him from all directions. There was no up any more. The sun couldn't reach him, he belonged only to the water. It tried to fill him up, to make him entirely ocean.

He woke up with his heart pounding in his ears. He propped himself up on his arms and took some deep breaths.

"What happened?" Jeff asked groggily from the other couch. Stewart said nothing, hoping his friend would just fall back asleep without coming into full consciousness. "You okay, man?" Jeff continued. No such luck.

"Sure, no problem," Stewart said, but his voice shook.

Jeff stood up. He bumped into the coffee table and shouted, "Christ!"

"Hush or Claire will hear you," Stewart said.

Jeff felt his way along the sofa. His eyesight was bad in the dark without his contacts. He sat down on the edge where there was space next to Stewart's thin legs. "Were you remembering what happened?"

Stewart wished he could say no, that he could prove that he had different problems now. But no, they were the same old problems. "Yes," he said, "The same old dream."

"Didn't think you'd had it in a long time."

"No," Stewart said. He thought back. No, not since he started dating Elizabeth.

"You're okay," Jeff said.

"I know that, tell it to my subconscious."

"Don't get all college on me," Jeff said, "Keep to the short words."

"Go back to sleep," Stewart said.

"Tell me about the girl."

Stewart sighed. "She's a freak," he said.

"Really?" Jeff said, "Sounds great."

"Not like that," Stewart said. "Really, honestly a freak."

"It seems to me people have been known to say the same about you."

Why was Stewart reluctant to tell him? Was he embarrassed for Elizabeth? No, he was afraid that her fetish had been obvious to everyone else and he had been suckered. "She has a fetish for disability," Stewart said.

"Say what?"

"Wheelchairs make her hot."

"Kinky," Jeff said.

"I knew I shouldn't tell you."

"So let me get this straight. This girl actually wanted you like this and you kicked her to the curb?" Jeff said.

"You could put it that way," Stewart said.

"Damn, Stewart, what's wrong with you?" Jeff said.

Stewart laughed. "A lot of people have wondered that

over the years." He released his arms and fell back against his pillow.

"I know you think no one can understand what you've been through or what you've given up, but we all make compromises," Jeff said.

"Didn't you get what you wanted?"

"I have the apartment next to the Pacific, sure. But I never had the talent you had. No matter how hard I tried I could never be as good as you were."

"Is that supposed to make me feel better?"

"I'm just pointing out that it wasn't my fault, but I couldn't have the skill that I most wanted to have. I always trailed you. There are some things in life that I want, but I'll never have."

"You were out there practicing with us, though."

"My inabilities never got in the way of me enjoying the sport."

"And you're drawing a parallel now?"

"You were given a gift and you're wasting it. I think you should take the risk with the water and with this girl. You've never been one to shy away from something out of fear."

"It isn't about what happened to me. Jeff, someone died."

"People die everyday."

"Harsh."

"There's a reason you lived. You shouldn't let two lives end that day."

Jeff knew his point had been made and he stumbled back to his own sofa. Stewart lay awake for a long time. It was only moments after he had finally gotten back to sleep that children were jumping on him.

"Wake up, Stewart, it's time for presents," they shouted.

"Are you sure?" he grumbled.

"Yes, yes, we're sure."

Julia tugged on his arms and Joyce pulled his legs off the couch. "Okay, okay," he said, "I'm awake."

"Breakfast first, you know that," Claire said, as she came into the living room.

The children bounced in their seats and, even though they loved pancakes, had only one serving.

"All right," Claire said, "Let's go open presents."

The family was all crowded into the living room again. Joey, as the youngest, got the job of passing out the gifts, but Joyce helped by reading the tags.

Julia insisted on carrying her own gift to Stewart. She stood in front of him and waited as he untied the dental floss around the package. Inside was a box that had been divided into compartments and decorated with construction paper.

"It's to hold ties," Julia said.

"Thank you," Stewart said, "That's very thoughtful." He had never worn a tie in his life, not even for his father's wedding.

Uncle John gave Stewart a watch, also a first for him. Every year John gave Stewart some gadget. At least a watch was something Stewart could get some use out of. Jeff had a bumper sticker for the back of the wheelchair: Hell On Wheels.

Stewart himself gave mostly joke presents, such as an egg timer for his grandmother who always burned everything she cooked, and an air freshener for the truck John took fishing. For the children he made an effort.

He gave Joyce a purse that looked like the one Elizabeth carried. Julia got a set of hairclips in a different color for each day of the week, and for Joey he had a model airplane.

"He's too young for that," Claire said.

"But we'll save it for him," John added.

"Who is your friend, Stewart?" Grandma asked when the presents were finished.

"Jeff," Stewart said, "He surfed with me."

"Oh." She made a disappointed face. "He looked like such a nice boy."

Stewart whispered to Jeff, "She thinks all surfers are bums."

"She may be right," Jeff whispered back,

"Well, Stewart, it's been great, but I have to get back."

"You're leaving Christmas Day?"

"It's still beach weather in California and people are off work, I can't keep my bar closed for that."

"I'll drive you to the airport," John said.

Jeff stood up, clapped Stewart on the shoulder, said good-bye to everyone and grabbed his bag. After he was gone, Claire said, "It's time to go see the winter tableaux."

"Can I bring my game?" Julia asked.

"Yes, fine, everyone pick a small present to take. Come on Mom and Dad."

As Claire tried to single-handedly get all her children and her parents out the door, Richard and Stewart hung back. "Aren't you coming?" Claire said to Stewart.

"I don't think so," Stewart said.

Claire turned to her brother. "And you?"

"I'll keep an eye on Stewart for you."

Claire threw up her hands in an I-give-up gesture, took her keys, and was out the door. The house went from filled with noise to silent as the door swung closed.

"You don't need to keep an eye on me," Stewart said, "In fact, please don't. Just go upstairs and I won't even know you're here."

"Sure, sure, you don't need anybody," Richard said.

"Don't start with me, Dad."

"Of course, whatever you say goes."

Stewart rolled past him, into his room, and shut the door. He took a deep breath as he enjoyed his first moment alone since he got here. He was ready to go back to school. Robert's attention seemed a blessing compared with Claire's. He loved his aunt, but it was easier to love her from a distance.

He opened the top drawer of his dresser and pulled out an old address book. He flipped through it and wondered if there was anyone from high school he should get in touch with while he was here. None of the names seemed familiar anymore. There was a time when these were the people who filled his life. Now he couldn't imagine going out drinking with any of them. Funny how they had all disappeared when he got hurt. In an instant his life went from filled with people to almost empty. Every once in a while he ran into one of his old friends in town and it was as though they had never met before. Some of them didn't even look at the guy in the wheelchair long enough to realize it was him. Others stumbled through a greeting and hurried on.

There was a crash in anther part of the house and

Stewart dropped the address book into his lap. He rolled out into the kitchen.

"Dad?" he said, "What was that?"

There wasn't any answer. For once the house was totally still. Stewart moved through the kitchen, the living room, the hallway and there was no sign of his father.

"Dad?" he shouted.

"I'm fine." The voice came from up the stairs.

"Okay," Stewart said. He turned around to go back to his room, but he stopped because the house continued to be completely silent. "Are you sure?" he shouted.

"Fine," the voice huffed, but Stewart heard the groan.

Stewart looked at the stairs. Other than passing them on the way in and out the door, he hadn't been near them in years. Stewart knew his father; something had happened and Richard just wanted to be stubborn.

Stewart pushed to the edge of the wheelchair and reached out to put his hand on one of the steps. He leaned his weight onto his arm and grabbed the railing with his other hand. The stairs were covered with a strip of carpet and Stewart gripped it, and then yanked the rest of his body onto the step.

"Stewart?" Richard's voice came drifted down to him.

"Yeah?"

"When Claire gets back, send her up here?"

Stewart rolled his eyes. He straightened himself and began to push up the stairs. He knew there was a reason he had worked on developing his remaining muscles. He placed his hands behind him on each step and pulled his butt up, then stopped and pulled each leg up by the knee.

Very slowly he saw the walls go by, backwards from how he had seen them six years ago, the last time he had been on the second floor. He had run down them then, not looking at the pictures on the wall. He had a duffle bag on his back and he was late getting to the airport.

Now when Stewart reached the top he stopped and looked around. There was a chair where a hall table used to be, and a painting he had never seen before hung on the wall at the end of the hall. Several of the doors had children's decorations on them; posters, signs, tape, and stickers.

When Stewart lowered his gaze he saw his father sitting at the far end of the hall looking at him. They were like bookends, sitting identically at either end of the hallway.

"What are you doing?" Richard said. He was lying against the wall, in front of an open closet with a toppled chair beside him.

"You didn't sound fine," Stewart said.

"So you've come to save the day?"

Stewart started toward his father again, pulling his body with his strong arms. When he arrived beside the older man, he also leaned against the wall in order to free up his arms and hands. "Let me see it," Stewart said, reaching for the ankle he could see starting to swell.

"What are you going to do to it?"

"Would you relax?" Stewart took the ankle in his hands and touched it carefully.

"Don't make it worse," Richard said.

"It's not broken," Stewart said, "It needs ice and you'll be fine in a day or two."

"Forgive me if I don't take your word for it."

Stewart rested his head against the wall and sighed. He wanted to say to his father, "You stopped looking at me when I was six years old. It's been twenty years, I've learned things." Surfing had taught him a lot about minor injuries and how to fix them. But what was the point? Richard wouldn't stop seeing Stewart as useless just because he said to. Richard didn't change for anyone. Father and son sat silently side by side at the end of the hall until Claire and John got home.

They both heard the front door open, but stayed silent. Stewart heard his aunt find the wheelchair and begin to make frightened huffing noises.

"Where is he?" Claire said.

"I don't know," John answered.

"What if he's hurt?"

"I think he'd be closer to his chair if that were the case."

Upstairs Richard said, "She doesn't wonder where I am, just worries over you."

"Believe me," Stewart said, "If I could get her to pay this kind of attention to you instead, I would."

Claire's voice warbled below, "Stewart, sweetheart?"

Stewart sighed. "Upstairs," he shouted.

"What in the world?" Claire muttered as she huffed up the steps. She stopped at the landing and looked at the two Masterson men with a hand on her hip. "What have the two of you been getting into?"

"He fell." Stewart nodded his head at Richard.

For once all the concern was directed another way.

Stewart watched while Claire fussed over her younger brother. Soon she was helping Richard down the stairs. Stewart sat alone in the upstairs hallway and smiled. He let himself slide down the wall and lie on the carpet, listening to the world below going on without him.

13

Stewart was relieved when Christmas was finally over. He packed his bag and hauled it to the car. He spent the last day of the vacation on the couch watching TV. Joyce came over and wanted to play with his empty wheelchair and he let her.

"This is fun," she said, "So relaxing. You're lucky you don't have to walk, you get to just ride."

Stewart laughed. "Try doing that all day, everyday, it'll wear you out."

"Do you really have to leave, Stewart?"

"Yes, I have school."

"When you're done with school, will you come back?"

"I don't know." The truth was he did know that he wasn't going to live in South Carolina when he was finished with school. But he didn't know exactly where he was going to go. Massachusetts was nice enough, but the winters were rough on anyone, particularly someone who couldn't trudge through the snow.

The phone rang and Joyce leapt up to get it, leaving the wheelchair far from Stewart's reach.

"This is Joyce," he heard her say behind him. Then, "Yeah, he's here." She dropped the phone onto the kitchen table and yelled, "Stewart! It's for you!"

"Well then get back here, you little monkey, and give me my wheelchair."

Joyce laughed and returned it to him. He was heading for the phone when Claire came in from the basement. "Who is it?" she asked her daughter.

Joyce shrugged. "She wanted cousin Stewart."

"Hello?" Stewart said.

"There you are, my angel."

"Ms. Morris. How are you?"

Claire turned on Joyce. "It's that woman," she said. "Next time you need to ask who it is. Stewart does not need to talk to her."

Stewart waved his arm in her direction to get her to be quiet.

"I'm doing well today," Ms. Morris said.

"I'm glad."

"You know what day is coming up."

"Pete's birthday," Stewart answered. Claire was standing in front of him with her arms crossed now. His aunt and uncle didn't understand why he took on Pete's mother's grief.

"I knew you wouldn't forget," Ms. Morris said.

"I'll remember."

"You're such a good boy."

Stewart's stomach twisted. Being a support to Ms.

Morris was the only thing Stewart had to try to atone for what he had done. So he ignored his own pain and stayed focused on her. "I do my best," he answered.

"I want to send you something for Christmas."

"I'm all set," Stewart said. "Really."

"Pete would have wanted you to have something from him. He thought very highly of you."

Stewart already had five of Pete's T-shirts folded under his bed, one for each year.

"He would be proud of how you're holding up," Stewart said.

"Thank you," Ms. Morris said, "I think I'm doing better. Lately there have been more good days than bad."

John was pointing at his watch now. "Listen," Stewart said, "I have to go and catch a flight."

"Oh."

"Do you have my new phone number?"

"No," Ms. Morris said.

Claire whispered, "Don't give her that. She'll pester you to death."

Not like anyone else Stewart knew. He gave Ms. Morris his dorm number. When he hung up, Claire said, "You're too good, Stewart."

"I have to go," Stewart said.

He gathered hugs and kisses, and got settled in the car. Stewart watched from the window of the car as he drove away from Claire, the kids, his father, and grandparents. Going away to school had accomplished what he had hoped it would. He had a life outside of theirs.

The airport checked his bag and an attendant whisked Stewart away in an airport chair with a long pole on the back while John pushed the now empty one back to his car. At the security check Stewart was pushed to the side of the metal detectors. As he sat there and the metal-detector wands were swirled around him, he watched people going by. They all glanced over at him. He understood their curiosity. He had been in this airport many times on his way to Florida or Hawaii or California and had idly watched the old people who boarded the plane before everyone else. At twenty-five years old, he was one of those people.

He was free to stare back at people, since no one looked him in the face. It was like being invisible. People glance over slyly as though they think they've seen something from the corner of their eyes, but it turns out to be nothing. Just a boy in a wheelchair.

He hadn't used to care about other people and their lives. He had had his own agenda and wasted no time on people. Now he noticed how their fears and pains were clearly marked on them. Every person seemed heavy and over burdened. No one seemed innocent anymore. Like Elizabeth, he was sure they all harbored strange secrets.

Stewart felt an emptiness he hadn't felt in a long time. Elizabeth had left a hole in him. He hadn't realized how deeply she had entered his life until she was gone. It had been many years since he had let himself care about anyone. This hole wasn't exactly a new one. He remembered feeling it when he lost his mother. He thought he had closed it by ceasing to care. Then Elizabeth showed up and undid it all. He had been foolish to begin to care about her.

The attendant pushed Stewart toward the gate while talking on a radio with a friend. He talked and talked, barely paying attention to where he was going, ignoring Stewart as though he were another piece of luggage.

People continued to sneak glances all the way to the gate. All that changed when he got seated in the airplane. Then no one could tell. Could his affiliation change that easily? Was he still disabled when no one could tell? His wheelchair was a badge of his identity in some way now. It negated the rest of his image; the long hair he used to have, the tattoo, and the state of disrepair his clothes were usually in. People treated him well, if condescendingly. Stewart didn't understand that attitude. Everyone had tragedy in his life; everyone was hurt by something. Stewart didn't think he had a special right to suffer.

The flight was short and Stewart had barely fallen asleep when it was time to get off the plane. Everyone else left the plane and when he was the only one in the vast cabin, a stewardess brought the narrow aisle chair for him to get onto. From that he was transferred to an airport chair, then an attendant pushed him down to baggage claim where Robert was waiting with his well-missed wheelchair.

Even though the school was still on break and almost deserted, Stewart went back to his job at the gym right away. It gave him something to do besides think about himself. He looked up surfing statistics on the computer while he waited for anyone to show up.

After his shift, he went down to the pool as usual. The entire room was empty and he could even hear against the high ceiling the echoes of the water gently lapping at the edges of the pool. The chlorine smell spoke of warm days and defied the snow he knew was waiting for him outside. He pulled his wheelchair close to the edge of the water and simply watched the reflection of the lights on the surface. He looked up when he heard the office door open. Lisa emerged in her red swimsuit.

"Hello, Stewart," she said, "You're back early, or didn't you go home for break?"

"Yeah, I left," he said, not sure that he could call his aunt's house home, though he had lived there for ten years.

"It's been quiet here," Lisa said, "Hop in, I'll join you."

Stewart went to the changing room and the handicapped bathroom stall. There he grabbed the handle bar with one hand and pushed his pants off with the other, revealing his swim shorts underneath. He carefully emptied and removed his catheter and stowed it in a plastic bag in his backpack. On the way out he stopped at the mirror and examined himself. He wasn't bad looking, he decided, and Lisa had gotten to know him now. She had always been friendly, perhaps it was time to see if she had gotten beyond her preconceptions about paralysis.

When he reemerged in the pool area, Lisa was already in the water. Her short dark hair fanned around her head and her swimsuit, now wet, clung to her curves. Stewart rolled close to the edge, put on his break, and crashed into the water.

It was over his head, bubbling above and around him. The lights of the gym were far, far above and Stewart relaxed his body and allowed himself to float to the surface. He felt the cold in his arms and chest, and beat his arms to keep his head above water as well as to warm up.

For a long moment Lisa and he treaded water side by side. Stewart swam closer. He held onto the edge of the pool with one hand and then he reached around Lisa and grabbed it with his other hand, encircling her in the middle. He was close enough to smell the chlorine on her skin.

He looked into her eyes and saw curiosity there. The water rippled around his arms. Before she could decide what to do, he said, "Come to New Year's with me."

She searched his face. "Yes, all right," she said.

"Good." He smiled, then let go of the wall and drifted back.

By New Year's Eve, Travis was back and he had big plans for the evening. "You've got to check out this club with me, Stewart," he said.

"We could do something here," Robert said. They were sitting around the common room. Robert and Travis were on the couch and Stewart sat off to the side in his wheelchair. The TV was on in the background, but none of them were watching or listening.

"That's the lamest New Year's possible," Travis said with a scowl.

"Everywhere is going to be crowded and the traffic will be awful, and there'll be drunk drivers on the way back," Robert said.

Stewart just watched them argue. He tried to picture Lisa out at the clubs or here in the dorm, but he couldn't imagine her anywhere except in the water.

"Stewart is coming with me," Travis said, "You can sit here and do whatever it is that you do."

"Stewart?" Robert said.

Stewart shrugged. "Going out is what New Year's is all about."

Robert slouched back in the couch and crossed his arms. "And here I thought New Year's was about a new year starting," he muttered.

"No, not really," Stewart said.

"Totally off," Travis agreed.

"Well, if we're going out, we better start now," Robert said. He pulled himself off the couch and disappeared into the bedroom.

"What a sad bastard," Travis said, shaking his head.

They all got ready and picked up their dates. Robert didn't have a car, and Stewart's was too small to fit all of them, so they piled into Travis's truck. Travis drove, and Stewart got the passenger seat, so Robert, Courtney, Lisa, Travis's date, and the wheelchair rode in the bed.

At the club, Travis's date complained about her dress. "Your truck ruined it," she said. She turned in circles, trying to look at her own butt. The boys all examined her, and could see nothing wrong at all.

Robert helped Stewart down out of the truck, but Lisa was hovering close by. As soon as Robert stepped away, Lisa took hold of Stewart and started pushing him.

"Lisa?" Stewart said.

"Are you okay?"

"Yeah, fine. Listen, why don't you come around here and walk next to me, okay?"

The sidewalk was choked with people and Lisa went ahead and said loudly, "Make some room people. Wheelchair coming through."

Everyone turned to look at Stewart while he navigated

the sidewalk. He put a tight smile on his face and looked down. "You don't have to do that," he said to Lisa.

"People are so oblivious," Lisa said, "They'd just trample you."

"I don't think the sidewalk is as dangerous as all that," Stewart assured her.

Travis led them to the end of a long line and they all waited. Courtney leaned her head on Robert's shoulder. They were quiet because they had dated for so long that they felt comfortable just being next to each other. Travis and his date weren't talking either. Shasti was still upset about her dress and was trying to make Travis make it up to her. Stewart didn't know why he and Lisa were silent. She leaned against the brick wall and watched the people passing on the sidewalk. He couldn't think of anything to say to her.

When they got inside there was almost no space to move. Travis pushed his way in and found them a table at the edge of the dance floor. There were already people sitting there, but they slid around the bench and made room. Stewart parked at the end.

Travis found them some drinks. Robert and Courtney got up to dance. The others watched as Courtney tried to get Robert to loosen his formal dance moves. Stewart looked over at his date. Lisa was focused on the dance floor. She tucked her brown hair behind her ears, but the top strand fell back across her face.

"Do you want to dance?" Stewart asked.

"Dance? But you…I mean you can't, can you?"

"Never mind," Stewart said.

Shasti wanted to dance and she got up and started grooving by herself. Travis sat back with a grin on his face. "Does my girl have a great ass or what?" he said. Shasti looked back and smiled. She shook her butt some more and Travis got up to smack it. He had worked his way back into her good graces and they squeezed their way further onto the dance floor.

"What's the matter?" Stewart said to Lisa, "You aren't having any fun."

She looked at him earnestly. "In the water it's different," she said.

Stewart knew what she meant. Without the water rippling around them, there was nothing to connect them.

"I guess this wasn't the best idea," Stewart said.

"I'm sorry," Lisa said.

When the New Year countdown ended Stewart and Lisa just looked at each other.

14

Amy, Becky, Maureen, and Elizabeth clinked their glasses of sparkling grape juice together over the top of the coffee table.

"Happy New Year's," Becky said.

The house was dark. The four girls were the only ones awake in Maureen's house. Their sleeping bags were spread on the floor below them and they snuggled into the well-stuffed couches.

"What do you think this year will be like?" Elizabeth asked.

"I'm going to learn to cook," Becky said.

"Don't you already know that, Miss Future-Housewife?" Amy said. She put down her glass on the coffee table.

"No," Becky said, annoyed.

"I'm going to figure out what I want to do with my life," Maureen said.

"Deep," Amy said, "I'm going to fall in love with a

guy in my core English class. Oh," she added, "Sorry, Elizabeth. I won't talk about guys."

"Don't worry about me," Elizabeth said.

Her three friends gave her sympathetic looks. Elizabeth was the first to have a boyfriend and the first to have a break-up.

The spirit of the new year had gotten into her and when she got home she felt ready to face the thing Stewart had called her head on. As much as Elizabeth used the computer, she had never thought of looking up the thing that was wrong with her. She didn't know what words to use, for one thing. But Stewart had solved that problem for her. Now she could type in those words and find out the truth about her own experience.

With some amount of trepidation, she reached out her hand and put it back on the mouse at the computer in the den. Into a search engine she typed what he had given her "disability fetish."

The links to which she navigated were terrifying. People told stories of following disabled people, and of pretending to be disabled. They sounded so desperate, obsessed with the desire to be around disability. Stalkers and sickos. Elizabeth felt a knot grow in her stomach, its tendrils spread out from her gut to the rest of her body. This was disgusting. These people were sick.

These people were her. If she were to write out the story of her life in what simple language she was able, it would amount to exactly the same thing. She knew now what it must have felt like to Stewart to be suddenly confronted with this information. To her it was a part of her. Even though she had tried to destroy it or put it aside, it had always been there. It was inside her and had been for years.

A few people on the sites tried to explain away the phenomenon. They spoke of possible childhood triggers. Perhaps wanting more love from your father, and seeing him be kind to a disabled neighbor. But Elizabeth had none of these experiences. Her childhood had not been painful or upsetting in any way, except for the secret that she had kept herself. There was no explanation. There was no answer. She didn't even know why she had kept it a secret. At four years old, watching a movie, she saw a man fall and hurt himself. She was aroused. It was not the first time, because she remembered thinking that if someone had told her about the man hurting himself, she wouldn't have been reluctant to watch the movie. A little girl cannot know what the itch between her legs is. She only knew the pleasure, the desire to press, and the sudden compulsion to never let anyone find out.

Elizabeth clicked all the windows closed. Then for good measure she turned off the computer too. She didn't want her parents to see the kind of sites she had just seen. She didn't want to ever see them again herself.

Elizabeth realized now how silly it was for her to assume that she was alone in her shame. No one's problem was unique. No matter what it was, someone somewhere else in this vast world had it too. Was that disappointing or good? On the one hand Elizabeth suddenly felt not so dirty or disgusting. This was a known thing, a thing with a name, it wasn't unrestrained evil. But then it meant that she had lost something.

Before she knew about it, she was unique. Now she was just sick like other people were sick. It didn't belong to her and she couldn't claim it. She couldn't claim all knowledge that there was of such a thing. It used to belong entirely to her, and now it belonged to someone else and she was just a person who was experiencing someone else's problem.

Did she detect shame in the words of the people on these sites? They spoke about pride, about accepting and growing to love one's own unique sexuality, but Elizabeth thought she still sensed fear and trepidation underneath it all. Perhaps she was just projecting her own onto other people. Maybe they did feel pride. Maybe they had always felt pride, but she saw that many of them related to her fear. They also spoke of secrecy and sneaking around.

The strange thing was, none of them seemed to be concerned with how disabled people felt about it. Shouldn't their ability to feel pride be contingent on the people they lusted after? Apparently not. Then again, frat boys didn't care whether the girls with big breasts and blonde hair liked them or not. They could still look at magazine centerfolds and not worry about how the girl in the picture felt about their behavior.

It didn't quite feel like the same thing. Maybe because she was a girl. Girls supposedly felt differently about sex than boys did. She closed her eyes and tried to imagine what it was like to feel lust for an able-bodied man. She pictured supposedly sexy men, saying sexy things, but in each scenario he turned cripple by the end. Here was a sexy young soldier with lean figure and well-defined arms and stomach. She imagined him dancing with her and walking her home in the moonlight. Apparently it was sometime in the 1950s. Then his old war wound bothered him and he started to limp. No, no, no. Start over. Here was an athlete, a jock at school who was popular and still friendly. He came to her for tutoring and they started kissing in the library stacks. In their wild passion, they pushed each other out of the stacks, onto the floor, then right out the library door. Then he fell down the stairs and broke his legs. No, no, no. She just couldn't do it. She couldn't feel the physical symptoms, she couldn't really get into the fantasy until there was pain. How could sex, supposed to be this amazingly good feeling thing, be related to pain? What wires were crossed in her brain?

She sat in the den on the swivel chair and she felt ill. She had always been disgusted with the pleasure that disability brought her, but now she was ashamed for more than herself, she was ashamed for all these people who would tell the world and let the world see their darkest and ugliest places.

She felt a tear hit her knee and then her face screwed up, her nose itched, and she started sobbing uncontrollably. It seemed to be a way to get all that sick, twisted feeling out of her body. She drew her knees up to her chest, and cried and cried.

Afterwards her head hurt and she felt tired and worn out. Though she had drunk some alcohol in her life, she had never been drunk enough for a hangover. She imagined that this is what it must feel like.

She dragged herself up and went to the bathroom for a Tylenol. On her way up to her room she was about to pass her Dad's study. She stopped and knocked on the door.

"Come in," he said.

She opened the door and stepped into the brown

study. It was like a mole's cave, but lined with books with dark spines; from Plato, Kierkegaard, and Marcilio Ficino to Joyce, Bronte, and Shelley.

"Sweetheart," her father said, standing up from his desk and coming over, "You don't look very well."

"Oh Daddy," she said and threw her arms around him. "I feel awful."

"What kind of awful? Do you need some ice chips and a bucket?"

"No."

"Do you need some tissues and a cough drop?"

"No."

"Do you need your mother?"

"Yeah," Elizabeth said, "I think so."

"Come on." David led her out of the room and down to the kitchen. He picked up the telephone and dialed Susan's number. Elizabeth sat at the table and put her head on her folded arms. David came over. "She's on her way. In the meantime, she told me to warm you up some apple cider."

Elizabeth smiled. Sometimes she hated living at home and longed to be out on her own, making her own choices. Then there were days like this when there was nothing more wonderful than having people who loved you there to give you apple cider.

"Can you tell me what's wrong?" David asked.

Of course she wasn't going to test the conditions of their love by telling the truth. "I don't know," Elizabeth said. "I just feel bad."

"It's tough being a teenager," he said, sitting down next to her on the couch. "Everything feels bigger and more important and more tragic than it really is. You'll see when you reach your twenties that a lot of the drama is just part of being a teenager."

"Don't take my feelings from me. I feel what I feel."

"Yes, but it all depends on how seriously you take those feelings. Trust me, you can step back and see a bigger picture."

"I don't know how."

"You're just in the midst of it, that's all. Believe me, it gets better."

"But people say if I'm not happy now, I won't ever be happy."

"Why do they say that?"

"Because you're not supposed to depend on outside circumstances to make you happy, you're supposed to rely on yourself and how you feel about yourself. But right now with school and friends and trying to get into a good college, it's so much pressure all the time."

"I know. But remember, I see college kids everyday and most of them have let go of that stuff."

"They don't care about school?"

"They do, but the problems that stem from low self confidence will go away and you'll be able to deal with the rest of it better. So have faith, and don't let a break up discourage you. That's what happens in high school. The vast majority of high school relationships don't last, and those that do maybe shouldn't. Because you have to go out there into the world and discover what you want from life. I don't want you held back by some boy."

"Yes, daddy," Elizabeth said.

She drank her cider and curled up on the couch, wrapped up in the old brown and green afghan. They watched TV together until Elizabeth fell asleep.

Elizabeth lay on the couch and dreamed. She dreamed about wheels spinning and fingers wagging, voices saying no and a man falling and falling and falling. Then it was her falling and she tumbled through black emptiness. There was nothing to break the fall, nothing to grab hold of and not another person around.

When she woke up, her parents were both there.

"Do you feel up to going to the temple with Bubby?" Susan asked.

Elizabeth nodded. She couldn't explain to her parents what she was feeling. She couldn't tell them that she had just discovered that she would never be happy because the things she wanted were wrong. The only thing for her to do was deny her feelings and live without passion and love.

Like going to Susan's mother's for Christmas, the family showed only a few obligations to the grandparents. Going to temple with Bubby was a planned event that took place only about three times a year.

"This is my son, David. His daughter." Bubby introduced the family around to all her friends at the temple. David pushed her wheelchair into place and they all sat down. They went so rarely to visit Bubby, particularly on a temple day, that Elizabeth could never remember the service. She flipped through the service book and tried to remember how to pronounce the Hebrew.

She looked up at the cupboard that held the Torah up at the front. Was God watching her at this moment? Did He see her thoughts and know the evil that grew inside her? If she reveled in someone else's misery, then she must be evil. How could there be another explanation? It made her feel wrong to be here, worshiping.

Her parents didn't mind going through the motions of religion, but it seemed wrong to Elizabeth. She didn't want to fake it, it seemed disrespectful to God. But she couldn't just walk out. She couldn't get up and go and she couldn't tell anyone that her heart wasn't clean.

The rabbi stood up and began the service. Elizabeth stood and sat and bowed her head to Adoni. Judaism was a nice religion and she was sometimes sorry that she wasn't really raised in it. Adoni did not seem as judgmental as her mother's Catholic God. Sure, He expected her to be good and do good works, which may have been the same thing. If she just behaved like a good girl, was she? Here she thought that was possible.

In Judaism perhaps she could ignore her desires and the voices of her mind, and just do good things for people. She could volunteer, just not with disabled people. That would be a conflict of interest. She could volunteer with children's reading or taking family photos for the elderly. Was that her subject? Would her camera be used for that purpose?

Her father poked her. Time to stand again. People rocked onto their toes and bowed forward every few moments. Elizabeth was always at least one word behind. She hoped Bubby didn't notice. Her dad's mother was very ashamed of how Elizabeth had been raised.

During supper, back at home, Elizabeth watched her parents. Every once in a while one of them said something, perhaps asking for the saltshaker to be passed, but mostly it was quiet. Elizabeth wondered what had attracted her parents to one another.

Why her mother had felt such a strong need to be with this man and only this man that she had alienated her family for his sake? What had Susan Whittamore felt when she first met David Foster? Did she still feel it? Had the sacrifice of her family been worth what she got?

Or perhaps Susan no longer thought about it, her love for her husband now no more than a habit like brushing her teeth. He was just there, the way the toaster was just there. Were her parents satisfied living this way or had they not yet noticed how sedated their lives had become? Was it inevitable for all couples who were once young and eager to lose their excitement? Perhaps losing Stewart was not so bad, since she was now spared a life of boring complacency. It was hard to imagine that Stewart could ever be that way, though.

For the first time Elizabeth tried to take a moment to see what her life was going to look like now that she had lost the love that had been delivered so perfectly to her. But horror at those thoughts swelled up around her and she dropped her fork with a loud clang. Her parents were both looking at her. Elizabeth murmured an apology and they all went back to eating.

Spring was on its way. Snow was lower against the side of the house than it had been and in some patches was gone completely. Pointy red ends of flowers had begun to show, piercing the snow. Some flowers would bloom too soon and die in a late frost. But they still heralded the coming of the next season. Soon it would be time to put away the long sleeved shirts and the heavy jackets. Spring would be full of short-sleeved shirts covered with light jackets.

Elizabeth was ready for it. She had missed her spring

clothes, and was ready to bring them out again. She remembered how good she looked in her spring jacket. She thought about all the things she could do in the spring; put flowers out on the kitchen table, and maybe have a vase of them in her room. Press some flowers to make cards later.

In the bare tree branches, blanched white and gray by the cold, she caught a glimpse of red and she knew it was the other sign of spring; the robin redbreast. Soon there would be multitudes of birds and her mother would clean out the birdbath and put new seed into the feeders. Her father would take her out on walks with binoculars.

Once spring came it was hard to concentrate on classes because summer was close enough to taste. The kids began to dream of chasing butterflies and trekking to the community pool with their little membership tags clicking on their wrists and towels dragging on the ground behind them. Elizabeth looked forward to lemonade and sitting outside without a coat at all. Opening the windows in her room and praying for a breeze. That would be a welcome change from the cold winter of huddling under three blankets and watching frost form patterns on the windowpanes.

On Monday Elizabeth woke up to the sounds of the birds crying. One in particular always annoyed her. Its sound started early in the morning and it was just two notes: a high one falling to a low one.

When Elizabeth's Bubby still lived in her own place she used to bake muffins and send them over for Elizabeth to have for breakfast. But now Bubby lived in a nursing home and no one else could make muffins just like hers.

That was one springtime tradition that had changed

and Elizabeth missed it. More than anything else she liked the ritual of it. Spring wasn't really its own season, it was only a transition period between winter and summer. Sometimes it had been known to snow in April or May. But usually this was the time when the snow became rain instead. Every time it rained Elizabeth watched from the window, looking for a rainbow. Once she had seen an amazing rainbow in a hazy, gray sky. The sun had come through, but shone through the curtain of rain, making everything change colors. The grass looked emerald, the sky looked like blueberries and the rainbow arched across the entire sky with wide chunks of each color. Elizabeth had never before or since seen both ends of a rainbow touching down on earth.

The tall crocuses and yellow clusters of forsythia had awoken from winter and were in bloom when Elizabeth and her Dad backed out of the garage on the way to school and work. In the front yard her mother would soon plant bulbs for tulips. And the spiria bush would begin to bloom with its delicate lace. After Mother's Day there would be more flowers crowding their lawn, flowers in every imaginable color, many with two colors on one blossom. Elizabeth's mother liked elaborate blooms that made the eye dizzy.

It seemed strange to Elizabeth to plant new flowers every single year, only to see them wiped out by the summer's heat or frozen to death in the winter. She imagined that when she grew up and had a house she would plant flowers that kept coming up year after year. And more flowering bushes, like rose of Sharon, lilac or holly. Their neighbors had a holly bush and Elizabeth would go and clip some branches near Christmas time to put on their table. It was an amazing shock of dark green and bright red sticking out of the pure white around it.

The drive to school was through mud colored slush, but there were more flowers and plants to see and more birds appearing in the sleeping trees. There was more to see on the morning trek in the spring.

Everyday at school it was as though a crank was turned tighter and tighter. The conversations at the cafeteria got shorter and everyone just ate their food, staring blankly at the table. Stress seemed to crawl the walls. In every class every teacher scared them, talking about the future and how bleak and hopeless it was without a fantastic college.

Elizabeth became aware that her friends and she were not going to pursue the same futures. Amy was talking about going to community college and Becky was aiming for Ivy League. Elizabeth had applied to a range of schools, but the only one she had researched at all was Stewart's school because she had planned to go there to be closer to him. Was that a bad reason to pick a school? People seemed to think so. She knew that everyone was advising Ted and Sarah, who had started dating when they were ten years old, that they shouldn't try too hard to go to the same school. It could compromise their futures.

The future was such a delicate thing. Every tiny movement in this year at school could jeopardize it, cause it to fall to the ground and crash. Though they had all been taught growing up that they could do and be anything, now was the do or die moment when they had to choose what that anything would be and see if they really could reach it.

Elizabeth used to think that the future was just

something that would happen by itself, inevitably. But now she was learning that it needed careful crafting or it might not come at all. She could see it dangling like a gold bangle covered in delicate parts. Everything she did caused it to shake and rock and the thread holding it up became thinner and thinner.

Elizabeth's determination not to respond to the desires within her body was taking a toll on her. It surprised her how much strain it was to not feel something, to not do something. Always a loner, she became even more withdrawn as the days dragged on. There was a new tone to the voice that whispered in her mind. *Is your desire really so bad? It's not hurting anyone.* And when Elizabeth recognized the trickery in this seduction the voice changed. *Do you suppose yourself strong enough to deny it?* Even that voice was too afraid to test out the actual word for Elizabeth's problem.

She sat in the cafeteria during a free period and just listened to her mind battling. The big round tables sat empty around her. From a window opened an inch a warm breeze moved torn bits of napkins on the floor.

"You okay?" A voice said.

Elizabeth looked up. "Oh," she said, "Hi." It was George. She had never spoken to him before, nor he to her. She knew who he was because everyone knew the one out gay person into the entire school.

"I'm fine," Elizabeth said.

"You don't look it." He sat down on the purple plastic chair across from her.

"Look," Elizabeth said, "It's nice of you to care, but I don't know you."

"I'm just being the person I wished I had when I was trying to come out. Someone to listen."

"You think I'm gay?" Elizabeth said.

"There are a lot of different kinds of closets. It doesn't have to be a gay one."

Elizabeth spread her arms in front of her on the table. "If you want to know the truth," she said, "I am stuck in some kind of closet. I'm not gay. That would be okay. At least there's a real word for that. People know what it is."

"It isn't ever easy," George said, "But you didn't choose to be the way you are."

"Maybe it doesn't matter. Maybe we're just unlucky," Elizabeth said, "Maybe no matter that we didn't do anything wrong, there's something wrong in us anyway."

"What if there's nothing wrong with either of us?"

A powerful, almost frightening question. How would Elizabeth even recognize herself without the guilt and the shame? Could she truly live without it? Wouldn't some karmic force destroy her for being arrogant enough to decide that sexual deviance didn't have to be a bad thing. *I'll never let you go.* But Elizabeth's attention was elsewhere. George had opened a window in her mind and she was focused on the sunlight she could vaguely glimpse through it. She sensed the end of her darkness.

Why was the thing inside her frightening? She had never dared to ask herself that question. It seemed sacrilegious. Wouldn't God be insulted if she dared to question how terrible this condition was? He couldn't have created it. Even though Elizabeth wasn't religious, she didn't like to disobey the rules, just in case. Her fetish didn't fit the order of the universe.

But disabled people still deserved love, didn't they? If

every girl only went after the stereotypical good-looking guy, there wouldn't be enough to go around. There was variety in the world. Some women loved fat men and some women loved black men and some women loved tall men and some women loved military men and some women loved hippie men, and some women loved women. So she loved disabled men. It was helpful, it spread the love around.

Could she really learn to be okay with this part of herself? She almost didn't want to. She had spent so long beating herself up about it. It was a part of her personality now that she hate herself. It was the shadow in her mind. The secret loved to hold her in bondage. It was like an entity unto itself, who hounded her and whispered in her ear. She wanted to live without it, didn't she? Maybe she could still have the pleasure of the fetish without the evil secret trying to tear her down. Could the two things be separated? She felt guilty at the thought.

What if it went away without the secrecy? What if the two were dependent on each other? If the desire for disability went away, would there be anything to take its place? Suddenly she didn't want it to go away. At least she knew what it was she liked. She knew exactly how to get her body to respond. And if she could just let go of the guilt, she could just enjoy her sexuality.

She couldn't just separate the pleasure from the guilt. That was crazy. The possibility felt intoxicating. It wouldn't be right, would it? Stewart had shown that it wasn't possible. His reaction proved that the whole thing was wrong, not just a piece of it. She was still not allowed to start liking herself. Maybe she would never be able to destroy it, but she could spend her life battling it. God would forgive her then, because she would have done her very best. She didn't choose to be this way; she was made this way.

Back at home Elizabeth developed the pictures she had taken of Stewart. She watched him emerge from the paper and look at her. Every face looked like an accusation to her now. There were the pictures of him almost naked, and also shots of him getting into his wheelchair, shots of him moving ahead of her. One in particular that she liked was a photo of him getting up a curb. His arms were flexed and muscular beneath his T-shirt, the bottom of his tattoo barely peeking out, and he had the small front wheels up and was pushing hard on the back wheels. At the moment of the photo he was looking down at the sidewalk ahead of him and concentrating on getting up onto it. When the camera button was pressed, Stewart had looked over at her and said, "You could help instead of just taking pictures." She had gone over and given him a push from behind to get him up.

The picture spoke to her. She looked at it and she saw his struggle and his quiet perseverance. This was why Stewart was her hero, her knight. He overcame obstacles everyday, as they came up and presented themselves to him. He didn't make a fuss about it, he just solved each problem that arrived. Most of the time he seemed charming and laid back, but at moments like this his true drive appeared from deep within him.

Next to the playground pictures, this one shone. It had a real message. In that tiny bathroom in the near total darkness, Elizabeth sat on the cold tile floor, her knees touching the toilet seat and she knew she had found her topic. There would be a purpose to her sickness after all.

People who looked at this photograph would see Stewart the way she saw him. They would look past his disability, to the face of pure determination. Stewart was still a champion. Elizabeth knew it and she hoped soon everyone else would know it too.

15

Robert shut down his computer and turned to his roommate. "Hey, Stewart, are you doing anything tonight?"

"Writing a paper. Or maybe just thinking about the possibility of writing a paper," Stewart said without looking up from the book he had open on his desk.

"Want to come with me to Courtney's parents' house? They're having a Super Bowl party. Or an anti-Super Bowl party. Or something. Courtney's dad is quirky about these things."

"You could just take my car."

"I don't want to leave you here alone. It will do you good to get out. They'll have food."

"Okay, okay, you don't have to work that hard to convince me." He looked up. "What is an anti-Super Bowl party?"

Robert shrugged. "He watches curling or something instead."

"Are there stairs?"

"It's an old house in New England, what do you think?"

"All right," Stewart said, "Long as I know what I'm in for."

As they drove, snow was lightly covering the ground and specks of it drifted from the roofs and trees onto the roads.

The house, when they parked in front of it, looked warm from the glow of electric candles in the windows. Stewart got out of the car and locked up, then bumped down the curb and crossed the street with Robert. Courtney was standing in the doorway of her house waiting.

"Hello, Stewart," she said as he and Robert reached the front steps.

"Come down and get his wheelchair," Robert said. He got his arms under Stewart's from behind. "Ready?"

"Let's do it," Stewart said.

Robert lifted him onto the stairs and Stewart used his arms to push up the steps while Robert held his legs by the ankles. Courtney came out into the chill night air with a sweater wrapped around her shoulders. She grabbed the back of the wheelchair and dragged it past them up the steps.

"Remind me to get gloves," Stewart said, "These stairs are freezing."

"I've reminded you to get gloves at least twenty times already," Robert said, "You always ignore me."

They reached the top of the stairs and Robert lifted Stewart back onto the chair. Stewart quickly grabbed his wheels before his roommate could start pushing him.

However, Robert still had to apply a little push to get Stewart up over the high door ledge.

They found themselves in a living room and Courtney's father sat on the couch watching TV. He craned his neck as they came in and greeted them warmly. He told them to come watch with him.

"Harold, this is my roommate, Stewart," Robert said.

Harold reached over the back of the couch and shook Stewart's hand.

"Welcome," he said.

"Thank you," Stewart said.

Stewart positioned his chair beside the couch and looked over at the TV. His breath came in sharply through his nose. He stared transfixed at the screen. Robert had said they would be watching curling, not surfing.

This was Massachusetts, far from big waves, sun, and surfboards. Yet here was Courtney's father watching a home video of a surfing competition while snow fell outside his window.

Stewart heard a voice from the screen, the person holding the camera was narrating what was happening, but Stewart didn't watch. He looked down at his hands in his lap and against his will his mind drifted back. He remembered the rush of wind in his face as he flew toward the shore; the cold water that splashed up when he ran back and slammed his board against the ocean. He remembered hot days of half-sleep, waiting for the waves; sitting in a wetsuit next to Lee's sister on the sand while the water lapped their toes. The sun glinted in her hair and she shyly touched her pinkie finger to his hand.

"Stewart? Stewart? Are you okay?" Robert was saying.

Stewart blinked, looked up at his roommate. "I'm fine," he said, startled to find himself back in a quiet New England home. Courtney, Robert, and Harold were all looking at him. The voice continued on the television. He tried to smile in a friendly way, but his stomach felt so tight he could hardly breathe.

"I'm surprised you're watching surfing," he said.

"Oh yes," Harold said, "All they play today is football. My buddy from college videotapes these competitions for me and sends 'em to me. It's a little joke. I can't stand football, you know?"

"Right," Stewart said slowly. Every time Stewart tried to get away from surfing, somehow it followed him. How bizarre was it that he was sitting here in Massachusetts watching someone's home video of the CA surfing finals from eight months ago?

Harold looked back at him suddenly and frowned. "Wait a minute, it couldn't be," he said, "You're not... Are you Stewart Masterson?"

Stewart was about to deny it when Robert said, "How did you know that?"

"It really is you," Harold said, ignoring Robert.

"Have you two met before?" Courtney asked.

"My boy, I should have recognized you right away, I just hardly expected Stewart Masterson in my own living room." To his daughter and her boyfriend he said, "I used to follow this kid's career. The most promising surfer in the country he was."

Robert looked at Stewart in shock. Stewart knew Robert was used to seeing him as a paraplegic and had given little thought to what Stewart's life had been like before that.

Courtney said, "Is he serious, Stewart?"

Stewart nodded reluctantly.

"You never told your roommate," Harold said. "This guy is so modest. I can't believe I have you in my very own home. I have to get your autograph, Derek will never believe it."

Stewart couldn't help smiling, it had been a very long time since anyone had asked for an autograph.

"Derek and I were sorry when you disappeared. We knew something must have really happened. It's a shame. Such a promising career…" Harold looked blankly at the TV screen for a moment. Stewart looked away. "But," Harold continued, "You did the right thing."

"Thank you," Stewart said. As usual, he swallowed his guilt and accepted the image of himself as a good person. Easier to accept praise for trying to save a life than to try to explain that he was the reason the life was in danger.

Before Robert and Courtney could ask what they were talking about, Courtney's mother came into the room, carrying a bowl of pretzels and a six-pack of beer. She passed cans to each of them, but stopped when she got to Stewart.

"Do you want something else? I mean, should I…" she said, tripping over her words.

"Jesus, Gladys, don't treat the man like an invalid," Harold said. He stood up and walked over to Stewart, throwing a thick hand against Stewart's shoulder. Harold grabbed a beer and pressed it into Stewart's hand.

"Come here, let me show you what I've got," Harold

said. He took hold of Stewart's shoulders and pushed him closer to the TV. Harold unpaused the action and pointed to a figure Stewart recognized immediately. "It's Lee Sharpton," Harold said.

"Yes," Stewart agreed.

"He knows all kinds of fancy tricks, and he rides a wave real smooth, but you had more talent in your left hand and everyone knew it."

Harold was ignoring everyone else in the room. Robert, Courtney, and Gladys stood back and just watched as Harold crouched down on his knees next to Stewart and pointed out each movement on the screen.

Stewart was overwhelmed by Harold's enthusiasm. He had forgotten what fame felt like. It reminded him of what it was like to be eighteen. He was surprised to find that the memory wasn't that bad. At the time his life had been nothing but stress. There was the stress of maintaining an image and the stress of fighting with his family and the stress of wanting to be the best in the world. He no longer worried about any of those things. Looking back he knew that the best part about the life of fame was the people. People like Harold and Pete and all the kids who looked up to him. Why couldn't he see that then?

During a break in the action on the television Harold went for the telephone and gripped it tightly in his hand.

"Derek?" he said, "It's Harold. Hey, how are you? You're not going to believe this. You'll never guess who just showed up at my house. Stewart Masterson. Yes, *the* Stewart Masterson, what do you think I called you for?"

Harold held the phone out to Stewart. "Go on," he said, "Say something."

"Hello?" Stewart said.

"Are you really Stewart Masterson?"

"Yes," he said.

"Where have you been? I thought you disappeared off the face of the earth."

"Well, off the face of the ocean maybe. I'm going to college in Massachusetts."

"Oh come on, now. You belong with us and you know it," the stranger's voice said.

"Um," Stewart said, trying to lower his voice even though everyone in the room was watching him, "I never recovered. I mean, that day, I was paralyzed. I can't walk."

"Oh…well, it's a miracle you got out of there alive at all. We all miss you, you should think about coming back."

"All right," Stewart said to placate him, "I'll consider it."

Actually he felt his guard loosening and for the first time he thought maybe he really could go back. He hung up the phone and found Harold still grinning at him.

"So have you ever thought about going back, Stewart?"

"Harold!" Gladys said, her eyes shifting to Stewart for a moment.

"They're announcing the winners," Stewart said, nodding to the TV and successfully taking the attention off himself.

Even with Jeff and Elizabeth pushing Stewart to go back to California, today was the first time that it really seemed possible. Maybe it wouldn't be too much of a shock to his fans to see him like this. It didn't seem to bother Harold at all. Stewart knew that the media had never been told what became of him after he was carried off that beach six years ago, but people must have had some idea when he didn't come back. And after all this time, would it even matter?

When he first got out of rehab and hid out at Aunt Claire's house there had been a lot of contact from magazines wanting to know what had become of him. At the time he didn't want his injury exploited. That news might have overshadowed the true tragedy of the day. He didn't mind if people forgot about him, but no one should ever forget Pete. He had worried that letting the magazines learn the truth might turn into a media circus and he would become the poster child for the fallen surfer. But the purity of Harold's excitement convinced Stewart that enough time had passed. At this point people would probably just be glad to know what happened. How many would even remember him now? That was a fast paced world with new celebrities and heroes to be made every year.

After dinner, Harold followed Stewart and Robert outside. "Come back anytime," Harold said at the top of the steps.

"I will," Stewart said.

Robert got his arms under Stewart and tried to lift him out of the chair.

"Here, let me help with that," Harold said, pulling the wheelchair back and helping to untangle Stewart.

"Be careful of your back, Dad," Courtney said from where she stood in the doorway.

"No trouble, no trouble," Harold said.

As Stewart and Robert began the strange climb back down the stairs, Harold hovered nearby. "Can I do anything?"

"We got it," Robert said.

At the bottom Stewart got back on the wheelchair for just the brief trip across the street and then he was lifting himself out of it again. He got into the driver's seat and found that he was too exhausted to deal with lifting the pieces of the wheelchair into the car. He knew that he had overworked himself and spasms might start at any moment. Robert noticed the pause and came around the car. He leaned over and said quietly, "Is everything okay?"

"Yeah," Stewart said, "Just, could you put the chair in the back for me?"

"Sure you're okay to drive?"

"Yeah."

While Robert was putting the wheelchair in the back, Harold opened the passenger door and leaned in to say, "I'm glad to see you're okay. Do come back soon."

On the road, Robert said, "I can't believe Harold knows you."

"Yeah," Stewart said. It certainly had been a shock.

"Where you're from you must be really famous," Robert went on.

"In some circles I used to be famous, now people don't usually recognize me."

"I never knew that about you. Why didn't you tell me?"

Stewart shrugged. "It was a different life," he said.

16

On his way to class Stewart checked his mail and flipped through missing person cards, coupons for the local pharmacy, and credit card applications. One of the larger items was a long manila envelope from Jeff. When he had seen Jeff, his friend hadn't mentioned sending anything. They had already exchanged gifts. Stewart sat next to the trashcan in the student post office. He tore open the envelope and a magazine fell out. It was a photography magazine, not something Stewart had much interest in. The picture of the camera on the front immediately made him think of Elizabeth, though. Did Jeff know Elizabeth was a photographer or was this just strange irony?

A note was attached. Stewart pulled the tape off the note and unfolded it.

Thought you should see this —Jeff

There had to be a reason. Stewart laid the magazine

on his lap and opened the first page. Was he supposed to be looking for clues to some mystery? Page by page he went through the magazine. He was close to giving up when he came to an article about young photographers and their subjects.

He remembered the first time he met Elizabeth and how concerned she had been that she didn't have a theme to base her photography around. Then he turned the page and knew what Jeff had seen. It was him.

Stewart was looking at a picture of himself. He remembered the day it was taken. She was showing him around the city. A moment after this picture she threw her weight against his back and together they got him up over the curb.

Weren't people supposed to get permission before using other people for subjects? He didn't want his picture in magazines. He had been there. His picture had been in surfing magazines and now he was firmly retired from being famous. What right did she have to try to bring him back?

He read the box of text beside it. "When asked why she chose her subject, Elizabeth Foster had this to say: This picture shows an everyday challenge to a person in a wheelchair. I think it also shows that he is lucky that his challenges are physical ones. There are a lot of us who have emotional disabilities and social challenges. It is my belief that there is no such thing as a divide between the disabled and the 'normal.' Disability is a spectrum because not one of us can claim that our body always does everything we wish it could. We all fall somewhere on this spectrum. Some of the disabilities are emotional and social and psychological and many are physical. It is time to stop thinking of ourselves as incomplete because of them. What would a whole human being look like? I don't think we would even recognize such a creature. This is a man who understands that there is nothing to fear. I envy him that and I hope to follow in his footsteps."

Stewart couldn't help chuckling at the word "footsteps." He could feel her next to him for a moment. Though they were apart, she had shared the joke with him.

But even as he laughed he remembered the moment he had seen the truth on her face. It had to be one of the rarest fetishes in the world. It had been a joke in rehab. Elizabeth was probably the only person he had come in contact with who had it. And why did it have to be her?

Although, if not for this, would she have never given him a chance? Would she have been like those girls who said yes to a date for fear of hurting him and then never showed? Would he have even noticed her? It was she who had looked across the room at him while dancing with Robert and held his gaze.

In the same way that paralysis was a part of him but only a small part out of many other aspects, her fetish was one aspect of her. She had seen beyond his chair, he was sure of it. Maybe she had been initially attracted to his disability, but he couldn't claim he had gone out with her without giving a thought to her body. Everyone finds something attractive, why shouldn't it be his legs? Maybe they were good for something after all.

He tucked the magazine in his backpack and continued to class. He knew now that he had treated her unfairly. He had asked for acceptance from her, but he had not given it. In his drive to be independent and take on the world alone, he had not let himself relax around her. In all that time he hadn't truly let her in. She had seen him anyway. She had seen him as he was and not as he presented himself to the world and not as the world wanted to see him. She saw him and now he thought he might be able to see her.

The next day Stewart parked his car at the high school and got out. He navigated through streams of teenagers. High school kids looked younger than he remembered. Some of these little people were the same age he had been the summer he was injured. He didn't remember being that small at the time. He saw the front stairs and started hunting for the ramp.

Eventually he discovered it around the side of the school. Once inside he didn't know where to go. Kids still streamed by him and one hallway looked the same as the next. People jostled him, bumped into him, occasionally turning their heads and calling back, "Sorry" or "Excuse me," while still rushing on.

Then a buzzer sounded and almost instantly there was no one. Stewart stopped and looked around, stunned at how quickly every other soul had vanished. Even without all the bodies in the way, he still couldn't see which way to go.

So he did what he always did when in doubt. He wheeled slowly down the middle of the hallway and waited for the answer to become clear. Finally he saw a person, a girl who looked like she was late for class. She was going to rush right by him.

"Excuse me," he said, "Can you tell me where the main office is?"

She jumped in surprise, then pointed her finger and

didn't say anything. Stewart followed where she had pointed. A little while later he saw what had to be the front office, right next to the entrance with the stairs.

He pulled open the heavy door and it closed on him faster than he expected. It pinched his hand and he yelped out loud. The secretary looked up. He smiled sheepishly caught half in and half out. He was in the process of extracting himself when the secretary jumped up from her desk and scrambled over to help him. She got in the way more than she helped, but eventually they were both inside the office.

"Hello," Stewart said.

"Can I help you, sir?" she said. She looked like she had just recently hit forty and hadn't adjusted to it yet. Her makeup was overdone and her dress shorter than the kids'.

"I need to find one of your students."

"Oh?" she said.

Stewart realized that he was going to have to come up with a good lie. How likely was it that this secretary would know Elizabeth? He didn't have much on him, but he did have his backpack. He turned on his charm. He smiled wide and pulled a notebook from his backpack. "Yes," he said, "I've been staying at my aunt's house and she asked me to bring this to my cousin Elizabeth. Apparently she forgot it this morning and needs it this afternoon."

"Oh sure, I can have one of the students deliver it to her."

Stewart thought about that. It was too bold to ask to deliver it himself. But he could follow the student and see where her classroom was. Of course he would stand out, it would be obvious he was following and the classroom could be on the second floor.

Stewart handed over the notebook and silently prayed that she wouldn't open it and see Stewart's notes from religion class. "Thank you," he said, "Her name is Elizabeth Foster. Can you have the student tell her that Stewart dropped it off?"

She frowned, not understanding why that could possibly matter. Stewart smiled wider and tried to look comfortable and confident, and not like a liar.

"Sure," the secretary said at last.

"Thanks," Stewart said. He headed for the door again and this time the secretary ran ahead of him to open it. In the hallway Stewart suddenly realized that he could have written a note inside the notebook telling her where to meet up with him. He smacked his forehead. Too late now. He moved backwards and waited for the student to emerge.

She did a few minutes later and Stewart followed. He could hear his wheels squeaking against the floor, so he stayed far back. The girl was absorbed anyway. He didn't know what she was concentrating on, but she walked quickly, her feet banging down with each step, and she stared at the floor with deep concentration.

He stopped short when the student knocked on a door. What was Elizabeth going to think when someone handed her his notebook?

He found out less than two minutes later. First the messenger student appeared, walked past him without even looking at him on her way back to the office. Stewart waited. He looked down at his hands in his lap.

The harsh fluorescent light of the hallway cast dingy shadows over them.

He heard the door creaking open and crashing shut. Looking up, he saw Elizabeth standing still in the hallway three yards in front of him. She looked different than he remembered. It saddened him that his memory could not hold a perfect image of her. How could he have forgotten the different shades of brown and gold in her hair that lay like the different grains of sand? How could he have forgotten the proportion of her eyes to her nose or the constant chapping around the bottom of her lip?

"How are you?" he said, smiling.

She frowned. "What are you doing here?" she said, holding up his notebook and shaking it.

He shrugged. "It got you out here," he said.

"I'm here," she said.

"Come with me," he said, nodding back down the hall, "And let's talk."

"I have class," she said.

"You're a senior in her second semester," he whispered, "live a little."

"I'm a good student, okay? I'm not all rebellious and too cool for everybody like you are."

"Ouch," he said.

"I already know what you think of me and I wish I didn't." She walked away quickly down the hall. Around the corner she went, and up the stairs. Stewart was following fast and slammed his feet against the bottom step.

"Elizabeth!" he shouted up at her heels, rounding another corner, "That isn't fair."

The words "Life isn't fair, don't you know that by

now?" fell back down on him. He should have seen that one coming.

Stewart checked his new watch and wondered what else he had to do that day. Also, how long could he stand to just sit here? He waited.

But classes let out and she didn't come back. The hallways were flooded with people again and Stewart was pressed back against the wall. He saw belts and skirts and underwear hanging out of boy's pants, but he didn't see Elizabeth.

When the stream finally subsided she had never appeared. He needed a new plan. He was tempted to try something bold and ridiculous. Teenage girls were crazy about that stuff, the movie romantic crap. He had a feeling that those kinds of stunts probably fell flat in real life.

Defeated, he rolled back the way he had come, to the handicapped entrance in the back, beside the dumpster. As he pushed the doors open with his knees he saw that Elizabeth was sitting on the side of the ramp. Sunlight sparkled off his spokes and glittered in Elizabeth's eyes.

"Say whatever it is you have to say," she said.

"I'm going to California this summer," Stewart said.

Elizabeth frowned. "Is that right?" she said slowly.

Stewart nodded. "If you come with me, I'll teach you to surf."

"You personally would?"

"Yes. I will teach you to surf."

"In the ocean?"

"In the ocean."

"What's the catch?"

He took the photography magazine from his

backpack and held it out to her. "Look, I don't know how I feel about this fetish thing. But I think we deserve the chance to figure it out."

"You want to give our relationship another chance?"

He nodded.

"So how do we do this?"

"You mean, how do we pretend that nothing has happened?"

"I don't want to go back to secrecy. Not ever again. This thing is a part of who I am and I'm finished with hiding it."

"No," he said, "No more secrets. I want you to tell me about it. I want to understand."

"Do you promise not to look at me like I'm a freak?"

Stewart laughed. "I promise I won't look at you as a freak if you promise not to look at me like a freak."

"I'm not ugly and shameful and a monster and a pervert?"

Stewart shook his head. "You're the same Elizabeth you've always been."

"Not quite," she said with a smile, "Now I'm free."

He reached for her hand and squeezed it. "I'm sorry for what happened. I have my own issues, you know. I'm very screwed up, little girl."

Elizabeth laughed. "You don't seem so bad to me," she said.

She looked at him with such trusting eyes, so clear and unclouded, with a trust that he knew he couldn't live up to. Most people would be willing to concede that if you managed to end up in a wheelchair, you must be screwed up. Not Elizabeth.

"Come back to my place," he said.

"Right now?"

"Right now."

Should she call her parents? Probably. But she didn't. "Okay," she said, "Let's go."

As they went toward the parking lot, she walking and he gliding, she saw the eyes of her classmates follow them. These people had known her all her life and she knew them, in that very surface way of knowing. They had seen each other grow from children into adults. But there were sides of each other they never knew. Stewart was a part of the life she had far away from childhood acquaintances. She saw in their eyes a vague wondering about the part of her life she had lived away from them, the part that included a devastatingly handsome man in a wheelchair.

Under their gazes Elizabeth felt a contentedness come over her. She didn't have to hide, because this was a real man and not a fantasy. Maybe it was actually good that there were people in the world like her. Stewart deserved love and she was here, able to give it.

She got into his car and pressed the window button up and down and up and down. "What made you come back?" she said.

"I know you talked to Jeff about me."

"He told you?"

"Under torture he confessed that Christmas was your idea."

"I'm sorry, I know you like to do things your own way, but…"

"It was good to see him again. He also showed me the picture you published."

"Are you sure you're not mad?"

He turned his head and fixed her with his steady hazel eyes. "Listen, I've heard it said about me that I don't know how to express affection. I don't know if that's true, but I'm working on learning to express emotion better. What I'm trying to say is I love you, Elizabeth, or I wouldn't be here."

"I love you too." She took a deep breath and forced herself to say the word she was afraid of. "Not your wheelchair, you."

"I know."

He pulled the car onto the road and drove toward the college.

17

In the quiet they could hear people playing videogames in the common room and faint music from a neighbor's computer. Elizabeth sat on Robert's computer chair across from Stewart. "Well," she said, "Go ahead and ask. Whatever you want to know."

"Is it the chair itself? That…excites you?"

"No. I mean, the chair is beautiful and graceful, but there's more to it than that. The limbs, the movement, the disconnect of upper and lower body, the lack of control over your body. I love the wheels and the way they move with you and flow almost as part of your body. I also love your feet and your knees."

"Could you just put an able-bodied guy in a chair? Like when Travis was using mine, did you feel it then?"

Elizabeth pondered this. "No," she said, "It's not a game and the chair isn't a toy. There is something about identifying as disabled that matters. And the paralyzed body is beautiful too, even without the chair."

"Have you ever thought about why?"

"Of course I have. I just haven't ever found a good answer."

"So you don't know how it started?"

"I've been living with it for eighteen years and I've analyzed it to death and never understood it."

"You had this when you were a baby?"

Elizabeth nodded. "Don't believe anyone who tells you that kids aren't sexual. Babies touch themselves and little kids might not know what they're doing, but I know I used to put my heel between my legs and rock back and forth. I didn't know why. It was like an itch I wanted to scratch."

"When I read about the fetish in a magazine they said something about it being about nurturing and mothering a disabled guy."

Elizabeth raised an eyebrow at him. "And when have I ever mothered you?"

"Point taken," Stewart said, "That's not it."

"Actually," Elizabeth said, "I talked to my friend, Amy, about it recently and she had the most reasonable explanation I've heard. She thinks I like that you're really tough and can handle anything and that the wheelchair kind of proves that you're able to deal with things."

Stewart thought about this. "You tend to put men on pedestals, don't you?"

"I suppose so."

"So my disability humanizes me, brings me to your level, maybe?"

Elizabeth shrugged. "Maybe. Doesn't really explain why I felt it when I was a baby, though."

"And nothing else has ever turned you on?"

Elizabeth shook her head. "I've never been attracted to an able-bodied guy," she said. "I've tried to destroy this thing I have, to force myself to stop wanting disability, but it never goes away. I'm not sure that I really want to destroy it anymore. Some part of me holds back. I mean, it feels so good. And if I got rid of it, what if I never felt that desire again? Maybe I'm lucky because I know exactly what I like, exactly what turns me on. I just don't want to be someone who takes advantage of someone else's suffering."

Stewart shrugged. "Well, you didn't cause anyone's suffering, right?"

"I hope not!" Elizabeth said. She smiled.

Stewart rolled back so she could see his full body. "And does the reality live up to the fantasy?"

Elizabeth smiled. "What do you think?" she said. She stood and bit her lip while she slowly peeled off her pants and underwear and held the underwear out to him.

He took them, frowned and said, "These are wet."

She nodded.

"Really, really wet. That's from me?"

Elizabeth nodded again, looking at the floor.

"Wow. Well, I've got to say, I hope it doesn't go away."

Elizabeth stepped forward and knelt on the floor in front of his chair wearing only her shirt. She put her hands on his sneakers. "May I?" she said. She looked up at him and waited until he nodded. She pulled the shoe off one of his feet and felt the dead weight of the foot in her hands. She peeled off the other shoe, then his socks. His upper body squirmed.

"Don't be embarrassed," she said, "Your feet are beautiful."

"Come closer," he said.

Elizabeth stood with his knees touching hers. He couldn't feel it, but she could. Through the material of his pants she felt the pressure of his legs.

His hands reached out and encircled her waist. He pulled her closer and she surrendered into his arms. She sat on his lap, her long legs dangling over the side of the wheelchair. With one arm he held her steady, his hand flat against her back under her shirt. The other hand reached under her shirt too and lifted it up over her head.

Stewart unhooked her small white bra with one hand and flung it to the side of his room. It hit the wall and slid down onto Robert's bookshelf. The sensitive skin of her breasts was pressed against his shirt, then he relaxed his arm and leaned her back. The muscular arm held her remarkably still as she leaned back against it. With his other hand Stewart touched the bare skin of her right breast.

Elizabeth shivered, feeling almost as though she was being tickled. She felt the tightening in her nipples and looked down, surprised to see the one Stewart was touching turning into a hard little point. He ran his hand over her skin and it left a trail of warmth across her always chilled body.

"Stewart," she said.

"Yes?"

"Nothing…" Her voice was unusually deep and raspy.

She reached out her arm and touched his face, pushing the strands of hair away from his forehead. She looked at his face, the stubble coming back in across his chin, and the angular lines of his features. She saw his deep eyes and felt herself falling into them. It was as though she could see him and everything that he was for one split moment.

Without realizing that she had moved forward, her nose touched his and she was still deep in his eyes. His lips moved forward and tried to hold hers. They broke apart, then they each started forward at the same moment, their lips pressed hard on one another's.

She had turned off her mind and didn't worry about whether this was sick or whether God was going to punish her or whether she was doing it right. She followed the feelings and the sensations, one to the next.

He released her to support herself balanced on the wheelchair with her legs locked around the back alone. With his free hands he reached down and slowly pulled his own shirt off over his head. Elizabeth touched the muscles and the scars. His body was unbearably beautiful.

She could feel his warm breath on her neck, and then on her ear and she shivered with a tickle. She smiled and raked her fingernails over his bare chest. He picked her up by the shoulders and lifted her onto his bed. She giggled and moved over to make room for him to join her.

"Sure you're ready for this?" Stewart asked.

"I've never been more sure of anything," Elizabeth said.

"Okay, give me a minute. Spontaneity and spinal cord injury don't exactly go together." He pulled something from the mini-fridge on the other side of the room and slipped out the door toward the bathroom.

When he returned, Elizabeth brought her knees to her chest and bit her lip while Stewart grabbed the side of his bed and pulled his body over, lifting the dead weight of his legs after. He concentrated on that, and then looked up at her.

Elizabeth crawled to him on all fours and pushed him back against his pillow. She straddled him and kissed his lips. He held her back and looked over her body. Elizabeth squirmed and tried to press herself closer to him.

"You are beautiful," Stewart said.

Elizabeth blushed. "You don't mean that," she said, "You've seen real surfer girls."

"You're different, but definitely beautiful."

"Does being disabled make it harder to date?"

Stewart laughed. "It can be a challenge."

"If you could be with anyone at all, who would it be?"

"You just want me to tell you that I'd still choose you even if women were falling over themselves to be with me."

"Yeah, I guess so."

"I don't have to be with anyone. I'm choosing to be here with you. Now, hush and enjoy."

He touched her bare body with his fingers and Elizabeth grabbed his shoulders and dug her nails in.

Sex was different from how Elizabeth had imagined it. She thought she would be a different person when it happened; that she would shed the skin of her childhood. She felt no different afterwards, though. There was a contentedness beyond anything she had known, and she let herself sink into it as she fell asleep.

Stewart woke her before Robert came back and she put her clothes back on. "Just give Robert and me a few minutes and then come back, okay?" he said.

"I get to actually spend the night in your bed?"

"Yes, just let me get situated. Come back in thirty minutes or so."

Elizabeth wandered the hallways of his dorm and tried to figure out if she was an adult now. The mystery of sex gone, she did feel a bit more grown-up, more worldly wise. When she thought of Stewart and the way he had looked at her, her face flushed. How had she been so very lucky? It was as though he had been made for her, or maybe she had been made for him.

When she returned to the room Robert was putting some things away and Stewart was lying on his back in bed. Elizabeth smiled at Robert, then climbed into bed with Stewart and pressed up beside him. Stewart put an arm around her and she smiled as she closed her eyes and Robert shut out the light.

18

"Stewart and I are getting back together," Elizabeth declared. She sat down at the kitchen table and picked up her fork. Her parents looked at each other over her head in alarm.

"What is this now?" Susan said, coming over and sitting down next to Elizabeth, putting her hand on her daughter's arm.

"The man you met," Elizabeth continued blithely, "We had a rough patch, but we've smoothed it over and we're getting back together."

"Elizabeth," her father joined in, "Next year you start college and make choices about the rest of your life. Wouldn't it be better to start fresh?"

Elizabeth started to eat. "No," she said, "I don't think so."

She was past being hysterical or even trying to convince them. It was her life and the reconciliation was a done deal. There was no need for argument or explaining. She had realized that she couldn't tell her parents the truth even though she wanted to.

It would be selfish of her to tell them about her fetish. They didn't want to have to deal with that. Elizabeth was getting a high from having it off her back, from having it be open and known, but she couldn't keep creating that high by telling people who couldn't deal with the knowledge. If Stewart himself had so much trouble with it, there was no way her parents could handle it.

"Pass the salad, please," Elizabeth said.

Susan moved the salad farther away. "Elizabeth, we need to talk about this."

"No," Elizabeth said, "We don't. There isn't anything to talk about, I just thought you would want to know."

"Why are you being like this?" Susan said.

"It's supper time and I want to eat supper."

Susan looked at David again. He shrugged. "She's a teenager after all," he said, "Let's eat." He got the salad back and gave it to Elizabeth. He sat down and settled into his chair. "Have some food, my dear," he said to Susan.

During supper they were all quiet. The wind could be heard rattling the blinds on the back door's window. Elizabeth swept her bare feet back and forth over the brown linoleum floor. She wasn't going to let the silence get to her and she wasn't going to let it change her attitude about the situation.

This second time around with Stewart was different. In the intervening months she had grown up. Maybe they both had. Now their relationship was different and she didn't have to worry about defending it.

"Good supper," Elizabeth said. She picked up her

plate and carried it to the sink and walked out of the room. She went upstairs. Her room felt different to her too. Her eyesight had snapped to a different perspective. Slowly she stretched out on her bed on her back and looked at her ceiling.

She sat up and looked over at the bureau that had hidden her notebook for so many years. She didn't feel the desire to take it out. In fact, she didn't care if she never saw it again. Funny how she was finally free now. Before she met Stewart she tried to get rid of her desire, but she could never manage it. She had needed Stewart and now that she had him, she no longer needed the pictures and fantasies. Yes, funny.

It really was amazing having this man know the darkest part of her and pull it out into the light. She was ready to face the adult world now, ready for anything if a man like Stewart was with her. He gave her courage and he gave her strength and she hoped that she gave him something too.

epilogue

"Stick your butt out more," Stewart said.

Elizabeth stood up straight and put her hands on her hips. "Are you serious?" she said.

"Now you're underwater," he said.

She was standing on top of a surfboard that was lying on the sand. Stewart was sitting next to her in his chair. The California ocean roared gently below them.

"When can I get in the water?" Elizabeth asked.

"When you stick your butt out more," he said, "Come on, try again."

Elizabeth lay down on the board, grabbing the sides with her hands. At Stewart's mark she pulled her knees in, and jumped up to a crouched stand with her arms spread. She closed her eyes and pretended she was on a wave.

"Better," he said.

"You're going to be a terrible teacher," Elizabeth said, "You're stingy with the praise."

"I'll let you know when you've done it well," Stewart said, but he was smiling. The sun glinted off his sunglasses. He wore only swimming trunks and the sun had tanned his body. The white scars were more evident against the darker skin.

Elizabeth stood with her hands on her hips and squinted at him against the sun. He could not have looked more like a cool surfer guy than he did at that moment, with his sculpted tan chest, and the tattoo on his bicep. He seemed so out of her league. She stepped off the board and walked toward him.

Standing in front of him with her feet planted firmly in the hot sand, she leaned down, grabbed his armrests, and kissed his lips. When she pulled back she pressed her forehead against his.

From the water, Jeff came running straight for them. He arrived breathless and dripping, with Lee trailing behind him. Lee stopped a distance away, but Jeff ran right into Elizabeth, knocking her to the sand. He said, "Sorry to break this up, but it's time for the champion to show us his stuff." He looked behind him, "Come on, Lee."

Lee edged closer. Stewart smiled at him. "How have you been?" he said.

Lee shrugged. "Not bad," he said.

"Enough chit-chat. Let's go," Jeff said. He scooped Stewart into his arms and carried him down the beach, with Elizabeth and Lee running behind.

At the edge of the water, a boogie board was waiting. The wind whipped off the water and blew their hair in wild circles. Lee held the board still and Jeff lowered Stewart onto it.

Jeff backed away and stood next to Elizabeth, their feet barely touching the water, while Lee pulled Stewart into the swirling ocean.

Elizabeth and Jeff jumped, cheered, and hollered, as Stewart negotiated the waves again. He came at them, shooting at the crest of the racing water, his chest lifted and his body flying.

"I'll be damned," Jeff said.

"He's still good, isn't he?" Elizabeth said. Even with her inexperienced eyes, she could see how he seemed to become a part of the ocean.

"Nothing can stop that man," Jeff said.

Other people on the beach began to gather. A few close to Jeff and Elizabeth said, "Who is that?"

Jeff said, "That there is Stewart Masterson."

"That's the tiger?"

Jeff nodded.

"I didn't know he was still alive," someone said.

"Is that really him?" someone else said.

More people arrived and Stewart's name was whispered from person to person. Stewart and Lee went back into the water and rode waves in again and again. When they stopped at last, Stewart lay back on the sand. The water rushed up over him and retreated again.

People gathered around and looked down at him. Elizabeth was there, smiling proudly. Jeff, Lee, and a handful of other surfers who still almost lived at the beach were close. Farther back was a layer of strangers. They were people who used to watch him surf or had read about him at the height of his fame. Someone moved and the sun filled his eyes.

Elizabeth knelt and helped him to sit up. As Jeff

prepared to carry Stewart back to his wheelchair, Lee's twin sister moved through the crowd and arrived in front of them. Stewart met her eye and they assessed one another for a moment. Then she smiled and said, "Welcome home, Stewart."